Queen of the Darkest Hour

Queen of the Darkest Hour

KIM RENDFELD

Cover design by Jennifer Quinlan of Historical Fiction Book Covers

Copyediting by Jessica Knauss

Printed by Kindle Direct Publishing and IngramSpark

ISBNs
Paperback: 978-0-9975695-7-5
Kindle Digital Publishing edition (MOBI): 978-0-9975695-8-2
Smashwords edition (ePub, MOBI, PDF, etc.): 978-0-9975695-9-9

Dedication

For my stepdaughter, Suzanne Thomas.

.

Dramatis Personae

All are historic personages unless otherwise noted.

Charles, king of the Franks
Himiltrude, his first wife, divorced
Lombard princess, his second wife, divorced, daughter of the Lombard
    king deposed by Charles*
Hildegard, his third wife from the important Agilolfing family, died
Fastrada, his fourth wife, from east of the Rhine

Charles's children (in order of age)
By Himiltrude
Pepin

By Hildegard
Karl
Hruodtrude
Little Pippin (originally named Carloman)
Louis
Bertha
Gisela

*By Kunigunde (concubine)**
Hruodhaid

By Fastrada
Theodrada
Chiltrude

Gomeric, Himiltrude's brother and Pepin's uncle**

Radolf, Fastrada's father
Sigibert, Fastrada's brother**
Nantlind, Fastrada's maid**
Irma, wet nurse to Fastrada's children**
Wilberga, midwife in the royal household**
Fardulf, a Lombard deacon, poet, and courtier

Pepin, Charles's late father
Bertrada, Charles's late mother
Carloman, Charles's late brother, and his widow and sons

Tassilo, Charles's cousin and duke of Bavaria

Luitperga, Tassilo's wife and Charles's former sister-by-marriage
Their sons and daughters

Gerold, Hildegard's brother

Severinus, Frankish aristocrat who owns land near Bavaria**
Richilde, Severinus's daughter**
Meginfrid, Charles's chamberlain
Hardrad, a Thuringian aristocrat
Amalwin, Charles's legate

Widukind, ruler of the pagan Saxons
His wife and children

Lucas, steward of Oppenheim**
Offa, king of Mercia
Alcuin, a Northumbrian scholar and teacher in the Palace School
Angilram, royal archchaplain and archbishop of Metz
Adalgis, Charles's former brother-by-marriage and son of the deposed
Lombard king

*Historic personage but name is unknown
**Fictitious

Chapter One

October 783, Worms

Fastrada forced a smile to hide her unease with the short fourteen-winter-old youth King Charles had introduced as his eldest son. The cause wasn't his stooped shoulders—she had long known about that deformity. In fact, he was better looking than she had expected. His dark blond hair framed a handsome face with her betrothed's long nose. But something seethed beneath the surface of his large, dark blue eyes.

"A pleasure to meet you, Lady Fastrada," Pepin said politely.

Fastrada shivered in the chill of the morning air and drew her marten-fur-lined cloak close with gloved hands. A breeze scattered red and gold leaves on the palace's courtyard, which was framed by a colonnade and three large rectangular stone buildings with many windows. The royal manor and the curved-end chapel flanked the barracks. Guards in the manor's tower could see past the city walls but not much farther. This land was so flat, unlike her hilltop fortress at Büraburg. Of course, she reminded herself, this palace sat in the middle of a guarded city, and the Saxons were across the vast Rhine and leagues to the north and east. Yet she doubted she would ever shake her fear of those heathens no matter how far away they were.

Shoving aside her worry about the Saxons, Fastrada focused on her immediate concern: her place in the royal family. She wanted to be a good mother to Charles's children. Would they accept an Easterner who spoke and dressed differently, especially one who had seen only two more winters than the eldest child? Did they pine for Queen Hildegard, dead only a few months?

"And this is my son Karl," Charles said to Fastrada and her father, Count Radolf.

About to see eleven winters, the boy was large for his age, close to surpassing his older brother. If he did grow to be as tall and brawny as his father, Fastrada wondered, would he obey her when Charles was away?

"We must get you a new wooden sword," Charles told his son in a tenor Fastrada was still getting used to. "The hilt on this one is worn."

Karl frowned. "I want a real one."

Charles chuckled. "When you're old enough."

Pepin scowled, and Fastrada's brow creased. Why did he seem envious of his brother? Her gaze fell to his belt, where he had only an eating knife and a dagger. She hadn't expected to see a sword, not for the youth destined to rule the archbishopric of Metz. Why would Pepin want a costly weapon that would sit unused at his hip? For vanity? One look at him revealed he was from a noble family—he wore a fine wool tunic fringed with silk and had plenty of gold and silver around his neck and on his fingers. Why was he unhappy, when Charles had been so generous? Fastrada had heard about a mother selling her misshapen baby into slavery to forget the sin that had brought God's curse upon the child. Instead, Charles had his stoop-shouldered bastard at court with his siblings. No one would accept a hunchback on the throne, but someday, Pepin would control the riches of the see of Metz and wield all the influence that went with it.

As the king presented his daughters, Fastrada turned her attention to the girls. All three were staring at her. Charles's features softened, and his voice took on a tender note as he uttered their names.

"My lord king," cried a high-pitched voice.

Both Fastrada and Charles turned. A young woman about Fastrada's age, her gem-studded girdle tied above a swollen belly, hurried toward them from inside the royal residence. Charles glanced at his bride, then at the noblewoman, and stood a little straighter, like a soldier bracing for a punch.

The noblewoman gazed up at Charles, her eyes pleading. "Is it true, my lord king? Are you going to marry this woman from east of the Rhine?"

Fastrada bristled but held her tongue. How could this woman not know? Oh, was she the concubine the merchants had gossiped about?

"Kunigunde," Charles said calmly, "Lady Fastrada will be my queen tomorrow."

With a gasp that sounded like a sob, Kunigunde laid her hand on her heart and hunched over as if she had been hit with a stone.

"Don't get overwrought," Charles said. "I will acknowledge the child just as I acknowledged Pepin."

Fastrada's throat tightened, and she pressed her lips together. *Don't cry. Not with her watching. Not with Father watching.*

"You told me you were not going to remarry," Kunigunde said, her voice choked. "You didn't want any more heirs."

I heard the same thing. Obviously, he changed his mind. Fastrada clenched her fists, trying to cage the jealousy roaring within her. She dared not speak and release a torrent of tears.

"After this summer's battles," Charles said, "I realized I must marry again for the good of our people."

"But what will happen to me?" Kunigunde asked.

Why should he care about a slut? Fastrada's throat grew tighter. Her eyes stung.

"My lord king," Radolf said, seizing Fastrada's elbow and dragging her away, "my daughter is not well and needs air."

"Of course," Charles said. Was that relief Fastrada heard in his voice?

Still holding Fastrada's arm, Radolf pushed his way through the crowd, and soon, people moved aside on their own. Although age had stolen most of his hair and lined his face, Radolf was still strong enough to wear armor and command soldiers. As Fastrada fought back tears, she and her father rounded a corner of the manor, passed its south wall to their right and apple trees to the left, and turned again. A garden still vibrant with radishes, cabbages, and other fall vegetables greeted them. Several cart lengths away, she spied servants coming in and out of the kitchen.

"She's trying to steal him from me!" Fastrada bawled.

"Stop that!" Radolf said in a low growl. "How many times have I told you never to cry in front of anyone? They'll think you're weak."

"But ... but she claims to be carrying his child!"

"He believes her." Radolf shrugged.

"Why won't you defend me?" During negotiations for the betrothal, her father had refused to insist Charles send the concubine away—to even discuss the matter—and it still irked her.

"She's nothing to you."

Fastrada had let herself believe that until she saw Kunigunde's round belly. "The baby will tie Charles more closely to her."

"No one cares about a bastard. You need to make sure Charles is fair to the sons you'll have with him. We need a man with *our* blood ruling our lands and Saxony."

"And he will."

Her father smiled. "That's my girl."

"I don't want to be only a duty to Charles!"

"You will be queen of the Franks, and your sons will be kings. Most women would be happy with that, even if her husband swived every maid in the palace."

Fastrada envied Kunigunde's curves, so unlike her own tall, willowy figure. Did Charles and Kunigunde share only lust or was there something more? And if there was something more, she might face a more difficult battle on her own sons' behalf, especially if Charles wished to strengthen his bond with Hildegard's brother, Gerold, by favoring his late wife's boys.

"He could heed Kunigunde and ignore me," Fastrada said softly. "She could turn her son against me and mine. How do you know Charles won't do to me what he did to his first wife? She bore him a son, and Charles threw her away like a threadbare rag."

"You're confused," her father said with an eerie calm. "The Lombard princess bore him no children, and she got what she deserved."

Fastrada glared at him. That was only half-true. Her father had told her just a few weeks ago that Himiltrude, Pepin's mother, was Charles's first wife, not a concubine, and Charles had divorced her to wed the Lombard. In fact, Radolf pointed out that Himiltrude's appointment as abbess of the royal double monastery at Nivelles was the price for peace with her family. Why would he attempt to deceive her now by repeating what Charles wanted people to believe?

Oh. Her father wasn't trying to trick her. He was warning her: she had better act like someone was always seeking an opportunity to use her own words against her, even if no one was within earshot. *It was never this way at home.*

She swallowed, loathing the lie she had to accept. "Your pardon, Father."

"You were a little girl at that time," he said, "much too young to remember."

That much was true. And that was what she would say if anyone brought up Charles's early marriages. She would not talk about the tension between Charles and his late brother. Or the Lombard princess Charles had set aside to marry Hildegard or the war that resulted between Charles and his enraged former father-by-marriage. But she would never forget that first war in Lombardy taking her father away for almost a year and the vengeful Saxons' attack on Büraburg while he was gone.

Our people paid the price. Again, she was seven winters old in a chapel crowded with monks from the Abbey of Fritzlar and refugees from neighboring villages, all praying before the stone box with the relics of Saint Wigbert. Boulders from Saxon catapults thundered into the fortress walls and rattled the floor, even the air. The smoke from burning houses and the fields filled her throat.

Her father's voice brought her back to the present. "The king stayed true to Hildegard."

"She was an Agilolfing." To seize his late brother's lands, Charles had needed an alliance with one of the realm's most powerful families, which included the duke of Bavaria.

"We're just as important," her father replied. "We have allies right where the king needs them."

"But I will never capture Charles's heart. It still belongs to Hildegard. Or Kunigunde." Fastrada looked down.

"Marriage is about the head, not the heart. Charles is fond of you, and that is enough for most brides."

"It wasn't this way for you and Mother," she mumbled.

"At first, it was. We married to bind our families and barely knew each other when we made our vows." He sighed. "She was a good wife."

With those words, the ground felt more solid under Fastrada's feet. Maybe there was hope to win Charles's affection. She raised her chin.

"And, Daughter, don't lose your temper with the concubine or anyone else. I won't be there to rescue you."

Fastrada nodded slowly. Her father loosened his grip.

While she was growing up, Charles had been the hero who fought the Aquitainian rebels, the Lombards who threatened the Church, the Saracen tyrant in Hispania, the Saxons burning their way through East Francia—the man who avenged last year's disastrous battles against the Saxons in the Süntel Mountains. She had wanted her father to promise her to a handsome, young count as brave and intelligent as Charles.

Over the past few months, she had wavered between dread of marrying a man old enough to have sired her and pleasant surprise at how her charming suitor showed as much vigor as a warrior ten winters younger. Her father's announcement that she would marry Charles had been like a draught of the strongest wine, but now that wine had become vinegar, sour in her mouth.

Chapter Two

A meaty hand clapped Pepin's shoulder, and he turned away from where his father's bronze-haired bride had gone.

"Uncle Gomeric!" Pepin embraced his mother's brother, a stocky man of thirty years, one of the few people not to look at him as if he were carrion.

"Pepin, your voice changed. You no longer sound like a little boy."

Pepin grinned, glad his uncle had noticed. Pulling back, Pepin beheld a bend in Gomeric's hawk-beak nose and pointed. "Did that come from a Saxon?"

"One that tried to kill me with a cudgel. You should have seen how I finished him off—one swift stroke." Gomeric moved his hand as if he were hacking into the Saxon's neck.

"I would have witnessed it," Pepin grumbled, "if Father had taken me to war with him. He refuses me a sword. Not fair that my little brothers have kingdoms and I get a bishopric."

Gomeric lowered his rough voice. "Your father cannot force you to take holy orders."

"Your father didn't try to force the priesthood on you."

Gomeric smiled. "Actually, he did. He wanted me to be a bishop so that all the land could pass intact to my brother. He sent me to an abbey school, and I liked it not one whit."

Pepin raised his dark blond brows. That explained why his kinsman spoke and read Latin as well as a bishop. He looked nothing like a priest now. No longer young, Gomeric was still strong; the only signs of decline were a few strands of gray in his thick, light brown hair and a couple of blackened teeth.

"What did you do?" Pepin asked.

"I kept saying I needed more time to deliberate before I took the vows, and prayed for a miracle. Suddenly, my brother had pains in his belly and died." Gomeric shrugged. "Must have been God's will."

This was not the first time Pepin had seen a lack of grief over a brother's passing. His nurse had told him no one mourned for his father's brother and he was not to mention his name.

Pepin had heard Gomeric mention his own late brother from time to time, always with an undertone of bitterness, but had known little else. All Gomeric had wanted was what Pepin wanted now: his share of the inheritance, something Hildegard had stolen. Two years ago in Rome, she'd made sure two of her sons, barely out of swaddling, were anointed monarchs. Seeing Carloman emerge naked from the baptismal font with their grandfather's name, Pepin knew he would never be a king. In name, Louis ruled Aquitaine, while Little Pippin reigned over Italy. *Cursed shrew! Deserves to be dead.*

He dared not voice his thoughts. Everyone but his uncle and his real mother thought the late queen was so pious, founding abbeys, befriending abbesses, teaching Psalms to her children. And God had blessed her with three healthy sons and three healthy daughters. No one mentioned the three babies who had died. Even his nurse—God rest her soul—thought the queen charitable to have Pepin educated with his siblings despite God's curse for his mother's sin. His nurse guessed God was angry that Pepin was conceived on a Sunday. Or maybe Himiltrude had seen a deformed man during her churching. Whatever she did caused a curse that could not be removed by Charles's prayers or Pepin's own, and she took the veil to repent. In Pepin's memory, she had always lived at Nivelles. He had seen her only a few times but had many letters. Was she moved by affection or guilt?

Gomeric's voice broke into his thoughts. "When do I get that puppy?"

Pepin made an obscene gesture. Gomeric laughed. They had wagered the offspring of their favorite hunting dogs over whether Charles would marry again.

"Why can't Father just have concubines like Kunigunde?" Pepin groused. "Three challengers for the throne is enough."

"And have a king be distracted with the royal household and the treasury? You jest."

"Kunigunde was doing that for him after Grandmother died. Why would Father want to marry an Easterner? His letters said we slaughtered the Saxons."

"We did, thanks to Radolf and his allies. We need them."

"Our house doesn't need a weakling given to humors," Pepin said.

"That was an aberration. In Büraburg, I saw a strong-willed woman ruling her father's household. So don't be a fool and underestimate her. The king is fond of her, and she may very well bend him to her will."

"He would listen to someone who probably says her Latin like a peasant, all gabble?"

Gomeric grinned. "That's one weakness we can exploit. We need more. You have stayed friends with Kunigunde, haven't you?"

"I did as you told me. She wept when the clerk read that my father was marrying." He rolled his eyes. "She kept whining about how she thought he loved her. Stupid girl."

"You did not call her that, did you?"

"I'm not an idiot."

"Poor Kunigunde, so tenderhearted," Gomeric said. "Perhaps, if you went to comfort her, she would be grateful and let us know what she has heard about Lady Fastrada."

Pepin gave his uncle a puzzled look.

"We need a spy among the women," Gomeric said in a low voice, "and she's perfect."

"I'll talk to her."

***

Pepin entered the royal residence and searched for the concubine. He found her in the great hall, where servants had already assembled trestle tables. The vast room smelled of wood smoke and the thyme and mint strewn on the floor. Clerestory square windows covered with parchment let in light, adding to the firelight from the hearth. Frescoes of past kings, heroes, and other scenes covered the plaster-coated walls.

With slumped shoulders, Kunigunde sat near the hearth, holding a cup of wine and staring at her knees. When Pepin took a seat beside her on the bench, she did not look up.

"What did Father say?" he asked.

"He is fond of me, but he needs allies on the east side of the realm," she replied, her face half-hidden by her dandelion-yellow tresses. "And he will acknowledge the babe and raise him with the rest of the royal children."

"And you?"

"I will get an abbey."

A nice prize for a steward's daughter.

Kunigunde wiped her face with her sleeve. "I don't want an abbey. I want to stay here."

"But you will have land and influence, as my mother does, and she is happy with that. Besides, Father will be married tomorrow. Why would you want to stay and see him with her all the time?"

"A small price if I could be with my babe and not leave him to that shrew's mercy. I am willing to be Charles's concubine. But ... but he ..." Her words were lost in sobs.

"He what?"

"He refused. Said he has enough battles to contend with already and cannot have a war within his own household. She must have allowed him no peace unless he consented to send me away."

He can face Saxons charging him with spears but is afraid of two women? Pepin suppressed the urge to smirk. Regarding Kunigunde's red-rimmed eyes, Pepin wondered if his mother had wept when she had left him as a baby. A couple of years ago, Gomeric had told him she had been so heartsick that she neither ate nor slept for days. Aloud, he said, "What have you heard about my father's bride?"

"Very little about her. I mostly heard about Count Radolf and what a great warrior he is and how many allies he has," she said bitterly.

"It's the only reason my father would marry Fastrada. If Father's heart could choose, you would be his wife."

"You think so?" Turning toward him, Kunigunde brightened a little.

"Yes." He did not know if his words were true, but they had the desired effect. Uncle Gomeric would be proud.

"We should see what we can find out about Fastrada," Pepin continued, "perhaps something that will make Father turn away from her."

"My servants will no doubt gossip with hers."

"Let us speak after dinner." Pepin smiled, pleased with how easy it was to get Kunigunde to spy on the soon-to-be queen.

***

Along with the maids and nurses, Fastrada, Kunigunde, and the princesses entered the bathhouse, a large, square, wooden building forty paces away from the manor. A fire burned brightly in the warming room, closed off by a curtain. The last thing Fastrada wanted to do was share space with the concubine, but she would not refuse a bath, especially after days of travel. She could not find supporters if she stank. Nor would she allow Kunigunde to claim a victory, no matter how small.

Fastrada's maid, Nantlind, was the only familiar face, the only one she could trust. The petite servant with dimpled cheeks and plump fingers had been with her three years, and at nineteen winters, her figure was in the full bloom of womanhood.

"Life here will be different from Büraburg, my lady," Nantlind said. She unfastened the brooch that secured Fastrada's cloak below her throat.

"God's wounds, yes." As the maid untied her girdle, Fastrada scanned the women around her and added: "But this palace is beautiful. Did you see the frescos in the great hall? With Siegfried slaying the dragon?"

Fastrada removed her bangles, the diamond betrothal ring Charles had given her, and her glass-bead necklace. She stole glimpses at Kunigunde. No matter what her father said, the shapely concubine was her rival, especially if she bore Charles a son.

9

"Lady Hruodtrude, what dress will you wear after the bath?" Kunigunde asked.

Charles's eldest daughter, a pretty, fair-haired, eight-winter-old girl, held up a vermillion gown.

"How pretty," Kunigunde said. "The color flatters you."

Hruodtrude smiled, and Fastrada looked away. Not only must she compete for Charles but for his children as well.

Nantlind undid Fastrada's braids, letting her bronze-colored hair fall to her waist. The maid tugged off her lady's boots and untied the garters that held her stockings at the knees. Fastrada stood and doffed her dusty green gown, then her yellow underskirt and white shift.

Letting the maids put the clothes and jewelry into baskets, the noblewomen ventured beyond the curtain. Fastrada's jaw dropped. Although she had seen other baths at other castles, the pools in the palaces still amazed her. In a room flooded with the scent of lavender, two pools—one hot, one cold—awaited the bathers in the flickering light of the candles. Through the wooden wall, Fastrada could hear splashing and murmurs from the men's side of the structure and could distinguish Charles's voice.

Hruodtrude and her four-winter-old sister, Bertha, ran to the hot pool and leapt in, shrieking and laughing, and splashed at each other. Their nurses climbed in after them and ushered the princesses to a corner. A nurse took Gisela, Charles's toddling daughter, to a nearby tub.

"I want swim," Gisela whined, pointing to her sisters.

"Not yet, child," the nurse said gently. "You are still too little."

Fastrada slid into the hot pool, followed by Kunigunde. The servants, now undressed, entered the room and the pools to attend to their ladies.

A small, high voice pierced the chatting and the splashing.

"Where Mother?" asked Gisela.

The room fell silent.

"She is in heaven," answered Bertha, who had her father's large eyes, his mouth, and even his bearing.

"And she would not want us to cry," Hruodtrude added. Her maid nodded.

Fastrada gave the girls a sad smile. Having lost her own mother two years ago, her heart ached for them, yet their loss made her queenship possible. Leaning forward to let Nantlind wash her hair, Fastrada wondered how she was going to teach Gisela and Bertha to be proper ladies. Hruodtrude had a greater challenge: she was promised to the young Byzantine emperor.

Kunigunde's voice drew her from her thoughts. "I hear you come from East Francia, Lady Fastrada."

Fastrada blinked back her surprise. After what had happened in the courtyard, she expected the concubine to be coldly polite at best. Instead, Kunigunde sounded like they were two noblewomen meeting for the first time. As much as she disliked the woman, Fastrada remembered her father's advice. "Büraburg in Hesse. And where are you from?"

"My father is the steward of the royal villa in Thionville."

A steward's daughter. Charles would never marry her. Still, she needed to be careful with this woman. No telling what word would get to Charles.

"I've heard of Büraburg," Kunigunde continued. "Is it close to Saxony?"

"Across the River Eder. What is Thionville like?"

The conversation continued in this manner, pleasant but awkward. Gisela's nurse was the first to leave for the warming room with the toddler in tow, and it did not take long for the other women and girls to quickly finish their baths in the cool pool and head through the curtains for the warming room.

Already dressed, Nantlind handed Fastrada her drying cloth. When Fastrada rubbed the wet from her skin, her maid gave her a clay bottle. Lifting the stopper, she paused for a moment, lingering over the aroma of violets, her favorite. She slathered the perfume under her arms and on her neck. The room was filling with the smells of imported sandalwood, roses, and other fragrances.

After donning a fresh shift, Fastrada sat on a stool and handed the bottle to Nantlind. She again smelled violets as Nantlind drizzled the scent on her lady's hair and combed it. Three arms' lengths away, Kunigunde was seated on a stool while her maid pulled a comb through her wavy tresses, a contrast to Fastrada's straight-as-a-pin locks. Hruodtrude sat still as her maid attended her, but her sisters' nurses pleaded with their charges. Gisela's nurse gave Fastrada a beseeching look.

Fastrada's eyes widened. This was happening too soon. "Bertha, Gisela, let your nurse comb your hair," Fastrada said.

"No!" Gisela cried, stamping her feet. "I want swim! I want swim!"

Wailing, she threw herself on the floor.

Fastrada mouthed a vulgarity. She would know what to do with a servant who was that defiant. A good slap across the face and the threat of the whip. But she was not about to hit any of Charles's daughters; he just might beat her. In the men's side of the bathhouse, what was Charles thinking of his daughter's screams, which drowned out all other sounds in this room? Fastrada pressed her fingers to her temples.

"Nurse," Kunigunde ordered, "take Gisela to her bedchamber."

A flush seared Fastrada's face. *I will not let you steal my rightful place, concubine.*

"Want swim! Want swim!" Gisela shrieked.

The nurse looked to Fastrada. Fastrada had to assert her authority. "Nurse, take her to the bedchamber," Fastrada barked as if Kunigunde had said nothing. "Gisela is not to come out until she looks and acts like a lady."

With a nod, the nurse picked up the child and headed toward the door. "No!" Gisela howled, flailing her arms and legs.

Fastrada turned toward Bertha, who was on her feet and watching the scene intently. "Child, you have a choice: let the nurse comb your hair or join your sister."

Bertha sat down on her stool and held the edges, submitting to her nurse. Hruodtrude raised her eyebrows. Gisela's screams faded as the nurse struggled to carry her away.

Kunigunde sighed. "I wonder if the children will ever stop missing Queen Hildegard."

"Did you know her?"

"Of course. The royal family spent last winter in Thionville."

Fastrada wanted to sink through the cracks in the wooden floor. She should have remembered that. Aloud, she asked, "What was the late queen like?"

"A true lady, so kind, so faithful to Our Lord and our people even in the end. As she lay dying in childbed, she said I was doing my duty to Francia as Charles's concubine."

"How so?" Fastrada asked, ignoring that Kunigunde spoke of her betrothed in such a familiar way.

"She was protecting her sons' rights. She didn't want Charles to ..." She covered her mouth.

"Remarry and bear him more heirs," Fastrada said coldly.

Kunigunde looked down.

Fastrada fumed. She had grown up admiring Hildegard as Charles's beautiful, pious queen. Fastrada did not doubt Kunigunde had spoken the truth: Hildegard would have disapproved of the pending marriage. Would Kunigunde use that knowledge to poison Fastrada's nascent relationship with the children? Was everyone comparing her to Hildegard and noting where she fell short? Was Charles? How could she equal a wife who had borne three princes? One living rival was difficult enough.

"My lady," Nantlind said softly, "the king has had much to grieve him this year. He lost his baby daughter and his aged mother as well as the queen. But remember how he said you cheered him?"

"He told me that, too," Kunigunde said with a tremulous voice.

Fastrada turned away. Had all of Charles's kind words at Büraburg and the journey to Worms been empty? Her father would tell her all that mattered was that she would carry the keys to the treasury. She wished she could believe it. Perhaps then her heart would not ache.

Chapter Three

At the head of the high table in the great hall, Charles sat on an ornate chair, one built for his husky frame, and had Fastrada occupy a chair to his right. On the dais, she had a good view of the people Charles had introduced her to earlier: the castle steward and his wife, courtiers, and clerics in the Palace School. How would she recall all their names—and the servants'? She was still trying to remember the counts and holy men who had traveled with her and the army from Büraburg—Pepin's uncle, Count Gomeric; Fardulf, a deacon from Lombardy; Angilram, the archchaplain and current archbishop of Metz, among others. The vast room hummed with the conversations of the men and women crowded at the lower tables, and it was warm with the heat of bodies and the fire.

On the bench beside her were Pepin, then Karl, the princesses, and the nurses of the youngest two. Other nobles and clerics filled out the table. After wary glances Fastrada's way, Bertha and Gisela turned their attention to their dolls. As musicians played their flutes and lyres and cupbearers rushed to bring wine to the table, servants scurried with bowls of water for hand washing.

Dipping her hands in the water, Fastrada regarded her betrothed. When she had explained why Gisela had been screaming, Charles chuckled and said something about Hildegard ignoring a toddling Karl, howling because he couldn't hunt.

"We have surely pacified the Saxons after this last war," Karl said, drawing Fastrada from her thoughts. "We've taken much booty and hostages."

"I wish it were so," Fastrada said, drying her hands with the cloth the servant handed her, "but nothing has pacified them yet. Not slaughter. Not oaths."

"You think they will rebel again?" Charles asked.

That's why you want me as a wife. "As long as Widukind rules them, yes."

"What would a woman know?" Pepin said.

Fastrada glowered.

Before she could respond, Charles cut in. "Pepin! Show respect. Lady Fastrada will soon be your queen and your mother. A woman who lives on the frontier with the Saxons knows plenty."

For a moment, Fastrada was too astounded to speak. Charles was defending her.

"A woman has not been on the battlefield," Pepin retorted, washing his hands vigorously.

"And you, Lord Pepin, have not been inside a fortress while Saxons tried to smash the walls with their catapults. I have," Fastrada said. She did not raise her voice, but it carried an undercurrent of fury. The high table became quiet. "I was seven winters old when the Saxons attacked Büraburg. I will never forget the sound of crashing stones or the smell of smoke from the crops they burned. Do you know what it's like to see an entire village starve in winter and stuff themselves with leaves and dead grass?"

Pepin scowled. Her father stared at her. Fastrada gave him a slight nod. She would not speak of his rage at the war in Lombardy leaving Büraburg vulnerable or her nightmares, but she would press her point. "In Hesse, we hate the Saxons more than you ever could. I have listened to every word from my father's spies, every merchant's tale, every warrior's story. And I tell you: Widukind has rallied the Saxons as no one else has. If he tells them to fight, they will fight without question."

Fastrada looked toward Charles, wondering if she should have been so blunt. No matter what the priests said at Mass, no matter how much she desired him, she could not pretend to be meek. A loyal wife told her husband the truth, even if he didn't want to hear it. She would not be a helpmate and queen to Charles if she didn't. Her betrothed laid his beefy hand on hers. His touch was surprisingly gentle.

"My dear, we will be ready for them," he said.

Pepin glared.

Fastrada heard clattering and footsteps from the door closest to the kitchen. Cooks and maidservants carried platters laden with sliced pork and roasted ducks and chickens, bowls of stews and vegetables, and many loaves of white bread—too many dishes to count. The huntsmen followed with hunks of venison on spits. And this was the first course.

The aromas of meat and spices washed through the hall. Brandishing his eating knife, Charles cut into the venison, his eyes gleaming. He laid some on the stale round of bread that served as a plate and gave a few slices to Fastrada.

"Lady Fastrada," Pepin asked, "what have you studied in *De Civitate Deo*?"

"Pepin," Hruodtrude said, "you know it's *De Civitate Dei*."

"What I have studied in …" Fastrada frowned, trying to understand what Pepin had just said.

"*De Civitate Dei*. It's one of my father's favorite books."

To her left, Charles sat up a little straighter. Fastrada's blush heated her face and ran down her neck.

"I have not read that book," Fastrada mumbled, staring at the tablecloth.

"What have you read?" Pepin asked.

"A little of the Psalter." *Very little.*

"That is all?" Pepin laughed. "Why, I've read all of the Psalter, *De Civitate Dei*, and …" The rest of his words disappeared into Latin.

"As you can see," Charles said, patting Fastrada's shoulder, "my children are eager students. Pepin, what did you study in *De Civitate Dei* while I was away?"

"Where Saint Augustine says …" Then he quoted the Latin. Charles listened intently.

The conversation shifted between Latin and Frankish. Unable to follow it, Fastrada picked at her meat. She had wondered what the Latin prayers at Mass meant, but her lack of understanding never bothered her. No one comprehended the words, save Büraburg's clerk and a handful of learned monks at Fritzlar, less than an hour away from the fortress on a slow-moving horse. Nor had she worried that her mother had taught her only two Psalms. They were two more than most people knew.

But in Charles's family, it did matter. Fastrada stifled a groan. Hildegard must have studied these books, and Kunigunde was smiling and nodding. Even Hruodtrude comprehended it.

Hoping for support, she looked toward her father. He was turned toward Severinus, a count with lands near Bavaria. Judging from her father's gestures, he was bragging about a stag he had hunted when she was ten winters old, a story she had heard countless times, but at least she understood it.

Her father, having never learned to read more than the letters to make his mark, could not help her here. She was alone in this struggle, out-armed and out-armored. But if she admitted defeat, Charles would think her a fool, and no man wanted a fool for a wife, let alone a queen. She needed allies. Straightening her posture, she eyed the clerics at the high table. Could she persuade one of them to teach her? She noticed Deacon Fardulf was watching her and the royal family.

***

Pepin was right! Fastrada was nothing but an ignorant Easterner, and he was exposing her true self. His father would know not to heed her now. The more Fastrada squirmed at the table, the merrier Pepin became. Of course, Karl had to ruin it.

"When can we go hunting, Father?" he asked. "I want to try my new bow."

Fastrada's bright blue eyes glowed. "Could we have a hunt the day after the wedding feast, my lord?" The words seemed to rush from her mouth. Did she thirst for blood?

Karl, Hruodtrude, and Bertha gave Charles pleading looks, while Gisela prattled with her doll. Pepin watched his father.

Charles chuckled. "When would I refuse a hunt?"

"Thank you, my lord." Fastrada beamed. "What have you caught on these hunting grounds?"

"Stags, boars, aurochs, bears—we had one bear that was a giant even among its kind," Charles said. "I should have the musicians make this battle into a song one day."

As soon as his father spoke those words, Pepin rolled his eyes. He had heard this story so many times he could repeat it word for word. How could his siblings stand to listen to it again? He glanced at Fastrada. She was leaning toward her betrothed, nodding eagerly.

Charles launched into his tale about the beast, determined to bite, claw, and crush its way past the army of dogs, huntsmen, and nobles. *Anything to make yourself look like a hero, Father.*

Fastrada was giggling, her cheeks and lips rosy. Talk of a hunt revived her. How could this pretty young woman be attracted to his father? He was almost old enough to be a grandsire. No girl looked at Pepin like that when he told his stories. The only thing he saw was pity or revulsion, except for Fastrada's maid, sitting at one of the low tables. He admired the curves on Nantlind's petite figure and wondered what she looked like without the brown wool dress.

Dinner went as it usually did. Three more courses, laughter, discussion, stories, songs from the musicians. As the meal ended, a woman tapped a lively rhythm on a tambourine. The murmur of conversation paused. Merry notes from the flutes, lyre, and zither soon joined the beat. Rising from the bench, Pepin watched his father and the soon-to-be queen. Charles helped Fastrada to her feet and patted her hand when she took his arm. Scowling, Pepin moved away from the high table. Servants hurried to clear the plates and tablecloths. His uncle approached him.

"Nephew," Gomeric muttered in his ear, "who pissed in your wine?"

"Look at my father. An Easterner as stupid as a peasant is leading him by his rod."

"How do you think the king should act in the presence of his father-by-marriage, especially when he has a concubine with child? If you were king, would you not want him to think his daughter will be treated with the respect due a queen?" Gomeric clapped his hand on Pepin's shoulder. "Now smile. This is a joyous occasion, and Kunigunde needs a dance partner."

The servants made short work of the tables, stacking the planks against the wall and making the vast hall seem larger in the midafternoon light. Soon, men and women started to join a circle of dancing pairs. When Pepin approached Kunigunde and asked her to dance, she accompanied him but did not take his arm.

"What have you heard?" Pepin said, his voice just above the musicians' melody and the stomping of feet against the wooden floor. He and Kunigunde took their places, joined hands, and advanced three steps.

"I pieced together what she told me with my maid's gossip. She is bringing a fat dowry, but her much younger brother—named Sigibert, I think—will inherit all of their father's lands," Kunigunde said while they danced three steps back then three forward. "She does not know what to do with your sisters."

After a turn, Kunigunde described Gisela's tantrum in the bathhouse.

"Clever Kunigunde," Pepin said. "You have done well."

Chapter Four

Fastrada awoke to a slight draft the next morning; a maid had opened the bed curtains. The scents of the lemon balm and thyme on the guest bedchamber floor wafted to her nose, along with wood smoke from the hearth. Her eyes still closed, Fastrada smiled at the memory of yesterday afternoon and evening. She could almost hear the flutes and zither from the dances.

"My lady," Nantlind whispered, "your father sent me. It's time. He awaits you in the hall."

Making the sign of the cross, Fastrada opened her eyes. Through the part in the curtains, she saw that a maidservant had dragged a chamber pot from under the bed and was stoking the hearth. The night candle on a nearby table was the only other source of light in the still-dark room. Although tempted to sink farther beneath the covers, Fastrada thrust her blankets aside despite the chill on her bare skin. After relieving herself, Fastrada quickly donned the shift Nantlind held for her. As she hurried to a basin near the hearth, she heard a maidservant rushing to take the chamber pot away.

The fire warded off the chill in the air while Fastrada washed her face and hands. She took the drying cloth from Nantlind. When Fastrada was finished, Nantlind handed her a clay bottle of lavender water. Stroking the fragrance on her throat and behind her ears, Fastrada hoped the scent would increase Charles's ardor and make her more desirable than Kunigunde.

"Are you certain Kunigunde was not in Charles's bed last night?" Fastrada asked, sitting on a stool near the fire. She crossed her arms over her chest, trying to keep warm.

"I overheard her maid say she was angry about being moved to the princesses' room." Nantlind set the bottle and drying cloth on a small table, picked up a comb, and drew it through Fastrada's hair. "What's more important, my lady, is that you will be in the king's bed tonight."

The thought of seeing Charles naked, his brawny chest and powerful shoulders bare, made Fastrada's heart flutter. Desire kindled in her breasts and between her legs as it had for a guard at Büraburg. She and Nantlind had whispered about the young man while watching him spar and admiring how the sweat made his tunic cling to his muscles. She didn't breathe even a hint of her attraction for him to anyone else—it would have meant a beating for her and death for him. But her lust attracted an incubus who took his shape in her dreams. The Paternosters and Ave Marias she said could not keep the demon away. Maybe leaving the young man behind in Büraburg would. Her desire was for her betrothed now, and the Church would not frown on that.

She felt a twinge in her belly. "I wish Charles and I didn't have to undress in front of everyone."

"All nobles do it. It's for your own protection."

"True." If Charles approved of her in front of witnesses, he could not claim she concealed a diseased body and repudiate her. She frowned. "But he set two other women aside, and he surely had accepted them."

"An alliance with your father is too important. The king would probably take you if you were covered with warts."

Fastrada grimaced and stuck out her tongue.

"I'm sorry, my lady," Nantlind said. "Try to think of something more pleasant. Like what will happen when they leave you two alone."

Fastrada smiled. Finally, she could press Charles's skin to hers, kiss him, and ... Her eyes widened. "Will it hurt, Nantlind?"

"I've heard it hurts some the first time, but if he is a good lover, you will not feel much pain."

"What if he calls out Hildegard's or Kunigunde's name?"

"You must stop fretting! You will be his queen. That's all that matters."

"You sound like Father."

"You should heed him."

From a chest against the wall, Nantlind retrieved a vermillion underdress and Fastrada's favorite gown, which matched her eyes. Dyed with woad, the cloth was embroidered with dark blue thread and sewn with blue and crimson glass beads. She sighed.

"Is there a loose thread, my lady?"

"I used to think my clothes were pretty." She pulled the vermillion garment over her head.

Nantlind knelt to straighten the skirt. "They are. What's wrong with them now?"

"Hildegard probably had sapphires and rubies sewn into her skirts, not glass. I look like a beggar next to her."

"My lady, please, stop comparing yourself to her. Just be the best wife and queen you can be."

As Nantlind held open the neck of the dress, Fastrada plunged her arms into the long sleeves and drew it over her head. Her maid pulled it over her torso and hips.

"What would I do without you, Nantlind?"

Smiling, the maid ran to a small table and brought back a casket, from which Fastrada picked out her bronze cross along with bangles, the diamond betrothal ring Charles had given her, and the enameled brooch of Saint Wigbert. Nantlind wrapped a beaded girdle around Fastrada's waist, then placed a dark blue woolen cloak lined with marten fur on her lady's shoulders and fastened it at the throat with a bronze brooch. Fastrada slipped her feet into beaded leather shoes and left the bedchamber. She crossed the reception room for the guest apartment and hurried to the palace's great hall, where her father paced amid waiting guards and servants setting up tables for the feast and cleaning the hearth.

Hearing her light footsteps, Radolf turned. He was dressed in his best tunic and marten-fur-lined cloak fastened at the shoulder with a bronze brooch. In his left hand, he held a rolled parchment listing her dowry. For a moment, his lower lip trembled. Surprised by her father's affection, Fastrada blinked back her tears.

"Daughter," he murmured, offering his free arm, "be a good wife like your mother."

"Am I not like Mother?"

"You very much are."

They stepped into the entryway, where one of the guards opened the door to the outside. In the pink light of the sunrise, Fastrada, her father, and their escort traversed the courtyard and passed through the colonnade. They turned and strode toward the gate in the walls surrounding the cathedral, about three hundred paces away. To their left, people crowded the street, watching her and her father. Her pulse beat in her throat. *Stay calm. Stay dignified.*

To their right, the sandstone structure, with a round tower in the front and a taller square tower in the back, loomed over the walls. Fastrada and her father entered the cathedral's courtyard, so crowded the people gave off heat despite the cool fall air. Charles and the bishop awaited them on the porch atop the steps. When she met Charles's eyes, he smiled, and that reassurance beckoned her.

"Make way for Count Radolf and Lady Fastrada," one of the guards shouted.

The crowd parted. As she and her father approached Charles, she heard murmurs and whispers. Were they saying how she would never be as good as the late queen?

Joining her betrothed, she scanned the crowd. The royal children were in front with their tutors and nurses. Karl and Hruodtrude watched intently. A nurse squatted beside Bertha and Gisela and whispered to them. Arms crossed, Pepin sulked, regarding her through narrow eyes. Standing with the courtiers, Kunigunde had her girdle pulled tight above her waist. *Showing off the child in her belly.*

She knew why her rival wanted to remind Charles of the baby, but Pepin's expression puzzled her. Why was he vexed that his father was marrying her? The boy had met her but one day ago, and she had done nothing unkind. She was not as educated as Hildegard or Kunigunde, but she came from a good family and knew how to look after a household. Although they were too close in age for him to see her as a mother, she had no intention of shirking her duty to him. She would see that he had the clothes, servants, and guards befitting a prince. If anyone had cause for annoyance, it was Karl, who would inherit less of the realm if Fastrada bore a son. But the younger brother seemed merely curious.

Just be the best wife and queen you can be. Fastrada silently praised the Blessed Mother for such a good servant. Refusing to let a sullen boy and jealous concubine mar her day, Fastrada turned her attention to Charles. Her betrothed handed Radolf a rolled parchment that listed the bride price, then Radolf gave Charles the parchment with the dowry. Excitement surged up her spine as she and Charles clasped right hands. The bishop nodded to Charles.

"I, Charles, by God's grace king of the Franks and the Lombards and patrician of Rome, will have you, Fastrada of Büraburg, as my wife to honor and protect, as a faithful husband should to his lady. This oath I swear by the king's cross and shall keep for all my days, so help me God, creator of heaven and earth."

Fastrada hoped her voice sounded strong. "I, Fastrada of Büraburg, will take you Charles, king of the Franks and the Lombards by God's grace, as my husband to obey and serve, as a faithful wife should to her lord. This oath I swear by the king's cross and shall keep for all my days, so help me God, creator of heaven and earth."

Charles drew her close and kissed her. She closed her eyes, savoring the tenderness of his lips, the strength of his hands.

The bishop turned his attention to the crowd. "With these vows, God has joined Charles and Fastrada in marriage as man and wife. A good wife is important to all laymen, yet she is especially important for a king. Who more needs a helpmate to take the burden to keeping a household, looking after the treasury, finding worthy nurses and tutors for the children, preparing the home for honored guests, and managing his affairs while he protects us, his people, from heathens?

"In Fastrada, we have a pious woman from an important family. Count Radolf has defended our churches against the raiding Saxons and given generously to our Church. May God bless King Charles and Lady Fastrada."

The bishop's words gave her strength. As a priest handed the bishop a silk veil, she bowed her head and silently wished for God to bless the bishop as well. After laying the veil over Fastrada's hair, the bishop said a prayer in Latin and finished by making the sign of the cross.

"And now, Bishop," Charles said, "I present my queen for anointing."

The double doors opened behind the bishop, who led the way toward the marble altar in the curved end of the center aisle, bright with sunlight from the large, square upper windows. In the aisle to her right, she caught a glimpse of the gold reliquary for Saint Sencia, one of the women martyred at Cologne with Saint Ursula. Hand in hand, she and Charles followed the cleric and waited while the church filled. Soon, the mass of people prevented her from seeing frescoes of saints on the walls of the low-ceilinged windowless aisles to her left and right, and still, the crowd overflowed through the doors, as if this were a Mass for the Feast of the Resurrection.

Fastrada's breath quickened when the bishop started chanting in Latin and ascended to his chair. She knelt before the bishop and kissed his foot.

"In the name of Christ," she vowed, folding her hands, "I, Fastrada, queen of the Franks and the Lombards and wife of the patrician of Rome, promise, undertake, and protest in the presence of God and His Merciful Mother, that I will be the handmaid of the Holy Church in all ways that I can be of help so far as I shall be supported by supernatural grace, according to my knowledge and ability."

Rising, the bishop held up a vial of sacred oil and said prayers in Latin, pausing for the response of "*Kyrie Eleison,*" dipped his hand in the oil and made the sign of the cross on Fastrada's forehead, then her right hand, then between her shoulder blades. After more prayers, he took a diadem from a cushion held by a priest and placed it on her head. She trembled, unable to contain her joy.

"Rise, my daughter," the bishop said.

Holding Charles's hand, she listened to a priest sing the lauds in a soaring baritone. Now she was queen, and her people east of the Rhine were fully a part of the realm! If only she had Charles's heart, this moment would be perfect.

***

Dark had settled in the great hall when the moment Pepin hoped for and dreaded arrived. The wedding feast had gone on for hours, and he was gorged with food and wine. On the tables, the platters were covered with bones and crumbs. The laughter and shouting of boisterous men and women almost drowned out the musicians' bawdy tunes and echoed throughout the hall, warm with bodies and the fire in the hearth. Pepin's father rose and helped the bride to her feet. With the wedding guests and his siblings, Pepin followed the couple into their bedchamber within the royal apartment. Gomeric sidled up beside Pepin.

"Kunigunde has taken ill," his uncle muttered.

Pepin snorted in derision but envied her. She had an excuse not to witness what happened next.

When Fastrada unfastened her brooch and handed her cloak to her maid, the room erupted in cheers. Both Charles and Fastrada continued to disrobe, but Pepin watched only the queen. She removed her gown and underdress. To his horror, the sight of her long, pale arms and legs was awakening his lust. He knew he should look away, perhaps sham a sickness as Kunigunde had, but his ardor blazed through him. He could not stop staring.

"Off! Off! Off!" the crowd chanted, Gomeric's voice among them.

The women gasped when Charles removed his shirt, revealing a muscular chest scarred by hunts and battles. Fastrada gazed at him with wide eyes.

"Don't worry, my queen," a drunk shouted. "The king has never been so wounded that he can't please his woman."

Rolling his eyes, Charles took off his drawers. The women cheered and applauded. "Oh, he is eager," a female voice said.

Fastrada's bosom rose and fell as if she was taking a deep breath. Then she pulled off her shift, and the guests hooted and clapped.

Aching with desire, Pepin wanted to sob. Her naked figure was like the white marble statues of pagan goddesses that he had seen in Rome, except they did not have bright red cheeks. She was his mother by Church law, but he wanted to squeeze those round breasts and enter her.

The words of the theologian Tertullian whispered in his mind, *Tu es ianua diaboli—you are the doorway of the Devil.* He clenched his teeth, trying to fight her temptation, but his desire swelled even more. Scorched with lust, he hated her. *She is damning me!*

"She will keep you up all night in more ways than one," a guest shouted.

Fastrada's blush deepened and spilled down her neck. Pepin's throat tightened. He would never be where his father was, smiling as if he were about to savor a fine wine.

Amid more ribald comments, Charles nodded to the archchaplain, who held up his hand for silence.

"The bride and bridegroom have seen each other in front of witnesses. Do they accept each other?"

"Yes," Fastrada said quickly and dove under the bed clothes. She looked pleadingly at her husband.

"Of course." Charles eased in beside Fastrada and held her hand.

The archchaplain blessed them. The guests and family filed out of the bedchamber, passed through the corridor and reception room, and left the royal apartment to return to their merrymaking in the great hall. As soon as

Pepin passed the threshold, he grabbed Nantlind's wrist and dragged her away from any firelight.

"I need you," he whispered.

"Need me? How?"

Not knowing what to say, he tightened his grip.

She gasped and pulled against him. "My lord! I am an honest woman!"

All Pepin knew was that he desired her and he wanted her to want him. In this dark corner of the hall, the shadows hid her face. He kissed her and held her close. She stiffened like a corpse. Through the layers of fabric, he could feel the curves of her breasts against his chest and her soft belly against the hardness of his lust. Then a shudder ran through his body. He heard himself grunt.

His shoulders heaving with deep breaths, Pepin backed away. "Leave," he said in a choked voice.

He heard the hurried steps of her wooden soles against the floor.

God's curse on him was complete. He had spilled his seed in his clothes. He was an abomination, unable to satisfy a woman. If he could have lasted longer, he would have pleased her. No doubt Nantlind would gossip about his inadequacy. He kept his back to the revelry and bit his knuckles to stifle the howls burning in his throat.

Chapter Five

Listening to the laughter and bawdy songs from the wedding feast, Pepin struggled to compose himself. Saints be praised, he was still in the shadows beyond the firelight, and his bodyguards had not followed him. When he finally managed what could pass for a calm expression, he arranged his cloak to hide any stain that might have seeped through his drawers and shirt and showed on his tunic. With soft strides, he emerged into the hall's firelight. Men and women danced to the lively tunes from the flutes and lyres.

Unable to smile, he had no wish to stay, but he did not want to retire to the room he shared with Karl, across the corridor from his father's bedchamber. The last thing he needed to hear was grunts and moans of pleasure. Looking down, he tried to figure out some sort of escape and paid no heed to the approaching footsteps. A familiar meaty hand clapped his shoulder.

"I saw you hand-in-hand with the queen's maid. Just what were you thinking, swiving her?" Gomeric hissed in his ear.

"I ... I ..." Pepin was torn. He wanted to say he hadn't sarded her but didn't want to reveal the reason to anyone, including his uncle.

"Even an idiot knows not to swive what belongs to the queen," Gomeric scolded in Latin, his voice low. "Of all the pretty maids in this palace, why her?"

"I thought I could make her desire me," Pepin said in a small voice. "She ... she doesn't look at me the way other women do."

"Did she desire you?"

"I don't know." If he could have lasted longer, maybe he could have awakened her lust.

"What do you mean you don't know?"

"Not your concern," Pepin snarled.

He raced for a door to the outside. He would rather face demons than his uncle or any of the revelers. In the starlit interior courtyard, he gulped cold air. He would need to confess his sin and do penance. *Curses on you, Fastrada.*

"Pepin?" Gomeric said behind him.

"Go away, Uncle. It's between me and the priest."

"Nephew," Gomeric said as if he were talking to a seven-year-old, "you would be right if this happened with a whore or any other maid here. But this girl is Fastrada's property, and I don't want the queen to get revenge by denying you money or guards or new clothes. And who knows what she'd tell the king and how vexed he'd be with you."

"I didn't sard the maid," Pepin muttered, hoping Gomeric would not ask why.

"Good. Let us hope no one tells the queen. I don't think anyone else noticed."

"My guards might have."

"I already bought their silence. If the coin doesn't work, my threats will."

"That's not necessary," Pepin said. "They are loyal to me."

"They just need to understand fidelity means not gossiping about their master," Gomeric replied. "You must understand your guards' true loyalty is with the woman who feeds and arms them."

"The queen? An Easterner who has been here but two days?"

"Don't underestimate her." Gomeric sighed and laid a hand on Pepin's shoulder. "Ah, Nephew, you are growing up. Next time lust overwhelms you, sate it with a whore. I will introduce you to my favorite girl tomorrow."

"But it's a sin," Pepin said, turning toward him.

"And swiving a maid isn't?" Gomeric chuckled.

"It's not the same. I like her, and I want her to like me."

"Nephew, stop letting her tempt you. You are better off with a whore."

"But all the harlot wants is money." Pepin scowled.

"Like the maid wouldn't?"

"It's different with her."

"Yes, it is different. You're using a whore for an agreed-upon price instead of ruining a virgin, and that's better than making an enemy of the queen. Besides, the Church would have little funds if men did not swive whores and repent. I'll give you some coins for penance afterward."

***

Pepin had been barely able to drag himself out of bed for sunrise Mass the next day, and it was torture to stand in the half-empty palace chapel and listen to the archchaplain's homily about marriage echo off the frescoed walls. Saints be praised for the cold that kept the windows shuttered and covered with tapestries; the light from the walnut oil lamps overhead and the beeswax candles at the altar were easier to bear than daylight. Pepin attended with his father, Fastrada, and his siblings, but many guests were still sleeping or sick from too much wine. Pepin peeked over his shoulder. Behind Fastrada, Nantlind kept her head bowed and her hands clasped across her belly.

The pale and sweaty archchaplain hurried through the rest of the prayers, and to Pepin's relief, the Mass ended sooner than he had expected. In glances, he watched Nantlind speaking with her lady, then approaching a priest so old he no longer needed a razor to maintain his tonsure. Clever girl. She must have asked the servants who was the most lenient with penance. Pepin would have chosen the old man, especially because he served the steward and not his father.

Pepin knew he should leave the church with his family and let her be, but worry gnawed at him. What if she told the priest how monstrous he was? He muttered something about needing to pray to Saint Georg, whose wooden painted statue was a few paces away from the maid. Her back was to him. Pepin, trailed by his bodyguards, knelt near the statue of the warrior on horseback, mouthed the Paternoster, and listened.

"That's all that happened?" the priest asked.

Nantlind cleared her throat and paused. "Did I sin, Father? I don't know what I did to tempt him."

"How old is he?"

"Fourteen winters, I think."

"Boys who are not yet men lust after every woman, even in their sleep. They confess to that sin all the time."

"Is there nothing I can do? He's a nobleman's son."

Pepin swallowed. Was she going to expose him?

"He sees me as just a servant," she continued, "another piece of property he can use whenever he wants."

Pepin winced. *Not true, Nantlind. Not at all.*

"I thought you serve the queen," the priest said.

"I do, Father."

"Could your lady help you?" the priest asked.

"She would protect me. She's good that way. But she gets rash when she's upset. If I told her, it would make things difficult for her. The boy is from an important family, and you know my lady is new to the royal household."

The priest was silent for a moment. The back of Pepin's neck tightened. Would he guess Nantlind was talking about him?

"Sounds like you didn't want to tempt him," the priest said.

"I don't want to be a slut that no man would ever marry."

"You didn't sin, but let me say a prayer for you, then you hail Our Lady ten times."

The cleric intoned a prayer in Latin so flawed Pepin couldn't guess at what the priest meant to say. He snuck a glance at Nantlind, who was turning toward him. When her eyes met his, she started, then her lips drew into a taut line. She straightened her posture and headed for a statue of the Virgin across the chapel.

Pepin let out a breath. His worst fears were not realized. Nantlind had not mocked him or called him a monster. Nor had she revealed him. He could hear her murmur but not make out the words. Did some part of her desire him or was she truly trying to not cause trouble for Fastrada? Was there a potion he could buy to make her want him as he wanted her?

He made the sign of the cross and rose to his feet. His uncle would tell him Nantlind was leading him to more sin. Better to sard the whore and forget the servant. If only the latter were so easy. Why did she have to be Fastrada's maid?

God curse you, Fastrada.

***

On the fourth morning after the wedding, the aristocrats gathered in the palace courtyard to prepare for the hunt. With the murmur of conversations in his ears, Pepin placed one hand on the horse's withers, at about the level of his collarbone. Facing the stocky horse's rump, he stepped forward with his left foot and hopped with his right. In midair, he turned and lifted himself. His arms strained as he swung his leg over the horse's back, but he was in the saddle. He patted his stallion's neck and straightened as much as his spine would allow. He scanned the crowd. His father had mounted a Roman military horse, two hand-widths taller than everyone else's animal. Karl, Hruodtrude, and Bertha were astride their steeds, as were Fastrada, Radolf, and Gomeric.

Heeding his uncle's advice to avoid wine sickness, Pepin had drunk little at yesterday's dinner, the third day of the wedding feast, yet he saw a few pale faces among the courtiers and guests. Kunigunde had stayed behind, again saying she was ill. Gisela was bawling at the manor entrance. Pepin glanced at his littlest sister.

"Want hunt! Want hunt!" Tears streamed down her face while her nurse struggled to hold her back.

His father blew his ivory hunting horn, the signal to ride out of the courtyard, which for a moment drowned out the toddler's cries. Charles and Fastrada headed the procession, with Pepin and Karl behind them. Their sisters followed, then the nobles. As the party rode on the city streets, Pepin tried to keep his mind on the stag they were about to pursue, rather than the whore Gomeric had hired for him two days before. His uncle's "favorite girl" was in her mid-twenties and already starting to age, but she kept him from thinking of Fastrada or Nantlind for a little while. A few kisses and a few touches, and it was all over. To his surprise, she apologized, promised to do better next time, and begged him not to tell anyone. He gave her an extra coin to quiet her fears.

A chill breeze stirred Pepin from his reverie. With gloved hands, he drew his cloak closer to his otter-fur vest. The overcast sky made the morning seem cooler. The party made a sharp right just past the cathedral's walls and soon filed through the west gate. The horses' hooves clopped against the paving stones as they passed a smaller church and its burial grounds before entering the forest, where the reds and yellows of the oak and ash trees blazed against the pines and the leaves crackled underfoot.

After another half hour, Pepin guessed, they took a path away from the road and followed it into a large clearing. While the rest of the party waited, huntsmen ran ahead with two dog-handlers and their charges. The remaining hounds tugged at their leashes.

About five paces away, Pepin spotted Gomeric chatting with the courtier Severinus. Frowning, he could not understand his kinsman's friendship with a nobleman who kept speaking on behalf of Duke Tassilo of Bavaria. *Oathbreaker owes his lands to Grandfather Pepin but listens to his loathsome Lombard wife instead of Father, his own cousin. Why does Tassilo let that shrew sway him? Let her be angry that Father divorced her stupid sister and overthrew her father. Tassilo pledged loyalty to our family.*

A cacophony of barks interrupted Pepin's thoughts. His father was speaking with one of the huntsmen. Pepin could not make out the words, and Fastrada seemed to be straining to hear as well. When Pepin saw his father reach for his horn, he smiled. The hunt was about to begin in earnest.

Charles sounded a series of short notes. With the hounds pulling their leashes taut, the dog handlers and huntsmen led the group through the trees to where they had seen tracks. The dogs jumped and wagged their tails as the handlers untied their leashes. Freed, the dogs buried their noses amid the leaves on the ground and paced the area. Pepin held his breath.

One of the dogs woofed. The other hounds raced to their fellow, their barks forming a chorus. Almost as one body, the hounds rushed forward, their paws barely touching the ground. Charles was the first to give chase. Fastrada followed. Pepin urged his stallion on. Beside him, Karl easily maneuvered his steed. As more joined the pursuit, the horses' hooves were like many drums to the dogs' music.

Pepin dodged between the trees, some so vast several men could fit inside, then ducked under a low branch. From behind, he heard a heavy body smack against wood, followed by a thud and vulgar shouts. Radolf. Pepin stifled a laugh. *Old fool.*

In the distance, he saw their quarry and kept the hounds within sight. The heat of the chase banished the chill in Pepin's flesh. Bits of twigs and leaves stuck to his sweaty face, and his breath came in sharp gasps. He did not know how much time had passed when the party found themselves in another clearing. Barking dogs had surrounded the stag, a large, magnificent beast with a shaggy coat and horns like branches. Its hair on end, the stag flattened its ears and regarded them with narrow eyes. It tensed its whole body and uttered a grunt that sounded like a growl.

Pepin's father, five paces ahead, turned. "Hruodtrude, Bertha, stay back!"

Pepin glanced behind him. Twenty paces away, his sisters pouted but obeyed their father. Beside Pepin, Karl was panting; his face wore a look of exuberance. Charles dismounted and unsheathed his seax. Three paces to Pepin's left, Gomeric did the same. Fastrada, two paces to Pepin's right, called for weapons. She was handed a javelin, and Karl received bow and arrows. When he slid off his horse, Pepin got a spear. He frowned.

"Pepin, is the weapon defective?" Charles yelled over the baying of the hounds.

"It should be a sword."

"The spear is good enough." His father turned away.

Pepin glowered. From the corner of his eye, he saw the stag paw the ground. Pepin's pulse pounded in his ears and throat while the dogs barked and bared their teeth. Lowering its head, the stag charged forward and thrust its large antlers. Two dogs yelped and fell. Blood covered the points on the antlers. As the other dogs fled, the stag chased Pepin's favorite hound and reared. Its forelegs landed on the dog's neck. She went limp as if made of rags.

"No!" he cried.

A javelin and arrows landed in the stag's side. The beast moaned and staggered.

Fastrada spat out a curse. Her bright blue eyes glowed with more bloodlust than Pepin had seen in most men.

Amid the baying of the hounds, Pepin, Charles, Gomeric, and other men dashed to their prey. The smell of blood and the stag's scent intoxicated Pepin. Before he could jam his spear into the beast, the stag lowered its head again and lunged at Pepin. Pain seared his left arm and chest.

"Pepin!" Gomeric screamed.

With an upward stroke, Charles hacked into the stag's massive neck. Blood burst from the wound, and the next moment, the beast crashed, the impact shaking the ground.

Dropping his spear, Pepin leapt back. He looked down. Blood flowed from the slashes on his arm and chest.

"Fetch the physician," Fastrada yelled.

In a daze, Pepin heard feet running toward him, and the whines and whimpers of the surviving hounds who wanted a huntsman to slice open the deer's belly so they could feast on its entrails. Still standing, he felt hands undoing his belt and peeling back his vest, tunic, and shirt.

"Thank God!" Charles cried. "The wounds aren't deep."

Gomeric pressed his hands against the cuts. "This will staunch the bleeding. Are you in pain?"

Pepin shook his head. He felt only the excitement of the hunt. He gazed about. His family had gathered around him. For once, his sisters looked worried instead of frightened of him. Karl's face was stern.

Pepin turned toward his father. "I was brave, wasn't I?"

"Yes, son."

"Can I have a sword now?"

"You have no need for one."

Pepin's elation blew away like dust.

Chapter Six

Naked beside Charles, Fastrada could hear the maids stirring outside their curtained bed. Listening to an iron rod poking against logs in the hearth, the scrape of a chamber pot dragged from under the bed, and the splash of water in the basins, Fastrada laid her head against Charles's large, scarred chest. As on their wedding night, he had been gentle with her, kissing and stroking her until she begged him to enter. Her pleasure far exceeded the few moments of pain on the first night. The only name Charles called out was dearling.

"We had better get dressed, my dear," Charles murmured, resting his hand on her hip. "Tell me, what have you heard about the gossip at my court?"

"The merchants say only half of it is true."

"They exaggerate." He chuckled. "Half is too much. The only truth you will know for certain is when they extol your beauty. When they ask you to tell me something, say that you will tell me what I need to hear. You decide what I truly need to hear."

"B-but I am so new to court," she stammered. "How can I ..."

Charles put a finger to her lips. "I need a queen who will give me counsel. If there is anything I have learned since I met you in Büraburg, it is that you are honest, intelligent, and strong willed. Come, my dear, we do not wish to be late for Mass."

Fastrada hoped she could prove Charles right. When her mother had died, looking after her father's household had daunted her. Somehow, she had managed to order servants and settle their quarrels and entertain the occasional guest, but the palace and its politics were more complex. So many more nobles sought her husband's favor, and he was asking her to determine whom he could rely on. She knew the nobility in East Francia and Thuringia but was uncertain about families on the western side of the realm.

No time to worry now. She and Charles parted the curtains on each side of the bed at the center of the room and rose. A bright fire illuminated two stools near the hearth, along with the huge tapestry of the Blessed Virgin and Her Child on the far wall.

After washing her hands and face, Fastrada pulled on her shift and let Nantlind help her into her vermillion underdress. She crossed the room and sat on a stool so Nantlind could drizzle violet-scented perfume into her hair and comb it. Someone scratched at the door. Already clad in drawers and his shirt, Charles glanced at Fastrada.

"Come, Meginfrid," he called.

The chamberlain, an East Frank with the broad shoulders and solid legs of a warrior, entered the room while all the maids except Nantlind left. Although Meginfrid was only in his twenties, he had already lost half his hair. He bowed to Charles and Fastrada, then opened a chest near the night candle, lifted one of Charles's tunics, and handed it to the king.

"What is today's business?" Charles asked. He donned the close-fitting tunic, sat on the edge of the bed, and stretched out his right leg.

Meginfrid knelt with his back to Fastrada and slipped on one of Charles's leggings. "Count Radolf has asked that his cousin be named the new bishop of Erfurt."

"Any reason not to grant this request, my dear?" Charles asked.

"No," Fastrada answered, letting Nantlind pull knee-high silk stockings onto her legs and tie the garters. "Our cousin is a learned man. He has been at an abbey since he saw seven winters." *He would know that book by Saint Augustine.*

Meginfrid cleared his throat. "My lady queen, there are rumors."

"An interesting story," Fastrada said. "Spread by families jealous of my lord's favor and God's blessing."

"You learn quickly, my dear." Charles lowered his voice. "But is it true?"

Her husband tilted his head toward the door, and Fastrada caught his meaning. Although they were alone with the chamberlain and her maid, a loose-tongued servant might suddenly decide to clean the corridor outside the royal bedchamber.

Her lips thinned. Charles was already testing her loyalty. She pitched her voice to carry no farther than Charles's ears. "He didn't touch boys or beasts. He loved another monk."

Charles smiled, and Fastrada let out a breath.

"Saint Paul says we've all sinned," Charles said. "Your cousin's transgressions are between him and his confessor."

"Thank you," Fastrada sighed.

"Meginfrid, who else today?"

As he continued to help Charles dress, Meginfrid listed the nobles seeking an audience. Listening to the names and the requests, Fastrada slipped her feet into short boots. When she rose, she thrust her arms through the long sleeves of the gown Nantlind held and allowed the maid to smooth the garment.

After Nantlind wrapped an emerald girdle around the queen's slender waist—one of Charles's many morning gifts—Fastrada walked to the casket with her jewelry and picked out her gold cross and the diamond betrothal ring.

"Will we have the Palace School today?" Fastrada asked as Nantlind laid a silk veil over her hair and secured it with the diadem that showed off a large beryl.

"Yes, my lady queen," Meginfrid answered. "The greatest minds in the realm."

Fastrada forced a smile. Charles often boasted of the scholars he had brought to court, among them Fardulf, a Lombard deacon and poet, and Alcuin, a Northumbrian deacon and former master of the church school in York. When she had first learned of the Palace School and that Charles's daughters were educated with his sons, she had been curious. Perhaps she could finally comprehend those Latin prayers at Mass. But her curiosity changed to anxiety after Pepin asked her about ... God's wounds, she couldn't remember the title of the book. Was she going to make a fool of herself again?

***

As soon as prime Mass ended, counts and clerics flocked around Charles and Fastrada like pigeons around a piece of bread and stayed with them while they left the chapel and crossed the courtyard. In the chill air, the courtiers' words smoked with bits and pieces about an ally's virtue or a foe's vice.

The chatter did not stop even as she and Charles entered the manor and broke their fast with bread, apples, cheeses, and slices of cold meat, and they kept talking while servants cleared the tables and put them away. The voices lowered a little when Charles stepped up on the dais and sat on his throne, specially made to support his hulking frame. After a moment, Fastrada followed her husband, bowed to him, and took her seat on a chair beside his. Clerks with wax tablets dangling at their waists surrounded them.

Smelling wine and boiled yarrow, Fastrada knew Pepin was nearby. The physician had used the concoction to clean and bind Pepin's wounds yesterday. Helped onto his horse by servants, the boy had ridden back to the palace at a slow pace and had not danced after dinner, but saints be praised, he seemed well otherwise. She looked in the direction of the scent and found Pepin's eyes boring into her. Sitting up a little straighter, she turned away from him.

Why was Pepin always so sullen? She had told a manservant to tend to him and ordered new clothes to be sewn to replace the ones ruined by the stag. She knew of nothing else she could do for him. The other children weren't like their eldest brother. Two paces away from Pepin, Karl was laughing with a count's son, perhaps exchanging jokes. She heard Bertha ask Hruodtrude's tutor, sent by the Byzantine emperor's mother, about the red star she had seen.

"Stop it! He is *my* tutor," Hruodtrude scolded.

Bertha hit her sister.

"Father," Hruodtrude said, "she ..."

"My dears, this is no way to act in public," Charles said. "Your mother will speak to you later. Wife, I will leave it to your discretion."

"If you disturb the court again, you're both going to your room and will stay there until after dinner," Fastrada said, keeping her voice even. *I just sounded like Mother.*

Both girls fell silent and dropped their hands to their sides. To her relief, the tutor stepped between the girls, and Bertha's nurse tempted the four-winter-old with a doll.

Fastrada scanned the crowd. Two cart lengths away, Gisela cradled her doll. Radolf chatted with two courtiers named Gomeric and Severinus. Kunigunde was nowhere to be seen. Come to think of it, she had not been at Mass this morning either. She would have Nantlind find out why.

When Meginfrid handed Charles his scepter, the hall quieted. Charles started by announcing that he was appointing Fastrada's cousin to be the bishop of Erfurt. One of the clerks scratched the decision on his tablet. Whispers hissed through the crowd, but her father's smile broadened. Pepin scowled.

Fastrada could not understand the boy's reaction. *What is a bishopric in East Francia to him?*

* * *

Pepin could already see the queen's influence over his father. Why else would Charles bestow a bishopric on her kinsman with unnatural desires? This girl had been at court less than a week, and his father was listening to her, a pretty Easterner who butchered Latin at Mass. He had grown up in the court, paid close attention to his tutors, yet his father never talked to him about what bishop or abbot to appoint.

Hruodtrude and her tutor were whispering to each other in Greek, and Bertha kept pestering them to tell her what they said. Karl nudged his friend and patted his wooden sword. Grinning, the other boy nodded and the two sneaked through the crowd toward a door to the outside.

In moments like these, Pepin envied Karl and his straight back. His hand strayed to the place where a sword would be and felt nothing but the leather of his belt.

Pepin stayed rooted, listening intently while his father appointed bishops, abbots, and abbesses. Fastrada's eyes were bright as she asked questions. How Pepin wished she would just hold her tongue. Yet he could not stop

35

watching her, admiring how her blue dress, the one she wore for the wedding, flowed over her breasts and hips. He clutched the cross that hung from his neck. He needed Gomeric's whore as soon as he could send for her.

He hoped Kunigunde would remember what to do this afternoon. If she did, he could defeat this succubus that took the shape of a queen.

Chapter Seven

Fastrada enjoyed her first day of court, but it had been intense. So many noble families asking Charles to give them church lands. As menservants set up trestle tables for dinner, she was relieved to descend the dais and ask the nurses and tutors about the children. She learned Pepin and Alcuin were discussing philosophers, Karl was more interested in history, especially about war, than Scripture, Hruodtrude spoke Greek well but still had a pronounced Frankish accent, Bertha was insisting on picking out her own dresses, and Gisela was outgrowing her tunic.

Fastrada tried to curb her annoyance at Hruodtrude and Bertha's bickering but could not help throwing up her hands and saying, "Bertha, stop whining! You'll learn Greek soon enough." She turned to Hruodtrude's tutor. "But kindly teach Bertha a few words."

"The Byzantine court sent him to be *my* tutor," Hruodtrude protested. "I am going to be an empress, not her."

"Daughter, you will be a fine empress," Fastrada said. "Having Bertha learn a few Greek words in no way hurts you. Stop being so selfish. Now I must see to dinner or you will all complain of hunger." *Just sounded like Mother again.*

While she and the steward's wife were inspecting the tablecloths, Fastrada spied Kunigunde near the door to the royal apartment. Charles approached the concubine, and she reached for his hand. Behind Fastrada, Radolf cleared his throat. Startled, she turned. With a stern look, he shook his head almost imperceptibly. Fastrada choked back the urge to spew obscenities. She seethed when Kunigunde gave Charles a weak smile and lay her hand on her swollen belly, and wondered if her rival had faked an illness to elicit Charles's sympathy.

When it was time to eat, Charles took his seat at the head of the table. Fastrada said nothing of the concubine and reminded herself that she, not Kunigunde, had the place of queen near him. Yet she could not quiet the whisper that Kunigunde was fat with her husband's child. Laying a hand on her own flat belly, she hoped Charles's seed would quicken there soon.

Dinner passed with laughter and song and gossip, but Fastrada fidgeted in her chair, nervous about the Palace School. After the last course, Charles helped Fastrada to her feet and led her to the hearth. They were followed by the royal family, the other noble children in the palace, guards and clerics, many of them older men, including Deacon Fardulf. As ordered, Nantlind hurried to the archive to fetch her lady's Psalter. A few of the courtiers joined them; other noblemen, her father and Gomeric and Severinus among them, went outside, probably to spar. Fastrada almost wished she, too, could go outside and escape the murmur of voices forming an undercurrent to the rattle of platters and cups servants cleared from the tables. Instead, she took her seat in a chair to Charles's right. Kunigunde sat on a stool to his left.

Fastrada's nostrils flared. "Lady Kunigunde, perhaps it would be better for you and the child if you were closer to the fire." *And farther away from my husband. He is mine. He swore a vow to me, not you.*

Kunigunde smirked. "How kind of you, my lady queen, but I am most comfortable here."

Charles frowned, then beckoned to a manservant. "Fetch a cushioned stool for Lady Kunigunde and place it near the hearth."

"My lord—" the concubine began.

"You're shivering," Charles said. "You must keep yourself and the babe warm."

Kunigunde, who hadn't shaken in the least, scowled. Fastrada allowed herself a small smile of satisfaction.

Panting, Nantlind brought the Psalter, a gift from Fastrada's late mother. Fastrada caressed the leather cover and opened the book to her favorite Psalm, the words swirling around the colored illuminations.

"Your Excellence," Kunigunde said, "I learned a new Psalm. Would you like to hear it?"

Charles grinned. Kunigunde spouted incomprehensible Latin. Fardulf corrected her but a few times.

Fastrada's heart felt as if it were made of lead. She could never recite a Psalm, even her favorite, so well.

"Queen Fastrada," Pepin asked, "what does that Psalm mean?"

"I don't know," she mumbled. She knew only what it wasn't. It wasn't either of the Psalms her mother had taught her. Kunigunde had made her look like a fool to her husband and the court. Her shoulders sagged as she thought of sinking through the cracks in the floor. *No!* said a voice within her. *No weakness. Not in front of the court. Not in front of your rival.*

Fastrada lifted her chin. If she could survive the Saxons' attack on Büraburg, she could endure the Palace School. She would not flee from another woman.

"My dear, this is a good Psalm to learn." Charles put his arm around her shoulders and turned the pages with his free hand. "This one. Alcuin, explain it to us."

Leaning into Charles's solid body, Fastrada felt safe. Kunigunde glared.

"We shall read it again," Alcuin said with a Northumbrian accent. "Hruodtrude will read the Latin, and Lord Karl, you give the Frankish meaning."

"I can do it," Pepin said, sounding annoyed.

"Yes," Karl said, "and he wants to."

"Yes, my lord," said Alcuin, "but Karl needs the practice."

Pepin snickered. Hruodtrude read a line of Latin, Karl rendered it into Frankish, and Alcuin led a discussion, often contradicted by Deacon Fardulf and a Visigothic monk. Fastrada felt as if a veil was lifted from her eyes. The squiggles on the page were starting to have meaning!

***

Pepin gritted his teeth. Gomeric's plan was failing. He had hoped for his father to praise him and Kunigunde for being so bright and learned, leaving Fastrada bent over her Psalter, weeping. Instead, the queen was smiling and nodding, even asking questions. And Kunigunde's brow furrowed as if in distress.

Why did his father care if his wife learned the Psalms? And why was it so important that Hruodtrude and the other girls study the liberal arts? All a woman needed to know was how to run a household and bear babies.

He was close enough to Fastrada to smell her violet perfume. *Ianua diaboli—doorway of the Devil.* He would expose the she-wolf even more. At some point, his father would see her true nature.

When the discussion of Psalm Thirty-six ebbed, Pepin asked, "Lady Queen Fastrada, what is your favorite Psalm?"

"My mother taught me this one," Fastrada replied, turning the pages. "*Dominus reget me et nihil mihi deerit.*"

Pepin held his breath to hold back his laughter. He didn't dare vex his father by openly mocking her lumbering over the Latin. Fardulf, however, politely corrected the queen's pronunciation.

"But that's how the priest said it back home," Fastrada protested.

Pepin bit his lip to keep from guffawing.

Fardulf folded his hands and said with a pronounced Lombard accent, "I teach you how we say in Rome, my lady queen."

Hruodtrude bounced in her seat. "I want to say what it means in Frankish. Karl got to last time."

Charles smiled. "Go ahead, dearling Hruodtrude."

"The Lord rules me and I shall want for nothing."

"Very good," said Alcuin. "This is a Psalm about faith."

"I want to read the next line in Latin," Hruodtrude said, which she did without waiting for an answer. Fardulf made only a couple of corrections. Fastrada was shifting in her chair.

"Lady Queen Fastrada," Pepin said, careful to keep his tone innocent as Gomeric had instructed, "what does it mean in Frankish?"

Fastrada made a choked sound. "Something about taking me to pastures and water."

"He has set me in a place of pasture," Pepin said. *"He has brought me up on the water of refreshment."*

"Excellent as always, Pepin," Alcuin said. "What this means is that God will provide for us."

To Pepin's satisfaction, Fastrada's flush ran down her neck.

***

After vespers Mass in the palace chapel redolent with incense, Fastrada paused near a painted wooden statue of Saint Ursula. She had promised Charles she would follow him and the children soon. In the light from the walnut oil lamps overhead, her bored bodyguards lingered near the doors. Before Fastrada could start her prayers in her best guess of the Latin, Fardulf sidled up beside her.

"Perhaps, I help you with Latin," he said in a low voice.

She turned toward the deacon. He wore a long-sleeved, ankle-length white tunic overlaid with a stole, both showing longtime use. Judging by the gray flecks in the dark hair left from the tonsure, she guessed he was a few winters older than Charles. She tried to remember what she had heard about him. He had been a favorite in the Lombard king's court and had supported the rebellion in Friuli a couple of years later. Yet Charles must have trusted Fardulf when he met him in Rome two years ago and asked him to come to the Frankish court. Her husband spoke of how he enjoyed Fardulf's poetry. Fardulf had a gift with Latin, but that didn't make him loyal.

"Why do you wish to help me?" she asked.

"I know what it like to be new to court," he said. "I know what it like when people talk language I do not understand. And maybe you help me with Frankish?"

Fastrada smiled, flattered. She knew she needed to be careful. Yet he had come right before she was going to ask Saint Ursula to send someone to help her learn Latin. Perhaps, her prayers had already been answered.

"Meet me in the archive tomorrow between tierce and sext," she said.

***

A few weeks later, Fastrada clutched her cloak against the chill and stood in the courtyard, struggling to keep her sadness in check. Her father was leaving for Hesse. It was a gray day, like the time her father had left to do battle in Lombardy ten years before. She almost felt her mother's fingers on her six-winter-old shoulders, heard her scolding, *Show tears in front of the servants, and they will be like wolves on a lame lamb.*

Here in Worms, she had watched over Büraburg's servants while they packed. Her father's possessions, his bed, chests of clothes, his leather tent, supplies, weapons, were in many carts. The only thing that bore her touch was a few tunics she had embroidered for him. *Is this the last time I will see him?*

He would be back in Büraburg before the Feast of the Nativity and could attend the three Masses in the church where she was baptized. The stone structure was smaller than many she'd seen in her travels, but it was the only one she had known for sixteen winters. Already, she longed for its painted wooden statues of the Virgin with her bright blue veil and Saint Georg skewering the dragon. She would never see Büraburg again! Nor would she hunt in its beech and oak forests or stand in the tower and behold the fields of barley and wheat outside the thick fortress walls. She had known this since her father announced her betrothal, but seeing the carts in the palace courtyard made the reality slap like a sharp wind.

"Daughter, what troubles you?" Radolf asked.

"I miss Büraburg. I miss knowing that our enemy is beyond its walls, not within them." She gazed at the stone manor and its many windows.

"What are you talking about?"

"Kunigunde makes me look stupid. She asks questions expecting me not to know the answers. Sometimes, she speaks to me in Latin."

"Young women and their humors." Her father shook his head. "You're comparing Saxon murderers to a concubine who's jealous you're queen? How many times must I tell you to stop letting it bother you?"

"Because I think she's swayed Pepin to her side. He does the same thing. He seems determined to dislike me, and I don't know why. We barely know each other."

Her father shrugged. "Don't trouble yourself about the little bastard. Make sure he has food, clothing, and a retinue, and you've done your duty."

"But his sullenness is like a dark cloud sometimes."

"Daughter, some people just can't be pleased no matter what you do. Pepin sounds like one of them. It's not your fault God cursed him and denied him a kingdom. What about Karl?"

"He worries me."

"How so?"

"Have you seen him spar? He might hurt himself or one of his friends."

"Is that all? Boys will get bruises. It's the only way they'll learn."

"And the girls are starting to accept me," Fastrada said. "If only they would stop bickering. I don't like always having to correct them."

Her father grinned. "Now you know how your mother and I felt. You will be fine."

She embraced her father, clinging.

"I am so proud of you," he murmured.

Fastrada's throat tightened. She had never heard him say those words to her. They released each other and took a half step back. Her father's eyes were welling.

"I will send messages," Fastrada said, her voice choked. "I will pray for you."

"You're in my prayers, too." Radolf managed a smile. "You will always be in my heart."

Fastrada felt a pang in her bosom. For a moment, she wanted to mount her favorite mare and ride back to Hesse. Anything not to be separated, perhaps forever.

"Daughter, this is no time for tears," Radolf said, wiping his face.

"Thank you," she whispered. She dried her eyes with her sleeve. "Thank you for this marriage. I will miss you."

"And I, you. God be with you."

"God be with you, also."

***

Preparing for the departure to Herstal, Fastrada checked on the servants packing the treasury's contents—her responsibility as queen—several times throughout the day. The archive with all its books, maps, and letters was next. She hurried past the garden and kitchen to the stables behind the barracks, where the groom promised he would say the incantation to protect each horse from injury. Then Fastrada rushed to the kitchen to make sure the men and maids packed enough rounds of hard travel bread and salted meat and filled the carts with wine.

Even with Meginfrid's and the seneschal's assistance, she was exhausted at the end of the day and retired soon after the evening meal. The next morning, she watched the servants disassemble beds and load them in one of the ox carts. Before they were to leave, she hurried through the rooms in the royal apartment, making sure all the chests had been filled. Having to do this every few months annoyed her, but such was life at court. The lands at the palaces could sustain the royal household, guests, and servants only a few months—a year at best. Very different from life in Büraburg.

Charles helped Fastrada onto her mare then mounted a gelding large enough to carry him. Surrounded by bodyguards, Charles and Fastrada headed the procession, with Karl and Pepin behind them. Riding smaller steeds, Hruodtrude and Bertha followed their brothers. Their sister Gisela was carried in a horse-borne portable cradle, and Kunigunde used a horse-borne litter. Fastrada hoped she'd never been so infirm as to need a litter, which resembled the cradle too much to her liking. Both were boxes attached to long poles on the right and left. Leather straps connected the poles at the ends and were placed over harnesses for the horses, which were led by grooms.

Along with the children's nurses and tutors, courtiers followed the royal family, then guards and soldiers. At the rear were servants and the horse and ox carts loaded with supplies, protected by the rearguard.

As the procession advanced, peasants in woolen and sheepskin cloaks stood in front of their wattle-and-daub huts to watch. Fastrada noticed parents talking to their children and pointing her way. Fastrada shifted in her saddle. She had drawn attention from the villagers in Büraburg but never like this. Were they wondering if she would ever be as good as Hildegard? After the guards opened the north gate, the travelers rode through a large area with a mix of Christian burials and Roman monuments to the dead. Fastrada was glad to leave the city's stink of refuse behind, but graves made her uneasy, even in daylight. Her hand strayed to her cross then her enameled bronze brooch with Saint Wigbert's image.

The back of her neck relaxed when they crossed fields with burnt stubble, probably wheat and rye, but the forest loomed ahead, most of its trees bare. The reds and yellows that had greeted Fastrada when she had first arrived had browned and fallen and filled the forest with their smell. The party passed the last sign of civilization, swine tended by boys who wore stained, patched tunics. The leaves crackled while the sleek, fat pigs rooted for the last of the acorns. Soon, the swine would be slaughtered to feed the steward's and bishop's households through the winter.

Shivering, Fastrada pulled her marten fur-lined cloak closer to her body. With the leaves off the branches, she could catch glints of the Rhine to her right. It seemed empty without the ducks and gulls, now in their distant winter homes to the south. To her left were a mass of trees and shrubs, where starlings roosted and squirrels scurried on the trunks. Bandits could be hiding in the dense forest, watching them now, yet she felt safe. The battle-scarred guards all displayed their weapons. But outlaws were not her only worry. The forest was home to demons, fairies, and who knew what other creatures. She touched her jeweled dagger, comforted by the cold iron that spirits loathed, and focused on the journey ahead.

"What is the Herstal villa like?" she asked over the clop of the hooves.

"Smaller than the palace at Worms," Charles answered, "but a good winter home."

"Think we'll hear from Tassilo while we're at Herstal?" Pepin asked.

"He and his wife would like to think we have forgotten them, but Gerold keeps me apprised."

"Count Severinus says Tassilo and Luitperga are not a threat."

"Of course, he would." Charles snorted. "But I don't forget oath-breakers, especially when they conspire with the Avars."

Saints be praised that Gerold remains loyal, Fastrada thought. Hildegard's brother had lands in Swabia just west of Bavaria, and he had allies in the Tassilo's territory. East of the duchy, the pagan Avars were powerful, with an empire stretching through the Transylvanian mountains. Yet she remembered something her father had told her. "Was there not a delegation of Avars at last year's assembly?"

"They were strange!" Karl said. "When we took them hunting, they stood in ... what are those things called, Father? Those loops they had hanging below their saddles, where they put their feet?"

Charles thought for a moment. "Stirrups."

"What an odd thing," Fastrada said.

"You should've seen them," Karl said. "They stood in their stirrups and shot at the stag. God's wounds, you never would have expected a bow so thin to shoot so far."

Fastrada hoped her cloak hid her shudder. She dreaded the idea of the Franks facing those weapons on the battlefield.

"They promised peace," Charles said, "but they lied, just like the Saxons. Had Widukind not roused the Saxons to rebellion, we could have conquered them."

Fastrada tightened her grip on the reins but loosened her fingers when her mare shuffled. She had not forgotten last year's disastrous battle in the Süntel Mountains north of her home, the fault of a few Frankish noblemen who had rushed into battle without enough men rather than follow the original plan. Was it for glory? Or was it as her father said—that they feared the Saxons would strike first? Following orders, Radolf had been lucky to escape with the large gash in his side. *They paid with their lives and their men's. Had it not been for Charles, we would have lost more.* She hoped no one would distract her husband from that fight as the Lombards had.

"Are the Lombards still causing trouble?" Fastrada asked.

"They are peaceful in the north of Italy, restless in the south," Charles said. "The Holy Father tells me what they are doing. For now, they are quiet."

"The Saxons are quiet now too," Fastrada said. "They won't be in the spring."

Chapter Eight

December 783, Herstal

By the time they reached Herstal, the days were very short, and a thin layer of snow covered the frozen fields. As they passed peasant huts and shivering commoners, Fastrada thought it strange for the villa to be near the waterway rather than atop one of the forested hills. Then again, these hills were much lower and easier for an enemy to climb than the one on which Büraburg sat. Still, the defenses impressed her. The River Meuse to her right provided one barrier against attackers. A curved earthen wall, with a trench of water, protected its other three sides. Battlements rose above the walls to give the guards a view of anyone approaching. As Charles had said, the villa was more modest than the Worms palace, but she had not expected it to be smaller than Büraburg nor to have only two towers, compared to the four at her birthplace.

Inside the villa's walls, Fastrada discovered one tower fronted the chapel, a stone structure with arched windows and three curved apses. To her left sat the royal residence, a rectangular stone building with square windows and the second tower. Beyond the wooden barracks between the residence and chapel, she glimpsed the kitchen and bathhouse behind it. The steward and his household had gathered in the courtyard to greet them. After introductions, Fastrada was watching over the palace servants as they unpacked the contents of the treasury in its stone room across an interior atrium from the great hall. The steward, or more likely his wife, had made sure the space was clean and free of any signs of vermin, as was the archive next to it. Inside the great hall, Fastrada breathed in the scent of fir and pine boughs decorating it for the Feast of the Nativity. She reminded herself to speak well of the couple to Charles.

The Nativity was joyous with the Masses and feasting. In the ensuing weeks, whenever the villa received a message from a nobleman or a spy, Fastrada was at Charles's side as he and his magnates retreated to the archive to study maps and speculate where the pagans would attack. Her husband encouraged Karl to accompany them to talk about strategy and weapons, and Pepin tagged along. Each seemed determined to outdo the other with their questions. *I hope my own sons will be as intelligent.*

When a letter from her father finally arrived, it was no help. One of his spies said the pagans would try to retake the fortress of Eresburg. Another said they would be bold enough to attack Charles's palace in Paderborn. A third said they would come from the Saxon settlement at Lübbecke.

"Where do you think they will strike, my dear?" Charles said.

Fastrada blinked in surprise. He had asked her the question just like he would one of his magnates. At Büraburg, her father had threatened to expel her from the room if she did not hold her tongue. After a moment, she found her voice. "It would be like Widukind to seek allies in Frisia this winter rather than flee to his father-by-marriage in Nordmannia. Some place to the north, near the River Weser, would make sense."

Fastrada felt most certain of herself when she and Charles spoke of war. She knew war. The Saxons' weapons and ferocity were as familiar to her as Latin was to the clerics of the Palace School. She did her duty to Charles's daughters, asking the Byzantine tutor about Hruodtrude and the nurses about the younger girls. But this was where a queen belonged, where Kunigunde had no place.

Thanks to Nantlind, Fastrada knew her rival was going to rule an abbey after the birth, and she was so glad Kunigunde was leaving that she didn't care about the concubine's animosity. But Fastrada worried Charles would change his mind. The rounder Kunigunde became, the more solicitous Charles was. To Fastrada's disappointment, her own belly remained flat. When Kunigunde confessed her sins to the archchaplain and began her stay in the lying-in room next to the royal bedchamber, Fastrada was glad her rival was out of Charles's sight but dreaded the birth that would come. She prayed the baby would be a girl.

On a cold, dark morning, she awoke to Nantlind's shaking her shoulder. "It's Kunigunde's time," the maid whispered.

Anxiety surged through Fastrada. "Has the midwife been summoned?"

"Yes."

"Good." Fastrada leaned over Charles's ear. "The child is coming. Servants are fetching the midwife."

Charles made the sign of the cross. Both he and Fastrada crawled out from under the furs and dressed quickly.

"I will be in the chapel," he said. His voice was tense.

Fastrada held both his hands in hers. "I will send word when the child comes."

Charles squeezed her hands before she rushed to the lying-in room. The chamber's huge bed and the low ceiling, two hand widths above Fastrada's head, made her feel confined. Already full of women, the room was warm despite the wind rattling against the tapestry-covered shutters. The fire had been stoked and more logs piled upon it, and the thick night candle and several beeswax candles added to the warmth and light. Fastrada hoped the men and royal children had all hurried to the chapel to pray for Kunigunde and her baby.

Fastrada scanned the room, making sure it was worthy of the king's child. Straw and strewing herbs of thyme and mint covered the floor, giving the space a pleasant scent. A maidservant was shaking out a coverlet for the birthing chair. Other maids were bringing water for a bath. The baby's nurse, an upstanding woman whom Fastrada had hired, was suckling her own infant on a stool in the corner of the room. *Why won't Charles's seed take hold in me?*

Kunigunde groaned as she and her maid threaded their way among the women. Fastrada felt a sudden sympathy for her rival. *This must be worse than the pains during womanly courses.* She stepped back to let Kunigunde pass.

"Wilberga will be here soon," Fastrada said. "She brought Queen Hildegard's children into the world." Fastrada bit her lip, wondering if she should have spoken of the late queen. Childbirth had caused her death, and the baby had lived only forty days.

The concubine's cries became louder and louder. Although Fastrada suspected only moments had passed, it seemed like hours before Wilberga, a stout old woman, arrived with her assistants. The midwife reached under Kunigunde's skirts and felt her belly.

"Any pins in your hair?" Wilberga asked.

"No," Kunigunde murmured.

"Good. Are all the knots untied? Are all the cupboards and drawers open? Are the chests unlocked?"

Every woman in the room, even the courtiers' wives, rushed to do the midwife's bidding. One of the assistants handed Wilberga an open clay jar smelling of fennel. The old woman rubbed the oil on Kunigunde's belly. After wiping her hands on a rag, she tied a piece of jasper to the concubine's thigh.

"Keep walking, my lady," the midwife said. "It will help the jasper hasten the birth."

When the church bells rang the hour for prime Mass, Wilberga held a crane's foot to Kunigunde's belly. No effect. An hour later, Wilberga whispered in Kunigunde's ear. "A spell to make the baby come forth," she said.

Kunigunde kept walking and moaning. All Fastrada and the women could do was wait and watch the midwife encourage Kunigunde. Moments after the tierce bells, Kunigunde stopped and looked down.

"Are you wet?" Wilberga asked.

"Yes," Kunigunde answered in a small voice.

"Good. The baby is coming."

The midwife ordered her assistant to get the birthing stool ready. After a maid laid the coverlet over the horseshoe-shaped seat, Kunigunde hiked up her skirts and sat down. Wilberga washed her hands in a basin of water and oiled them. As the midwife reached under Kunigunde's skirts, Fastrada and the other women gathered around. Kunigunde strained and grunted. Fastrada held her breath.

"Keep pushing, my lady; you're doing well," the midwife coaxed. "There's the crown. Very good. Now the face. Just a few more pushes. Oh, very good."

Wilberga pulled back with the baby in her arms. "A girl! A big girl!"

Fastrada covered her mouth as she beheld the child, perfectly formed, with Charles's round face. She could not stop the tears. A girl! Her prayers had been answered! *Thank you, Jesu. Thank you, Mother Mary. Thank you, Saint Wigbert.*

A hush fell over the room as the midwife wiped the baby's mouth with a cloth. The newborn started sobbing and was soon drowned out by the women's cheers.

"Go tell Charles he has a daughter," Fastrada choked out to Nantlind.

Nantlind ran. An assistant pushed on Kunigunde's belly, releasing the afterbirth and a torrent of blood. Gasps filled the room, and Wilberga's face fell. Kunigunde's eyes grew wide.

Fastrada spat out a profanity and grabbed a maidservant's arm. "Run to the church and tell them to pray for Kunigunde!"

Fastrada turned back to Kunigunde and the baby. The assistant was frantically massaging Kunigunde's belly. Cutting the cord, the midwife called for ergot.

White-faced and sweating, Kunigunde stared down. Fastrada covered her mouth. She had seen maidservants at her father's house bleed like this. Sometimes, the midwife could stop the bleeding. Other times ... Fastrada made the sign of the cross.

A grim assistant offered a potion to Kunigunde. Another untied the jasper from Kunigunde's thigh and held it to the new mother's belly.

"What's going to happen to me?" Kunigunde whimpered.

"Pray to the Virgin," the assistant said.

Fastrada swallowed hard, trying to suppress the nausea. She had prayed to be rid of her rival but not this way. She murmured, "*Ave Maria gratia plena.*" *Please, Mother Mary, let her live. Let her go to the abbey.*

Chapter Nine

er eyes glazed, Kunigunde slumped against the birthing chair.

"How strong a dose was the ergot?" Wilberga asked as she washed the infant.

"Any more now and she will be poisoned," her assistant said.

"Get her to the bed. Make her comfortable."

With the metallic smell of blood filling the room, Kunigunde's maid started to undress her lady.

Fastrada shook off the panic that gripped her throat. "Why are you gawking?" she snarled at the women. She pointed at each maid as she spoke. "You, put straw on the bed and cover it with a sheet. You, help the lady get to bed. The rest of you, get rid of this mess."

As the women scurried about, Kunigunde's maid stuffed rags between her lady's legs and secured them with a cord around her waist, then helped her to bed. The concubine lay limp while her maid covered her with blankets.

Fastrada approached the bed, wondering if she could leave matters to the midwife and go to the chapel. She tried to hide her shock when she beheld Kunigunde. The concubine was paler than the sheets.

Kunigunde glowered. "You've witnessed the birth of the king's child as is your duty. Now leave. You can gloat out of my sight."

Son of a whore's sow! Kunigunde, you've left me no choice. "We will leave when *we* will it so, not you." Fastrada was surprised by the ice in her own voice, but it was either that or she would scream. "It is beneath us to gloat. We are queen. We are responsible for the king's children."

"She is *my* baby!"

"She is the king's daughter."

The newborn cried out. Fastrada turned toward the sound, and her lower lip trembled. Months ago, she had accepted the duty of providing for the infant, but the sight of the helpless girl stirred something in her heart. *God made me that child's mother.* Fastrada took a deep breath to steady her voice and grasped her cross. "Lady Kunigunde, the baby will have her rightful place with the other girls. She will not want for anything—food, clothes, nurses, or tutors. I swear this to you by God, creator of heaven and earth."

Wearily, Fastrada sank to her knees, pressing her weight against the straw on the stone floor, and called to the other ladies. Kunigunde gaped at her.

"We are to pray for Lady Kunigunde until the Good Lord restores her to health or takes her home. Wilberga, after our little Hruodhaid is fed, present her to His Excellence."

Kunigunde let out a sob. "How dare you! You have no right to name her."

Fastrada gave Kunigunde a puzzled look. "His Excellence has every right. He said if the babe is a girl, call her Hruodhaid, after his late sister."

Kunigunde turned away.

"He never talked to you about the baby's name?" The words tumbled out of Fastrada's mouth before she had a chance to stop them. *Father was right. Kunigunde never was the enemy.* "I ... I didn't mean to cause you pain. I just thought Charles ..."

Fastrada could feel the other women's eyes on her. Kunigunde turned toward her. She was no longer a rival. Just a frail, anguished woman.

"After he brought you home, he rarely talked to me about anything. It's your fault he's sending me away." The weakness of Kunigunde's voice did not conceal her bitterness.

"You ..." Fastrada stopped herself from saying, *You have no right to complain that Charles is a steadfast husband.* Kunigunde's fading vigor squelched any urge to argue, especially when Fastrada had won this fight months ago. She could not rue Charles's repudiation of the concubine, but she wanted to say something to comfort her. Fastrada fumbled for words and settled on, "I know my marriage caused you sorrow. I wish it hadn't."

Kunigunde raised her eyebrows slightly. "Thank you," she finally whispered. "Will you pray for me and my daughter?"

"Let us start with the Paternoster." Fastrada blinked back the mist in her eyes.

***

Pain shot through Fastrada's legs. She did not know how long she had been at Kunigunde's bedside, murmuring the prayer to the Blessed Virgin and the Paternoster as best she could. Her voice blended with the other women's. Kunigunde lay silent, even when the women paused to allow Wilberga to give her a little more potion.

The old woman shook her head. "Bleeding's slowed but not enough."

Fastrada ordered the maids to change the concubine's rags and slip clean straw underneath her. Kunigunde opened her eyes briefly, but Fastrada couldn't read her expression. As the hours passed, Fastrada suppressed the

50

urge to weep that a woman's life was being cut so short. *It was not supposed to be like this.*

Sometime after vespers, she heard a rustle near the head of the bed. The midwife pressed her hand against Kunigunde's neck and shook her head.

Fastrada swallowed back her tears and held them in the pit of her belly. If she cried now, it might cause Kunigunde's soul to linger. "*Requiescat in pace*," she murmured, imitating the priest in Büraburg.

Making the sign of the cross, she rose. She ordered one of the maids to tell the sexton to ring the bell and sent another to fetch carpenters to build a coffin.

"Nantlind, help Lady Kunigunde's maid wash her and find fine linen for a shroud."

Fastrada left the lying-in chamber and made her way through the royal apartment's dark corridor. In the reception room, now cold and dim in the light of glowing embers, she shivered and drew deep breaths, relieved to escape the smell of blood. The space seemed to spin. Bracing her hand against the plastered wall, she realized she had not touched any food that day. The church bell started to ring.

Weariness flooded through her. She only wanted to feel her husband's arms encircle her and hold her close. *Find Charles.*

After retrieving her cloak and gloves from the bedchamber, she stumbled out of the royal apartment and into the great hall, gloomy in the waning light of the day, with shadows starting to cover the bright murals of Charles's grandfather defending Francia from Muslims. When she saw the boards for the tables and benches stacked against the walls, Fastrada vaguely remembered that the steward's wife had left the lying-in chamber to make sure the household was fed. Except for a few whispering guards and servants lighting torches, the large room, smelling of thyme and mint on the floor, was quiet, unnaturally so. A male voice startled her.

"My lady queen, our lord king ordered me to take you to him." The guard took a torch from its holder in the wall.

Fastrada muttered her thanks and trudged beside him through the hall to the entryway. When they stepped outside, she welcomed the wind that slapped her face and made the torch's flame waver. It reminded her she was alive. Then she was chilled. Holding her cloak close, she quickened her steps to the chapel, a small stone structure dedicated to Our Lady.

Inside, she made out the shapes of the men and children against the candlelight at the altar in the apse at the far end. She could see only a little of the mural of Christ in Majesty above the cross. The dark gray light masked the frescoes on the other walls, painted wooden statues, and the apses flanking the marble altar and its gold box embedded with gems. She felt empty.

Charles and his sons stood near the altar while the girls knelt before a statue of the Virgin. She approached the group with her husband but waited for them to end the Paternoster. After the amen, she softly said her husband's name.

When he turned toward her, his usually bright eyes seemed dull. Then he furrowed his brow. "My dear, are you ill?"

Beside him, Pepin snorted in derision. "You don't fool me," he sneered. "You're glad she's dead. You prayed for it."

Fastrada trembled, unable to still the rage. "Hold your tongue, you twisted little boy! If not for your father, I would have you flogged for such a lie."

Everyone in the room turned toward her. Charles's features hardened into stern lines. He was going to scold her in public! Fastrada stood up straighter, clenched her fists, and braced herself. Her eyes stung. *Don't show weakness. Don't give him the satisfaction of tears.*

"No bitch orders me around like a common servant!" Pepin snarled.

Fastrada heard gasps from the girls. Charles laid a heavy hand on his son's stooped shoulder, turned the boy, and slapped him. Pepin's head snapped back.

"You will not speak to the queen that way again." Charles's steady voice held only a hint of anger.

Fastrada's throat tightened with the effort to hold back the tears. The whole room was still.

"But she called me ..."

Charles slapped him again. "You insulted the queen. To insult her is to insult me."

"You never side with me!" Pepin's voice was on the edge of a sob.

Charles turned his son to face Fastrada and shoved him forward. "You will ask the queen for her pardon."

Hatred blazed in Pepin's deep blue eyes. "I apologize," he mumbled.

"Louder," Charles said, raising his voice.

"I apologize, Queen Fastrada." It came out as a growl.

"It will not happen again, will it, Pepin?"

"No."

"I ... I give you my pardon," Fastrada replied, willing her tongue to move. "Because you are the king's son, I give you my pardon for falsely accusing me of praying for a countrywoman's death."

Charles arched a brow.

Fastrada met his eyes. "I cannot pretend to have liked her, but I would never ask Our Lord to strike down a Frank, especially the mother of the king's daughter. I am not a traitor, and I did my duty to her when she was alive. She wanted for nothing as a guest of this house.

"And now that the Good Lord has taken her, I will do everything within my power for the repose of her soul and care of the baby. With your permission, my lord, I must go to the treasury for alms to be given on her behalf."

"You are a good wife and a good queen," Charles said. "The courtiers and the servants are to obey and serve you as they would me. Pepin, you may go to a priest and confess your sins."

***

When the matins bells rang in the middle of the night, Fastrada was drained and wanted to crawl under the furs and blankets and lie next to Charles. She had spent the last few hours planning Kunigunde's funeral feast and deciding what alms to give.

She and Charles, along with Nantlind and Meginfrid, entered the reception room, but he grabbed her elbow, preventing her progress to the bedchamber, where maidservants already slept on cots and pallets. Fastrada frowned.

"Stoke the fire and leave us," Charles said. "I must speak to the queen in private."

As she watched the maid and chamberlain do her husband's bidding, Fastrada felt her throat go dry. Charles was going to berate her for what she had said to his son! She held up her chin, refusing to show any sign of fear or weakness. She would not cry out, lest the children or servants in the nearby rooms hear, and she hoped Charles would keep his voice down. The servants already would gossip plenty about this; she did not want them to have proof.

Once they were alone, Charles told Fastrada to sit in one of the two chairs near the fire. He took a seat in the chair made specially for his massive frame. In the flickering light, Fastrada scanned her husband's face.

He sighed. "Disciplining Pepin in public is like holding a hot iron in my sword hand. But he left me no choice. Respect for the queen is essential to the court. If he did not apologize, the courtiers would take advantage of you in my absence. We can't have that."

His voice was calm. Not knowing how to respond, she nodded that she understood.

"My dear, I will always defend your honor as my wife and queen, but you must learn to control your tongue. Don't call my son names again."

"You heard what he said!" she whispered. "Do you expect me, the queen of the Franks, to say nothing?"

"I expect you to remember you are queen and act accordingly," he said coldly.

"You never spoke to Hildegard like this," she muttered.

"I didn't need to."

His voice was level, but Fastrada flinched. Those words hurt more than a slap.

53

Chapter Ten

March 784, Nivelles

It took Pepin and his guards five days of riding through the woods to reach his mother's double monastery at Nivelles. He had left a week after Kunigunde's funeral, in the early days of Lent. The weather was cool enough for him to need his leather gloves, otter-fur vest, and heavy cloak, but he and his guards did not encounter any sudden ice storms. Asking to come here and pray to Saint Gertrude had been easy. His father even handed him a bag of coins to give to his mother as alms and ask for her prayers in the coming war.

He still fumed about his father's blows the night Kunigunde had died. How dare Fastrada come into the chapel and pretend to be distressed? Did she think the court was populated with fools? He had merely spoken the truth and was forced to apologize to a she-wolf.

If that shrew had been his wife, he would have beaten her bloody and then used her. That night, he listened for clues that his father had punished her in private but heard nothing. When he watched her the next morning, she still held her head high. Instead of cringing when his father held her hand, she smiled up at him. Her manner toward Pepin was icy. She made sure he had enough food and supplies for the journey and said she'd pray for his safety. But her tone made it clear her prayers were only a duty, something she would do with her mouth, not her heart.

If only Gomeric had been at Herstal instead of tending to his duties as count at his home in Maastricht. Pepin needed to talk to someone who understood. He wondered whether Gomeric had gotten the message he had sent.

Pepin dug the wire points on his heels into his horse's flanks to spur the beast along in the twilight. He longed to be near a fire amid the smells of hot food, even if it was fish and bread. Passing squat peasant huts in the gray light, he made out three rectangular sandstone structures that seemed smaller than he remembered. The funerary church where he would pray at the tombs of Saint Gertrude and her mother, Saint Itta, sat to his immediate right. The church dedicated to Our Lady stood about one-hundred paces away, and farther to his left was the chapel. The abbess's residence, a large wooden building, lay between the two churches.

After dismounting and handing the reins to a groom, Pepin strode into his mother's home. A guard greeted him in the entryway and led him to the great hall, where tapestries covered the walls. His feet crunched the thyme and lemon balm, which smelled fresh, like they had been strewn on the floor that day for an important guest. In the firelight, he saw Gomeric sitting on a cushioned stool near the stone hearth, next to a woman wearing a dark blue silk veil secured with jeweled pins. She was already turned toward Pepin, her eyes eager.

"Abbess Himiltrude, Lord Pepin has arrived."

"You may leave us," she said to the guard.

Beaming, she rushed to Pepin and hugged him fiercely. As he returned the embrace, his mind flooded with the memory of their last meeting six years ago. Her touch was loving and strong then, too. No hesitation. No shudder of revulsion. The only difference was that now he was almost as tall as she.

Himiltrude pulled back slightly. "You were a beautiful boy when I last saw you, but look at you now. Gomeric, you didn't tell me what a handsome young man my son is."

Pepin regarded the stranger who was his mother. She had seen thirty years, he guessed, but she looked younger, with pale skin unwrinkled by the sun. Her gown was white over a brown underskirt, her sole concession to humility. Hildegard and Fastrada would have envied the glittering girdle at her waist and the blue woolen cloak lined with marten fur.

As she stepped back, she glanced at his belt and frowned. "Did my guards take your sword? I ordered them not to. I want to see the blade your father gave you."

"I don't have a sword, Mother."

From the look she gave him, he might as well have said his father was covered with boils. "You're a king's son! You should have a sword," she said in Latin as good as a clerk's.

"My father wants me to take holy orders," he replied in the same language, surprised to hear his mother speak it.

"Hildegard's doing, isn't it?"

Pepin nodded.

"I should have known," she said in a low voice. "And I hear your father's new wife is a shrew."

Pepin blinked as if hit by a sudden wind. No one would have dared say that about Fastrada at home. He glanced about. The room was empty except for the three of them.

Gomeric winced. "Perhaps, you shouldn't say …"

"It's my abbey, and I will say what I please. Charles wouldn't dare take it away, not if he wants my sisters and brothers to keep praying for him and the kingdom." She laughed. "Oh, Gomeric, do you think I'm a simpleton? I allow only those loyal to me to learn Latin beyond the prayers. Pepin, stop gawking. Refresh yourself and have a seat by the fire." She gestured toward a small table bearing a tray with wine, cheese, and rolls.

"I've never heard you speak like this, not in person, not in your letters," Pepin said when he could finally find his voice.

"You had seen only nine winters when you last visited me. I thought there was a chance your father would still provide you with your rightful inheritance."

Pepin took a gulp of wine that burned as it slid down his throat. "He would if you had not sinned!"

Himiltrude bristled. "What sin?"

"Don't play ignorant with me!" Pepin cried. "Your sin bent my back."

"It wasn't *my* sin." Her words came out slowly as if her fury were a dog straining at its leash.

Pepin put his hand to his chest as if an arrow had struck him.

"When you came out of my womb," Himiltrude said, "you were perfect. Why else would Charles give you his father's name?"

"My back was straight?" His hand reached over his shoulder and felt the top of his spine under his shirt. For as long as he could remember, it had been curved and had gotten worse in recent years.

"Your spine started to bend about a year after you learned to speak," Gomeric said, "about the same time the king married Hildegard instead of restoring his rightful queen. Although your mother had already taken the vow, the Holy Father surely would have granted a dispensation."

Pepin's jaw tightened. His *father's* sin had caused his deformity!

"Charles was greedy," Himiltrude added. "He wanted all of his dead father's realm for himself, so he stole it from his own nephews. And he needed Hildegard's family to do it."

Hildegard. The woman Pepin had once considered a mother had convinced his father to deny him a kingdom. His face felt hot. "Grandmother Bertrada said you took the veil to do penance."

"I took the veil because it was the only way to preserve what was left of my honor. Our family let your father think we were appeased."

"We never forgot your mother should be queen," Gomeric added, "and you should be the heir. That's why we're seeking allies like Severinus."

"And it's the reason I learned to speak Latin and read and write," Himiltrude said. "Son, I know you can read. Promise me you will learn to write. I want letters from your hand, not from a clerk prone to gossip. It will help us place you on the throne when the time is right. Tell your father learning to write will make you better suited to serve the Church."

"I promise, Mother." Pepin felt as if a blindfold had been removed from his eyes, one he had never known existed. *Place me on the throne.*

***

After Pepin's return to Herstal, his father continued to spend hours planning for war against the Saxons. Charles frequently asked Karl to accompany him, the queen, and his magnates to the archive, the store of maps and messages, some from Radolf about East Francia and Saxony, others from Little Pippin's guardian about unrest among the Lombards in Italy, and still others from Hildegard's brother, Gerold, and his Bavarian friends about Duke Tassilo forming alliances with malcontent Lombards. Although not invited, Pepin had followed and watched, as Gomeric had instructed.

The days became more temperate, and the windows were open more often, revealing the river behind the chapel outside. Swollen with spring rains, the waterway reflected the trees studded with leaf buds and blooms, and Pepin could see storks and grebes returning from their winter homes. He welcomed the Feast of the Resurrection and its Holy Communion and great procession with censers, holy water, and crosses—and the end of Lent.

Eight days later, Pepin, his father, the queen, Karl, and the magnates surrounded a table, where a map of Francia and Saxony was spread. Pepin glanced at his brother beside him. Although three years younger, Karl was almost as tall as he.

"Karl," Charles asked, "if the Saxons make trouble near Frisian lands, where should we cross the Rhine?"

"We should ..." Pepin began, pointing to the map.

"Be quiet, Pepin. I asked Karl."

Pepin crossed his arms and glowered.

Karl smirked. "Lippeham."

"Very good, Karl."

A scratch at the door interrupted the conversation. Charles nodded to the guard, and a servant burst in moments later trailed by a stranger. "I bear a message from the East," the stranger said between breaths.

"Fetch wine and rolls for our guest," Fastrada said to the servant. "Is this about the Saxons?"

"Yes," the stranger gasped.

Pepin's frown deepened. The queen had shown more warmth to that messenger than she had toward him in the past few weeks.

The messenger handed the piece of parchment to Charles, and the room hushed. As Charles's eyes went back and forth, grim lines formed on his face.

"Where did they attack?" Fastrada asked her husband.

"Lübbecke. They killed my vassal. A priest escaped to Paderborn and dictated the message." Charles's voice was calm but carried an undercurrent of fury.

"Any Frisians with them?"

Charles nodded. "We will send word for our forces to meet us at Lippeham in May." Charles laid his hand on Karl's shoulder. "It is time to gird you with a sword."

"A real one?" Karl beamed.

"He's in his twelfth year! He's too young!" Pepin cried.

"I had seen about as many years as Karl when I went to battle in Aquitaine with my father," Charles said. "What say you, my dear?"

Pepin's face felt hot. Why was his father asking a backward Easterner and a woman?

"It's dangerous." She twisted the edge of her sleeve. "But if Karl is to be a king someday, your vassals must see him proving himself in battle at an early age."

"Exactly," Charles said. "I am doing for Karl what my father did for me."

Rage flashed across Pepin's eyes, blinding as lightning.

***

After sunrise prayers three days later, Pepin, his family, and his father's magnates watched Karl kneel before Charles. His brother had to raise his little boy's voice to be heard above the rain drumming against the chapel's roof. The clouds were dark gray through the clerestory windows and made the space as dim as dusk, a gloom broken by the candles and lamps.

With folded hands, Karl spoke first in clumsy Latin then Frankish: "I, Karl, son of Charles, king of the Franks and Lombards and patrician of Rome, do swear fidelity to my king. I am your faithful servant as a vassal should be to his lord, and a son to his father, in the service of your righteous rule. May God make me worthy of wearing the sword."

Their father laid his stout hands over Karl's. "And, I, Charles, king of the Franks and Lombards and patrician of Rome by the grace of God, do swear my protection and bestow on you the sword forged by our best smith."

Pepin rubbed his tired eyes. Neither brother had slept well the previous night. Pepin had been too angry. Beside him in their shared bed, Karl, too excited for rest, whispered his oath over and over and over again. Whenever he heard Karl's whispering stop and his breathing become slow, Pepin had jammed an elbow into his brother's ribs. Whenever Pepin had been about to drift off, Karl had punched him in the back. Neither brother had relented.

A gust of wind rattled the windows in their frames and startled Pepin from his brooding. Charles released his son's hands. Karl approached a jeweled golden box, the reliquary of Saint Lambert, brought from Liège for this occasion. He knelt before it and placed his right hand on the box.

"By this bone of the holy martyr Lambert," Karl said, "I swear this oath and will keep it all my days, so help me God, creator of heaven and earth."

He said the Paternoster, rose, and returned to his father, who now held a sword sheathed in leather in his outstretched hands.

Fury tightened a cord between Pepin's shoulders.

He glanced at his sisters and Fastrada. Hruodtrude and Bertha were smiling while Gisela sat on the floor and talked to her doll about her brave brother Karl, using Fastrada's words and cadence. The queen held Hruodhaid, asleep in her swaddling. Pepin snorted. How could anyone believe the she-wolf cared anything for this bastard infant, especially when she hated the mother?

Pepin looked back at the altar. Meginfrid strapped a belt with an empty jeweled scabbard on Karl's waist. Karl grasped the sword's hilt and withdrew it from the leather. His gaze lingered on the weapon before he slid it into the scabbard.

Charles wiped his eyes. Pepin wanted to howl. He would never be where Karl was now, with his father so proud. Silently, he vowed he would learn to write—and tell his mother everything.

Chapter Eleven

August 784, Worms

Even as she kept her eyes to the page and sounded out Saint Augustine's words, Fastrada could feel Pepin smirking at her awkwardness. Near the hearth in the palace's great hall, she fought to keep her face impassive. With Charles away, the court and the Palace School were greatly reduced, but her husband had wanted Alcuin to continue her lessons and the children's. Fortunately, Fardulf stayed at court and continued tutoring her. Despite Pepin's silent mockery, she was glad for the books. Those parchment pages gave everyone something to think about other than their worry for Charles and Karl. Even she could not admire the murals of Siegfried and past battles forever.

How she longed for Charles's touch, his shouts of triumphs during the hunt, their discussions about politics. She missed Karl, too, and their conversations about history and warfare.

Would these absences ever cease to bother her? When she was a child, she had fretted over whether she would see her father again. At Büraburg, she had confided to her mother. Here, she had no one except Nantlind. Fastrada had to be strong for the children and for the court. How many times had her mother spoken words she didn't know were certain, that her father would come back whole?

The last time she had heard from her husband, severe floods had forced him to take his troops through Thuringia to fight the eastern Saxon tribes. He had gotten as far as the Elbe and sent Karl with a detachment against the Westphalian Saxons. In name, Karl led the men, but Meginfrid commanded them in deed.

Her hand strayed to her belly. Her courses had come every month since Charles had left in April. Why was her womb empty, when Hildegard and

Kunigunde had conceived so readily? She attended Mass every morning and evening and gave alms, hoping Mother Mary and Saint Andrew would answer her prayers when Charles returned. *What if a Saxon blade* ... She dared not finish the heart-shattering thought. Nor did she want to imagine the noblemen's rivalries shredding the kingdom.

Pepin looked up from the wax tablet where he was scratching out letters. "What does the passage mean, my lady queen?"

How predictable. Every time she struggled with a passage, he asked such a question. Did he think she would never guess he used an innocent tone to hide his true purpose—to embarrass her? When she had first realized it, anger had stolen her tongue, and her words came out in stammers. But now she refused to satisfy him.

Pretending Pepin was sincere, she said, "Something about pagan Romans and the Christians."

She looked toward Fardulf, who smiled and nodded.

Rapid footsteps interrupted them. Fastrada turned and saw a guard and another man bowing to her. "The king's messenger," the guard said.

Fastrada set the book aside. Holding out her hand, she searched the messenger's face. "How fares my husband?"

"Well, my lady queen."

She let out a breath. The lesson forgotten, the children leaned toward her. "Where did you come from?" she asked the messenger.

"Schöningen," he said.

Charles has gone far into Saxony. Ordering a servant to fetch refreshments, Fastrada unsheathed her eating knife. She tore through the seal, a profile of a warrior in wax, and glanced at the letter. She traced her finger over Charles's signature, the letters in the form of a cross, and handed the parchment to Alcuin. As he read the formal introductions, Fastrada sat on the edge of her seat, and the children fidgeted.

"*Almighty God, in His mercy, has granted us victory.*"

Fastrada's own cries blended with the shouts of joy from the court. Once the hall had quieted, Alcuin read about the battles and the Masses that were held.

"*We will return to Francia in a month.*"

Hruodtrude squealed. "Father is coming home."

When the hall again quieted, Alcuin read on: "*The Westphalians have been stirred to wickedness again at the Lippe River. Our beloved son Karl will march with a host of men.*"

Fastrada stiffened her spine. Meginfrid was an experienced warrior, she reminded herself, and Karl was skilled at the hunt. Still he was a boy, not much older than her brother.

"Don't be scared, Mother," Gisela said. "Karl is brave. He will make short work of the Saxons."

Fastrada smiled to hear her own words coming from the child. "We will pray for Karl at vespers. God will help him win this battle." She sighed. "If only it were our last with these heathens."

***

When Alcuin finished the letter, Pepin headed for the palace chapel, trailed by two guards. On his way out of the hall, he spied the queen hurrying toward the door that led to the kitchen. Apparently, she realized once the messenger's travel was taken into account, his father would return home in two weeks, and she needed to make preparations.

Pepin stepped outside. Golden sunlight bathed the courtyard and the palace, but his heart was clouded. He wished he were riding into battle with his father while Karl contended with all these little girls. How often had he seen his father tell Karl how to hold his wooden sword and where to place his feet while the boy played soldier? *He never did that for me!* Bertha and Gisela irritated Pepin, constantly asking for their father. Hruodtrude acted like a little queen, arguing with her Byzantine tutor in Greek about Homer, which annoyed Pepin even more.

Yet Fastrada scorched his thoughts. He clutched the silver cross that hung at his neck, trying to ward off the succubus who haunted his dreams. Attracted by his lying with whores, the demon assumed Fastrada's shape, tore off her clothes, and leapt atop him rolling her eyes in pleasure. Pepin wanted her like a starving man wanted bread. He would awaken having spilled his seed.

Why did the demon choose to resemble the woman he most loathed? Why could she not look like Nantlind all the time? The dreams were the closest Pepin got to the maid, who either stayed near Fastrada or was running errands for her. Such a demanding mistress.

Pepin shuddered, despite the warmth of the day. Would the demon use his seed to conceive a changeling? Before his manservant entered the bedchamber to help him dress, Pepin draped the top sheet over the mattress to hide the stain. When he retired for the night, clean sheets lay on the bed. Why had God made him so monstrous? What were the maidservants who made the bed saying?

His confessions—never even hinting at Fastrada—and prayers kept the succubus away for a few days. But she would return, and he was powerless.

Memories of the demon caused Pepin to quicken his steps to the chapel, where the scent of incense lingered within its frescoed walls. Pepin scanned the nave; he and his guards were the only people here. As he strode to the altar, his steps on the wooden floor echoed. He lay down two coins for alms and knelt.

Although his guards didn't understand Latin, Pepin kept his voice below a whisper. After the Paternoster and a Psalm for victory in battle, he added, "Father in heaven, smite her. Save my soul."

***

Charles's return was a happy day for Fastrada. He was still whole, still had both hands, both feet, both eyes. As soon as he dismounted in front of the church and the crowd of nobles and commoners, she and the princesses ran to him. Amid the cheering, laughter, and tears of the families, all that mattered was Charles, his kiss, his enfolding arms.

Charles kissed her again, then embraced each of his daughters. Finally, he hugged Pepin. The boy who had sulked all summer put on a face of cheer.

Charles held Fastrada's hand, then nodded to a man with a hunting horn to sound for silence. When the crowd had quieted, he announced what he had written in his letters, added that his youngest sons, Little Pippin and Louis, were in good health in their kingdoms in Italy and Aquitaine, and exhorted the folk to pray for Karl and for the Franks.

After the feast to celebrate the Franks' victory, life resumed its normal patterns, with one exception. Each time Charles heard a messenger had arrived, he straightened, then his shoulders slumped slightly when he learned the letter was not from Karl or Meginfrid.

One night when they were abed, Charles constantly shifted positions, and his restlessness kept Fastrada awake. She propped herself on her elbow and stared into a darkness, broken only by the light of the night candle peeking through the opening between the bed curtains.

"What troubles you, Husband? Does your new scar hurt? I can send for the herbalist."

"Pay no mind to the scar, my dear. The Saxon who gave me that is dead. No need to fret about me."

"I worry about you all the time."

She felt him turn toward her. His finger stroked her cheek. "I've lived through many battles."

"It's Karl, isn't it?"

"I can't stop thinking about what happened in the Süntels. What if some count gets reckless, this time taking Karl with him?"

Fastrada winced, remembering when the clerk read her father's message. Two of Charles's emissaries and twenty-six noble Franks fallen. Her father wounded. All because of a few fools. "Our men can't have forgotten already. It was only two years ago."

"Do not underestimate the idiocy of young men."

"But Meginfrid is with them. Surely, they respect him."

"They paid no heed to my kinsman."

October 784, Worms

Fastrada awoke, feeling as if clawed hands were wringing her belly. *Not now,* she thought, *Karl will come home in two weeks. There's still much to do for the feast.*

The morning should have been chilly, but she was sweating. Her belly lurched. She shoved aside the blankets and the bed curtains, dropped to the floor, yanked the chamber pot from under the bed, and vomited. Light footsteps ran toward her. Nantlind's hands draped a blanket over her bare shoulders. Fastrada heard Charles shift in the bed.

She retched again and after a few minutes, unsteadily rose to her feet, clutching the blanket to her body. Now she was shivering. One of the maidservants stoked the fire. Another took the chamber pot away.

"Do you think ..." Fastrada asked Nantlind.

"You haven't bled since the king returned home."

Fastrada beamed. Finally. Her prayers had been answered. After almost a year, God had opened her womb! Then a cold terror swept through her. *What if I die as Kunigunde did?*

"Fastrada, are you well?" Charles asked.

She climbed back into bed and placed Charles's large hand on her belly. She wanted to sing. "Husband, your seed might be growing here."

Charles blinked, startled. For a moment, he gazed at her. "We are blessed."

"Are you not happy?"

"Of course, I am, my dear," he said too quickly. "Why wouldn't I be?"

Fastrada pursed her lips, unsure how to interpret her husband's reaction. Perhaps, he was thinking of what happened to Kunigunde and Hildegard. No point in dwelling on that. "What should we call him?"

"Him? We should decide on a girl's name, too. God may give us another daughter."

Fastrada's eyes widened. "Do you not want another son?"

"I already have three healthy heirs," he said, stroking her cheek, "and I must make sure each has a kingdom when my time comes. If all goes well, Little Pippin will rule Italy, and Aquitaine will go to Louis. And that leaves Francia intact for Karl. I would be overjoyed with another healthy daughter."

"Are you going to pray for a daughter?" Fastrada's voice cracked.

His brow creased, Charles hesitated.

"You are going to pray for a girl!" Her eyes welled.

"I will pray for your safety and the child's," he said calmly. "Most wives would be happy if their husbands cared only for that."

"I ... I am overwhelmed." Fastrada could not utter her true reasons. Her father would have more influence in East Francia and Thuringia if he were the grandfather of a future king. As the boy's mother, she would be equal to Hildegard.

"Perhaps the midwife or the herbalist can give you something for your belly," Charles said. He squeezed her hand and kissed her cheek.

Fastrada kissed his hand and strode to the basin, where she splashed water on her face and let its cold sting revive her. She cupped her hand, took a mouthful of water, and spit into the empty cup that had held her sleeping draught. Although her belly still roiled, she had to go to Mass. She would pray to be carrying a future king and to survive his birth.

After she dressed, she pinned her enameled bronze brooch of Saint Wigbert to her gown. She needed to ward off evil, especially spirits that would harm her unborn child.

***

Tarrying with the crowd outside the church for Karl and his men, Pepin used his smile as a mask, just as he had when he had learned Fastrada was with child. Although pale from her morning sickness, she preened about the palace. Why didn't God answer his prayers to strike her barren? When he wrote to his mother, he carefully worded his request as Gomeric had instructed: *"Pray God will bless our house with a healthy girl, beloved in a house with four sons."* Three rivals for the throne were enough.

Chief among them, Karl. A month before, his brother had sent a message: victory against the Saxons in Dreingau. His father's eyes moistened. The queen whispered, "Praise God." Over the next few weeks, the household busied itself to welcome Karl back. *It's just Karl, not Siegfried.*

And now the wait was over. The procession turned a corner and came into view in the distance. When it was three hundred paces away, Pepin heard the shouts and applause from the peasants outside their wattle-and-daub huts as if they truly were welcoming the long-ago dragon slayer. *Those cheers should be for me!*

As the procession approached the church, Pepin made out Meginfrid and Karl at its head, followed by noblemen and soldiers, along with a small baggage train and captives. Not only was Karl still whole; he had grown. He held his head high, like other boys returning from battle after their first kill. Karl dismounted at the church and handed the reins to a servant. He strode to their father and bowed.

Pepin clenched his teeth and kept smiling, even though his face ached. If not for his father's sin, the crowd gathered in front of the church would be chanting, "Pepin, Pepin."

***

The elation over Karl's return did not last long. A week later, Charles spoke to Fastrada when they were abed for the first sleep. With her head on Charles's bare shoulder, Fastrada's eyes seemed to shut themselves. Morning sickness had drained her of vigor.

"My dear," Charles said, "you still believe the Saxons will rebel again, don't you?"

"Yes." Shifting onto her elbow, she wished she could see her husband's face, but the bed curtains were drawn.

"I do, too. We've waged war against them for over a decade. They will not change unless we do something drastic."

65

"What are you thinking?" Fastrada shivered.

"We march against them this winter."

Fastrada gasped. "You could freeze! You could starve! And for what?"

"Widukind." The calmness in his voice stunned her.

"How?"

"Our spies say that Widukind is still in Saxony, not fleeing to his wife's family in Nordmannia. He would never expect us to strike in the winter."

"For good reason," Fastrada muttered. Charles and his men could be caught by a sudden snow or bone-cold winds. Illness could plague them or their steeds. The horses would depend on the hay cut a few months ago—better than the previous drought-stunted harvest but still limited. The army's only food was what grew last summer, whatever game they could find in the forest, and what little they could forage from Saxon farms.

"My dear, if we make their hard winter even harder, they will realize we are bolder and stronger. Widukind will have no choice but to surrender." His fingers caressed her cheek. "How else do we stop them?"

Fastrada stared into the dark. Six years ago, a merchant held back tears as he told her father of churches along the Rhine in ashes, of nuns being raped, of monks with crushed skulls. What was to stop Widukind from leading these brutes to burning more churches? What was to stop them from marching on Büraburg again?

"Fastrada?" Charles asked, his fingers brushing her shoulder. "Are you ill?"

"I am well. I miss you terribly when you're away. We won't even celebrate the Feasts of St. Martin or the Nativity together. But you're right. We must capture Widukind."

Charles's hand moved to her hip. "I need you to help me convince the court this is the right strategy."

"I'm frightened."

"Don't worry. We will take plenty of provisions."

"I will pray for you," she whispered.

Clinging to Charles, she raked her mind for what else could get the Saxons to follow God's will but could find nothing better. Even with the hard-won Saxon lands, the wars would not end, not as long as Widukind led the fight.

Charles's lips found hers, and she yielded to the temptation. Was it truly a sin to enjoy her marital right when she was already with child? To forget the Saxons for a few hours was worth the penance of alms and prayers. Surely, she and Charles could give enough to placate God and avoid any curses.

***

After sunrise Mass, Fastrada sat before the fire in the royal apartment's reception room and sipped mint tea mixed with a little wine. Her belly was too unsettled for more than a few bites of bread to break her fast.

"My dear, you must eat," Charles said.

"Later, husband."

"Are you well enough to ..."

"Of course, I am," Fastrada snapped, hoping to hide her tiredness.

Charles frowned.

"If it is your will," Fastrada murmured, leaning toward him, "I will rest after dinner."

"It is my will." His voice was stern.

She took his proffered arm, and they entered the great hall, crowded with courtiers and the visiting counts Charles needed to persuade. His tread crunched the thyme and mint strewn on the floor. Letting go of her arm, he ascended to his throne on the dais. Feeling the noblemen's gaze on her, Fastrada followed her husband, folded her hands and bowed to him, and took her seat beside him.

The room quieted when Charles raised his scepter. Pepin stared intently at her. Karl elbowed a count's son who was whispering to him. Hruodtrude sat on a bench while her younger sisters played on the floor with their dolls. Hruodtrude's tutor stood behind her. No doubt he would write to the dowager Byzantine empress about the plans for war. Well, as Charles said, at least they knew this informer.

"Count of the Palace," Charles said, "will the Saxons revolt again?"

"Yes, my lord. Our slaughter of the rebels at Verdun failed to pacify them. They have been just as vicious the past two years."

"Who is the author of this wickedness?"

"Widukind," Meginfrid said, "God curse him. Instead of paying for his sins, the coward flees into Nordmannia."

"Lord Karl," Charles said, "tell the court what our spies told you."

"Widukind is still in Saxony."

Whispers rippled through the hall. Charles paused for a moment before giving his chamberlain an almost imperceptible nod.

"We should march against him—now!" Meginfrid shouted. "Bring him to justice. Make him accept God's will or join his devils in hell."

"Alas," Fastrada cried as she and Charles had agreed, "winter is but weeks away."

"Are we to let a little snow stop us?" Meginfrid asked. "We are Franks!"

Other noblemen spoke of the risks, the same perils that had haunted Fastrada since the previous night, but she would not contradict her husband in public. Meginfrid and his allies argued if they were doing God's will, He would give them good weather.

"Are we warriors or scared little girls?" he added.

Fastrada bit her lip to stay silent, but she could not stop thinking of the crashes against Büraburg's walls. Charles gave her a sidelong look and reached over to lay his hand on hers.

"Are we to forget the churches the Saxons burned?" Charles asked. "Are we to forget the murder of innocents?"

Against her wishes, Fastrada was crying. She wiped her wet cheek with her free hand. Oh Sweet Mary, she was embarrassing Charles! But the harder she tried to staunch the tears, the more they flowed.

"My lord king," she said softly. The hall quieted. "I beseech you not to forget Büraburg. Do you know what it's like to see people stuffing themselves with dead leaves in the winter because the Saxons burned their crops? Everyone was so thin, so sick. The babies ..."

Her throat was too tight for her to speak. Pressing her fingers to her mouth, she heard a few murmurs, probably the nobles sneering at how weak she was.

"I'm sorry, Husband," she choked out.

Charles squeezed her hand. When she turned toward him, she was surprised to see his face held not a trace of anger. So unlike her father. Was that admiration she saw in her husband's eyes? "Beloved and most loving wife, do not get overwrought." His voice was gentle. "By God, creator of heaven and earth, we will have justice. My loyal men, this is why we must march into Saxony."

***

The week that followed was a blur of packing, packing, packing: barrels of salted pork and beef, fodder for oxen and horses, blankets, tents, supplies. In the glow of fires through their workshop windows at all hours, smiths repaired armor and weapons. Fastrada focused on what she needed to do, shoving aside her disappointment that Charles would leave so soon and be far away for the birth, and her fear that he might not return at all.

On the day of departure, she stood in the courtyard with the children watching her husband and his men ride away. As the wind billowed her cloak and veil, she cradled Hruodhaid in her arms and held the blanketed infant close. The men's armor—leather tunics with tiny metal plates—would be rolled behind the saddles as they traveled through Francia, but they would don their heavy second skins as soon as they crossed the Rhine. The warhorses, now led by mounted grooms, would be ridden into battle within a few weeks.

Fastrada did her best not to sob. Left in Worms, Karl frowned like a boy denied the chance to hunt again. All she could do was let the twelve-winter-old glower—this war needed men who'd seen years of battle. Pepin sulked as usual, but Fastrada no longer let it bother her. She would fulfill her duty to this hateful boy, but the other children, especially the baby, needed her.

"Your father will return soon," Fastrada whispered to Hruodhaid, stroking her fine hair, hoping her words were true.

The child looked up at her and whimpered. Her nurse stepped forward and held out her arms.

"Mother must give you to Nurse so she can feed you," Fastrada said.

"Don't be sad," Hruodtrude said to her sisters. "Karl will protect us."

Fastrada smiled at Hruodtrude, such a sweet girl to say something so kind to her siblings. Perhaps, the girl was too worried to pick a fight.

"Karl," Fastrada added, "remember what your father said: you must practice with the guards. This is no time for sloth."

Brightening, Karl nodded. Each day, he looked more like a young man and less like a boy. Pepin glared at his brother.

***

As the days grew colder and shorter, Fastrada's bouts of morning sickness passed. Excused from the Advent fast because of the unborn child, Fastrada was able to hold food down again and was getting plump. She attended Mass at sunrise and vespers, praying for Charles and her baby. As the days grew into weeks with no word from Charles, she became uneasy.

Two weeks before the Nativity, a messenger arrived. She laid her hand over the fluttering in her swelling belly as she listened to the clerk. Charles was in Lüdge, a villa on the Emmer River, a tributary to the Weser. The march had gone well. It had rained and snowed, but it was nothing to stop the Frankish army. Thus far, they had encountered little resistance.

Fastrada tried to make the Nativity and the holy days that followed joyous. She and the children attended the matins Mass with its veils of black, white, and red. The Feast of Donkeys was followed by the sunrise Mass, then back to the palace for feasting and dancing. Still, she felt Charles's absence keenly.

A month later, another messenger arrived with word from Charles. On her chair in the hall, Fastrada leaned back, letting what was left of the court see how Charles's seed had grown in her. She felt the baby move. *My little Bernard.*

She read the message silently first, understanding more than half of it, before handing it to the clerk to read aloud. Much to her relief, Charles was well. He had marched as far as Rehme on the Weser before being turned back by severe floods. He was now at the fortress of Eresburg, which he was rebuilding, and having a new church constructed.

"*As soon as you are able, join us here, along with our darling daughters and beloved sons.*"

Amid the whispers and mutters, Fastrada worked to keep her face impassive. Part of her was overjoyed. *He needs me.* Yet she was terrified. Winter was far from over.

"When do we leave?" Karl asked, his hand caressing the hilt of his sword.

"Alcuin," Fastrada said, "what do the stars say?"

"Clouds have covered the sky for two weeks," he answered. "I have not been able to see them."

"What did they say when you last saw them?" She did not bother to hide her irritation.

"They seemed to bode well. I saw no omens."

"Then we leave in three days."

"What about provisions?" Pepin asked. "The surplus harvest went to the army."

Stop trying to make me look inept. She pitched her voice to carry through the hall. "We are well aware of that. But we have some food and supplies here. We will take what we can and buy the rest along the way."

"What if our hosts have nothing to sell?" Pepin asked.

Why must you say this in public? Courtiers were staring at her. She kept her chin up, her back stiff. She would show no weakness. "They *will* have something to sell. Otherwise, they're traitors who deserve no mercy."

A few in the crowd gasped.

She did not intend to have anyone executed, but she needed the courtiers and whoever received their messages to believe they would pay a steep price if they refused her and the children.

"B-But these are our own people," said Pepin.

Since when have you started to care? She gazed at the courtiers. Some had their mouths open in horror. Maybe she had gone too far. Charles still needed their allegiance. She laid her hand on her brooch of Saint Wigbert and chose her next words carefully. "We will pay a fair price. We only ask that they follow the will of our God and our king."

Chapter Twelve

January 785, Oppenheim

In a chair near the hearth, Fastrada drew her fur-lined cloak close with gloved hands. Although she had been indoors for a couple of hours, she was still chilled from the full day of travel on the snow-covered road through the woods. For most of the day's journey, she could see the vast Rhine, quiet and empty of birds, to her right through the leafless trees. Refusing a litter, Fastrada had mounted a steady mare she had grown up with. She would not have the servants gossip that she was delicate, yet she heeded the midwife's advice and rode at a walk in front of the procession of sixty-five.

How she wanted to go at a trot or canter. Despite the noise of hooves and wheels, she could sometimes hear Hruodhaid fussing under layers of blankets in her portable cradle borne between two placid horses led by a groom; Bertha and Gisela, old enough to ride small steeds, whined questions about how much farther the journey was. Knowing Oppenheim was close, Fastrada pushed the party on. In the waning light of the day, she had been relieved to behold the estate. Carved from the forest on the slope of a hill, the large fields and vineyards, now dormant under a thin blanket of snow, had been a generous donation ten years before from Charles to Lorsch, an abbey across the Rhine. Amid several small buildings was a two-story wooden manor that could have fit inside the palace's great hall.

Even crowded with servants and guards in the modest quarters, Fastrada was glad to be inside, out of the wind. Leaning back in her chair, she listened to the musician singing about the long-ago hero Siegfried slaying the dragon on a Rhineland mountain to the north. The girls were already in bed upstairs, and the boys were nodding off. If not for the need to buy food and fodder, she, too, would have retired. She regarded her host, reeking of wine on the bench next to her chair. Lucas, the estate's new steward, was an angular monk of about twenty winters. During the evening meal—one with little bread—he kept repeating himself and was quick to slap a cupbearer who did not return soon enough from the cellar. His manner confirmed the gossip Fastrada had heard from merchants. A cousin of the abbot of Lorsch, Lucas did little more than drink wine all day. Just the type of man Charles would despise.

She wrinkled her nose. The evidence of the gossip was at her feet. The strewing herbs on the floor were crushed into powder and smelled of mice and rats. All the other nobles she had ever visited had ordered their maids to sweep out the old herbs and replace them. Even if the host did not think of it, a loyal maid would make the place suitable. A faithful cook would ensure bakers produced enough loaves. Fastrada had sent the message two days ago, plenty of time to prepare for guests. Either Lucas had not told his servants of visitors, or the servants loathed him and hoped to anger a queen.

Not my concern. She shoved aside her own budding dislike. *Get what we need to feed ourselves another week and go to sleep.* "Brother Lucas, we must replenish our supplies. We will pay a fair price."

He blinked as if awakening from a stupor. "I will sell you the meat of half an ox for one hundred deniers."

She repressed the urge to laugh. Only one way to answer hagglers who started with ridiculous prices. "I will give you three deniers for one-eighth an ox."

"That's thievery! I'm not selling you anything."

Fastrada gaped at the monk. She had expected Lucas to counter with a higher price the same way merchants did. It was all part of the dance, one without scorn.

The legs of a stool scraped against the floor. Fastrada turned to see Karl on his feet, his hand on the hilt of his dagger. Anxiety flooded through her, sweeping away fatigue the way wind blew browned leaves.

"Are you calling the queen of the Franks a thief?" Karl said through clenched teeth. At twelve winters, his voice was still that of a boy, and he was still shorter than she. But he was stout, and she lacked the strength to wrest a dagger from him. She could order a guard to do it, but that would humiliate him.

"Karl," she said as if they were waiting for dinner, "please sit down."

"I'm not going to let him insult you!"

"He's an unarmed monk," she said. "Don't lower yourself."

"But he ..."

"I am with child, and your father will be displeased if you upset me," she said in a tone reserved only for the children.

Karl frowned, his hand still on the hilt. She glanced at Lucas. The young monk was staring at the prince.

With great effort, she kept her voice cold, even. "Karl, you should pity Brother Lucas. We will send a message to Lorsch in the morning, and the abbot will need to decide between appointing a more worthy steward or losing royal favor and our gifts."

"Y-You c-can't," Lucas said. "The abbot is my kinsman. He will tell his monks to stop praying for you. Do you want God to deny His favor?"

"That's treason," Karl snarled, moving forward.

"Karl, don't!" Fastrada held up her hand. "We will defend our honor in a civilized way. Nantlind, fetch the clerk. The messenger and his guards will leave at first light."

Trembling, the monk threw himself from the bench and groveled at her feet. "I beg you, have mercy. State your wishes, and I will obey."

"You have shown remorse and have our pardon." Fastrada leveled her gaze at Karl. The boy returned to his seat and leaned forward. The knot between her shoulders relaxed. "Brother Lucas, you will provide the meat we asked for. You will replenish our wine, ale, travel bread, and oats. We will pay ..." Fastrada calculated a fair price; she would not be accused of breaking her word. "Ten deniers."

Lucas's eyes blazed with hatred.

Fastrada's patience for the man was as exhausted as her body. She aimed her last barb carefully. "As queen, we have a duty to inform our lord about the disgraceful state of his donation. And we will make no effort to stop his message to the abbot about the property's need for a new guardian."

✳✳✳

The monthlong journey fatigued Fastrada. Snow covered the roads, and the wind whipped through the trees' bare branches, stinging her face. It took all her will not to snarl at the children when they yet again complained of the cold or asked how much longer they would need to travel. With the baby swelling her belly, her back and breasts ached, and her legs and bottom were sore. The bargaining for food and fodder from reluctant hosts at castles and abbeys tired her even more. After crossing the Rhine at the stone bridge near Cologne, Fastrada felt more at ease, even though civilized areas were farther apart. This forested, hilly territory, with its share of kobolds, demons, and bandits, was more like the lands of her childhood.

The last part of the journey was on a road that was little more than a path alongside a river swollen with rain and melted snow from a midwinter thaw. At midday, barges ferried them across, and the road led to the foot of a high hill. Fastrada beheld a limestone structure through the bare trees. Eresburg. She still had her baby teeth when Charles had first conquered the Saxon stronghold so close to Büraburg. Four years later, the Saxons destroyed it, but Charles had retaken the hill months after the attack and rebuilt the fortress.

As the horses lumbered up the steep, winding road, she caught more glimpses of the fortress. When they reached the plateau, Fastrada gasped. Across the burnt stubble fields spotted with snow, she beheld the village, whose wattle-and-daub peasant huts resembled Frankish ones. The close look at the fortress was just as pleasing. Its walls were thick and solid, and the recently dug ditches surrounding them enhanced the defenses. As her party crossed a small bridge, Fastrada looked up at the ramparts where the guards stood, and she nodded her approval at the spaces to pour boiling water. This place felt more like home than any of Charles's palaces. Ahead of the travelers, gates of thick wood and iron were open to the courtyard. Fastrada admired the stone manor, a spacious, rectangular building with arched windows. Nearby, men were laying the timbers for the roof on the church, also made of stone and almost the same size as the manor.

Meginfrid greeted Fastrada and the children. He and other courtiers helped Fastrada and the royal children dismount.

"You look well, my lady queen," the chamberlain said. "My lord king is expecting you and the children."

He escorted them past the entryway and into the great hall. Diffuse light from parchment-covered windows added to the light from the roaring fire in the hearth. Seeing Fastrada, Charles stopped midsentence in his conversation with a courtier and rushed toward his family. The children dashed to their father. Fastrada could manage only a stiff walk.

Charles kissed and hugged the children. "Karl, you are as strong as ever. You will have to show me how well you wield your sword. Hruodtrude, my dear, are you still correcting your tutor on his Frankish?"

"And his Latin," she replied.

Charles chuckled.

"I'm learning my letters, Father," Bertha said, "and can read some words."

"I want a tutor!" Gisela said, clutching her doll, worn and stained from her love.

"Your mother will find one for you when the time is right. Ah, Hruodhaid," Charles said, lifting her from her nurse's arms, "how you have grown."

Fastrada said, "She is taking a few steps, Husband."

After setting Hruodhaid on the floor, Charles kissed and embraced Fastrada. Her desire stirred. "How I have missed you, my dear! How do you fare?"

"I am well."

"You look lovely. Pepin, how go your studies?"

"Very well, Father. I have finished Boethius's *De Consolatione Philosophiae.*"

"You will make a fine bishop, indeed."

A shadow crossed Pepin's face. Would that boy ever understand that his father was making the best choice for him?

"Come, let us eat," Charles said, "and I will tell you how we have been fighting the Saxons."

"I want to lead a campaign against them," Karl said.

"You will have plenty of opportunities to fight," Charles said.

As they approached the high table, Fastrada took a moment to savor the murals on the plastered wall. One that caught her attention showed soldiers felling a pillar that divided itself into two branches at the top, then setting it aflame. The yellows and reds were so bright they almost created their own light.

"The burning of the Irminsul," Fastrada whispered. A thrill ran down her spine. Charles had destroyed that monument to heathenism during his first war at Eresburg.

"Do you like it?" Charles grinned.

"It's glorious." She gazed about the immense room, taking in its beauty. "Any guest here will know the power God gave you."

"I was thinking that as well." He took her hand. "And how our estates in Francia should reflect our true glory."

"Like the palace at Worms?"

"And the places I saw in Italy."

"We have good villas at Aachen and Ingelheim." Fastrada's heartbeat quickened.

Charles gave her a broad smile. "We could make them magnificent."

***

Pepin finally got a chance to speak to Gomeric in private in the late afternoon while his father and Fastrada napped in the royal apartment. He and his uncle stood in the great hall gazing at a mural commemorating the Irminsul's destruction when he was three years old. The nurses had taken the two youngest girls to their room to sleep. Hruodtrude sat by the hearth and embroidered one of Karl's tunics, while Bertha and a young cleric talked about the stars. Karl and some of the courtiers had gone outside to spar.

Gomeric nudged Pepin. "The king and queen are doing more than sleep."

Pepin felt his face go crimson. The image of Fastrada's nude body on her wedding night seared his mind, and her belly fat with his sibling had not extinguished his lust. The demon in her shape still haunted his dreams. To keep her at bay, he had used maids at the castles and paid them as often as he could. If only Nantlind did not belong to the queen.

"Is the queen's tale of what happened at Oppenheim true, Nephew?" Gomeric asked in Latin, his voice low.

"Yes," Pepin answered in the same language.

"God has given us a gift with the queen's actions. It would take little for people to believe that she took everything she could from Oppenheim and let Brother Lucas and the tenants starve. Think of how the story will spread. Your mother will be pleased."

"How? It didn't happen that way."

"But it's close enough. If you hear rumors of Queen Fastrada's cruelty and Karl's complicity, do not undeceive the speaker unless they ask you directly. Think of it, Pepin, if the realm despises her—and they think Karl is weak—you will be that much stronger."

Then maybe the demon will leave me be.

***

For the sake of her unborn child, Fastrada tried to keep herself calm when her husband was absent. Throughout the winter, Charles sent detachments to raid Saxon castles, and many times, he and Karl rode out with soldiers. A priest held Masses in the unfinished church, and Fastrada attended every sunrise and sunset. She always left alms and prayed for her husband, the children, and her baby.

God and His saints must have heard her prayers. Charles's worst wounds were a few scrapes and bruises. With each territory he conquered, he appointed a Saxon ally as its count.

Charles's baby continued to grow in Fastrada's belly. *Let it be a son*, she thought while whispering the Latin words to please the Blessed Virgin. *Let him be a future king.*

Winter melted into a wet spring, soaking the fields and gorging the small river at the base of the high hill. Green shoots poked through the ground. In the two weeks before the Feast of the Resurrection, the church crawled with penitents making their confessions. On that holiest of Sundays, the church, bright with light through the clerestory windows, was packed and warm despite the open doors, and Fastrada could see only a little of the statues carved and painted by the best artists. In the murmur of the crowd, she could distinguish the prattle and cries of babies baptized the day before. Fastrada laid her hand on her distended belly. She would need to wait until the day before Pentecost for her own child's rite. *Soon, very soon, I will hold my son.*

When the priest stood before the crowd and raised his hands, the faithful hushed.

"Today is a joyous day," he bellowed. "Today, we will consecrate our new church."

Amid the smoke of incense and chants of "*Stetit angelus,*" the priest prayed over the gold-and-marble altar in front of a vibrant mural of Christ in Majesty. Then he blessed the embroidered altar cloth, clay vases, and silver and gold ornaments, and made his way through the crowd to anoint the crosses painted on the walls.

Fastrada's eyes misted. She hoped God would be pleased and grant her people victory.

April 785, Eresburg

Fastrada wished her son would come soon. Over the two weeks since the church's consecration, it seemed as if she had become even more bloated.

76

Her breasts and belly weighed down upon her; her hands and feet were swollen. Wilberga the midwife told her the time was near, so she confessed her sins to a priest but delayed entering the lying-in chamber, despite Charles's gentle urging. She suspected her husband did not order her outright because he knew how much she disliked the cramped chamber and did not want to upset a woman with child. Like the room in the palace at Herstal, the lying-in chamber here was low-ceilinged and dominated by a bed, and with its sole window shuttered, it made her feel caged. Worse, it would keep her away from Charles for more than a month.

One bright spring morning in the royal apartment's reception room, Fastrada felt as if a dagger twisted in her belly. Forgetting what she was going to say to Charles and Meginfrid, Fastrada doubled over, almost falling into Nantlind.

"My dear?" Charles asked.

"Did you feel a pain like that with your womanly courses?" Nantlind asked.

"Worse," she managed to say.

"It's your time! I will fetch Wilberga."

Fastrada grasped Nantlind's hand. "Stay with me! I need you. Meginfrid, send for the midwife."

"Go, Meginfrid," Charles said.

Sweating, the chamberlain quickly bowed to his king and queen and hurried out of the room.

Stone-faced, Charles strode to his wife and kissed her and held her close. "Wilberga is one of the best." He sounded like he was telling himself this. "My dear, I will go to the church. My prayers are with you and the babe. May God bless us with a safe delivery."

Giving Charles a final embrace, Fastrada longed for her husband but knew a man at a birth was as useless as a broken knife. He could do much more good at the church, appealing to God and His Mother. But Kunigunde died despite his prayers. So had Hildegard.

She clutched her cross. *Don't let my fate be like Kunigunde's.*

Chapter Thirteen

Despite the untying of knots and Wilberga's fennel ointment, pain ripped through Fastrada's belly and back. She sweated in the lying-in chamber, warm with a vigorous fire, bright with many beeswax candles, and smelling of the straw and sweet woodruff strewn on the floor. Like Kunigunde's time, the room was crowded with women: the midwife, her assistants, the priest's grown daughter, the steward's wife, maids, and Hruodtrude. A week ago, the ten-winter-old girl had said she wanted to help, and her younger sisters begged to join her.

After some thought, Fastrada told six-winter-old Bertha and four-winter-old Gisela that they needed to go to the church to pray and help the nurses watch baby Hruodhaid. But she had allowed Hruodtrude into the lying-in chamber only if she promised to obey the midwife's every command. In a few years, Hruodtrude would be married, have a palace to manage, and babies to bear. She needed to witness this part of life.

Helped by Nantlind as she walked around the room, Fastrada wondered if she had made the right decision. Several times, she wanted to scream when pain stabbed her womb but saw the fear on Hruodtrude's face. Bottling her cries in her throat, Fastrada clutched her cross, pressing its edges into her hand. Would she live through this? Would her baby?

"I will be fine, Daughter," she said when she could speak without gasping.

The girl nodded but seemed too frightened to utter a word.

"An incantation will help," Wilberga said. She approached Fastrada and whispered in her ear, "As the Earth Mother makes the seedlings arise from the earth, come forth from your mother's womb."

The midwife reached under Fastrada's skirts and laid a hand on her belly. The older woman held up her free hand for silence and counted with her fingers. "The movements are closer together. You're doing well, my lady queen."

As she had done for Kunigunde, Wilberga tied a piece of jasper to Fastrada's thigh and held the foot of a crane to her belly, but all Fastrada could do was walk and wait.

About an hour after the nones bells, Fastrada felt a pop beneath her belly followed by a rush of water on her thighs. She lifted her skirts and looked down.

"Good. You're wet," Wilberga said. "Nantlind, take your lady to the birthing stool."

Soothed by the midwife's calmness, Fastrada hiked up her skirts and sat on the horseshoe-shaped stool. *It's almost over.*

Wilberga reached up. "Time to push."

Fastrada did with all her strength. When would this pain end?

"Very good. Again."

Fastrada was not sure how long the midwife continued to coax. She only knew to do the older woman's bidding.

"Here is the crown," Wilberga said. Excitement rose in her voice. "Now the head. One more push. Perfect! A girl!"

"A girl," Fastrada whispered. Tears streaked her face. All that bloating, all that sickness, all that pain. For a daughter. A Theodrada instead of a Bernard. She had not wanted to talk about what to name a girl, but Charles had insisted.

Fastrada turned away. Soon the newborn squalled, then she was drowned out by the women's cheers.

One of the midwife's assistants pushed on Fastrada's belly, releasing the afterbirth. Fastrada looked down. Blood, but not as much as Kunigunde.

"Some blood is normal, my lady queen," the midwife said. "The mulled wine my daughter is giving you will help restore you."

The young woman shoved a cup into her hand. Fastrada downed the drink, letting its warmth spread through her face and throat. After the midwife cut the newborn's cord with a sharp knife and wiped her with cloths, Fastrada extended her arms, hoping the women around her would think her tears were of joy. What kind of a mother would she be if she did not hold her firstborn?

"She is beautiful and healthy," Nantlind said. "The king will love her."

Feeling as if she had swallowed the strongest wine, Fastrada regarded her daughter. Wrinkled and pink, Theodrada was perfectly formed, with wispy blond hair and Charles's lively eyes. Fastrada extended her finger and let the tiny fingers close around it. *She is strong, too. If only ...*

"My father ..." Fastrada sobbed.

"... is no longer your lord," Nantlind said. "The king is, and he will be happy."

Managing a smile, Fastrada took comfort in her maid's words and gazed at the newborn in her arms. She remembered Charles had never denied asking God for a girl.

"My little Theodrada, you are the answer to your father's prayers," Fastrada said softly. "It's God's will."

When Fastrada met her baby's eyes, love surged through her, tempering her disappointment. Kissing her baby on the forehead, she silently vowed that when she did bear a son, her daughter would not lose her favor, the way Fastrada had lost her parents' when her brother was born. He was Büraburg's longed-for heir and got the best of everything.

"May I hold her?" Hruodtrude asked. She was smiling; the earlier tension on her face had disappeared.

"Only for a moment," Wilberga said, "then she needs a bath and her wet nurse. She is hungry, just like you were when you took your first breath."

Fastrada handed the baby to Hruodtrude, who gently cradled her newborn sister. The infant started to shift.

"Daughter, let the midwife bathe her," Fastrada said. "It would please me if you went to the church and told your father about me and your sister."

As she listened to the girl's light, quick footsteps, Fastrada let Nantlind help her undress for a bath. Sitting in her own tub, Fastrada watched the midwife bathe Theodrada, massage her with salt, and rub honey inside her mouth. While Fastrada dried herself and stuffed a flux rag between her legs, the midwife wrapped the child in swaddling and handed her to Irma, the baby's wet nurse. The widowed peasant from Worms had joined the royal household shortly before the Nativity.

"Theodrada takes to the breast eagerly." Irma's voice was wistful. Her own infant had died of a fever a few days before.

"Good," Fastrada murmured. "Tell Nantlind if you need anything."

Suddenly, Fastrada's limbs felt heavy. She staggered to the bed, glad her father was leagues away. She would see him at the assembly in Paderborn in a couple of months. Maybe she would have the will to face him by then.

***

Pepin knew something had happened when he heard excited girls' voices from outside the church, where the nurses for Bertha, Gisela, and Hruodhaid had taken their restless charges. Inside, Pepin knelt before a cross painted on a plastered stone wall and cast a sidelong look to Gomeric beside him. His uncle stared up at the cross. Pepin hastily muttered the remainder of the Paternoster. He wanted to stand but knew what Gomeric was trying to tell him: better for the men in the church—his father, brother, and the courtiers—to think he was praying.

Moments later, the doors groaned open, and he turned toward the sound. Hruodtrude ran into the church. Her broad smile told him Fastrada and the baby were well. His sister fidgeted as she waited for their father and Karl to hurry through their prayers before the painted wooden statue of the Blessed Mother.

Charles had barely finished when the words burst from Hruodtrude and echoed off the walls: "Mother is well and so is Theodrada!"

At least it's a girl. Pepin smirked. His mother would be glad as well.

In the evening light, his father rose. "Praise be to God." His voice was low, as if his relief had stolen it. "Praise be to His Merciful Mother and Saint Margaret."

Pepin wondered if his father's face had the same expression when he was born. While Hruodtrude chattered about the baby, Pepin searched the faces in the sanctuary. The others, were they truly glad Fastrada had survived, not only survived but was well? His eye landed on his brother, his tall, straight-backed brother, whose singsong child's voice was starting to crack. Of course, Karl was happy. What was one more sister? She would not demand a share of the kingdom.

Fie! My prayers for the she-wolf's death were refused.

***

Fastrada passed the next few days in a haze of fatigue within the warm darkness of the lying-in chamber. She was still bleeding, but the midwife said it was nothing to worry about and that she was recovering well. Nantlind left the room only to use the privies or bring her food on a tray painted with a scene of a serene mother holding a newborn.

Theodrada slept in a cradle, tended by Irma. Fastrada would arise from bed and don a shift so that she could gaze upon the child, her lovely child, a blessing from God. That is what Charles told Wilberga when she presented the baby to him. She clung to Charles' words and tried not to think of her father's reaction.

Despite her exhaustion, Fastrada sent for the other girls. How she missed Hruodtrude speaking of her studies of Saint Augustine, Bertha expounding upon the stars, Gisela talking to her doll, and Hruodhaid taking faltering steps. She longed to see Charles and Karl, too, but knew not to allow men into the lying-in chamber.

"My queen, don't tax yourself," the midwife said.

"My daughters comfort me," Fastrada said, although her eyelids felt leaden. "Even confined in a cramped room, I will not stop being a mother or a queen. Must I stay here an entire month?"

From the corner of her eye, she saw Irma smile.

"If you try to do too much," Wilberga said, "it will be longer."

Hruodtrude, Bertha, and Gisela gathered around the crib and a few moments later started bickering over who would hold the baby first. Fastrada sighed heavily and wondered if she should have heeded the midwife.

"My ladies," Wilberga said, "this quarreling is too much for your mother and the baby. If you don't stop, your mother will order you to leave the chamber and let her have peace."

"But she—" Hruodtrude said, pointing at Bertha.

"Listen to Wilberga," Fastrada said in her mother tone. "You will all have a chance to hold Theodrada. Hruodtrude, you can hold her first."

Thankfully, the girls settled.

"How does your father fare?" Fastrada asked.

"He's well," Hruodtrude said.

"He left for battle at midday," Bertha said. "He wore a helmet and armor and had a sword."

"Why did he have two horses?" Gisela asked.

"One for riding, another for battle," Fastrada explained. "Have you prayed to Saint Georg and the Blessed Mother?"

The girls nodded in unison. "The priests said the litanies, too," Hruodtrude added.

Fastrada enjoyed hearing their voices, and when one of them let slip a piece of gossip about a courtier's interest in a betrothal to a girl from an important Thuringian family, it was like a dried apple soaked in honey.

When she was struggling to keep her eyes open, Wilberga turned toward the girls. "My excellent young ladies, your mother needs rest now. I will let you see her again when she has a bit more vitality." She met Fastrada's eyes. "I promise."

As soon as the girls left, Fastrada asked Nantlind the question most on her mind. "How does my husband truly fare?"

"He looked hale and hearty. As I was bringing food to you this morning, he called to me and asked about you and the babe. I assured him you both were well."

"How many men is he taking with him? Is he going to march along the Weser? Is it still flooded?"

"He does not tell me these things, my lady queen, but he told me to give you a message. He says for you not to worry about him, that your duty is to recover from the birth."

"How can I not worry? Widukind is out there."

Chapter Fourteen

Fastrada regained a little more vigor each day. Just as important, Theodrada continued to thrive. The nurse cared for the princess as if the infant were her own, and Fastrada was relieved to have made the right choice. Still, she became restless toward the end of her month in the chamber. To pass time, she altered her gowns to flatter her more rounded breasts and wider hips. When the midwife was in the room, she used the light of the candles and low fire. In the midwife's absence, she and Irma moved the tapestry of the Blessed Virgin and her Child aside and opened the shutter a crack, careful not to let the light fall on the baby and injure her eyes. Fastrada's peek through the narrow opening revealed the herb and vegetable garden in full leaf, a welcome sight even on a day darkened by rain clouds. She could see where cooks had cut sprigs of thyme, pulled radishes and carrots, and sheared leaves from the cabbages.

Every time she heard the prime and vespers bells, she prayed for Charles and her countrymen. She learned her prayers had been answered two days before her churching, when Hruodtrude and Bertha burst into the room with the news that the Franks had reconquered Lübbecke and Charles had returned as he had promised.

The night before the ceremony, Fastrada hardly slept. She was so eager for the feast and the gossip. Most of all, she longed to behold Charles. An hour before Mass, Nantlind helped her into the dress she had worn on her wedding day and pinned the enameled medal of Saint Wigbert near her collar. This time, she donned a silk veil and secured it with a headdress accentuated by a large beryl. Her jeweled girdle glinted in the candlelight. Before she left the room, she cradled the baby in her arms.

"My dearling Theodrada," she cooed, "Irma is going to move you to the princesses' chamber. Mother will return soon."

She gave her daughter a final embrace and handed her to the nurse. She let her hand linger on the child's cheek. Odd, how she had wanted nothing more than to get out of this cramped room but did not want to be away from her baby.

"My lady," Nantlind said softly.

Fastrada kissed Theodrada's forehead and left the room. Alone in the corridor, she quickened her steps toward the reception room, where Charles and the children awaited. Her husband rushed to meet her and swept her into his arms.

"How I missed you," he murmured.

"And I, you," she whispered.

She embraced Karl, and for Charles's sake, gave Pepin a brief hug. The young man was rigid, but Charles would know she tried.

"It's almost sunrise," Charles said. "Let us go to church."

The family traversed the great hall, which was starting to brighten with the growing light of the dawn and smelled of fresh woodruff on the floor. Outside, the clouds were becoming pink with the awakening sun. They strode to the church and paused outside its doors. A priest handed her a lighted candle.

After murmuring a few Latin words to please the Blessed Mother, Fastrada tightened her grip on the candle and stroked her medal of Saint Wigbert with her free hand. With her husband, the royal children, the archchaplain—who would vow to be Theodrada's godfather next week at Pentecost—and the courtiers, she entered the church. It was as magnificent as she remembered. The crowd of Franks and Saxons obscured her view of the painted wooden statues of saints and the plastered walls and their painted crosses. The worshippers turned toward her, their faces displaying curiosity.

A priest greeted her, made the sign of the cross and sprinkled holy water on her. She mouthed the Latin words to the Psalm he chanted, *Domini est terra et plenitudo eius*, "The earth is the Lord's and the fullness thereof." How she loved Jesu and His Merciful Mother. She was almost recovered, and Theodrada was strong and healthy.

With a broad grin, she held the end of the priest's stole and followed him to the altar while he sang more Latin. She could comprehend only phrases here and there. The crowd parted for her.

Fastrada knelt while the priest chanted a prayer and sprinkled her with holy water in the form of a cross. Then he ended with a blessing.

Fastrada smiled her thanks. She turned to the main entrance, keeping her eyes straight ahead. Her baby was most vulnerable at this moment. *Don't look at Pepin. Don't look at Pepin. Don't bring his curse on Theodrada!*

But Pepin leaned into her view. His eyes gleamed. Fastrada trembled, causing the light from the candle to waver. She staggered a step before resuming her pace. Once outside, she handed her candle to a guard.

"I must see Theodrada!" She picked up her skirts and rushed back to the manor. With her cross jangling on her neck, she murmured "*Ave Maria, gratia plena*" over and over and over. The guards easily kept pace.

"Are you ill, my lady queen?"

Fastrada shook her head. She repeated the prayer to Mother Mary as her breath would allow. She dashed to the princesses' bedchamber. If Pepin's curse took hold, her little girl would be reviled.

"My baby!" she cried to Irma. "I must see her!"

The nurse gawked at Fastrada. "She is sleeping, my lady queen."

"Take off her swaddling! Now!"

Her brow furrowed, Irma lifted Theodrada from her cradle, set the child on her lap, and stripped off the swaddling. Theodrada bawled at being roused from sleep. Fastrada turned her daughter on her side and felt the baby's spine.

"Sh-she's normal!" Fastrada sobbed. "Praise God for His mercy!"

"Why would she not be, my lady queen?" Irma gestured at the cross painted on the cradle. "I sing the charm against changelings every night."

"Good work," Fastrada mumbled. "Keep saying those charms. Wrap her back in the swaddling. We need to keep her limbs straight."

She wiped her eyes and cheeks and tried to regain her composure. She didn't know if the cross or the charm warded off Pepin's curse. All that mattered was that her baby was well.

***

Fastrada was too filled with rage against Pepin to feel any joy at the feast she had so looked forward to, and that made her rage hotter. She refused to let Pepin see a woman so mired in self-pity she could not eat. Fastrada stuffed meat into her mouth even though it was tasteless to her. *Hate me all you want, Pepin, but leave your sister be. She is innocent.*

"Did your gaze land on a little boy, my queen?" Pepin asked from his seat beside her.

"No." Fastrada's voice was colder than she intended.

"Your next child will likely be a girl as well."

Fury seized Fastrada's tongue. It took all her will not to scream that Pepin was a twisted boy lower than a worm.

From the head of the table, Charles leaned forward and laid his hand between her shoulder blades. "God has given me three heirs, a son to serve the Church, and five beautiful daughters. Boy or girl, any child you carry will be a blessing, my dear."

With a sideways glance, Fastrada saw Pepin's face turn crimson. It gave her little satisfaction. *The Church is too good for him.*

She knew she needed to talk to Charles about his eldest son, but they had not had a moment alone. Shortly after she had seen to Theodrada's welfare, Charles entered the princesses' chamber and asked what troubled her. With Irma in the room and the voices of courtiers floating from the hall, she had said only that she needed to behold Theodrada, and the answer had satisfied him.

During the feast, Fastrada tried to keep up the conversation, but even court gossip and talk of war failed to completely hold her interest. Her mind kept racing back to her daughter, her beautiful, helpless daughter. How could Pepin wish ill on a baby?

She finally got her opportunity when the last course was cleared from the table. She and Charles retired to their bedchamber, and she dismissed her maids. His eyes shining with lust, her husband placed his large hand on her knee.

"Are you healed from the birth, my dear?"

"No. The midwife said I could bleed again if I know you too soon." Fastrada burst into tears. She wished her body would long for him as it used to and wondered if desire would ever kindle within her again.

"Hildegard had to wait, too." Sighing, Charles patted her shoulder. "Sleep now."

"Husband," she said in a small voice, "there is something I must tell you."

"What is it?"

"Pepin, he leaned into my view as I was leaving the church. H-he was trying to curse Theodrada!"

"He must have been trying to get a better look at you."

"I know what I saw! He hates me and always has!"

"You are overwrought, as Hildegard was after she gave birth."

"Charles!"

"Wife." Charles's tone was an order to no longer discuss the matter.

Fastrada could not stop the sobs wracking her body.

Charles drew her into his arms. "Pepin is vexing sometimes, but so are all youths. He would never hurt his sister. But let us get Theodrada a medal of Saint Nicholas. Send for the silversmith after our nap, and we'll have her godfather bless it."

Fastrada's frustration threatened to choke her. How could her husband, so adept at persuading Frankish counts to invade Saxony in the winter, be so blind to his own son? *Pepin does not deserve that kind of love.*

Now she knew her true place in the royal family. To protect the children from their God-cursed brother.

***

Fastrada awoke to Charles whispering her name. She forced her eyes open. He was propped against pillows. "I must speak to you," he said. The urgency in his voice banished her sleepiness.

She sat up. "What is it, Husband?"

"While you were sleeping, Meginfrid brought a message. We might be able to end the wars with the Saxons. Widukind wants to negotiate."

"How can you even think of a bargain with that viper?" she spat. "Have you forgotten the slain monks? The raped women? Have you forgotten the winter my people starved because his men burned our crops?"

"Calm yourself, my dear. I will accept nothing less than Widukind's baptism and a vow of loyalty as my vassal."

"We cannot trust him—or any Saxon. Throughout their whole history, those worms have been nothing but thieves and murderers. Look what they did to the Thuringians, slaughtering them with hidden knives while pretending to want peace. Slime, all of them!"

"That was centuries ago, and you have not seen what we have wrought." He stuck out his scarred, muscled chest. "Their fields were red with the blood of their warriors, and we destroyed whatever was left."

"Tell me the truth, Charles," Fastrada muttered, her shoulders hunched, "not your boast to the courtiers."

"It is true! That's why Widukind wants to treat. We never exacted an oath from him. Once he takes the vow, the rest of his people will follow."

"I want him dead. Burning in hell. With devils slicing him open and eating his innards!"

"A fate he deserves, but how many of our people must die before we capture him? We have tried and failed for years. And now with Tassilo stirring trouble in the south with the Lombards and the Avars, we need all our men and Saxon allies as well. You have heard the messages. We can no longer be diverted by these wars in Saxony, not when one of their leaders is willing to turn to God."

Fastrada gaped at him. He would have never been so candid in court.

"And if we stop Widukind from accepting the True Faith, we will draw God's wrath," he added.

Fastrada shuddered. Her people needed God's favor. Defying His will would mean even more death for her people and disaster for Charles. A bitter taste filled her mouth.

"I need your aid," Charles said. "When your father comes to the assembly, I need you to convince him to support our cause."

"I will speak to my father, but it will be difficult. I ... he ... he thinks ... I'm a failure." She slumped.

Charles gathered her in his arms. She leaned against his solid chest.

"My dear, why would you say such a foolish thing?" His voice had the tone of a father soothing a child after a nightmare. "You are a good wife, a good mother, and a good queen."

"I bore a girl."

She felt him shrug. "Why does it matter to him? I already have sons. Your place with me will always be secure."

"Girls are not future kings."

Charles stared ahead, then nodded as if something had become clear. He stroked her hair. "The heirs God grants to my kingdom are not your father's concern," he finally said. "His loyalty as my vassal is."

Charles was right, although she knew telling her father so would only invite a quarrel. "Even if I can sway my father to accept this," she said, "the East Franks and Thuringians will see this as mercy to a murderer. Count Hardrad, especially. His losses were so great, he will not want peace on these terms."

"We must take that risk."

***

After sunrise Mass the next day, Fastrada lingered in the church and knelt before a statue of the Blessed Mother, the blues and yellows bright in the light streaming through the arched windows. Fastrada's only companions were the bodyguards a few paces away. She breathed in the scent of incense. How she needed this moment alone.

"Is mercy for Widukind the will of Our Father in Heaven?" she murmured, bowing her head.

She was bound by her nuptial oath and her vow as queen of the Franks, but her heart was torn.

"Widukind is a monster," she said softly.

But she could not argue with Charles on one point: if God wanted that monster baptized and she prevented it, she would be damned. She shivered, remembering a poem about a condemned soul hung upside down and dipped in ice. And His wrath would not stop with her. He could send plagues or droughts or floods or let the Lombards or the Avars overrun Francia. No, she could not let that happen. She must please God.

She touched the Blessed Mother's foot. "Pray for me," she whispered in Latin.

Still, every time Fastrada thought about how she would talk to her father about Widukind, her guts clenched. It was a relief to direct the servants to get ready to travel to Paderborn, where Charles would hold this year's assembly and receive his youngest son, Louis. The seven-winter-old boy would be another reminder of how she failed to produce a grandson for her father.

As the days passed, Fastrada barely spoke to Pepin, but she seethed whenever she laid eyes on him. Vengeance germinated in her mind. What would it be like if he lost those fine clothes and jewelry she provided to him, the baths prepared every week, the four-course meals rich with meat, those whores he wasted his uncle's money on? Life in a strict monastery would be most fitting, and he could do penance for his sin against Theodrada.

She toyed with the idea of letting him find out his guards spied on him and related his every activity to her but decided against it. The pleasure of unnerving him was not worth the price of the guards' learning nothing.

When she was healed enough to lie with Charles again, her desire was not what it had been, but she could not deny him his rights as her husband. He was as gentle as he had been on their wedding night. Wilberga had said the first time after the baby would be the most difficult, that desire would return, that she would again demand her wifely rights to the marriage bed.

Three weeks after Fastrada's churching, the court and the soldiers started their journey. They spent half a day on a narrow road that followed a river to their right and lay beside hills vibrant with vast pines and ancient oaks and ash trees to their left. At an intersection with a better road, they turned left and followed another river for a few hours before ascending a large, steep hill. The terrain became smoother, but at sunset, they were far from any village and camped in the forest, something that always made Fastrada uneasy. She checked that servants had placed bread in the trees—a bribe for kobolds to refrain from mischief—and that the children were wearing their charms along with their crosses to protect themselves from demons.

At midafternoon on the third day, the oaks and ash trees were giving way to beeches, a sign the travelers were getting close to a city: Paderborn. Fastrada could see the city walls as the party emerged from the woods and crossed fields of tall winter wheat and rye and short grass-like spring oats. Close to the great gate, Fastrada nodded her approval of the ramparts' height and sturdiness, with plenty of spaces to pour boiling water on invaders.

Inside the bulwarks, her jaw dropped. The palace and church sat atop an incline, and their towers peeked from the walls surrounding them. But she was equally amazed by houses and huts in front of her.

"It looks like a Frankish city!" she said.

Charles grinned. "We were not going to let Widukind's little fire defeat us."

Fastrada reached for Charles's hand. It had been seven years ago, when she had seen twelve winters, but she had not forgotten her father's grim face when he recounted how Widukind's Saxons had destroyed Paderborn while the Franks were doing God's work in Hispania. Now that the city was rebuilt, what better way to show Charles's power than to hold the assembly here?

Only the peasants who emerged from their homes were different. The men wore knee-length tunics and sheepskin cloaks similar to the Frankish style, but they had long hair and beards. The women favored sleeveless dresses held with brooches and covered their hair with voluminous veils. The expressions on their faces were mixed. Some people seemed curious; others were glowering.

The travelers rode toward the city's center, passed through another gate, and entered a courtyard. Among the smaller structures and livestock pens stood the manor, a large, rectangular two-story stone building with square windows. The stone church about the same size was a few paces away.

Fastrada straightened her shoulders. She was mistress of the palace and of these lands.

Inside the manor, the great hall would inspire awe in its guests. Bordered with delicate carvings near the ceiling, the plastered walls were painted with murals of saints and a Latin inscription in red letters. The columns were topped with thin pieces of marble forming geometric designs. Lamps overhead and a huge hearth would give the vast room its light after the sun set. Now, the windows were open for the summer air, and the hall was sweetened with the smell of fresh rushes on the floor. Opposite the entrance, Charles's throne, made even higher with five steps, sat on a dais, and Fastrada's ornately carved chair was beside it.

"This is what we need at Aachen and Ingelheim," Charles whispered.

***

When Radolf arrived two days later, Fastrada greeted him in the great hall and threw her arms around his neck. After returning her embrace, her father stepped back and gazed at her.

"You look well."

"You must meet your granddaughter," Fastrada said excitedly. She gestured for Irma to bring the child to him. "Is she not beautiful, Father? She is gaining weight every day and smiles now."

The baby regarded her grandfather as if she were studying him. Fastrada searched her father's face. He was not smiling. A weight sank in her bosom. How she wished she had been wrong.

Her father glanced at Theodrada and did not extend his arms to hold the baby. Instead, he sighed. "Perhaps your next child will be a boy."

Heat flooded her cheeks. Her little girl was perfect. Why could her father not welcome his own granddaughter?

"Charles is happy with a healthy daughter, and so am I," Fastrada snapped. She felt a stab of jealousy. Had her father been this disappointed because she was not a boy? She was six winters old again, standing in a corner, clutching her doll, watching the joy spread through the household with Sigibert's birth. "A strong boy at last!" her nurse had said. At the time, she had wondered why all this fuss over a boy. Had she not been a good daughter? Was she not a good horsewoman? Was she not skilled with the needle and learning her prayers? What was so wrong with her that her father needed a son?

Her father's voice drew her back to the present. "Do you not know what a future king in our family would mean?"

"Don't treat me like a simpleton!"

Radolf squared his shoulders. "You may be queen of the Franks, but you are still my daughter."

"Father, I am a woman grown, a wife, and a mother—and your queen."

His nostrils flared.

This is no way to ask for a favor. Fastrada took a deep breath to still the pounding in her chest. First, she would need to tell her father what he wanted to hear.

"I have not forgotten my duty to our family or our people," she said. "I prayed every day for a son. I gave alms. I slept on my right side. But God willed for my child to be a girl. Tell me, what else could I have done?"

Radolf's face softened. With a wave of his hand, he beckoned a maid, who handed Fastrada a girdle of green jasper set in silver. "The midwife said it will help you conceive a boy."

How many glass beads and bronze brooches had he traded to get this? "Thank you, Father. I will wear it until God blesses us with a boy." She glanced at the servants bustling around them. "I must talk to you about a matter that will affect the future of Francia. About Widukind."

Chapter Fifteen

As soon as Fastrada announced it was time for dinner, Pepin rushed out of the archive. He found Gomeric speaking with Angilram the archchaplain in the great hall, where noblemen milled about the trestle tables.

"Uncle," he cried, "I must speak with you!"

After a moment, Gomeric smiled. "I told you the fair lady would like your poem."

Pepin furrowed his brow.

Angilram frowned. "You should not be tempting maidens to sin. It is bad enough that you use whores."

"What Pepin does with fallen women is between him and his confessor," Gomeric said, "and the lady in question is not chaste. Now, if you will excuse us, I must speak to my nephew about making sure she doesn't pass a babe off as his."

His face still sour, the archchaplain stalked away. Pepin waited until the cleric was out of earshot.

"This is not about a maid," he said in a low voice.

"I know," Gomeric muttered, "but your father must not suspect you are telling me about his meetings or writing to your mother about them. Don't act so excited next time."

The words from his mother's last letter echoed in his ears: *Always heed your uncle. In your father's court, he alone has your interest.*

A wave of voices spread through the vast room. Pepin and Gomeric both glanced about. The magnates had entered the hall followed by Charles and Fastrada. Pepin had but a moment before everyone took their seats. He leaned toward his uncle and lowered his voice. "Swear you keep what I tell you secret."

Gomeric readily agreed. In hurried Latin whispers, Pepin told him what he had overheard about Widukind during his father's meetings with his magnates.

"It's a devil's bargain," Gomeric said between clenched teeth.

"Radolf used almost those exact words."

"Yet our queen supports this foolishness?"

"She argues most fiercely for it," Pepin said.

***

Each day brought more nobles—Frankish and Saxon—and their retinues to Paderborn, and Pepin was never more glad for the custom of the king's guests leaving their weapons in the treasury. Of course, the noblemen and their servants still had their eating knives, and Pepin wondered more than once if a Saxon warrior would use his blade to scratch the mural of the flaming Irminsul.

When a messenger announced his brother Louis's arrival a week later, Meginfrid and Fastrada hastened to the courtyard to greet the boy. Pepin scowled. He would never be able to come to his father with soldiers. No chamberlain or queen would ever rush to meet him. Then he forced a smile, remembering his mother's counsel to pretend to like his brothers. He could do so with Louis and Little Pippin. Karl would get suspicious.

In the hall, Charles ascended the steps to the dais and his throne, and the seneschal handed him the scepter. Pepin, his siblings, and the court bowed and gathered at the foot of the dais. A moment later, the crowd parted.

Fastrada strode to her husband, pressed her hands together and bowed to him, and took her seat on an ornate chair beside him. Pepin felt as if a fist was squeezing his heart. His brothers would someday have beauteous ladies at their sides. The only women in his future were the ones he paid. One by one, Aquitanian counts and bishops filed in and bowed to his father.

"His Excellence Louis," Meginfrid bellowed, "king of Aquitaine by the grace of God and by his father, Charles, king of the Franks and the Lombards."

Charles shifted in his chair. Fastrada was perched on the edge of her seat. A seven-year-old, dark-haired boy entered the hall. Tall for his age, he had his father's long nose but his chin recessed a little. He, too, was dressed like an Aquitainian: circular cloak, shirt with long, wide sleeves, baggy leggings, and boots with pointed spurs of thin metal bands. He held a javelin in his right hand—allowed in Charles's presence for the moment as a symbol of kingship—and bowed to his father.

Charles crossed his arms and smiled. "You make a fitting king of Aquitaine."

"Thank you," Louis mumbled.

"Lady Queen Fastrada has prepared a fine feast to welcome you."

Louis bowed to her and muttered his thanks. He glanced over his shoulder. A lanky cleric in his mid-twenties tentatively stepped forward.

"Tell me how my son fares with his lessons," Charles said.

The cleric bowed. "Your Excellence will be most pleased. King Louis is reading the Psalms, and we have just started lessons in arithmetic, geometry, astronomy, and music. He is a superb horseman and wields his wooden sword well."

Pepin flushed. Someday a metal sword would replace the wooden one at Louis's hip. Someday Louis would sit on a throne and have a wife he could lie with whenever he pleased. Everything Pepin wanted. Everything he might never have.

***

When the assembly started twelve days later, Fastrada still did not know if her father would support Charles. Their conversations had been heated or strained. Radolf had raged against baptism for Widukind, but when Fastrada brought up the Saxon's heirs and God's will, he had fallen silent and glared at her.

Again, she and Charles were on the dais. The royal children, except Hruodhaid and Theodrada, gathered nearby and the nobles formed a semicircle.

After Meginfrid took the scepter, Charles laid his hands on the arms of his throne and spoke. "This is the summer Widukind will follow God's will. He will accept baptism."

Count Hardrad, a Thuringian, snorted in derision. "After burning churches?"

"Amalwin," Charles said, "tell the court what our Saxon allies told you."

"Widukind is ready to treat with our Lord King Charles," said the courtier. "Otherwise, he will lose all of Westphalia, just as he has Eresburg and Paderborn and many other fortresses."

The Saxon nobles in the crowd nodded.

"We should tie Widukind to four horses and send them running," snarled Hardrad.

"I would like nothing more," Fastrada said, "but Widukind's baptism is the only way to end these wars." She tried to catch her father's eye. *Now everyone knows my place is with Charles.*

Radolf looked away.

"Why should we trust the Saxons?" asked Severinus, whose lands were near Bavaria. "They have broken all their vows."

"Widukind's influence is so powerful," Amalwin said, "the Saxon rebels let him escape after the battle in the Süntels, even though it meant they would meet the headman's ax. If Widukind follows God's will, so will the people who swore an oath to follow him."

Fastrada locked eyes with her father. *Please.*

"I hate that Saxon viper," Radolf said, his voice strong. "I will never forget his attack on Büraburg. That coward waited until I was in Italy with the rest of the army, saving the Church from the Lombards. I came home to scorched fields and starving peasants. My wife could not sleep for months, and my little girl ..." His voice rasped. He paused for a moment.

Fastrada started to raise her hand to put it to her mouth but then laid it on her lap. She pressed her lips together to mask their trembling. *I will not cry.*

"I want revenge," her father growled. "I want to cut out Widukind's eyes, his tongue, his hands, his feet, and let him bleed to death."

A stone sank in Fastrada's belly.

"But," Radolf continued, "if we kill him, another heathen will only take his place. The wars will continue. More of our churches will burn. More of our women will be raped. And more of our men will be slaughtered."

Thank you, Father. Hearing her own words from his mouth loosened the knot between her shoulders.

"Worm!" Hardrad spat. "You're afraid of the Saxon cur."

Radolf drew himself to his full height. His hand fell to the place where his sword usually hung. "I fear no Saxon. But I fear God. It is His will that heathens be baptized, and if we defy Him, woe to us."

"We should send Widukind and his ilk to hell," Hardrad shouted. "To do otherwise is a betrayal of our people."

"Saving souls betrays no one," Charles said.

As more nobles voiced their support for Charles, Hardrad's eyes blazed with loathing.

***

Five days later, Fastrada and her father stood in the courtyard with the morning sun casting long shadows. Hoping to placate him, Fastrada wore the green jasper girdle. With Irma behind her, she held her daughter, who stared at the servants and soldiers bustling about. Fastrada regarded her father. The wrinkles in his face had deepened, his cheeks seemed more hollow, and the hair he had left was grayer, yet he still wore his armor of small metal plates as if it were a second skin.

"Theodrada," Fastrada said, "Grandfather is going with your father to the Bardengau to bring Widukind to God."

Radolf frowned. "My support for your husband's plan has cost us allies."

"How many times must you say this, Father? I knew that as soon as Charles mentioned it to me."

"You have no inkling ..."

"I have more than an inkling," Fastrada said firmly. "But Alcuin pointed out a Scripture ..." Seeing her father gaze into the distance, she let her voice trail. There was no point quoting Scripture to him. "I will pray for you," she murmured.

"God be with you." Radolf's voice betrayed exasperation. He kissed his daughter on the cheek and his granddaughter on the forehead. The baby stared at him.

That's the only sign of affection he's shown for Theodrada. "God be with you, Father."

Turning away from him, Fastrada blinked back the tears. The people needed their queen to be strong, show no fear, not even a hint of doubt. As she approached Charles and the children, the tension in her chest eased a little.

Charles held out his arms. Fastrada handed Theodrada to him. The baby smiled.

"May God keep you safe and well," he whispered. He stroked the infant's cheek and kissed her before handing her to her nurse.

After hugging and kissing the children, he turned to Fastrada and embraced her. Within his arms, against his massive chest, she felt almost certain this plan with Widukind could work.

"I shall miss you, my dear," he murmured.

Fastrada's throat tightened. *Not now! You can weep all you want in your bedchamber after he leaves.* She clung to him, not wishing to let him go. She swallowed and straightened her frame. "I will pray for you. I will see to it we observe the litanies."

"I could not ask for a better queen."

***

While Charles and his army marched north, Fastrada and the three eldest children abstained from meat and wine for three days, hoping God would bestow His favor on their people. She gave alms on behalf of the royal children too young to deny themselves food. The bishop and priests read Psalms and litanies.

Still, the next month passed in anxiety. What if Amalwin was wrong and Widukind wanted to fight another war? Her relief overwhelmed her when a letter with Charles's seal arrived. Hastily, she grabbed her eating knife and sliced through the hardened wax. As she started to read silently, she held her breath and heard footsteps from many people approaching. Her face bloomed into a smile. She looked up and noticed the royal family, the remaining courtiers, and servants crowded around her, leaning in.

"Charles is well and victorious," she cried.

When the shouts of joy quieted, she handed the parchment to a clerk and clasped her hands in her lap.

"We marched throughout Saxony on open roads and encountered no opposition. When we arrived at the Bardengau, Amalwin persuaded Widukind of Westphalia and his followers to come to us. We warned them that if they did not submit to God's will, we would give them another winter of plunder and destruction. We swore their only hope was

to follow God's will. Widukind pledged to accept baptism. We agreed to send twelve hostages with Amalwin to affirm our commitment to Widukind's safety.

"We will come for you, our dearling daughters, and beloved sons in two weeks' time. Then we will travel to Attigny and witness God's triumph."

When she saw anxious faces among the courtiers, Fastrada knew what they were thinking. It was the same matter that troubled her, one she dared not voice in public: who among the nobility would send their sons to Widukind? If she were a countess instead of a queen, she would have railed against it. She would scratch and bite anyone who would hand Karl or Louis over to the heathen, no matter what the promised rewards. She could imagine the arguments: *It's only a few months. They will be honored guests. It's for the sake of the kingdom. It's God will.*

True, she thought, *but these children are going to a fiend's lair.*

November 785, Attigny

The Saxon messenger fidgeted, his feet crushing the thyme and mint on the floor in the great hall. Fastrada smiled but suppressed the urge to laugh. She knew she should not be amused by his nervousness or care if he was impressed with the villa. He would have no idea how the site was the perfect place for his master's submission. A synod of bishops throughout the realm had gathered here twenty-three years ago to settle their differences and unify the Church, and soon the Church would be even stronger. Fastrada had made certain the villa was ready for the Saxon leader, even though she would have rather seen Widukind brought here in chains. The paved courtyard was swept of dirt and browned leaves, the tables were clean, fires blazed in the hearths, and the baths would soon be ready.

On the stone walls, the tapestries, brilliant even with cloudy light seeping through the narrow parchment-covered windows, told stories from Scripture. Fastrada had made sure the one showing the Final Judgment was most prominent. She wanted Widukind to see his choice: either the golden clouds of heaven and the melodious songs of angels or the inky blackness of hell, broken with orange flames and the punishment of sinners—bodies hung by their heels dipped in pitch and ice, men with bellies slit open while demons gnawed at their innards, and more tortures than the eyes could take in.

"Herzog Widukind sends greetings," the messenger said with a Saxon accent. "He expects to arrive at midday."

"Your news cheers us," Charles said. "Thanks to our queen, a fine feast awaits him."

Again, bitterness filled Fastrada's mouth. If she had her will, this brute would be a feast for maggots. At least, she could send a message of her own.

"Our king will make sure Widukind is well protected," she said smoothly. "While your lord is our guest, his weapons will be safe in our treasury under lock and key in a stone tower. And as you no doubt have noticed, the mountains and river you just crossed deter any enemy, and the walls here are so stout that this castle has resisted attacks for well over one hundred years. We have many seasoned guards with well-honed swords and spears. Should anyone try to attack, they will be greeted with a volley of arrows and scalding water."

The messenger winced.

"So," she continued, "your master will be perfectly safe with us."

Charles gave her a sly look as if he was caught between a rebuke and a laugh.

When a guard announced Widukind's arrival three hours later, Fastrada strolled through the stone corridors to the courtyard. It was important, Charles had said, that Widukind be treated as an honored guest and be greeted by the queen. Her belly roiled. She wanted to spit on him, kick him until he was bruised and bloody.

She refused to hurry. Widukind would not forget she was the queen. She touched her jeweled diadem, checking to make sure it and the pins that held her embroidered silk veil were in place. Her blue gown glittered with the gems and gold threads sewn into it. Her enameled brooch and gold cross nestled amid her emerald and sapphire necklaces, and the furs lining her cloak were marten.

When she beheld Widukind, she blinked back her surprise. Oh, he was as the courtiers described, a tall, muscular warrior, but not as tall or broad as Charles. Nor was she shocked that his eyes were two colors, one blue and one brown, the mark of the Devil. She had already heard the stories. As with most Saxons, his clothes fit more loosely than the close-fitting costume Frankish men preferred.

What surprised her was how haggard he looked. He had seen perhaps fifty winters, older than her father. His face was craggy, and his blond hair, a little too long, was streaked with silver. *He is still the spawn of the Devil. His men burned our churches, hacked our monks to death, raped our women.*

Forcing a smile, Fastrada regarded the savage's family. Widukind's Nordmannian wife, about twenty years his junior, kept her face impassive but draped her arms protectively around her daughter and son. The Nordmannian had the prominent eyebrows and jaw of her people and fashioned her red hair in a knot at the back of her head with ribbons braided into it. She and her daughter wore belted Saxon gowns, fastened by gold brooches at the shoulders. The daughter was old enough to be Hruodtrude's playmate, and the boy, clad in loose clothes like his father, was Bertha's age.

Both of Widukind's offspring regarded her with wide eyes. For a moment, Fastrada saw them only as frightened children in a strange place. *Do not be deceived! Do not forget their sire.*

Widukind bowed to Fastrada as did his family and his followers.

Fastrada kept her pasted smile and spoke words she had thought would never pass her lips. "Welcome to our villa. We invite you and your companions to refresh yourselves in our baths and then come to our table."

"You are more beautiful than your husband ... told, Queen Fastrada," Widukind said in Saxon-accented Frankish. "He ... has luck to have you."

The Devil speaks honeyed words, too.

***

The next morning, the church adjoining the villa was warm with the crowd, which overflowed out the doors. Fastrada, clad in jewels and her richest garb, stood with her family and Widukind's near the square baptismal font, where two square apses and the curved apse with the altar intersected with the rest of the structure. Perfect for allowing as many witnesses as possible to watch Widukind's submission.

She and Charles had made sure the priests had enough walnut oil for the lanterns overhead, especially needed in this one-hundred-forty-winter-old building with its small circular and narrow arched windows. The crowd prevented her from seeing most of the murals, but she could admire the wall behind the marble altar several paces away. The image was crucified Jesu the Christ, with soldiers piercing His side with spears and the haloed Mother Mary looking on. *I hope this monster knows the sacrifice.*

The crowd parted to allow a priest to enter the church, swinging a smoking censer and perfuming the area with incense. When the archchaplain approached the altar, the murmurs fell still. He said a few prayers, then with two clerics, walked to the church door, where Widukind and Charles, his godfather, awaited. Widukind wore only a tunic and was shivering. Towering over the Saxon, Charles was clad in his best clothes, along with his diadem and jeweled shoes.

"I believe in the True Faith," Widukind said stiffly, "and the one true God and wish to enter the Church through ... baptism."

"Do you believe in God, the Father Almighty?" Angilram the archchaplain asked.

"I do believe." His face remained impassive.

"Do you believe in Jesu the Christ and the Holy Spirit? In the Trinity and in His Unity?"

"I do believe."

"Do you believe in the Holy Church of God? In remission of sins by baptism? In life after death?"

"I do believe."

The priest breathed on Widukind, exorcising evil spirits. Fastrada touched her brooch with Saint Wigbert's image.

"Do you renounce the Devil, his works, and his will? Do you renounce the blood sacrifices, idols, and gods of pagans?"

"I do renounce them."

99

"Do you renounce Wodan, Donar, and Seaxnot and all those fiends that are their companions?"

"I do renounce them."

Angilram placed salt on Widukind's tongue. Dabbing his fingers in holy oil, the archchaplain made the sign of the cross on Widukind's forehead, ears, eyes, nose, chest, and between his shoulders. Standing on her toes to get a better view, Fastrada squinted and scrutinized the Saxon. Was he sincere? She pressed her hand against her cross, praying Charles was right.

"Herzog Widukind of Westphalia, the Church welcomes you."

The archchaplain led Widukind and Charles to the font. Special curtains supported by rods and poles would be brought in and drawn for Widukind's wife and daughter, but everyone would see Widukind and his son take the vows. After renouncing the Devil again, Widukind doffed his tunic, revealing battle scars on his pale torso and legs. Fastrada put her hand to her mouth. He had as many as Charles. She glanced at the Saxon's wife, whose gaze was on her husband. Did she spend weeks wondering if he would come home? *No, don't think that! Harden your heart.*

Naked, the Saxon leader climbed into the marble font, knelt, and crossed his arms. Using a silver vessel, Angilram poured water over Widukind's head three times. Making the sign of the cross, he chanted, "Widukind, *ego te baptizo in nomine Patris, et Filii, et Spiritus Sancti.*"

Fastrada mouthed the words. If Widukind dared break his vows, he would answer to God.

Charles held out his hand. After a moment's hesitation, the Saxon took it and let Charles raise him from the font. Fastrada smiled. This was Widukind's first public sign of submission.

A priest handed the Saxon a white robe. Kneeling again, Widukind stumbled through the Paternoster three times. Then Charles and the archchaplain made the sign of the cross on his brow. The priest took Widukind by the hand and led him to the altar. Widukind prostrated himself for a few moments. As he rose, he mispronounced the Apostle's Creed and Paternoster.

Angilram gave the Saxon a lighted candle, said another Latin prayer, and ended with "Go in peace."

Widukind kissed the archchaplain's ring then bowed to Charles. Fastrada's heart fluttered.

"As your godfather, we welcome you to the True Faith," Charles said, draping a silver medal of Saint Peter around Widukind's neck.

Stone-faced, Widukind gave the candle to a priest. He knelt before Charles and folded his hands. Charles placed his hands over the Saxon's.

"To Charles, king of the Franks and the Lombards and patrician of Rome, I, Herzog Widukind of Westphalia, am your faithful servant. I pledge my loyalty and aid as a vassal should pledge to his lord in the service of his rule and righteousness."

Two priests stepped toward Widukind. Each held a wooden purse gilded in gold and set with colored glass discs, housing tiny relics of saints and martyrs, wrapped in scraps of a vestment. Widukind kissed each portable reliquary and paused, as if trying to remember what to say next.

"By the bone fragments of the holy martyrs Ewald the Fair and Ewald the Black, the hairs of the holy martyr Ursula, the oil of the lamps burning above the tomb of the holy martyr Boniface, the stone chip from the tomb of Saint Lioba, the dust from Saint Willibald's and Saint Walburga's graves, and a splinter from the True Cross, I make this oath and will keep it all my days, so help me God, creator of the heavens and earth."

Charles smiled his approval. "We promise our protection, as a lord should his vassal. We bestow upon you these two portable reliquaries upon which you swore your oath, to use in the chapel you will build at your residence and in a church you will found.

"We also bestow Westphalia from the Ruhr to the Aller, ten horses, fifteen hunting dogs, and two silver cups from which we have drunk."

Amid the gasps, Fastrada nodded grimly. She and Charles had discussed it. She loathed giving so much to Widukind, especially the portable reliquaries, but this was what the saints in those reliquaries had lived and died for. It was the price for peace. As Widukind's godfather, Charles all but assured the Saxon's safety. If any attack was made on Widukind, Charles would avenge it.

Fastrada remembered the fury burning in Hardrad's eyes during the assembly at Paderborn last June. She doubted Widukind's surrender to God and to Charles would cool it. Nothing but blood would satisfy him.

Chapter Sixteen

April 786, Attigny

You know the passage," Gomeric said. Then he switched to Latin: "Have you heard anything about Thuringia?"

Pepin smiled at his uncle's cleverness. He had puzzled over why his uncle had started the conversation by expressing disappointment that the priest did not quote Saint Augustine during his homily. Now it made sense. The two mounted guards trailing them would think they were discussing theology. No one else could hear them. He and his uncle had taken advantage of the temperate day and decided after sunrise prayers to ride beyond the farm fields and into the woods. They had slowed to a walk at a clearing dotted with evergreen broom and gorse. Sparrows flitted among the pines and blooming maples while squirrels chased each other on the trunk of an old oak.

Pepin welcomed the breeze on his sweaty face. It felt good to be in the forest at this hour, when the daylight kept the kobolds and demons away.

"The magnates said nothing new about Thuringia. They were talking more about Lombardy and Bavaria," Pepin said in Latin. "Can you believe that father asked Hruodtrude to join us? Why should he want a girl in the room, and one who has seen but eleven years?"

"She will be a marriageable age soon, and the Byzantine emperor will expect his bride. If she is to convince the boy to keep siding with Francia, she needs to know your father's wishes."

"Didn't you say the dowager empress holds the real power?"

"She does, and she will be loath to give it up when her son comes of age in a couple of years." It was the same thing his mother had said in her last letter: "*We pray the dowager empress will follow God's will and cede power to her son for the sake of the next king of the Franks.*"

"It's still unfair," Pepin muttered. "My siblings will have power, and I won't. Even eight-year-old Louis is back in Aquitaine playing king."

"His guardian needed to settle the problem with the Gascon count."

Pepin snorted in derision. "I would have shown him who was king and dragged him to court in chains. Exchanging hostages makes him think he's an equal."

"Your father exchanged hostages with Widukind."

"Widukind submitted to God and to my father."

"And the king estranged himself from the Thuringians. That's why they are denying Amalwin his bride."

"My mother said that, too, in her letter. They are playing games." Pepin waved his hand dismissively. "Amalwin's father-by-marriage would not be so stupid as to break his daughter's betrothal with a courtier. Amalwin will return from Thuringia with his bride."

"This is not about a betrothal. This is retaliation for the bargain with Widukind."

"How far will the Thuringians go?"

"Don't know, but it won't stop with Amalwin."

∗∗∗

Fastrada could tell by Amalwin's face that his visit to Thuringia had not gone well. Nothing ever seemed to bother the courtier, who had managed to get twelve Frankish families to agree to send their sons to Widukind as hostages. As much as she had despised the idea, she marveled at Amalwin's ability to carry it out.

Now, she noticed he had his guards but no woman. On top of that, his party had the misfortune to arrive in the late afternoon, just as the servants were clearing the tables of the sole Lenten meal of the day. The scents of cooked fish, bread, beans, and radishes lingered.

"Amalwin," Charles said, "let us talk in the royal apartment. Meginfrid, come with us and the queen."

Fastrada pointed to the servants. "You and you, show these travelers to a table. And you two, fetch some food and wine. Nantlind, bring a tray of refreshments for Amalwin to our apartment."

Amalwin murmured his thanks.

As she crossed the great hall, Fastrada could think only of her father's message from two months ago: Hardrad was tempting other Thuringian counts to conspire against Charles. Despite her pleas with her husband to bring the traitors to justice, Charles had chosen only to watch them. "Hardrad is an oaf," Charles had said. "This might fall apart on its own; any meddling from us might strengthen it."

They entered the reception room, where two chairs sat near a low fire in the hearth and light streamed through the narrow windows. As Fastrada took her seat next to her husband, he invited Meginfrid and Amalwin to sit on the stools.

"Keep your voice low," Meginfrid told Amalwin, "lest a maidservant suddenly decide to brush a speck of dust from a tapestry near the door. We've already drawn curiosity by going to the apartment."

"Sound advice," Charles said. "Amalwin, tell us what happened in Thuringia."

Amalwin sighed. "My father-by-marriage is flouting our laws. He refuses to deliver my bride to me. I tried to make my case and showed him our agreement, where we had both made our marks. He threw it in the fire, then summoned his guards and threatened to kill me and my men if we didn't leave. We were outnumbered."

Frowning, Fastrada stopped herself from telling her husband he should have heeded her advice.

"My dear, you think this is Hardrad's doing?" Charles asked.

"He's testing us."

Charles uttered a vile word for a catamite. "This cannot go unanswered," he said. "We will send a force to let Hardrad and his ilk know the dear price for trying to rip our realm asunder."

"They only understand strength," Fastrada added. "Show no mercy."

June 786, Worms

"My lady, a message from Thuringia. The king has read it and awaits you in the archive."

Dismissing the clerk, Fastrada forgot what she was going to say to the seneschal about preparing for the assembly in August and set aside her cup. The look on the clerk's face told her the matter was urgent. Was Amalwin wounded in Thuringia? Was Louis or Little Pippin ill?

With two guards trailing her, she lifted her skirts and rushed past the wine barrels with their now dormant presses and bellows to age the drink and dashed up the stairs from the cellar, adjacent to the kitchen. She hurried through the gardens, the greens blurring.

She passed through an arched opening, made a sharp left, entered the treasury, and ascended the stairs at the back of the room. The rectangular archive, crammed with tables, shelved books and chests of maps and letters, was bright with the windows open to a sunny day, and it smelled of the wormwood to repel vermin. Charles turned toward her. The lines in his face deepened, and he tightened his grip on a piece of parchment in his fist.

"We will speak to the queen alone," he said to the guards. "Leave us."

Still holding the message, he approached Fastrada and hugged her.

"What is it, Charles?" She wrapped her arms around him.

For a moment, he was silent. "My dear," he said so softly that she strained to hear him, "your father fell in battle."

Fastrada shook her head as if Charles had spoken a foreign language. Her father, her strong warrior father, had survived battle after battle. How could he be dead? Her knees buckled. Charles held her up against the blackness lapping at her feet and helped her to a stool.

Fastrada did not know how long she stayed hunched over, weeping, holding the edges of her sleeves to her eyes. She grimaced but did not make a sound lest servants were listening downstairs.

"We will have the litanies said for him here. We will appoint a good, pious guardian for your brother." It was Charles's voice, but it was distant as if from the depths of a cave. "I will see to it that his loyalty to Francia is never forgotten."

"What ... what happened?" Fastrada finally choked out.

"Your father joined forces with Amalwin to put down Hardrad's scheme. They devastated the rebels' lands and forced them to flee to the monastery in Fulda, but your father was slain."

Anger boiled in Fastrada. Her eyes were hot. In all those years that she had prayed for her father's safety, she had feared a Saxon sword or a weapon from the Lombards, Saracens, or Avars. Not a Thuringian. An ally.

"Letter," she said, her voice barely audible to her own ears.

Charles handed it to her. She translated the Latin to Frankish. "*Hardrad was seduced by the Devil ... conspiracy to murder Your Excellence.*"

Fastrada crumpled the parchment. Tears burned her cheeks. "Scum-filled cowards! The headman's ax is too good for them! Let them be tied to four horses and torn apart. The world must know what happens to those who betray our people and our king."

"My dear," Charles said, taking her hand, "we cannot make them martyrs. We would lose allies east of the Rhine."

"But they are worse than the Saxons. We knew the Saxons were our enemy. We knew they would try to kill our men in battle. Hardrad and his band of traitors threatened you personally. Do you know what would have happened to Francia if they succeeded? The courtiers would fight for power like wolves over a sheep and tear our country to shreds. Our sons are too young to stop them. It would be worse than Büraburg. If they don't pay the highest price for their treachery, what is to stop other counts from conspiring against you and destroying our people?"

"We will have the traitors brought to us at the assembly," Charles said as if he were comforting Fastrada from a bad dream. "We will have justice. I promise."

July 786, Worms

Fastrada awoke nauseated. She threw back the bed curtains, dropped to the floor, dragged the chamber pot from under the bed, and vomited. Nantlind scampered toward her, pulled a blanket off the bed, and draped it on Fastrada's bare shoulders. Fastrada sweated and shivered, despite the heat of the summer. She heard the rustle of linens from the bed then Charles putting his feet on the floor. He squatted beside her and laid his hand on her shoulder.

"My dear?" he said.

Fastrada met her husband's eyes. "Nantlind, when were my last courses?"

"You haven't bled since June."

Fastrada beamed. "This time, it will be a son."

Charles kissed her forehead. "All that matters is that you and the baby are safe."

He will pray for a girl again. Father would be vexed.

Tears welled in Fastrada's eyes. If she bore a son, she could have seen her father's proud face. Or his disappointment as he ignored his granddaughter. She would never again argue with her father about why she needed to bear a son. With a twinge of guilt, she was relieved. As soon as sunrise prayers ended, she would send for a clerk to write to Sigibert, but she wondered if the brother she hadn't seen in almost three years would care.

Father would be overjoyed I conceived again. She silently vowed those Thuringian murderers would feel the same crushing pain that afflicted her heart.

***

Fastrada tried to maintain a calm face during the two weeks to prepare the palace for the assembly. Mint leaves and licorice root sometimes helped calm her belly as she made sure servants washed the linens, cleaned the furniture and hearths, and strewed fresh thyme and lemon balm on the floor. Yet vengeance consumed her thoughts like a fire devouring kindling. In the great hall, she often found herself in front of the tapestry of the Final Judgment, where a giant figure of Jesu gazed out, a line of naked souls before Him.

She regarded the green jasper girdle her father had given her. He would miss taking Sigibert into his first battle, teaching her thirteen-winter-old brother to rule a countship. The guardian she and Charles appointed was a pious, intelligent man, but it would not be the same.

When the twenty Thuringians arrived in the great hall, it took all Fastrada's will not to call for the headman. She reminded herself that they had left their sanctuary of the abbey in Fulda and agreed to come in peace in the company of sixty guards. *Charles is right*, she told herself, laying a hand on her roiling belly. *They must go through a trial. The world must see him as a fair judge. But if they act penitent, he must show mercy.*

Sitting on her chair beside Charles, she studied the traitors. Several stood arrow-straight, watching their surrounding with wide eyes. Some fidgeted, kept tapping their feet, or twisted their sleeves. A few glowered. Scowling, Hardrad wore a glare that seemed to bore through stone.

Fastrada and Charles stood for the bishop's prayers, but her fury muffled her ears to the Latin chants. When she and Charles were seated again, she curled her fingers around the arms of her chair, watching the rebels and witnesses swear oaths on a small reliquary with a nail of the True Cross, drops of the Virgin's milk, and a pebble from Jesu's tomb.

"Hardrad," Charles said, "you and your fellows are accused of seeking our death. Is this true?"

"If we had our way," Hardrad sneered, "your rotting corpse would feed the wolves and crows."

To stop herself from cursing, Fastrada tightened her grip on the arms of her chair, letting its edges bite her palms. She would not give Hardrad the satisfaction of seeing her weep. She had never expected this slime-covered worm to almost boast of his plot against Charles. But Hardrad had always been a hothead, and he had just made it easier for her.

"No!" one of the counts cried, falling to his knees. "Have mercy, Your Excellence, I beg you. I only agreed to it because Hardrad threatened to burn my fields."

"My lord king," Fastrada said barely able to steady her voice, "they admit they are traitors, and traitors should be deprived of their lands and their lives."

"Oh, their lands are forfeit," Charles said with a calmness that thinly veiled his wrath.

The Thuringians' gasps and whispers rippled through the great hall. *What did they expect?* Fastrada struggled to keep her face impassive.

"But for the sake of their souls," Charles continued, "we will spare their lives and send them on pilgrimages to repent their sins and swear their loyalty on saints' relics to us and our children."

Many of the rebels blanched as if they had been struck in the belly with a cudgel.

"God bless our merciful king!" Meginfrid shouted.

"This is no mercy," Hardrad snarled. "What is a count without his land? How dare you give land to a heathen and steal it from us!"

Despite her nausea, Fastrada smiled at Hardrad. Some of the rebels drew back as if from a snake. *Good.*

"You should have thought of that before you defied our king's and God's will," she said as if speaking to a slow child.

She kept smiling even as Hardrad shot her a look full of rage. *A pilgrimage is not enough. He will not rest until Charles is lying in blood. I won't let that happen.*

Chapter Seventeen

Once the trial ended, the nobles turned their attention to foreign matters, much of which Pepin had heard the magnates discuss before. Saxony was quiet, although Alcuin complained of priests who cared more about collecting tithes than saving souls. Widukind had kept his word and was donating properties for monasteries. Yet the hall stilled when Charles turned to a monk in his mid-thirties, a cousin he had appointed as Little Pippin's guardian, and asked about affairs in Lombardy.

"Adalgis is threatening to leave his exile in Byzantium and attack the Italian peninsula," said the monk, his brow creased. "We don't know where or when."

Pepin's loathing for Adalgis, his father's former brother-by-marriage, had not diminished over the years. That viper, the son of the Lombard tyrant Charles had sent to the cloister fourteen years ago, had slipped away during the first war. Still, he had allies. The dowager empress of the Byzantines was sheltering him in Constantinople, even though Hruodtrude was betrothed to her son. The duchess of Benevento would welcome her brother back as would his other sister Luitperga, Duke Tassilo's shrew of a wife.

"I would not be surprised if Tassilo is seeking an alliance with the Avars and the Beneventans to place Adalgis on the throne," Meginfrid said.

Fastrada's nostrils flared. "The duke of Bavaria cares little for his oaths and ties of blood to our husband and our sons."

Count Severinus flushed. "Duke Tassilo would never treat with the Avars. It would be like treating with devils. He will keep his oaths, just like he did eleven years ago when he refused to support the plot to put Adalgis on the throne. Rumors of his disloyalty are lies spread by his rivals."

"Severinus," Charles said patiently, "we would like to trust our cousin's fidelity, but we heard no word from him about Adalgis. Count Gerold and our allies in Bavaria are the ones who send us messages."

"And Your Excellence's loyal friends in Rome and Italy," Little Pippin's guardian added.

Karl stepped forward. "We should march south!"

Pepin regarded his brother with hooded eyes. *Father told him not to do this.* "We cannot conquer Adalgis if we don't know where he is," Pepin said, echoing their father's words.

He looked to his father, hoping for a smile and a nod. Instead, Charles and Fastrada were exchanging a glance as if conveying their thoughts to each other. The back of Pepin's neck prickled. The queen's influence was so great she did not need to utter one word!

"We can watch for now," Charles said. "And let our friends know their vigilance will be rewarded."

September 786, Worms

Shortly after the tierce bells, a messenger entered the great hall, which was noisy with the chatter of courtiers and the scrapes and thunks of the servants assembling trestle tables and benches for dinner. Pepin stopped in midsentence in his conversation with Gomeric as his father and Fastrada arrived moments later through the door to the inner courtyard. Pepin and the courtiers formed a circle around the royal couple. The queen wore her gown more loosely, yet that did not conceal her swelling breasts. Fearing the demon would use him again in his sleep, Pepin tore his gaze from Fastrada to watch his father break the seal, read the message, and nod.

"The rebels took the oaths," Charles said, "but their leaders were blinded on their journey back here."

Pepin flinched. A few courtiers gasped, but many more shrugged. Karl, Hruodtrude, and Bertha leaned forward. Gomeric tilted his head as if listening for more.

Fastrada nodded grimly. "Their blindness is a blessing. Through it, they will keep the vows they made at the saints' tombs and save their souls. And they will never hurt anyone again."

Ice spread through Pepin's limbs and belly. "You caused this!" he blurted.

Glowering, Gomeric shook his head almost imperceptibly. Pepin stared at his kinsman. How could he say nothing? How could all the courtiers, who were educated clergy and practiced warriors, be silent? Were they that afraid of a woman?

"It was our decision as king," his father said. "We must do what's best for Francia."

"They are our own people!" Pepin cried.

"Only the most culpable lost their sight," his father said.

"They are murderers and traitors." Fastrada's voice shook. "They would have broken their oaths at the first opportunity and again tried to tear our country asunder. A handful of blind men who all but boasted of their guilt is far better than thousands of slaughtered innocents."

"My wife speaks wisely as usual," Charles said. "Karl, when you are king you must make choices, and it is important to have the right woman with you, one with intellect. That's why you should care for more than a maiden's fair looks."

Pepin's face and neck felt hot.

"I will only marry a beauty," Karl said.

"You will marry whatever woman I choose for you," their father said with a laugh.

Gomeric's nostrils flared, and his jaw was clenched as if he was holding back something he wanted to say. Pepin wondered what had made his uncle so angry now. A few moments ago, not even Fastrada's cruelty had upset him.

Early November 786, Worms

Too weary to rub the ache in her head, Fastrada leaned back in her chair and forced her eyes open as Hruodtrude kept reading Saint Augustine to family and courtiers gathered for the Palace School in the great hall. Why was she so exhausted these days? And constantly cold. Even a seat near the hearth and her marten fur-lined cloak could barely keep her warm. Unlike Theodrada, the child moving within her belly demanded all her vigor. She hoped she could last through today's Palace School; she had so looked forward to discussing *De Natura et Gratia*. Her Latin was now good enough that Pepin no longer smirked when she read.

She closed her eyes just for a moment. Drifting into sleep, she started when Charles nudged her. Puzzled, she looked up and beheld one of the palace guards standing with an unshaven messenger who wore a cloak that reached his calves and a long, loose-fitting tunic, a fashion favored by the Italians. Fastrada straightened her spine. No one would send a messenger over the sharp-peaked Alps and its trackless mountain ridges so close to winter unless it was urgent. Was something wrong with Little Pippin?

The messenger handed Charles a rolled parchment bearing Little Pippin's seal, even though it came from the almost ten-winter-old boy's guardian. Fastrada noticed a shadow cross Pepin's face, just as it had whenever Charles spoke of a wife for Karl. Charles broke the seal, read the message, and frowned.

"Affairs in Italy are worse than we thought," he said. "The duke of Benevento is planning to usurp Little Pippin and place Adalgis on the throne. He is amassing troops for an attack this spring."

"Is Duke Tassilo involved?" Fastrada asked. "Are the Byzantines?"

"They must be," he replied. "I must travel to Italy without delay, before the Feast of Saint Martin. I hate to miss the celebration you've worked so hard to prepare."

"God's wounds! Who cares about the feast? I'm worried about you freezing to death."

"No need for concern, my dear. I have traveled late in the year before. You will make sure the priests here will perform the litanies for God's blessing on us and our children?" His tone was more command than question.

Fastrada nodded. With her constant weariness, she would be a burden on the journey, but she could help her husband here.

Chapter Eighteen

Nothing Fastrada did could banish her illness. None of Wilberga's potions or herb-soaked cloths could shake her of this constant weariness and make her feel warm. After summoning the midwife to her bedchamber yet again, Fastrada sat near a bright fire and reread one of Charles's letters. The tapestries of vibrant reds and yellows shielded her from some drafts, but cold seeped through the parchment-covered windows. Fastrada needed the light to read and sew, and ordered they not be shuttered until night.

She looked up when she heard a scratch at the door and Nantlind's light steps running to admit the midwife. Beholding the grim lines in Wilberga's face, Fastrada knew she had more to worry about than discomfort. "Tell me the truth."

"I've seen this before, my lady queen," the midwife said. "When women have an ailment like yours, babies have come too early."

Fastrada felt the blood drain from her face. She grasped the seat of her stool to steady herself. "What must I do?"

The older woman used her fingers as if she had written a list and was pointing to each item. "Keep drinking mulled wine; the spices in it are all warm and will strengthen your yellow bile. Pray to Our Lady and Saint Margaret and give alms. Eat meat every day. And attend only to the most important matters. You need rest."

"The court will think I'm weak." Fastrada slumped.

"My lady queen," Wilberga said gently, "everyone knows a woman with child needs special care. That's why the Church excuses you from the Advent fast days."

"It also excuses little children, the old, and the frail," Fastrada muttered. When Wilberga opened her mouth as if to argue, Fastrada added, "But I will do what you say."

***

Karl's behavior taxed what little vigor Fastrada had. For weeks, he sulked about being left behind. About to see his fourteenth winter, his voice was that of a young man, but his complaints were those of a spoiled boy. And Pepin took every chance to remind him of how he was still in Worms. Then the brothers would argue. One day it could be about what to study in Palace School, and the next Pepin or Karl would demand a new horse because his brother's was better. Hruodtrude often sided with Karl, which only made the two brothers act worse toward each other. Fastrada wished she could awaken from a nap without hearing those three bicker.

"You are worse than Hruodhaid and Theodrada," she grumbled one afternoon. "They are toddling babes and don't know any better. You do!"

Finally, she ordered twelve-winter-old Hruodtrude to help her plan the Feast of the Nativity. Already drained, she needed Hruodtrude's assistance, but she also was glad to distract the girl from goading the princes. Hruodtrude welcomed the task, and together, Fastrada and Hruodtrude made sure the cooks had baked enough large pies of pork and dried fruit to exchange with the peasants when they brought chickens and grain. In a palace decorated with pine and fir branches, Fastrada wanted to weep with frustration on the day of Jesu's birth. Charles was absent from the Masses, the feasts, and the dancing, and she could barely stay awake through the meal and had to retire early.

Soon after the Nativity, the three eldest children were quarreling about when the next hunt should be. The family was returning to their residence from sunrise prayers, their breath smoking in front of them. Fastrada narrowed her eyes. The last thing the court needed was two princes near manhood who might use their weapons on each other instead of a boar. Only the king or queen could rebuke them and prevent it.

"There will be no hunt," Fastrada said. "It's too dangerous."

And that was when Pepin, Karl, and Hruodtrude were united, all angry with her. Bertha glared at her, but she always imitated her older sister.

"You act like we've never been on a hunt before," Pepin protested.

"I've led troops in battle," Karl snapped. "I can easily go on a hunt."

"Not until I am well or your father returns," Fastrada said. "And he will be angry if you defy me, especially while I'm with child."

The three of them looked away.

"When will Father be home?" asked Gisela, as she had every day since Charles had left.

"I wish I knew," Fastrada said.

Early February 787, Worms

Fastrada knew her prayers for the baby had been answered—the child had stayed within her belly. Wilberga cheerfully said this was a good time for the infant to come and was pestering her to go into the lying-in chamber and leave things to the seneschal. Fastrada ordered maids to prepare the room and confessed her sins to a priest, but she hesitated to start her confinement. She still disliked the dark, cramped space, and her malady was already causing her to miss too much at court.

For the next two days, she followed one of the midwife's instructions: to rest. She was so tired she had no choice. In the midafternoon, Fastrada awoke to Bertha's and Nantlind's voices.

"... message from Father! Hruodtrude says we cannot read it until Mother is in the great hall."

Fastrada's eyes popped open to dim light. The bed curtains had been drawn to ward off the cold, and she was in a pocket of warmth, curled under blankets and furs. She could hear Nantlind whispering but could not make out the words.

When Fastrada sat upright and parted the bed curtains, chill air hit her bare flesh. She wrapped her goose-fleshed arms around her swollen breasts and belly and tried to still her chattering teeth. From their spot near the door, Bertha and Nantlind turned toward her.

"Nantlind, help me dress," Fastrada said.

The maid rushed to retrieve her lady's clothes from the pegs on the bed post. Bright-eyed like her father, Bertha was fidgeting.

"When did the messenger come?" Fastrada donned the shift Nantlind handed her. The white linen was taut over her middle.

"A few moments ago. Pepin wanted to read it right away, but Hruodtrude grabbed it and said you need to read it first." Bertha's brow creased. "Then Pepin started screaming at Hruodtrude, and Karl was shouting at Pepin."

"Did Karl shove Pepin this time?" Fastrada said. Quickly, she pulled on her underdress, then an embroidered, wine-colored, woolen gown.

Bertha shook her head.

Perhaps, he is finally listening to my rebukes. At least, he has stopped sulking about being left at home.

Letting Nantlind put on her stockings and now tight slippers, Fastrada wondered if the messenger and his guards had been neglected. "Bertha, go order refreshments for our servants."

Bertha pouted. "Hruodtrude already did. She ordered the cupbearer to fetch mulled wine for you, too."

"What a good young lady. She will have a palace of her own soon." Fastrada was surprised by the wistfulness in her own voice. Hruodtrude was almost old enough to marry the Byzantine emperor. A shiver ran through her that had nothing to do with the cold. If she were to believe Hruodtrude's tutor, her daughter was about to marry a pious, intelligent, young ruler close to manhood. The messages from Charles's spies told a different story, that the dowager empress treated her son like a five-winter-old boy and excluded him from her meetings with her magnates. And the empress was still sheltering Adalgis the Lombard—the reason Charles was far away.

Fastrada shoved her worries about the Byzantines aside for the moment. She needed to know what was in Charles's letter. "Bertha, is Gisela in the hall?"

"She was practicing her stitches when the messenger arrived."

Fastrada smiled. The girl, who had lost a baby tooth the previous day, had threaded her first needle this morning.

"Have the nones bells rung?" Fastrada asked.

Bertha shook her head.

Hruodhaid and Theodrada are still napping. "Bertha, go tell your brothers and sisters I will come to the great hall soon."

Bertha ran, slamming the door behind her. As Nantlind wrapped a girdle around her lady's waist, accentuating her breasts and belly, Fastrada stared after the girl, longing for the vigor to run.

"I wish you had rested more," the maid said. "The message could have waited."

"I could not sleep if I knew there was a message from Charles. And the sooner I'm in the hall, the sooner I can stop Karl and Pepin from quarreling."

Nantlind placed a blue cloak lined with marten fur on Fastrada's shoulders and laid a matching veil on her head, securing the silk with a headdress. After putting on kidskin gloves lined with marten fur at the wrists, Fastrada walked slowly, keeping her carriage as straight as she could. If she could not run, she would at least look dignified. She passed through the corridor and reception room and into the great hall. The children were silhouetted against the hearth across the vast room in animated conversation. Bickering again. The courtiers who had not accompanied Charles turned away.

As she approached them, her feet crushed thyme and mint. The herbs' scent mingled with the wood smoke from the fire, blazing as if a servant had recently stoked it. The flames and sunlight seeping through parchment-covered windows would give her enough to read by.

"See, Pepin?" Hruodtrude said. "There is Mother now. Bertha said she was coming. Just wait."

"I give orders to girls, not take them," Pepin sneered.

Scowling, Karl raised his fist.

"Karl! Don't!" Fastrada barked. "And Pepin, you be quiet, or I will slap you myself. Do you want your father to hear you vexed me? Hruodtrude was right to insist on waiting. That message is for the queen. Daughter, thank you for seeing to our guests."

Karl lowered his fist. Glaring at each other, the children fell silent. When she was near the hearth, Fastrada braced herself against the arms of a cushioned chair, lowered herself into it, and held her cloak closer. The children and what was left of the court gathered around her. Her temples ached. The scents of cinnamon, nutmeg, and cloves wafting from the cup of wine beckoned from a small table next to her. She took a sip, hoping its heat would flow through her.

Hruodtrude handed her the letter. Fastrada broke the seal with her eating knife and unrolled the parchment. She hurried through the usual pleasantries, the greetings to her and the children.

"The king says he is safe and well," she translated. "He and his troops crossed the Alps with few losses and spent the Nativity in Florence, where he met Little Pippin. Pippin is also well. Our king will soon go to Rome to meet with the pope and speak about our affairs with Benevento and Bavaria."

Resting the parchment against her belly, Fastrada smiled and closed her eyes, glad all was well with Charles. Then pain tore through her womb.

***

As it was when Theodrada was born, the lying-in chamber was crowded with women: the midwife and her assistants, Nantlind and other maids, Hruodtrude and Bertha, and Irma, who had been such a good wet nurse to Theodrada that Fastrada asked her to suckle the newborn now that the toddler was weaned. With the sole window shuttered and covered with a tapestry of the Virgin and Her Child, beeswax candles brightened the room, and their scent blended with the fresh straw on the floor. As flames danced high in the hearth, Fastrada was glad to finally be warm.

But no matter how many knots were untied, how much oil the midwife rubbed on Fastrada's belly, or how many times the midwife retied the jasper to her thigh or held a crane's foot to her belly or whispered a spell, the baby would not come.

Fastrada managed to walk for a little while but soon became too exhausted to stand. She lay in bed, waiting. When a cramp stabbed her, she wanted to restrain the cry, but it escaped. Her maid and her daughters looked so frightened, and her murmurs that she would be well did not reassure them.

She turned to the most talkative maid. "Tell me your best gossip, whether it is true or not."

The young woman was eager to comply and embellished the story about a village wife tricking both her husband and her lovers. It helped Fastrada think of something other than the pains, which continued long into the night.

Fastrada thought she heard lauds bells when she felt water gush down her legs. Nantlind and another maid helped her out of bed and into a dry tunic and shift, then took her to the birthing chair and held her up.

The midwife reached under Fastrada's skirts. "Push!"

With great effort, Fastrada complied.

"Good. Again."

With each push, Fastrada wondered if it would be her last. Wilberga pressed strongly against her belly. Fastrada did not know how much time had passed when the midwife announced she could see the crown.

"Another push, my queen. Very good. Again."

Fastrada used what was left of her strength, grunting while the pain ripped through her.

"Another girl! What a tiny thing!"

Fastrada slumped on the stool, leaning against Nantlind. Her little girl had a round face like Charles's and wisps of hair the same shade as Fastrada's. She was a little pale but perfectly formed. After the midwife wiped the newborn's face, the infant whimpered.

"Is she well?" Fastrada's voice was just above a whisper.

"Yes," Wilberga answered. "Some babies are small and quiet, my lady queen."

Relieved, Fastrada could manage only a smile. Why was she so weak? She had not been so drained after Theodrada's birth. She felt the pressure of an assistant's hands, followed by expulsion of the afterbirth. Another maid supported Fastrada while Nantlind stuffed a flux rag between her lady's legs, secured it with cords, and smoothed Fastrada's skirt down.

"Will Mother be well?" Hruodtrude asked in a small voice.

That's why everyone has been so silent. "Of course, I will," Fastrada said, with more confidence than she felt. "I just need rest. Wilberga, let me hold our Chiltrude."

"Just for a moment. She will want her wet nurse soon." The midwife placed the newborn in Fastrada's arms.

Fastrada smiled down at the girl and kissed her soft forehead.

"Why does Father want to name her after Tassilo's mother?" Bertha asked.

My question, too. She repeated what Charles had explained to her. "She was your father's aunt, and your grandfather protected Tassilo's rights for her sake after she was widowed. Your father wants everyone to remember that."

"Can I hold her?" Hruodtrude asked.

"I want to!" Bertha said.

Feeling as if her limbs were weighed down with boulders, Fastrada sank against the maid holding her up. Why must the girls tax her so now?

Nantlind folded her hands and bowed to the princesses. "My Ladies Hruodtrude and Bertha, your mother will let you both hold her after the midwife bathes her and her nurse feeds her. Such a small girl needs to eat. Your mother just whispered to me that she wants you to tell your siblings they have another sister. She asks them to pray for the baby and her own recovery. Did I relay that correctly, my lady queen?"

Fastrada nodded. When she was well enough, she would give Nantlind an embroidered girdle and good wool for a new dress. For now, she hoped her eyes could convey her gratitude.

Hruodtrude pursed her lips, then assented and tugged at Bertha's sleeve. Fastrada handed the baby to the midwife as the girls hurried out of the room. Nantlind and another maid helped her undress and climb back into the bed, now with fresh sheets.

"Pray for me," Fastrada murmured.

Chapter Nineteen

Fastrada awoke to bells. For the first time in how many days ... five ... she wanted to eat instead of go back to sleep. In the light from the candles and fire, Nantlind sat on a stool beside the bed, mending her lady's clothes. Fastrada called to her.

"You're awake." Nantlind set aside her needlework. "Let me fetch you food and wine."

Without waiting for an answer, Nantlind leapt to her feet and grabbed a tray.

"I am hungry, Nantlind. You won't need to beg me this time."

"Jesu and His Merciful Mother be praised," Nantlind breathed. She made the sign of the cross and raced out of the room.

Watching her plump maid, Fastrada wondered if she would ever be able to run again. She sat up and leaned against the pillows, drawing the blanket over her bare body.

"Irma, I want to see Chiltrude," Fastrada said.

The wet nurse hurried toward her and placed the baby in her arms. Was the infant already heavier? Wrapped in swaddling, the newborn smelled of milk. Fastrada remembered hearing the girl cry a few times, soon to be quieted by Irma. She took comfort in those cries. Her daughter was healthy and wanted to eat. How Fastrada wished she was well enough to do more than hold her baby for a few minutes.

"Chiltrude's color is better," Fastrada said.

"She has taken to the breast readily," Irma said.

"And how are you faring? The maids were ordered to give you whatever you needed."

"I am well, my lady queen. They bring me plenty to eat."

Fastrada nodded and turned her attention to Chiltrude. "Your father will be pleased. He will love you."

And with Fastrada's own father gone, that was all that mattered. It was the first time she had thought of her failure to bear a son since the birth. These past few days, she had been too exhausted to care about more than Charles and the children. If her husband knew how ill she was, he would pray for her, and she clung to that thought in her moments between wake and sleep. Now as she was convalescing, she could see her father's disappointed face, the same one that beheld Theodrada.

I will never see that again. Her eyes welled for a moment, and she blinked back the tears, unsure if she was crying for grief or guilt over her relief. She shook her head. This was not a time for self-pity. She was still queen of the Franks and had responsibilities. If only she were not so weak.

Nantlind entered the room, carrying a laden tray, and Wilberga followed. The maid set the tray on a small table beside the bed. The aromas of beef stew, bread, and mulled wine had never been more welcome. With a kiss to Chiltrude's forehead, Fastrada handed the child back to her nurse. Nantlind was approaching her with a bowl of water and small piece of linen.

"How do you fare, my lady queen?" The midwife searched her face.

Fastrada sank her hands into the cold water and washed them. "You will not need to pester me into eating this time."

"Good. I'm even glad to hear that sharp tongue of yours."

Fastrada hurriedly dried her hands, then grabbed the wine. She took a sip and let its warmth slide down her throat. She could feel three sets of eyes on her when she reached for the eating knife that lay on the table and stabbed the meat. Three sets of shoulders relaxed as she ate.

"As you heal," Wilberga said, "you will get restless. Do not try to do too much. The birth was hard on you."

"I am well enough to bathe."

"A bath will help you feel better, and I will tell the maids to fetch water for you. Nantlind, don't wash your lady's hair. It's unhealthy in winter."

After Fastrada finished her meal, servants poured water into a small tub. Although cool, the water felt good against her skin, but soon she was tired again, craving sleep. She struggled to keep her eyes open while Nantlind combed her hair.

***

Fastrada did not know how long she had slept when she awoke to bells again.

"Nantlind, what hour is it?"

"Nones. I will get you more food."

Fastrada sighed. Her maid and the midwife would not let her do anything unless she ate every time she awoke.

"Nantlind has not left your side, my lady queen," Irma said, rocking the cradle.

"How is Nantlind?"

"Her health is good. Her heart will be better when you've recovered."

Fastrada clambered out of the bed and donned a shift, cloak, and slippers. She crept toward the cradle and beheld Chiltrude. The infant's eyes were closed.

"The baby is still faring well, my lady queen. She is finally sleeping."

Although Fastrada wanted to hold Chiltrude, she decided not to disturb the child and settled for stroking her cheek. Soon, Nantlind returned, carrying a platter with slices of roasted pork, bread, baked apples glazed with cinnamon and honey, and more mulled wine, and placed the food on a small table where her eating knife lay. Fastrada sat on a nearby stool.

"Any word from Charles?" Fastrada asked.

Nantlind shook her head. "I would have told you if there was."

"How do the children fare?"

"They are well."

"Still fighting?"

Nantlind hesitated.

"You don't need to protect me from their squabbles," Fastrada said. "But I do need you to help me dress when I'm done eating. I miss the younglings."

"Wilberga said ..."

"I know very well what she said," Fastrada snapped.

Nantlind looked as if Fastrada had slapped her.

Regretting her maid's hurt, Fastrada adopted a gentler tone. "Nantlind, I am grateful for your faithful service. I don't know what I would do without you. You must understand I cannot stop being a mother. I will see each girl one at a time, but Hruodtrude will be last. I have an important matter to discuss with her."

Fastrada sat near the fire but was still cold despite her cloak and gloves. Each of the girls was so well behaved that Fastrada wondered what Nantlind had told them. Or threatened. She guessed it was a reminder that their father would be displeased if they upset their mother. When Hruodtrude arrived, Fastrada bade the princess to sit on a nearby stool.

"Mother, are you well? You look very pale."

Fastrada envied the girl about to bloom into womanhood. To be so healthy, to have such strong limbs, to be so lovely with flawless skin and shiny fair hair.

"That's why I sent for you, Daughter." She pushed the words through. "This birthing, it has drained me of strength, but let us keep this from the court. When you are empress, you will understand that no one must think you're weak."

Furrowing her brow, Hruodtrude nodded slowly.

"I ... I ... need ..." Fastrada cleared her throat. "I need you to watch over our household while I recover. It will help you later with the Byzantines."

Hruodtrude smiled. "Yes, Mother, of course."

Fastrada could not bring herself to tell Hruodtrude that she did not know if her robustness would ever return.

***

When Hruodtrude announced that the queen had asked her to manage the household, Pepin realized Fastrada was ill. She had made no such request when Theodrada was born. He reminded himself to write about this to his mother, who had asked about Fastrada's health in her last letter.

Pepin thought his sister would leave most everything to the seneschal. For the first few days, he smirked as she struggled with her duties, and servants stopped working as soon as she turned her back. Then the seneschal ordered the flogging of a manservant more fond of beer than work, and none of them defied Hruodtrude afterward. To Pepin's dismay, his sister was becoming like Fastrada and Hildegard, giving orders and expecting to be obeyed. How he wished Gomeric were here instead of in Italy with his father.

Lent started as the winter waned. He, Karl, and Hruodtrude were reduced to fish, vegetables, and bread in the midafternoon while their younger sisters could still enjoy meat. Nantlind continued to bring beef, pork, and eggs to the queen, but the priests would not demand penance from a woman convalescing from childbirth.

For the next three weeks, Hruodtrude was too busy with the household to pay much heed to Pepin and Karl's arguments about what their father should do in Lombardy. As they awaited the midafternoon Lenten meal, both retreated to the archive and ignored each other. Pepin read Saint Augustine's *Confessiones*. A few paces away, Karl spread a map of Italy on a table and studied it. The day was temperate enough to open the windows and brighten the second-story room. Pepin's and Karl's guards stood near the entrance and stared dully at the shelves of leather-bound books they could not read. A clerk copied something from a wax tablet to a piece of parchment. The scratch of his quill mingled with the birdsong from outside.

When Hruodtrude entered, Pepin glanced up before returning to his book.

"Leave us," she told the guards and the clerk. "Lord Karl and I need to speak to our brother in private."

Hearing the guards and clerk shuffle out of the room, Pepin looked up.

Hruodtrude was standing before him. Her hand worried the edge of her long sleeve. After a pause, she said, "Our mother requires that you remain in the manor tomorrow while she is churched."

Pepin barked out a laugh. He had struck a blow at the she-wolf during her first churching. "You think I can be ordered around like a servant?"

"Pepin," she pleaded.

122

He grinned at her distress.

Instead of the bewildered expression he was hoping for, her features hardened, and she lifted her chin like Fastrada would. "This is the queen's will. And you are to obey."

"As if I would obey a little shrew like you."

Hruodtrude flinched, then she stepped forward and slapped him.

His cheek stinging, Pepin got to his feet and shoved her. He was still taller than she. "How are you going to stop me, little sister?"

Hruodtrude's eyes shifted to something over Pepin's shoulder. Pepin felt Karl grip his upper arm and pull him back. Pepin stumbled a couple of steps.

"You will not inflict God's curse on Chiltrude," Karl growled.

Although it strained his neck, Pepin met his brother's eyes. "What a brave boy you are."

Karl drew back his fist.

"No!" Hruodtrude cried behind him. "Karl, please don't. It will upset Mother."

Karl's fist shook before it fell to his side. When he released Pepin, his eyes carried a warning.

Rubbing his arm, Pepin slunk toward the stairs. A flush burned his face and down his neck. Why had God blessed his younger brother with a straight back but cursed him with shoulders that were getting more and more stooped and now causing pains at the top of his back? His frown deepened. His father had caused this curse. Why wasn't he the one to pay?

***

It had taken all of Fastrada's strength to get through the churching. After Hruodtrude had relayed the conversation with Pepin, she realized Charles's oldest son would stay away only if guards confined him to the room he shared with Karl. That would infuriate Charles, and just as bad, give the servants fodder for gossip. So she invited Pepin to attend. In fact, she insisted. Her gaze did not fall on him as she left the cathedral. Karl and Hruodtrude stood closest to the aisle and must have prevented their brother from moving. Or it could have had something to do with what she hissed in his ear in the royal apartment before the ceremony: "If I see so much as your eyelash while I leave the cathedral, so help me God, your guards will turn away any whore you wish to use, ever."

Hruodtrude had planned an excellent feast; the table was laden with twisted rolls, fish stews, platters of fish in parsley and mint sauces, and pies of fish and dried fruit. Fastrada lasted only an hour before retiring to her bedchamber, where she slept until morning. All she could manage the next two days was prime Mass and dinner.

Lying in her bed in midafternoon, she longed to be in the great hall hearing gossip and arguing politics. Why was she so weak? What had she done to displease God so much that He would not heal her, despite the alms

123

she gave to the Church? In a doze, she heard a tap on the door, then Nantlind scurrying to answer, then whispers, Bertha's and Gisela's voices among them. Fastrada raised herself on her elbow and drew back the curtain.

"We have a message from Father!" Gisela blurted. "Deacon Fardulf is waiting in the reception room."

The news gave Fastrada a spark of vigor, one she felt in her heart. Any message from Charles demanded her attention, but his choice of Fardulf, one of his trusted courtiers, as the messenger gave it urgency. "Nantlind, help me dress and have the cupbearer fetch some mulled wine."

As the girls paced and jabbered, Fastrada donned her clothes as quickly as she could without depleting what little vitality she had. Even with her fur-lined cloak and gloves, she was cold. She glanced at herself in the polished brass mirror Nantlind held for her. *Too pale. Sickly.*

Leaving the lotions to whiten her skin untouched, she chose her vermillion silk veil, hoping it would give her some color. As soon as she took a step toward the door, Bertha, Gisela, and Nantlind sprinted ahead. Fastrada wanted to hurry but worried the effort would exhaust her. Instead, she kept her pace measured as she traversed the corridor and entered the royal apartment's reception room.

The windows were open to let in the light of the temperate spring day, but the fire was burning brightly and the cushion on her chair had been plumped. Nantlind's handiwork. Fastrada smiled at her maid. What would she do without her? She settled into her seat while Pepin, Karl, and the girls gathered around her.

Standing stiffly, Fardulf handed her the rolled parchment. His look of concern was the same as the expressions that greeted her every morning at Mass.

"Is my husband well?" Fastrada asked, her words a rapid fire.

"Yes."

A cupbearer approached her a moment later. After taking a sip, he placed the wine on a small table beside her chair. She took a mouthful of wine, hoping its warmth would spread to her cheeks, then broke the seal and read Charles's letter.

"He says they arrived in Rome and were received with honor by the Holy Father," she said. "A few days later, the duke of Benevento's son arrived with rich gifts and demanded our army not set foot in his land. The duke promised to follow our king's will and not support Adalgis." She looked up from the parchment. "Fardulf, will the duke keep his word?"

"No one believes it," he answered.

The letter went on with plans for three days of litanies before the army set off for Capua. Charles asked Fastrada to see to the prayers at home and send him a message about herself and the baby.

"Fardulf," she said, "tell Charles I will make sure the litanies for his success in Benevento are carried out in Francia and that the children and I will keep him and our army in our prayers. His sons and daughters are all well and learning their lessons and send their love. Chiltrude is healthy and will be baptized on Easter eve, and I am ... recovering."

Pepin snorted. "You conceal your illness from your lord, my lady queen?"

Fastrada's heart hammered like it would burst from her chest. To give herself time to think, she took a swallow of wine, then another and another. She could feel several pairs of eyes on her.

"I appreciate your concern, Pepin," she said. "I am getting stronger each day."

"But my father wants to know everything."

"He must concentrate on affairs of the realm. To tell him more now would distract him. We know that he prays for all of us and will ask His Holiness to do so as well." She hoped Fardulf would agree.

Fastrada and Pepin locked eyes, and she felt her vigor seep away. *Was he praying for my death? Is that why I am so weary and cold? How could I ever prove it? Who would believe me?*

Chapter Twenty

April 787, Worms

Fastrada stared out the window of her bedchamber and sighed. The late afternoon spring breezes were warm, and the sky had only a few clouds. A perfect day to be atop a horse cantering through the forest with a tapestry of greens overhead. Instead, her malady, made worse by her recent courses, kept her trapped, unable to appreciate the beauty of the waves of mint, sage, and thyme in the garden. She turned when she heard a scratch at the door. Nantlind entered, followed by Wilberga.

Fastrada scowled.

"I answered your summons as quickly as I could," the midwife said.

"It's been ten weeks since Chiltrude's birth. Why do I need to sleep every afternoon? Why am I still cold when everyone else isn't? I want to hunt or at least ride. I don't want to be tired and weak anymore!"

"My lady queen," Wilberga said, "some women are left weary for months after childbirth. I have done everything I can."

"Am I ever going to be well?" Fastrada loathed the pleading note in her voice.

"It is in God's hand," the midwife said softly.

***

Some of Fastrada's strength returned in the ensuing days. One afternoon, too fatigued for riding but too restless for sleep, she climbed the steps to the archive. Whenever the royal family traveled, she as queen was responsible for the archive's safety, along with the treasury's valuables, the furniture, and the rest of the household. She had watched the clerks and servants pack the leather-bound volumes and rolled parchment, yet she had rarely examined the archives' contents, other than maps.

Here were all the letters her husband had received from the pope, the queen mother, Hildegard, Alcuin, the Byzantine dowager empress, and many other important people. Among the books, she spied many reflecting Charles's interest in history: hagiographies and the book he commissioned of the life of the late Pope Stephen. But something was missing.

Hearing the scrape of a stool being hurriedly shoved, she turned. Her favorite clerk, a middle-aged man with ink-stained fingers and sleeves, was standing near a table. A wax tablet lay near a quill and piece of parchment, one that had been written on before and had most of the ink scraped off, multiple times. Whoever was paying him to write a message did not want to spend much.

"Where are the records of our king's reign?" she asked.

The clerk laced his fingers. "We have some accounts of his father and Fredegar's work, but not our current king."

"Unacceptable. He has worn the crown for almost twenty years. Our story must be preserved. No doubt the Bavarians and Lombards are inscribing their lies." She looked him up and down. "You are our best clerk and will start a chronicle for our king at once. Begin with the year his grandfather died. The lord king and I want a complete record."

The clerk swallowed, causing his Adam's apple to bob. "I am humbled, my queen. I hope it will please you."

Was that terror she read on the clerk's face? She had never punished him. She thought for a moment, trying to remember who his friends were. Fellow clerics and scholars in the Palace School. She had done nothing to any of them. Perhaps, he had heard about Brother Lucas being removed from his post at Oppenheim. She smiled to herself. She was not so powerless, after all. *Let him fear displeasing me.*

Late June 787, Worms

Standing in the courtyard with the children, courtiers, and servants, Fastrada hoped her nervousness didn't show as she awaited her husband's return. The midsummer sun made the gems in her girdle and headdress glitter, and the blue and yellow threads in her embroidered wine-colored dress shone bright. Still, she could not shake the image of the too pale face she had seen in the mirror. The lotion of sheep's blood and fat on her cheeks was so garish she could not wash it off quickly enough. Even the pinches to her face fell short.

It had been seven long months since she had seen Charles. The affairs between Benevento and Francia were finally settled. The Beneventan duke and his two sons swore oaths of allegiance, and to secure that promise, the duke gave over twelve hostages—boys from noble families—in addition to one of his own sons. In return, Charles presented gifts. He then returned to Rome and met with Tassilo's emissaries, but they could not come to an agreement. Even the pope was frustrated. Charles had decided to come home and hold an assembly to determine what to do next.

As her husband came through the gate, Fastrada's heart quickened, and a smile spread across her face. Handsome and muscular as ever, Charles, too, was smiling astride his horse. Once he handed the reins to a groom and slid from his saddle, the children ran toward him. Pepin, Karl, and Hruodtrude seemed to be in a race. Fastrada wanted to rush into Charles's arms but knew she would falter after a few steps. Instead, she kept her pace measured, hoping the court would think she was maintaining dignity.

He greeted her with a puzzled look. Fastrada resisted the urge to wipe her sweaty hands on her skirt. Did he think she looked haggard? She would need to explain her illness to him and now wished she had told him earlier in a message. When she reached him, she savored the touch of his lips, the feel of his brawny body against hers. Her desire quickened in her breasts and between her legs.

"I missed you," he murmured. "Saints be praised, you and Chiltrude are safe."

"Thanks be to God, you're home," she whispered.

They lingered for a moment in their embrace before letting go. Fastrada beckoned Irma, who placed Chiltrude in Charles's arms. The baby looked even smaller.

"She is healthy," Fastrada said. "Everyone heard her cry when she was lifted from the baptismal font the third time."

Charles kissed the infant's forehead. "So did her brothers and sisters. Little one, you are beautiful, just like your mother."

Chiltrude shifted and smacked her lips. Irma held out her arms.

Charles handed the baby to her nurse and turned to Hruodtrude. "How are your studies going?"

"Very well, Father," she said. "I learned much when I tended to the household while Mother recovered. She says I will make a good empress."

A shadow crossed Charles's face. He had mentioned the Byzantines in his letters but said little. Affairs with Tassilo had consumed most of his messages. Charles turned to Fastrada. "My dear, Fardulf said you were tired but healing. Have you been ill?"

"Yes." Fastrada looked down.

"Our lady queen has needed much rest of late," Pepin interjected, "and she always wants the fires stoked."

"Pepin," Fastrada said in a clipped tone, "this isn't your concern."

"It is mine," Charles chided. "Your health is important to the kingdom—and to me. Why didn't you tell me?"

"I ... I didn't want you to worry. You had to contend with the Beneventans and Bavarians and ..."

"Let me decide what to worry about." He looked wounded.

Fastrada wished she could tell him she would be strong again, but she could not lie to him. All she could do was reach for Charles's hand and squeeze it.

***

In bed that night, Fastrada realized how much she had missed her husband, the kisses that sent fire through her body, the embraces that made her feel safe, the pleasure of his closeness. They had both climaxed quickly. As much as she enjoyed lovemaking, it left her exhausted. Charles's low voice startled her from her doze.

"I wish you could have come to Italy with me. You would have seen for yourself how treacherous my cousin is."

Snuggling closer to him, Fastrada remembered what Charles had said in his letters. She responded in a voice barely above a whisper, lest any maids were awake outside the bed's closed curtains. "It's good we have the Holy Father's support. What shall we do about Severinus? He always argues on Tassilo's behalf."

Charles shrugged. "And he will again. His lands are near the Bavarians."

"Coward. Bavarian families on the River Lech show sympathy for us."

Charles snorted. "Those families are always feuding with each other. They will say what they think Gerold and I want to hear. They probably pledge their cooperation to Tassilo when he's in earshot. They want to side with whoever is stronger. So will Severinus. He always has."

"Why keep him at court if he is so fickle?"

"We can watch him here. What troubles me more is that the Byzantines are still sheltering Adalgis."

Fastrada frowned to hear that the son of the Lombard tyrant was still in the Byzantine court. While Charles was away, the empress had asked for Charles to send Hruodtrude to Constantinople. Fastrada had not replied. "What about Hruodtrude?"

"The emperor still wants to marry her when they both come of age, probably because her tutor is sending messages extolling her beauty and intelligence. But I doubt the boy's mother will surrender her regency, and that would be bad for our little girl."

Fastrada wished she could read her husband's face, but she could see nothing beyond the night candle's flickering sliver of light between the curtains. "She is almost a woman grown, Charles, and she handled the affairs of the household well, after some help."

"My dear, the Byzantine court makes ours look like a church school. Even if that palace were not full of vipers, the empress's displeasing the pope is a problem. Adalgis is Rome's enemy as well as ours, and the empress keeps calling church councils His Holiness doesn't approve."

Fastrada's throat tightened. "Hruodtrude's marriage to the emperor would endanger our alliance with the Holy Father—and God's favor!"

***

The next two weeks, Fastrada spent her mornings making sure the palace was ready for the assembly and the guests who would come from all across the realm, from the west side of Francia to Saxony to Bavaria. Servants swept the hearths, beat the dust from the tapestries, and cleaned the rooms and furniture, while Fastrada decided what meals would be served. Between the preparations and spending time with the children, she was exhausted. She wanted to continue her work on Charles's annals but finally asked her husband to appoint his archchaplain to oversee them. She needed to sleep in the afternoons, although she was able to awaken in time for vespers and the evening meal.

Still, she lacked the stamina a hunt demanded. Fortunately, Charles was there to prevent Pepin and Karl from injuring each other. He was taller and broader than both of them and could slap them if all else failed. Gomeric's presence also helped. Pepin was always less troublesome when his uncle was at court, and Gomeric spared the royal treasury the expense of Pepin's whores and his penance for using them. Fastrada would soon need to talk to Charles about Karl's flirting with pretty servant girls. She hated the idea of paying for a harlot, but as Nantlind said, it was less loathsome than an innocent girl being ruined.

When the first guests entered the palace, it smelled of lemon balm and fresh rushes, the cleaned tapestries were bright, and water for the baths would soon be hot. Hildegard's brother, Gerold, was among the early arrivals. As he and Charles greeted each other heartily in the great hall, she wondered whether her own sibling would get such a welcome. Fastrada knew her husband needed Gerold's support. His lands were close to the Bavarians, and like Tassilo, he was from the Agilolfing clan.

Gerold bowed to Fastrada and remarked on how Hildegard's son and daughters had grown. "Your mother would be so proud," he added.

Fastrada felt her cheeks redden. From the corner of her eye, she saw Pepin frown and wished she could do the same. Of course, Gerold would see his nephew and nieces as Hildegard's children, and Fastrada reasoned, he was more likely to support Charles if he did. Yet she wished he had expressed a modicum of gratitude for her efforts to be a mother to *all* of Charles's children. She suspected it meant nothing to him.

Quiet. Save your strength. You will need it for Sigibert.

Her brother arrived a few days later, while Charles and Gerold were discussing war plans in the archive. Fastrada met Sigibert in the great hall. His blue eyes widened a moment. She could not be that changed in the past four years, even if she wore precious stones rather than glass beads and had gained some flesh with the births of her daughters. She tried not to think of her pallor. Behind her, Irma held Theodrada's chubby hand as Chiltrude lay sleepily on the nurse's other shoulder.

The years had transformed Sigibert more. When she had left Büraburg, his ten-winter-old head reached her collarbone. Now on the verge of manhood, he had the same cap of brown hair, but he was almost as tall as she. He was not done growing, and those slender arms and legs would thicken in a few years.

Her gaze dropped to his sword, a gift from her and Charles and a reminder of where his loyalty lay. It would be in the treasury during his visit, but she had ordered the guards to let her see it on him first. *He looks too young to wear it, but he must go campaigning with Charles this summer if men are to follow him when he comes of age.*

"Welcome to Worms, Brother," she said, clasping both his hands.

"Greetings, my queen," he said.

She blinked back her surprise. The piping voice of the boy she had left in Büraburg was gone, replaced with that of a young man.

"You may still call me sister in private," she said, smiling.

He nodded but did not return the smile. Why was Sigibert being so distant? Until Chiltrude's birth, she had sent messages to him once a month, and he occasionally responded. Was he vexed by her silence? No time to brood. She released his hands and gestured toward her daughters. "Come meet your nieces, Theodrada and Chiltrude."

Sigibert bent over, placing his hands on his knees, and grinned. Theodrada turned toward her nurse.

"No need to fear," he said in a soft voice. "I'm your Uncle Sigibert and will use my sword to protect you."

Fastrada swallowed back the thickness in her throat. If only her father had shown such tenderness.

***

At dinner, the great hall was warm with the guests and their servants. Fastrada seated her brother at a place of honor at the high table, both to flatter him and better hear him against all the noise from the conversations. But the warmth he had shown her daughters had disappeared. When she asked him about affairs at Büraburg or studies with the tutor Charles had appointed, he shrugged or gave one-word answers. Even questions about hunting yielded only a few words. Why was he so sullen? He had the voracious appetite of boys his age, so it was not illness.

As she had feared, Fastrada was too tired to talk to her brother about affairs of the realm when dinner ended and servants were clearing the tables.

"Brother, I must retire for a few hours." She rose from her chair. "Chiltrude's birth was hard on my body. Can Karl …"

Nothing from Sigibert, not even a nod.

She slapped her palm on the table. "You have been acting like a child denied his favorite game. Tell me: what is bothering you so much you are curt with your sister and your queen?"

He started. "Nothing."

Fastrada stared him down, like she did when they were younger.

"I've heard rumors," he muttered.

"What rumors?"

Sigibert cleared his throat. "You had the steward of Oppenheim castrated, then thrown out naked and bleeding into the snow."

Fastrada laughed. "If only the truth were so interesting. He was stripped of his honors for his rudeness to the crown, but his person was unharmed."

"You swear?"

"By Saint Wigbert. What made you believe such silliness?"

"I didn't." He tugged at his collar. "I defended you, of course, but the merchant was so certain."

"Don't believe all the prattle that comes from merchants. You're lucky if half of it is true. Now, you and Karl can go riding, and you and I will speak about Bavaria when you return."

"Why should I care about the Bavarians? Our family has no quarrel with them." He scowled.

"Sigibert," Fastrada said as if speaking to a child of six winters, "if your brother Charles has a quarrel with them, you do as well."

"Is that how you convinced Father to support that idiocy with Widukind?"

"You call peace with the Saxons and following God's will idiocy?" She struggled to keep her voice low and even, but it sounded icy even to her ears.

"It killed him," Sigibert said through clenched teeth. His eyes, the same as her father's, accused her of murder. Fastrada's heart raced, and the room started to spin. She leaned against the table and took a breath.

Her brother gaped.

Don't faint. Not in front of the court. Not in front of your brother. Concentrate. She straightened her spine. With measured steps, she descended the dais and strode toward the royal apartment.

Halfway across the hall, she felt another wave of dizziness and faltered. Was she going to swoon out here in front everyone? Charles rushed to her and offered his arm. She leaned on him and approached the apartment as quickly as her feet would allow. Once they passed the threshold, Charles swept her into his arms.

"You don't need to do this," Fastrada murmured.

"It's no trouble."

She clung to him as he carried her to the bedchamber. He settled her on a stool. Nantlind soon followed, bearing a cup of mulled wine.

"Rest now, my dear," he said.

Fastrada was too tired to hold back the tears. "I'm sorry I'm so sickly."

He kissed her. "Do not get overwrought."

"Why won't God answer my prayers? I've given alms and prayed to the Virgin."

"God's ways are a mystery. You will be stronger once you've had some rest."

Fastrada squeezed her husband's beefy hand.

"I will have a word with Sigibert about how he should not upset his sister's delicate health," he said. "If logic will not prevail, guilt might."

"You heard what he said?"

"I didn't need to. The look on your face told me everything."

"I thought I was doing God's will when I argued for my father to support Widukind's baptism," she said in a small voice.

"You were, my dear, and that will be another thing for Sigibert and me to discuss."

Chapter Twenty-one

After vespers prayers in the palace chapel, Sigibert asked to speak to Fastrada alone. With Nantlind trailing them, Fastrada and her brother passed through the great hall, where servants were assembling trestle tables for the evening meal, and into the reception room in the royal apartment. Through the closed door, they could still hear footsteps, chatter, and an occasional thunk of wood. While Nantlind stoked the fire, Fastrada took her seat and invited her brother to sit on a stool. Fastrada and Sigibert spoke in stilted sentences until Nantlind said she would fetch more mulled wine and left the room.

"Why do you need a fire?" Sigibert said. "It's midsummer."

"My humors are unbalanced."

Silently, he gazed at the ceiling, as if pondering something he had heard earlier.

"Charles told you, didn't he?" she said.

"Yes, he told me. He said you didn't tell him either."

"Father said to never let anyone think you're weak."

"Just like Father. He was always telling me to be tough, to fight the bigger boy, to not flee from the boar. He was easy on you."

"Easy?" Fastrada let out a laugh. "You were favored. You always got the best horses and hawks."

"He never slapped you and then told you to stop crying or he'd hit you even harder." He looked as if he had just felt the blow.

"Mother struck my knuckles with a rod and threatened to have Father beat me if I didn't obey." Fastrada kept her voice low.

Sigibert looked at his hands. "I ... I wanted to talk to you to ... I apologize for upsetting you earlier. I didn't know how bad ..."

"You have my pardon."

Sigibert's shoulders relaxed.

"Did Charles give you his as well, for what you said about Widukind?" she asked.

"Of course."

Fastrada blinked in surprise. "So you understand why Father supported …"

"His Excellence saw me sparring with Karl and said I'm a fine swordsman and I should put it to good use in Bavaria." Sigibert's eyes gleamed. "At last, a chance to cut a real enemy and be a hero."

That's how Charles changed Sigibert's mind. Talk of glory. She was caught between wanting to kiss and slap her husband. She knew her brother needed to prove himself in battle, but he was all too eager. In her mind, she saw Sigibert spurring his horse into battle. Right into a Bavarian blade.

"Promise me you will be careful," she finally said.

"You worry too much." He was grinning.

"Maybe," she said. "But I will still order the silversmith to make a medal of Saint Sebastian for you." If anyone could protect her brother, it was the patron saint of soldiers.

***

At the assembly three days later, Fastrada wished the warriors were as easily swayed as her brother by the faintest whiff of fame. In truth, the Thuringians cared little about Bavaria, and Fastrada's patience was further tested as she listened to Charles's Saxon allies, who wanted nothing to do with the Thuringians.

How will Charles get these men to his side? She watched the noblemen gather around the dais where she and Charles sat. Servants had cleared the remains of dinner and stacked the boards for the tables against the walls. Even with the windows open in the midafternoon, the hall was warm with so many men, sweating in their finery. Yet Fastrada felt comfortable. Karl, Pepin, and Hruodtrude stood at the foot of the dais and watched their father. Bertha was shushing Gisela, while Hruodhaid and Theodrada played with their dolls. Irma had taken a sleepy Chiltrude to the royal apartment.

Charles wore his diadem but otherwise was clad in his usual clothes, a wine-colored tunic hemmed with silk, silk leggings, and leather boots. Jeweled pins secured Fastrada's silk veil, its vermillion contrasting with her glass-beaded woad-dyed gown and golden underskirt.

The room quieted when Charles rose to speak. Fastrada stood as well. Even though he had rehearsed his speech with her only the previous night, she was amazed as the words poured from his mouth, his voice clear and steady.

"Many of you were not yet born when our uncle Grifo captured Tassilo and his widowed mother and tried to steal the duchy. We were barely outside our mother's womb. But Tassilo should remember. He had seen seven years.

"Whom could Duchess Chiltrude turn to? Her brother-by-marriage sided with Grifo, the same man who had made war on our father and our uncle Carloman, the rightful heirs to Charles the Hammer. We sometimes wonder if she rued marrying into such a disloyal family against her brothers' advice."

That remark drew many raised eyebrows in the crowd. Everyone knew about the scandal of Chiltrude fleeing Francia to join Tassilo's father a few months before her son's birth, but Fastrada guessed they were surprised Charles would allude to it.

"Duchess Chiltrude had one man who could help her and her son: our father," Charles continued. "Your late king did what was just. He rescued them and restored Tassilo to his duchy. Had our father ignored his sister's pleas, the current duke of Bavaria would have no land and no power. He might not have lived to see manhood."

Charles paused, letting the words sink in. The Franks nodded. The guests from the eastern side of the realm—the East Franks, Thuringians, and Saxons—stared ahead, stone-faced.

"Our aunt never forgot," Charles continued. "As Tassilo's regent, she remained loyal to our father and the Franks for the rest of her life. That is why my beloved daughter bears her name.

"At first, Tassilo returned the fidelity our father had shown to him. He rode into battle twice against the Lombards. When he reached his majority, he swore on the relics of saints to be loyal to our father and his heirs and to the Franks.

"But if Duchess Chiltrude were alive today, her heart would be heavy with sorrow. Again and again, her son has failed to fulfill that sacred promise. He shammed a sickness and fled to Bavaria when our father asked for assistance to put down rebels in Aquitaine, and he refused to come to Rome's aid when the Lombards threatened the Church herself."

Charles never raised his voice. His face betrayed no trace of the frustration he had expressed to Fastrada. "We were able to keep Aquitaine and preserve the Church without his help. But we can no longer ignore his disloyalty. We have heard that he and his Lombard wife are again conspiring with the Avar khagan."

The Easterners' shoulders straightened. Some men craned their necks. Charles had received a letter from the bishop of Freising, irritated with how Tassilo sided with the laity in disputes over land donated to the Church. He had said a conspiracy was possible. The archbishop of Metz had sent a message about what he'd heard from a traveling monk at an abbey near the Enns, the river separating the Bavarians from the Avars. The monk never used the word "conspire," but he did say Tassilo was too lenient with those pagans more vicious than Saxons.

"If Tassilo and the khagan agree to an alliance," Charles said, "what is to stop the Avars from expanding their borders into Saxony or Thuringia or Francia itself?"

Fastrada suppressed a smile as she beheld the wide eyes in the crowd. They had shrugged when she said the very same thing, yet now that the words came from Charles's lips, they paid rapt attention. *So now you see this is not the product of a woman's humors.*

"While we were settling our affairs in Italy," Charles continued, "we had hope for our relations with our cousin. Tassilo sent two emissaries to Rome and asked for the lord pope to foster peace between us and the Bavarians, as His Holiness had done before. Tassilo's emissaries are men of great integrity. Some of you have met one of them: the bishop of Salzburg. Of all Bavarians, he would understand our ways best from his time at Saint Amand Abbey a few years ago.

"When we saw the bishop and his companion, our heart sang. For years, we wished for nothing but peace with Tassilo. All our cousin needed to do was follow the oaths he swore to our father and us.

"We asked the emissaries to make an agreement with the lord pope as a witness. After all, had they not come to Rome for that purpose? But Tassilo had refused to allow his legates to commit to anything."

Charles paused again. A few whispers and mutters rippled through the crowd.

His voice remained smooth as the deep water of a river as he continued. "The lord pope saw how Tassilo was using two good men to carry out his deceit and at once threatened to excommunicate Tassilo and his supporters. So not only does our kinsman endanger his land; he endangers his soul, many souls."

Gasps erupted through the crowd. Charles waited but a moment for the wave to pass.

"His Holiness has given us a dispensation," he said. "If we must make war on Tassilo, we are absolved of any deaths or any other misfortunes. And now, my noble friends, tell me your counsel."

"We should invade," said Gerold, chosen beforehand to say these words because he was an Agilolfing. "You, my lord king, have shown patience for too long. If Tassilo will not heed the Holy Father, whom will he heed?"

"Surely by now, his envoys have conveyed the pope's warning," Severinus said. "Perhaps all you need to do is send emissaries."

"Oath-breakers deserve no mercy," Fastrada said.

"Would you blind an Agilolfing as Hardrad was blinded?" Severinus asked.

Some of the men near Severinus leaned away from him. Fastrada noticed Gomeric almost imperceptibly shake his head toward Pepin.

"Hardrad brought his punishment on himself," Charles said calmly. "Severinus, you should learn your history. Maybe then you will understand why rebels must be stopped at any price."

Fastrada smiled at Severinus, which only made the men shrink more. "I would blind anyone with my own hands, no matter how important his family, if it would keep our people safe from heathens."

A few jaws dropped, but many of the men nodded.

A hint of a smile flickered on Charles's lip. "Beloved wife, we doubt that will be necessary. We shall send emissaries to Tassilo and bring him here to reaffirm his oaths. Amalwin, Severinus, you will deliver our message."

Both Amalwin and Severinus bowed.

Now it was Fastrada's turn to speak, as she and Charles had agreed. "But my lord husband, Tassilo has not listened to you yet, not even after renewing his oath six years ago."

"That is why we will also make plans to fight Tassilo with an army from many lands."

***

Fastrada bade Sigibert farewell after two intense days in the archive with Charles and his magnates planning for battle. Her brother had barely glanced at the books, but he had pored over the maps spread on the tables and asked questions. He was going to be part of Gerold's force of Swabians, Allemans, East Franks, Thuringians, and Saxons, who would march for three weeks and converge on Pförring. Charles had sent a message to Little Pippin and his guardian to assemble a force that would attack Bavaria from the south.

Fastrada had overseen the packing of her brother's possessions as closely as she did her own household. In the courtyard, she tried to reassure herself he would be safe. With a few clouds in the sky and a light breeze, the day boded well for travel. Gerold was an experienced warrior, and Sigibert would be surrounded by skillful men. She had the blacksmith inspect the armor that now lay in a roll on the baggage horse. Still, he seemed too young for the sword at his hip.

"Sister, what is it?" Sigibert asked.

Fastrada kept her voice low. "If the talks fail, Tassilo will be a formidable enemy. Promise me you won't rush headlong into battle, no matter how much the enemy tempts you. Don't be like the men who fell in the Süntels."

"What's 'formidable'?"

"Strong."

Her brother rolled his eyes. "That won't happen to me."

"Those men thought that too."

"I promise not to be an idiot," he said. "You need to promise me something, too. Look after your health. Don't try to do too much."

"Charles has been talking to you again."

"Yes. And he's right."

"I will do my best. God be with you."

"And with you also."

His enthusiasm worried her. Fastrada prayed his new medal would protect him.

***

Over the next fifteen days, Charles and his magnates spent most of their time in the archive discussing the force he would lead from the west. She admired her husband's cleverness in sending Severinus to Tassilo; the duke would know a large army was going to attack but not the battle plans. Fastrada listened to Charles and his men when her health allowed. One week, her courses left her so enervated she did not rise from bed for two days, and even after they passed, she needed sleep in the afternoon.

When Amalwin and Severinus returned to Worms without Tassilo, Fastrada was not surprised. Amalwin looked crestfallen as the royal family and courtiers gathered around the emissaries.

"We made every entreaty," Amalwin said, "but neither promises of protection nor threats of war would move the duke."

Charles remained impassive. "We gave our cousin one last opportunity for peace."

Most of the courtiers nodded. Severinus pressed his lips in a tight line.

"Because Tassilo will not follow his oaths," Charles continued, "we have no choice but to invade."

Karl, who was going to travel with Charles, beamed. Fastrada jabbed him with her elbow. Would the boy ever learn that he needed to look stern? His puzzled expression told her he would need more reminders.

Frowning, Pepin flushed and his stooped shoulders rose slightly. Fastrada furrowed her brow. Why would he be angry about a war with the Bavarians? Surely, he bore no love for Tassilo.

***

Charles and his forces left five days later, heading east toward Tassilo's residence at Augsburg. For six weeks, Fastrada gave alms and prayed to the Mother of God and Sebastian, the patron saint of soldiers. On her knees, she pleaded for victory and safety for Charles, his sons, and her brother.

Finally, a message from Charles. Fastrada immediately left the kitchen where she was giving orders for dinner and walked to the great hall as quickly as her tired body would carry her. It did not take long for the children, servants, and what was left of the court to join her. She could feel their stares as she asked the messenger about Charles and Karl and Sigibert.

"Yes, my queen, they are well."

She tore through the wax seal with her eating knife and started to read. "He says Little Pippin marched through Italy to Trent, where he is staying while his soldiers go to Bolzano. Tassilo is still in Augsburg." Fastrada mouthed a profanity.

"What vexes you, Mother?" Hruodtrude asked.

"Before retreating into the city, peasants gathered the crops they could harvest and burned the fields." She lowered the parchment. "That means Tassilo is preparing for a siege. This war could go into winter, the way the first Lombard war did."

"Why did they burn their own crops?" Gisela asked.

Pepin rolled his eyes. "So our men can't use them to feed themselves."

"Lady Gisela asks a good question," Fastrada said. "And Lord Pepin speaks the truth." *Honestly, Pepin? Condescending to a six-winter-old?*

As the summer leaves changed from green to gold and scarlet and the swine were led into the forest to feast on acorns, Fastrada prayed at prime and vespers Masses for the Franks to avoid a siege, for Charles to have victory. It was becoming more difficult for her to put on a brave face for the children, the servants, the court. Her prayers were answered when one of the servants told her a messenger awaited her in the great hall. The man she greeted was red-faced and panting. Why had Charles made him hurry? Was Karl or Sigibert wounded? The children were coming toward them, as were servants and courtiers.

"How fares my lord husband? My son? My brother?"

"They are well, my lady queen," he said between breaths. "The lord king ordered me to you posthaste. He wanted you to know as soon as possible that Duke Tassilo submitted to him."

Fastrada gasped. "Saints be praised! Tell us what happened."

"When the three armies gathered, the duke sent a messenger with a flag of surrender. He said his master wanted safe conduct to the camp."

"That's all?" Pepin asked.

"The duke knelt before our king, placed his folded hands in our lord's, and surrendered his duchy. He promised to follow the king and his heirs, and the king returned the duchy to Duke Tassilo as a benefice."

Charles's letter did not say much more other than that he and his army were returning to Worms with thirteen hostages, including one of Tassilo's sons. Karl and Sigibert would be disappointed not to try their swords, but Fastrada could live with sulking boys. Better than losing either of them in a war. Why did Tassilo give up before a single battle? The answer came like a bucket of cold river water. Fastrada's smile became a mask.

Tassilo will bide his time and fight another day. If his wife's brother comes to Italy, those two could join forces. Tassilo is just like the Saxons. They swore oaths and gave hostages, too.

<h1 style="text-align:center">Chapter Twenty-two</h1>

March 788, Ingelheim

As Fastrada and Charles left prime Mass, she leaned on her husband's arm, grateful for his support. The children followed about five paces away. Her womanly courses had just passed, leaving her fatigued. And cold. Charles had left his otter fur vest in the bedchamber, but in the gray drizzle of the morning, she needed her marten fur-lined cloak and leather gloves. The walk was only a few minutes along the stone path, flanked by awakening rosebushes, yet Fastrada longed to be inside near a fire.

She had tried to fast during Lent but quickly became ill. She had never enjoyed waiting until midafternoon for a meal, and one without eggs, cheeses, or meat, and Charles especially loathed it. But her infirmity frustrated her. She wondered if the courtiers noticed if the trays brought to the royal apartment held more food than needed for the four princesses too young to fast. Was Pepin gossiping about her weakness?

She laid a hand on her belly. Part of her wished Charles's seed would take hold, yet she was relieved it didn't. A few days of weariness were easier to bear than months of exhaustion, if another birth didn't kill her. Had her father lived through the battles, would he have insisted she try to conceive a grandson at the cost of her life?

"What troubles you, my dear?" Charles asked. "Are you feeling feverish?"

"I was just thinking of my father."

"I still miss my mother from time to time. I wish you could have met her."

From what she had heard of the strong-willed lady, Fastrada was thankful she hadn't met Queen Mother Bertrada. She smiled up at her husband to cover her twinge of guilt.

"But if Mother were still alive," Charles continued, "she might say I would be at peace with Tassilo and Adalgis if I had not repudiated the Lombard." His lips drew a grim line. "I should have listened to the Holy Father and not agreed to the marriage in the first place."

"Why did you?"

"Mother was trying to make peace." He sighed. "In the end, it was not to be."

Fastrada cocked her head. Charles rarely ever spoke of his brother. "What happened?"

"When my brother died, I had a choice. If I let his widow be the regent for her young sons, Francia would remain divided. I could not rely on her or her counts to support us in battle. We'd lose Aquitaine. It would be a betrayal to let go of a land that had cost so much blood.

"I could unite Francia by marrying Hildegard. With an Agilolfing family's support, we would keep our hard-won territory. We could answer the Saxons with overwhelming force."

For the first time, Fastrada understood Charles had seized his brother's lands for the good of the Franks, not a lust for power. She gave his arm a squeeze.

"My mother warned me my former father-by-marriage would be angry," he continued, "and his daughters in Bavaria and Benevento would turn their husbands against us. She was right. But even she was surprised when the Lombards threatened Rome because the pope refused to anoint my brother's sons as kings."

"That would have divided our people again."

"Exactly. Yet I did not want war with the Lombards. No one in Francia did, not with the Saxons still a danger to us. I offered him gold to make peace with Rome."

"I didn't know about the bribe," she murmured. Had it worked, she might have never known nightmares.

"My dear, the decision to invade Lombardy and leave our eastern lands vulnerable was agonizing. But the Lombard tyrant refused our offer. We had no choice but to remove him."

Fastrada had shared her father's resentment over the war that took him away from Büraburg; now she understood Charles had faced two awful choices. "If only his son had not escaped."

Charles's voice took on a hard edge. "We can thank the Byzantine dowager empress for Adalgis's presence in southern Italy, just as Tassilo is talking to the Avars."

Fastrada and Charles had paid some heed to the message from the bishop of Freising, knowing he despised Tassilo, but they could not ignore the bishop of Salzburg, who had been the duke's emissary only a year ago. The letters from the pope and other Italian noblemen only complicated the situation.

"We cannot send the army the Holy Father is requesting," Charles said, "not if the messages from Freising and Saltzburg are true."

The back of Fastrada's neck tensed. "How can Tassilo let his Lombard wife convince him to ally himself with devil-worshipping brutes? Does he care that little for his son? I would gladly send that nuisance back to his father."

"Still fighting with Karl?"

"All the time. And he whines about Pepin touching him. You would think he was six winters, not sixteen. The only good thing is that Karl and Pepin are not quarreling with each other as much."

"In me, Tassilo and the Avars have a common enemy," Charles said as calmly as if he were speaking of a rain cloud, "and if Tassilo can help his brother-by-marriage get the Lombard throne ..."

"He would have more control of the trade routes, the salt supply, the roads to Rome." Fear shook Fastrada from her fatigue. "You should summon him to court!"

"Let us wait, my dear. He doesn't dare attack yet."

"But he will continue to conspire with the Avars!" She could not understand Charles's lack of anxiety.

Charles grinned. "And he will further divide himself from his countrymen west of the River Inn by plotting with the enemy they fear most."

"So when he does come here," Fastrada said, stringing her thoughts like beads, "he will have no support. But Adalgis is still a threat. We must do something."

A guard opened the door to the royal residence. As she and Charles went inside, Fastrada was glad to be someplace dry. Still, her hands and feet felt like ice.

"Can we sit by the fire, Charles?"

Charles patted her hand. "In our apartment, my dear."

And away from prying ears.

They crossed the vast audience hall. Such a difference than when she had last visited it on the way to Worms two years ago! Instead of wood, the floors were covered with geometric patterns of marble and porphyry imported from Italy. Charles's throne was on a dais opposite the main entrance. In bright yellows, greens, blues, and reds were the frescoes of Ninus of the Assyrians, Phalaris of Sicily, Cyrus of Persia, Alexander the Great, Hannibal, Romulus, and Remus. It was almost as magnificent as the villa's defenses. Framed by mountains, its walls were taller than six men standing on each other's shoulders and its six round towers provided a commanding view.

Charles led her to the hearth, where servants had set two chairs. Fastrada sank into her seat and pulled her cloak close. As Charles sat beside her, she stared at the glowing embers.

"We'll send the Beneventan back home," Charles said. "If his oath doesn't secure his loyalty, the warriors we send with him will. So will Little Pippin's men."

Fastrada nodded. With the old Beneventan duke and his elder son assassinated, the hostage in Charles's court was the rightful heir, even if the pope hated the young man's mother.

She heard a scratch on the door. Nantlind entered the room, carrying a cup, and took a sip before handing it to her lady. Fastrada cradled the warm vessel in her hands. The cinnamon and nutmeg wafted to her nostrils as she raised the mulled wine to her lips.

"The Byzantine empress is still asking for Hruodtrude," Fastrada said. "Would you like to give her an answer?"

"Good idea, my dear. Nantlind, fetch a clerk, but first tell Lady Hruodtrude to come here. We must speak with her."

Hruodtrude and the Byzantine emperor were old enough to marry now. The girl used to smile whenever someone spoke of her betrothal, as if remembering a pleasant dream. In recent months, she had become pensive at the mention of Adalgis or the emperor.

When Hruodtrude entered the room, her brow was creased. *Poor girl. Her heart will be broken.*

Charles took his daughter's hand. "When the clerk arrives, I am going to have him write a letter to the emperor. It will say if he or his mother persist in defying God's will by calling councils that offend His Holiness, supporting Adalgis, and adoring images, he will not marry you."

Withdrawing her hand from her father's, Hruodtrude gasped. She hunched over and covered her face. Her shoulders shook.

Fastrada ached for the girl. "We are about to face an enemy stronger and more vicious than the Saxons," she said. "We cannot risk losing God's grace."

Charles stood and hugged his daughter. "I know your tutor was extolling the emperor's virtues. Despite what he told you, this betrothal offers no gain for you or our people."

Hruodtrude looked up. To Fastrada's surprise, the girl was beaming. *Those are tears of relief!*

"You promise?" Hruodtrude said. "My tutor says the emperor wants me, but I so dread my mother-by-marriage."

"The Byzantine court is evil," Charles said, "and I will not send you into evil."

June 788, Ingelheim

Pepin welcomed the cooler air when he emerged from the great hall, overheated with people from all over the realm: Francia, Saxony, Lombardy, and Bavaria. Even his young brothers Little Pippin and Louis had come to the assembly. Like Karl, Pepin noticed, Little Pippin was girded with a sword.

Gomeric and Severinus accompanied him on his way to the stables, and Pepin's guards trailed a few paces behind them. Although cloudy, the afternoon offered a perfect opportunity for a ride.

"I no like how Tassilo treated," Severinus said in stilted Latin, keeping his voice low.

Pepin arched an eyebrow, wondering how Severinus could still support a man who had repeatedly proven his perfidy. There was no advantage in it. Every time Tassilo's name was mentioned, Pepin heard "traitor" and "oath breaker." Still, his father was treating the duke as an honored guest who had answered his summons. In the meantime, his father's legates were bringing Tassilo's wife and children to the assembly, along with their household and treasure. The message had said Duchess Luitperga did not resist.

Gomeric gave Pepin a meaningful look, as if to tell him to remain silent. Although he did not understand the reason, Pepin nodded almost imperceptibly.

"It's Fastrada's doing," Gomeric said. "Tassilo's cause is hopeless. If you speak in his defense, Severinus, you might be executed with him."

"King not murder own cousin!" Severinus said.

"Hold your tongue!" Gomeric said. He glanced over his shoulder.

Following Gomeric's gaze, Pepin saw only his guards. "Peace, Uncle. They don't understand Latin, not even the prayers. Severinus, you've heard the whispers—all for the duke's death. The court is like wolves that smell blood on the wind."

Gomeric's lips twitched. Pepin suppressed a smile at his uncle's approval, even if his behavior puzzled him. Pepin's mother despised Luitperga, sister of the Lombard princess his father had married after his first divorce. He remembered what she had said in her last letter: *Praise God that His Excellence will bring justice to this loathsome woman.*

***

A week later, Pepin joined the crowd in the courtyard when a messenger announced that Tassilo's family had arrived. Let Karl, Little Pippin, and Louis wait for the traitors in the great hall. Pepin was finally going to get a good look at them. He wondered if Luitperga looked like his father's former wife, even though the marriage had been so brief he had no memory of her.

The great gate ground open, and the crowd's murmur fell to a hush. A procession of at least fifty warriors and many carts poured through. Pepin recognized the leader: Gerold, Hildegard's brother. Although Gerold was stout, Pepin could see some semblance to the woman he had once called Mother in the high cheekbones and rounded chin. Behind him was a noblewoman whose dark eyes shone with defiance. She wore the jeweled coronet of a duchess, and a necklace of glass beads with an amethyst pendant graced her neck. A large cross lay on her bosom. *Interesting ornament for a woman hateful to God.* Her younger son was beside her and her two daughters followed. The children were hunched over as if trying to make themselves smaller.

The crowd surged forward, taking Pepin with it. Whispers of "vermin" and "oath breaker" became cries.

"Stay back," Gerold bellowed. "Our lord king wants Luitperga and her children alive."

Pepin pursed his lips. Luitperga? Not Duchess Luitperga?

Surrounded by guards, the duchess and her children dismounted and were led to the great hall. The murmuring crowd trailed them, and Pepin was swept along as if by a river. Inside, he pushed his way to the foot of the dais and stood with his siblings, just as Gomeric had instructed. Despite the room's vastness, it was hot with so many bodies, and the odor of sweat blended with the smell of wood smoke and the rushes strewn on the floor.

Accompanied by five guards, Tassilo and his elder son joined their family. The duke, a gaunt man, had dark circles under his eyes and half his hair was gray. He hugged Luitperga and patted her back, then embraced his younger son and daughters and whispered something to them. The girls' lips trembled. After kissing her elder son on the cheek, Luitperga gazed about the room, then her features hardened.

The crowd parted for Charles and Fastrada, who ascended three steps to the dais. Bowing to her husband, the queen was glittering with jewels. *Another show of Father's power.*

Pepin and the other royal children bowed to Charles and Fastrada. Nearby, the clerks had their styluses hovering over their wax tablets. The crowd stilled when Meginfrid handed Charles his scepter.

"Tassilo, duke of Bavaria," Charles said, "you are accused of conspiring with the Avars against us and trying to murder our vassals. You are accused of having said that if you had ten sons, you would rather they perish than keep the vow you made on the bones of saints. Is this true?"

Tassilo's lips drew a taut line.

"Cur," a man called out.

The duke briefly clasped his wife's hand. "I would rather die than serve a God-cursed tyrant."

Throughout the crowd, the nobles called for his death.

"He deserted our king's father when he was at war in Aquitaine!"

"He refused to stop the Lombards when they threatened the Church!"

Severinus was about to speak, but Gomeric elbowed his friend and mouthed *no.* Pepin doubted anyone else noticed.

"Tassilo should live," Fastrada cried. "Blinded."

Just as she and Father had agreed. With a sidelong look to his wife, Charles held up his hand for silence. "Tassilo, for the desertion of King Pepin in

Aquitaine, you are guilty of treason. For the love of God and because you are our kinsman, we offer you a choice: death and slavery for your wife and children or the cloister for all of you so that you can repent your sins."

Tassilo nervously glanced at his wife. Her back was stiff as if she was bracing herself for a blow. His eyes darted to his children.

"The monastery," Tassilo mumbled.

"Take them to Jumièges," Charles barked. "We have wars to plan."

"God curse you! God curse the Franks!" Luitperga shrieked.

Fastrada blanched. "May God give you a slow, painful death," she growled.

The guards took Tassilo and his family from the hall.

"And now for the most difficult question," Charles said, "how do we defeat the Avars?"

Chapter Twenty-three

August 788, Regensburg

In a fog of exhaustion, Fastrada wondered whether she was dreaming and blinked hard to clear her eyes. The immense Bavarian city walls still loomed ahead.

"Come, my dear," said Charles, who was riding beside her. "We can rest soon."

Fastrada urged her mare forward on the pontoon bridge that crossed the Danube from the river island they were on. Although the structure was held fast with ropes and anchors, it swayed slightly with the horses' weight and the current. The mare stiffened. Only a nudge from Fastrada's wire spurs moved the beast. When they reached solid land on the south bank, she felt the tension leave her and the horse.

How Fastrada needed rest, in a bed, surrounded by solid walls instead of the leather of a tent that moved with the wind. The travelers—the children, their nurses, the courtiers and other nobles, servants, guards, and soldiers—had spent three weeks traversing hills thick with trees so tall she could not see the sky, so broad not even three long-limbed men could wrap their arms around them. Here at Regensburg, pines, firs, and beeches sat to the fortress's left and rear, and she wondered how big the deer and boars grew in these woods. In the distance to the right of the gray stone structure, she could make out the square cathedral towers and the walls of the nearby monastery. Peasant huts dotted the landscape between the cathedral and palace. Just beyond the huts were fields of wheat, rye, and oats, enough to feed hundreds. Horses, cows, and sheep grazed in a fallow area. Beyond the fields, the forest blanketed the hills.

The closer she got to the city, the greater her awe. Built with huge square stone blocks, the walls were higher than four men and punctuated with many towers. As they passed under a high, wide arch flanked by two towers, Fastrada noticed the thickness—about a cart length.

Within the bulwarks, she beheld fountains and Niedermünster, an enclosed convent. As the travelers neared the center of town, they rode by a large stone building, rectangular with square windows—the church with the relics of Saint Erhard, whom the sisters perpetually venerated. The walls of the royal residence had the party turn left and then right to reach the main entrance. Across the courtyard was a portico with a series of stone arches supporting a roofed entryway to the structure.

Now she understood why Charles had waited until Tassilo lost support among his own people.

"It would take a year-long siege to conquer this place. Maybe longer," she said. "The Avars cannot hope to penetrate it."

Last month, the pagans had attacked the Lombard city of Fruili, but the Franks stationed there had repelled them. *Disgraced*, Fastrada thought, smiling, *that is what I will tell the clerk to write in the annals*. Her smile faded. In truth, the fight in Fruili had only bruised and bloodied the Avars, and they would likely try to avenge themselves somewhere in Bavaria and test her husband's might. Charles needed to prove to the Bavarians that he was their protector.

***

Pepin knew something was amiss as soon as his stern-faced father entered the great hall with Fastrada on his arm. The queen was pale, but Pepin could not tell if her illness or the last hour's message caused it. Since their arrival at Regensburg three days ago, she had left the royal apartment only to attend prime Mass and eat dinner. Even now, she seemed weary and wore a cloak although the day was warm enough for the clerestory windows to be open to the interior and exterior courtyards.

The king and queen crossed the rush-covered floor, passed the murals of battle scenes—with Agilolfing heroes, Pepin guessed—and ascended the dais at the opposite end. Pepin joined his siblings at the foot of the platform and heard Hruodtrude and Bertha whispering about Chiltrude, who lay in the bedchamber all the girls shared. The infant princess had coughing fits so severe she sounded like she would choke and made a whooping sound when she drew breath. The same illness had claimed Pepin's foster brother when they were both three months old. He made a silent promise to give alms after vespers Mass. In her letters, his mother urged him to act like he cared for his siblings, especially his sisters.

Next to Pepin, Karl tapped his hand against his dagger hilt, perhaps sensing the tension. Little Pippin and Louis stared about and shuffled their feet. Pepin frowned. *They are as ignorant as Theodrada and Hruodhaid playing with their dolls.*

149

The murmurs grew louder as the noblemen, including Gomeric, Meginfrid, and Gerold, gathered. When Charles held up his hand, the voices stilled. Pepin raised his head so he could better listen and remember everything to tell his mother, carefully phrasing his letter as praise for whatever his father decided.

"The Avars attacked Lorch," Charles announced, "just as Tassilo and Luitperga instructed."

A shiver ran over Pepin's misshapen spine, yet he was not surprised. Close to the Avars' territory, Lorch made an attractive target. From what Pepin had heard, he imagined a small town, not even half as protected as this fortress.

Karl squared his shoulders and stuck out his chest. "I want to fight."

"Me, too," Little Pippin said. "I want to blood my sword."

"I want a sword!" Louis cried.

Pepin felt the heat spread across his cheeks. He met Gomeric's eyes, but his uncle shook his head slightly. Pepin remained silent, just as his mother had advised. *Listen more than speak, my son, and heed the wise words said at the assembly.*

"Sons, we need you here," Charles said. "Gerold, my brother, you will lead a force of Franks and Bavarians to defend Lorch."

"It is my honor," Gerold said, bowing.

Pepin's eyes narrowed. His father was sending an Agilolfing to fight the heathens. Clever move to appease the Bavarians.

***

An hour before vespers, Pepin slipped outside through a side door with Gomeric and Severinus and felt the stifling heat roll off him. How could Fastrada still insist on such a high fire with all those people in the room? Even with a few open windows, some were fanning themselves.

Pepin and his companions said little as they crossed the interior courtyard. When they reached the garden, servants were cutting parsley and thyme and rushing back to the kitchen.

"I told you Tassilo was a traitor," Pepin said to Severinus. "The monastery is too good for him."

Gomeric's scowl puzzled Pepin.

"The king ..." Severinus began.

"In Latin," Gomeric said in that language, tilting his head.

Severinus glanced nervously over his shoulder. Pepin turned and saw only his guards ten paces behind. He shrugged. He rarely noticed them.

"His Excellence ... mistaken." Severinus kept his voice low. "Avars, um, attack, uh ..."

"Because?" Gomeric prompted.

"Tassilo ... not there to defend land ... lawfully his. Tassilo not talk to Avars if king not menace him."

"This is not the first time the king has dealt unjustly with a kinsman," Gomeric said. "My nephew deserves to inherit the kingdom."

Raising his brows, Severinus glanced from Gomeric to Pepin and back to Gomeric. "How so? Himiltrude ... a concubine."

"As you have heard with your own ears, my former brother-*by-marriage* lies."

Pepin blinked. Did his uncle really say that? If his father knew, Gomeric could be blinded or slowly strangle like a thief on the hangman's rope. Saints be praised for the guards' ignorance. He opened his mouth to warn his uncle but closed it when Gomeric's face betrayed no fear. *He said "lies" deliberately.* Pepin turned toward Severinus.

The count looked at Gomeric with wide eyes, then nodded. "That the word, 'lie.'"

"My sister and the king married on the orders of both our fathers. She has known no other man and did nothing to merit repudiation. By Church law, she still is his wife and the rightful queen of the Franks. Thus, Pepin is the only true heir. The other three boys are bastards."

Pepin tried to hide his surprise that his uncle revealed what they had discussed with his mother at Nivelles four years ago. Pepin raised his hand, but Gomeric waved him down.

Severinus pursed his lips. "Why no protest when king send her away?"

"The king heeded only his mother, and my sister's fidelity meant nothing to him. Had we protested, it would have been worse for Pepin. We needed to salvage Himiltrude's honor and protect her son's place in the court." Gomeric paused. "Had Charles done his duty as a husband and remained married to my sister, we would have never been at war with Lombardy. He would have left Tassilo in peace, and the Avars would stay in their lands."

And my back would be straight. And pretty girls would want me.

***

Fastrada spent the next sixteen days worrying more about Chiltrude than the Avars. She had seen Hruodhaid and Theodrada suffer through these fits wracking their tiny bodies, but it never became any easier. Irma, who had lost her own child to this malady, was even more fearful. Fastrada tried to hide her own dread for the nurse's sake, but only God knew if the baby would survive. Charles gave alms on his daughter's behalf, and to Fastrada's astonishment, so did Pepin. Was this the same young man who had tried to curse Theodrada and might have done the same thing to Chiltrude if Fastrada hadn't threatened him? Perhaps at nineteen winters, his heart was softening, and he finally understood that his place was with the Church.

Charles and Fastrada were in the archive, using the light of the slanted sun to study a map of Bavaria and discussing noble families' requests for land, when a servant showed a messenger into the room. The sweating, breathless young man handed Charles a rolled parchment with Gerold's seal.

151

"Show our guest to the great hall and fetch him refreshments," Fastrada told the servant.

Charles withdrew his dagger and broke the seal, unrolled the message, and held it for both him and Fastrada to read. At first, she smiled. Lorch's walls had held, and Gerold's warriors had driven the Avars away and sent them across the River Ybbs.

As she read on and deciphered the Latin, her smile disappeared. "Is he saying what I think he's saying? The Avars raided the fields before they left and are camped across the river? And there are now more heathens?"

Charles nodded. "They will try again. We must send more food and supplies."

If Charles failed to protect Lorch, the Bavarians would never follow his rule. Her heart sank. The Avars were attacking at the worst time, when peasants should be harvesting grain to feed themselves through winter.

She shuddered, remembering the murders and burnt churches at the Saxons' hands. The Franks needed God's help. It was time the holy women at Niedermünster knew where their loyalty should lie.

***

After sunrise Mass the next day, Fastrada led her guest to the reception room in the royal apartment. They had exchanged several messages the previous day until Fastrada demanded that her meeting with the abbess of Niedermünster take place inside the royal residence—a statement to show authority.

But the abbess had reminders of her own. Unlike her sisters, she was clad in a black silk widow's veil and blue gown of fine wool. In addition to a silver circlet, she wore a large cross and several rings, one of them with a seal. She had the pale skin of a woman from a noble family, but Fastrada guessed from the leanness of her face that she was past forty winters.

The windows in the reception room opened to the orchard and its ripening apples to the left and the interior courtyard with gravel paths and a fountain to the right. Fastrada settled in her chair by the hearth and a small table upon which a rolled parchment and bulging pouch sat. She bade her frowning guest to use a cushioned stool and ordered Nantlind to fetch wine.

Perched on the edge of her seat, the abbess let her eyes dart around the room, yet her alto voice was steady. "To what do I owe the honor of this invitation?"

"His Excellence and I are troubled about the confusion over the ownership of Niedermünster's land."

A crease formed in the abbess's brow. "Duke Tassilo and Duchess Luitperga donated the property to us."

"They are traitors and had no right to give land."

The abbess gasped and started to respond.

Fastrada held up her hand for silence. "So to avoid any disputes, His Excellence and I are bestowing the property, its buildings, its livestock, and its tenants upon the holy sisters. Our clerk wrote this charter yesterday." She handed the parchment to the abbess. "It is our will that you remain Niedermünster's abbess and continue God's work."

The abbess's shoulders relaxed. "I ... thank you and your husband, my lady queen."

"In return," Fastrada said, "we ask that you pray for the king and his family and the Franks' and Bavarians' victory against their enemies."

"Of course," the abbess said.

Fastrada picked up the pouch heavy with coins and placed it in the abbess's hand. "Alms on behalf of my little Chiltrude." She choked out the next words. "Remember her in your prayers."

The abbess sat up straight. A gentle smile replaced her frown. "I always worried when my son was ill. My sisters and I will ask the Blessed Mother for God's mercy."

***

Fastrada struggled to keep herself upright in the cathedral. The early morning sunlight flowed through arched clerestory windows, brightening the murals of saints and biblical scenes in the large central section. At the altar, a barefoot priest chanted prayers for God's favor and mercy, and she and the rest of the faithful responded *"Kyrie Eleison."*

She gazed at the mural of the Crucifixion the priest was facing. Blood flowed from where the crown of thorns pricked Jesu's forehead and the nails impaled His hands and feet. If she looked to her right, she could catch a glimpse of the gold reliquary that held Saint Emmeram's remains at the end of the aisle. If the Christ could endure this pain, if the Blessed Mother could endure the sight of her son's murder, if Emmeram could still praise God while he was hacked to pieces, could she not endure abstaining from wine and meat?

If only she could. On this second day of abstinence, standing through Mass took all her will. She had given alms to excuse the five youngest children, but the people needed to see their queen could make the sacrifice. She was going to fail them soon and wanted to weep. Once this Mass ended, she was going to give more alms, return to the palace's royal apartment, then send a maid to fetch wine and meat for her and the youngest girls. How she wished God would restore her strength. More important, she wished God would stop Chiltrude's coughs. A week after Fastrada's meeting with the abbess, the girl still suffered fits.

She snuck a sidelong glance at the other children, the eldest five who were abstaining. Even though he had seen ten winters, Louis was not restless, as she had feared. He stood, with his head bowed, arms crossed, and feet still.

Unlike eleven-winter-old Pippin beside him, Louis apparently understood that he must give all his mind and all his body to prayer. As she must.

Holy Mother of God, let me finish this Mass. I will have an ox slaughtered for the pilgrims and beggars.

***

Gerold's second message arrived five days later, just as Fastrada was recovering from her womanly courses. She would soon find out if the litanies had pleased God enough for the Franks to triumph over the Avars. She had one hopeful sign: Chiltrude's fits were occurring less often.

In the great hall smelling of thyme and mint underfoot, the flushed messenger was panting but smiling as if he had set aside a burden. Charles decided to read Gerold's letter in public. As he unrolled the parchment in a patch of bright light, the children and courtiers gathered. A hush fell over them, and they seemed to hold a collective breath.

"Victory!" Charles cried. "Praise God!"

Cheers filled the hall, rebounding off its walls. Fastrada blinked back tears.

When the noise subsided, Charles spoke again. "Our men slaughtered the Avars in great numbers. The heathens' hearts were so filled with fear, they tried to flee across the Danube. They were trapped by the whirlpools and drowned like rats."

The shouts and whoops of joy were deafening.

We must have murals of this triumph, remind the Bavarians that Charles kept them safe. She glanced at the space to the left of Charles's throne, where a painting showed Tassilo fighting Carinthians. *That's where it will go. Charles will send Gerold to war, then the Avars will flee into the water.*

***

The following two weeks were thick with gossip, like smoke on wet wood. Pepin learned of more rumors from men who wanted to enlarge their pieces of Bavaria. For his own amusement, he nodded and asked a few questions to see how ridiculous the stories could get. So far no one accused a rival of selling his soul to the Devil.

But when he spied a kinsman of the bishop of Freising in the great hall, he slipped out a side door to the interior courtyard. He had no desire to yet again hear the bishop's virtues and his opponents' faults. The air smelled of rain, but Pepin left the shelter of the roofed passage and strolled toward the fountain at the courtyard's center. Soon, he heard Gomeric's footsteps on the gravel path behind him, and his uncle appeared beside him.

"I have had my fill of drivel today," Pepin said. "I don't know why you tell me to listen to it. Father pays me no heed."

"Latin, Pepin," Gomeric said in that language. "The drivel, as you call it, is important because you need to know the alliances among the Bavarians, especially if any are angry at the king for deposing his cousin."

Pepin snorted. "What does it matter? Tassilo was vile."

"Perhaps. But stop saying that to Severinus. If you want to rule, you need to make friends of your father's enemies."

Pepin raised his eyebrows. Was it possible for him to be king someday? If he could stay out of the clergy—and not relinquish his inheritance—until his father died, perhaps he could wrest support from Karl. Time was on Pepin's side. His father was not young, and Angilram the archchaplain, although older than Charles, still lived, occupying Pepin's archbishopric.

"But what about my back? Who would accept me as king?"

"Nobles furious with your father. That is why you need their support."

"Any way to make friends with the dowager Byzantine empress?" The corners of Pepin's lips quirked.

"Not without offending His Holiness, but tell me what her letter said. I heard only that she was breaking the betrothal between her son and Hruodtrude."

Pepin shrugged. "Not much more than that. The empress said she will choose her own magnates and she will call councils as she sees fit. Hruodtrude laughed to hear it."

"She's not upset?"

"If she were, all those men gathering around her and bragging about their lands and hunting prowess would be happy to console her."

"Too bad. It would have helped our cause if she were vexed with your father. Still, you need to be courteous to her."

"Why? She's only a woman."

Gomeric gave Pepin a look as if he were a simpleminded five-year-old. "When you are on the throne, we will need your sisters to keep their husbands on our side."

Chapter Twenty-four

February 789, Aachen

When Pepin entered the archive, he was surprised to see the she-wolf. Pale and gaunt, she sat in an ornate chair at a table with wax tablets spread before her. A fire burned brightly in the hearth, yet she held her cloak close with gloved hands. Fardulf the deacon and a lanky clerk stood behind her. Nantlind, usually hovering near her lady, was absent, as she had been at prime Mass.

That day's sunrise was the first time Pepin had seen Fastrada in almost two weeks. A fever had swept through the palace, and Fastrada had been among the first to get sick. When he overheard Nantlind worry that her lady slept all day and barely woke up long enough to eat a few bites, he wondered if his prayers were finally being answered.

Then the fever struck him and left him bedridden for six days. It had vexed him to see Karl, already recovered from the illness, dressing for the hunt that morning and hear him boast to his manservant about the stag he would slay. Pepin turned away. At least he had been spared Louis's and Little Pippin's prattle. They were back in their kingdoms.

The faint baying of the hounds leaving the courtyard seeped through the parchment-covered window, and Pepin felt a tug at his heart. He longed for the assault of the deafening barks and the wind sharp on his face, although he could no longer ride at a full gallop. His back had become so hunched he could not sit upright to draw great gulps of air. Still fatigued, Pepin was certain he would go mad if he had to stay in his bedchamber any longer and stare at the tapestry of Saint Georg slaying the dragon. Even the archive was better, she-wolf or no she-wolf. Pepin strode across the room and sought a Tertullian among the leather-bound volumes.

"Pepin," Fastrada said, "how do you fare?"

He started, then reasoned she asked only out of courtesy. "Better," he muttered.

With an expression of longing, Fastrada turned toward the window and sighed. Then her stare roamed the room and lingered on a table at the far end as if she was contemplating where to order him to sit. Her gaze flicked to Pepin again, and she bit her lower lip.

"Fardulf, clear a spot at this table so the king's son can read near the fire"—she locked eyes with Pepin—"as his father wills."

Why was she being considerate? So he wouldn't complain to his father? He wished his uncle were here instead of his home in Maastricht. Pepin sat on a cushioned stool. "Where is Nantlind?" he asked.

A mist formed in Fastrada's eyes, and she blinked it away. "Nantlind has the fever."

"I will pray for her and give alms." He touched his pouch and was glad to feel a few coins through the leather.

Fastrada gaped at him. "How ... how kind of you."

Pepin truly wished Nantlind would recover, even though he and she never spoke more than a few words and she always seemed to be in a hurry. At least she didn't look at him like he was offal. Pepin turned to his book. For a few moments, the only sounds were the crackling of the flames in the hearth.

"This should say how happy Charles and I were when he returned from Rome," the she-wolf said.

Pepin snuck a glance. Fastrada was pointing at one of the tablets. *Who cares about whether the king is happy to see his wife? Stupid Easterner.*

Turning the parchment pages, Pepin could not appreciate the illuminations. Fastrada's voice kept breaking into his thoughts.

"The annals are to say nothing of the disaster at Roncevaux or the Thuringians," she said. "Do I make myself clear?"

The clerk nodded.

You do have some brains.

Fastrada pointed to another tablet. "Fardulf, does this say Aachen is still a villa?"

"Yes."

She turned to the clerk. "Call Aachen a palace. It will rival anything the Byzantines can build."

Pepin had to agree. With a new royal hall, the villa was twice its former size. He remembered the plan he had spied before he fell ill. The church was a circle with an octagon inside; his father had said he had seen one like it in Ravenna during the first war in Lombardy. Flanking the circle were two rectangles, basilicas, and with a large rectangle, the atrium, behind them. A new judgment hall and barracks would connect to the current royal hall and residence. The large bathhouse would remain. The stone was being mined from local hills now, and his father had asked the pope for marble and mosaics from Ravenna. As soon as the weather became more temperate, the archchaplain would bless the ground for the chapel, where workers would set pink stone along the base. *Father wants to show the Byzantines his might.*

"Should we not consult with the archchaplain first?" the clerk said, rolling the stylus in his long, ink-stained fingers.

Fastrada stiffened her spine. "I am the queen, and he is doing this at my behest."

You are still a woman. Ianua diaboli—doorway of the Devil.

April 789, Aachen

The message from Widukind made Fastrada almost wish he had remained a pagan and not pledged his loyalty to Charles. Then the Slavic Wilzi raiding the Eastern Saxons—and Widukind's fear of their pushing westward into his territory—would not concern her husband.

Charles needed to discuss the matter with his magnates but not in public. The archive, with its letters and maps, was the perfect place. Although any open window felt like a draft on a winter day to her, she ordered the servants to remove the coverings and allow sunlight and April's breezes into the crowded room. Charles, Pepin, Karl, Hruodtrude, Meginfrid, and the others had no need for a cloak. She still did. Nantlind hurried out of the room to fetch mulled wine. Saints be praised, her maid had recovered quickly from the fever.

Meginfrid took maps from one of the chests and spread them on a table. Everyone clustered around.

"Must we turn our attention away from the Avars?" Karl asked.

Pepin muttered, "We should let the Wilzi and the Saxons destroy each other."

Fastrada would have uttered those words only a few years ago, even if the Avars weren't still a threat. "I would like nothing better. But Widukind has kept his oath."

"And I must keep mine to protect him," Charles added. "The question is not whether to protect the Westphalian Saxons but how. Gerold has proven he can hold off the Avars for now."

And the Bavarians, Fastrada thought. After all, Charles was staying true to their law by appointing Gerold, an Agilolfing, as the count of Augsburg. It also helped that the bishop of Salzburg—Tassilo's former envoy—and the bishop of Freising declared their fidelity to Charles. *As long as they're on the side that's winning.*

"We will need allies besides the Saxons to fight the Wilzi," Charles said. "My dear, do you think the Frisians might side with us?"

"They have sided with the Saxons before," Fastrada replied, "and they hate the Wilzi."

"So do the Obrodites and the Sorbs," Meginfrid said.

"Father," Karl said, "let me fight them. If I can beat the Saxons, I can beat the Wilzi."

She gave Charles a slight smile. They had discussed this the previous night. As she beheld Karl now, she still found it difficult to believe this sixteen-winter-old man was the same boy she greeted in the courtyard the day before her wedding. How had he gotten so tall, almost matching Charles? How had he gained those muscles?

Charles laid his hand on Karl's shoulder. "Son, it is time for our soldiers to see your prowess with a sword again."

Karl beamed. Pepin scowled. Fastrada suppressed the urge to shake her head. Just when she thought Pepin understood God's will was for him to succeed Angilram as the archbishop of Metz, he showed her he didn't. As his back stooped lower and lower over the years, how could he believe otherwise?

Patience, said a stern voice in her mind. She, too, was struggling to accept God's will. She had yet to make peace with her constant fatigue and chill—and her ambivalence about her empty womb.

Worms, October 789

Bored with the counts asking his father to bestow church lands on their children, Pepin leaned toward his uncle to comment. Gomeric elbowed Pepin and tilted his head toward the back of the crowd. Annoyed, Pepin looked in that direction and fell silent. A messenger from a Saxon kingdom in Britain, judging from the loose tunic. As the messenger crossed the great hall, the people nearby quieted and craned their necks. Pepin turned his head to better hear.

"Your Excellence." The messenger bowed. "I bear tidings from Offa, king of Mercia."

Karl's shoulders straightened. His father was negotiating a betrothal between Karl and a daughter of the most ruthless ruler in Britain.

"We and our queen will read the message in our apartment," his father said. "Karl, come with us."

Nantlind rushed ahead of them. After a slight nod from Gomeric, Pepin followed. His father and the Frankish army had been home for a month. It had taken only a few battles for the Wilzi to sue for peace, swear oaths of fidelity, and surrender hostages. Seeing Franks, Saxons, and Frisians on the same side must have terrified them. *Might be the last time that happens.*

When Pepin entered the reception room, Nantlind was stoking the embers under a fresh log. Fastrada took her seat near the fire while his father stood by a parchment-covered window to use the mid-morning light. Charles broke the seal with one swift stroke of his dagger and stretched the letter between his brawny hands. Karl stared at their father.

"What does Offa want?" Fastrada asked.

"The old Mercian seeks reassurance Karl will inherit." Charles chuckled. "And he points out that his son rules alongside him."

"Subtlety is not his strength."

Karl's eyes gleamed. "Does that mean I get to be more powerful than Little Pippin or Louis?"

Pepin clenched his teeth but watched his father and Fastrada. The queen gave Charles a troubled look. *Worried if you have a son, he'll get nothing? Or be told that he belongs to the Church? Not so pleasant, is it, she-wolf?*

"I am not so aged that I need to share the crown," Charles said.

Fastrada's shoulders relaxed.

"Karl," their father continued, "it means you will have a domain between the Seine and the Loire. That should satisfy Offa."

A lot more than the archbishopric you want me to accept, Father.

"What does the girl look like?" Karl blurted. "Did he say anything this time?"

Idiot. Why do you care if she's ugly? You can still have any woman you want. The maids won't stop lusting for you.

"He didn't," Charles said nonchalantly.

"You should care more about her dowry and the bride price," Fastrada added.

"Every father will say his daughter's fair," Pepin taunted. He fought the urge to laugh when Karl scowled at him.

"Exactly," Charles said. "Karl, you might like her when you meet her."

"It's my betrothal," Karl muttered. "I should have a fair bride."

Pepin's eyes bored into his brother. *At least, you will have a betrothed and be a true man. I want a wife, even if I have to put a sack over her head to sard her. I'm sick of whores who look at me as if I were vomit.*

***

As soon as Pepin left the royal apartment, Gomeric sidled up to him. "You've seen twenty years," he said in Latin, keeping his voice low. "The king ought to be arranging a marriage for you before your younger brother."

"Did you not hear?" Pepin grumbled in the same language. "I am destined for an archbishopric."

Gomeric glanced about. "Let us go to the palace chapel, where I can give you a letter. Not many people there right now, if any."

The chapel was empty. While Pepin's guards idled near the door, he and Gomeric approached a statue of Saint Ursula near one of the windows. The wooden floor echoed with their footsteps. Gomeric and Pepin knelt near the statue, letting it conceal their movements from the guards. Gomeric reached inside his cloak and produced a rolled parchment whose seal was already broken. Pepin did not recognize the pattern of lightning bolts.

Holding the letter close, Pepin gazed about the room. In the light from the clerestory windows and walnut oil lamps, he could clearly see the frescoes of the saints and their sacrifices, Saint Lawrence over the grill, Saint Sebastian with the arrows. His bored guards chatted with each other. If he and Gomeric kept their voices low, they remained out of earshot. Yet he would speak Latin.

"It's from Minerva, sister of Mars," Gomeric said.

Pepin unrolled the parchment. To his surprise, the writing was his mother's. *"Tonight I saw Jupiter and Saturn near each other, and I marveled at how Jupiter outshone Saturn. The astronomer says it bodes well. God has shown us the time is right to sow the seeds. May supernatural grace bless our harvest and keep you safe."*

Pepin stared at Saint Ursula's shoes, the parchment slack in his hands. "Has a fever addled Minerva's brain? Saturn's recent victories make him stronger."

"Those battles will do nothing to placate Tassilo's allies. They are angry over the war with the Avars." Gomeric's lips hardly moved.

"Why does Mars support someone who favored setting Minerva aside?"

"Mars did not argue on Tassilo's behalf until after Saturn set aside the Lombard and married a Swabian." His frown deepened. His voice dropped even more. "Tassilo and Mars have their hatred of Saturn in common. Jupiter hates him too."

A chill ran down Pepin's spine. It was as if Gomeric saw into his heart.

"Mars also supported the duke of Bavaria," Gomeric continued, "because Severinus supported him. We need his connections to make Jupiter king."

The words hung in the air with the smell of incense. Pepin closed his eyes and savored them. He could feel the weight of a gold, jeweled crown on his head and an iron sword at his hip, one of the new kinds that made the shorter seax unnecessary. Against his skin, he would have the finest linen, the smoothest silk leggings against his calves.

"It will be you on the throne with scepter and orb," Gomeric said. "It will be you with a beautiful woman at your side."

"What woman would accept a man with a stoop?"

"Wouldn't matter if Jupiter were king. The bride's father has already agreed."

"You've chosen someone for me?" Pepin felt a flush creeping into his cheeks.

"Severinus's daughter. Venus."

Pepin blinked back his surprise. Severinus had rarely spoken of the girl, whose real name was Richilde. She had never been to court. "How old is she? What does she look like?"

"She has seen fourteen years. Mercury says she is healthy and fair."

"All fathers say that." The flush spread down his neck. "Is Jupiter not to have a say in his own betrothal?"

"Marriage is too important to leave to a young man alone. If Jupiter does not like the bride, Mars and Minerva will find him another one."

"Is she pure?"

"We would never let Jupiter marry a slut."

Oh, to know a virgin, a woman who is mine alone. Pepin could feel her curves against his hands, her lips against his. Perhaps she could banish the demon taking Fastrada's shape and haunting his dreams. *But Father...* Pepin bowed his head.

"What is it?" Gomeric asked. "The girl is from a good family."

"Saturn would never consent to any marriage for Jupiter."

Gomeric buried his face in his hands, and his shoulders shook.

How odd for him to weep.

Finally, Gomeric raised his head. His eyes were dry and his lips twitched as if he was fighting the urge to smile. "What makes you think Saturn's consent is required?"

Pepin furrowed his brow, trying to comprehend.

"Did you think we were simply going to wait for Saturn to die?" Gomeric asked.

Pepin's jaw dropped. Did his ears deceive him? His pulse raced, becoming thunder throughout his body.

"It's a sin!" Pepin hissed.

"Saturn is the one who sinned," Gomeric said through clenched teeth. "His death will appease God, and He might heal your spine."

"If God is so angry at Saturn, why does He not strike him down?"

"Look at how God afflicts Ops. Is that not proof enough of His wrath?"

Pepin pondered Gomeric's words. Why else would Fastrada be so sick all the time?

"It's still treason." Pepin's voice was barely audible even to himself.

"Is it treason to save our people from wars that can be avoided? Is it treason to bring about justice long overdue? Jupiter is the rightful heir, and he can rule a united empire so strong Francia's enemies dare not attack."

"What of Jupiter's brothers?"

"Usurpers cannot be allowed to claim the throne and divide our people," Gomeric said calmly. "There are only two ways to ensure that."

Blinding or killing. They could not merely send his brothers to the cloister, the way his father did Tassilo. Pepin gaped at his uncle.

"Is it a sin to prevent our countrymen from slaying each other for the sake of three bastards?" Gomeric whispered.

After a moment, Pepin shook his head. "We would rid ourselves of the she-wolf, too."

"Ops is our greatest treasure, the very reason the people will support Jupiter as king." Gomeric smiled.

Pepin arched a brow.

"Mars and Minerva have written to friends about Ops's cruelty," Gomeric replied, "how she crippled the monk at Oppenheim, how she raided her own countrymen's winter stores on her journey to Eresburg, how she had her countrymen blinded."

Anyone who received his mother's and uncle's messages about Fastrada would gossip with merchants, who would gossip with other noble families. Those rumors would turn the people against the queen and his father.

"Now, hand me the letter so I can burn it," Gomeric said.

Grinning, Pepin obeyed.

Chapter Twenty-five

February 790, Worms

Fastrada awoke to stabbing pains in the right side of her face, as if an invisible hand were poking hot needles, worse than the burning and aching sensation for the past five days. The herbalist's advice to apply a paste of flour and lily juice and drink goat's milk had soothed the scorching but only for a short time. She touched her forehead and flinched. Yet she was shivering and wanted to sink farther under the furs and blankets and curl into a ball. A splash told her Charles was washing his face at a basin near the fire.

Must get ready for Mass. Clenching her teeth, she sat up. Still fatigued, she grasped the curtains and thrust them apart. In the light of the night candle and the fire, Nantlind awaited with her clothes. The maid gasped and rushed to her.

"What is it?" Fastrada asked.

"Let me help you dress. Then I will fetch a physician."

"No physician! All he will do is bleed me and make me even weaker." What had Nantlind seen? Fastrada dreaded the answer.

She stood unsteadily. Her maid helped her to the basin.

Charles turned toward her and winced. "Nantlind, fetch a physician, regardless of what your lady says."

Fastrada's eyes widened. Charles distrusted physicians more than she did. "All Nantlind needs to do is make me presentable for Mass."

"You will obey me."

Fastrada gaped at her husband, unable to believe he had just ordered her as if she were three winters old.

"My dear," he said, "it's for your own good."

"I won't let the idiot bleed me," she growled.

"Very well. But you will heed me otherwise."

"Yes, my lord."

She splashed water on her face. When she used the drying cloth, the pain seared. She bottled the scream in her throat.

With trembling hands, Nantlind helped her lady into her shift, underskirt, and gown. Fastrada hurriedly donned her cloak and gloves.

"Mirror," she said.

Nantlind hesitantly held up the polished brass. Beholding her reflection, Fastrada felt a wave of nausea. Welts covered the right side of her forehead, her eye, and part of her cheek.

"Pray for me," she whispered.

***

Fastrada clung to Charles through Mass. She was too tired and weak to stand without his support. The bitter willow bark tea she had drunk for two days banished the chills, but it churned her belly and did little for the pain. She had barely eaten or slept. If only she had enough strength to discuss history with Karl, encourage Gisela as she learned to stitch, or even watch Hruodhaid and Theodrada play with their dolls.

She should have listened to Charles and remained in the bedchamber instead of insisting on accompanying him to Mass. She had thought if God or the Blessed Virgin saw her in the palace chapel, He would heal her. She wished she could hide the welts with a veil but could not bear even its slight weight. Were the courtiers whispering about her face? About how gaunt she was?

"I'm sorry," she murmured to her husband.

He gave her a slight squeeze. "Do you still want to pray to the Virgin?"

"Yes." She tried not to whimper.

After the benediction, she leaned against Charles as they approached a painted wooden statue, vibrant in a blue gown and veil. She sank to her knees, wishing her face were as flawless as the Blessed Mother's. If not for Charles, she would have collapsed. He knelt beside her. Slumping, she grasped the foot of the statue and murmured, "*Ave Maria, gratia plena.*" *Why is He letting this happen to me? Help me, Mother of God.*

She made the sign of the cross and waited for Charles to finish the Paternoster. After he crossed himself, Charles placed her arm around the back of his neck and slid his other arm around her waist. He lifted her to her feet. She leaned the left side of her face against his chest and closed her eyes. Just for a moment.

***

Fastrada awoke to voices, her husband's and Meginfrid's, both low. She didn't know how much time had passed. She opened her eyes a crack and realized she was lying in her bed, fully clothed save her boots, headdress, and girdle. The bed curtains were shut, but she could smell strong wine. She heard Charles's heavy tread, pacing.

"We must do something, Meginfrid. She is terribly ill. She made not a sound when I picked her up—not like her at all. And she was so light, too light."

Oh Father in Heaven, had she swooned? In church? In front of everyone?

"My lord king, may I suggest a pilgrimage to Saint Goar's church? He has done great miracles. Hruodtrude can oversee the affairs of the household. She enjoys ordering everyone about."

"Just like my queen. I want that strong-willed woman restored to me."

I want to be restored to you too and to our children. Fastrada made a quick calculation. Saint Goar's church was twelve days north of Worms, with stops at Mainz and Ingelheim to rest the horses—twelve days alongside the Rhine through the forest, thick despite its bare branches and trunks. Twelve days if no cart broke a wheel and no sudden storm pelted them with snow and ice.

Faint scrapes of tables dragged across the great hall's floor stirred Fastrada from her thoughts. It must be midmorning. The laughter and gossip of dinner would begin soon. How she longed to be surrounded by gossiping guests, enjoying the aromas of roasted meat, fresh bread, and wine. How she longed to have an appetite. She was exhausted, yet she hurt too much to sleep.

She tried to raise herself, causing the cloth to rustle. The bed curtains parted, and Nantlind appeared.

"Don't overexert yourself, my lady queen," the maid said, helping Fastrada sit against the pillows. "I will fetch willow bark tea."

Meginfrid left as well. Her husband approached and sat on the edge of the bed.

"My dear, how do you fare?" His eyes, not as bright as usual, studied her face.

"When can we leave for our pilgrimage?" Her voice was just above a whisper.

Was that relief she saw on Charles's face? "Tomorrow, if we can. Pray for temperate weather."

Fastrada reached for her husband's hand. She was willing to try anything, even travel in winter.

The next morning greeted Fastrada and Charles with snow flurries. A dreary day, but at least, they could start their journey. In the courtyard, the cold air stung her lungs, and the frozen ground shot ice through her legs despite the two layers of leather on the soles of her boots. Bidding farewell to the children hurt as much as the blisters on her face. This was the first time in six years that she would be away from the girls. Chiltrude bawled while Theodrada and Hruodhaid sobbed. The others managed to keep their composure. On the verge of tears herself, Fastrada didn't rebuke her youngest daughters but instead whispered for them to be good.

"Hruodtrude," she said, "if any servant is stubborn, tell them they will answer to me."

Hruodtrude smiled. "We will be fine, Mother."

With Nantlind's help, Fastrada plodded toward the litter. After she and her maid entered the wooden box, Nantlind drew the blankets and furs over them. Through small square windows, Fastrada watched four burly menservants lift the box by its two long poles and affix it between a pair of waiting horses.

"I hate this," Fastrada muttered.

As the party started its journey, Fastrada leaned toward a window to gaze one last time at the children in the courtyard. All of them seemed worried, except for Pepin. His eyes gleamed like a hunter's after the kill.

***

Kneeling before the tomb of Saint Goar, Fastrada murmured another prayer and heard the same words from Charles's lips. Besides their guards, they were alone in the room specially built for pilgrims on the east side of the church, a way to control the crowds seeking miracles in spring and summer and allow the monks to have their prayers in the sanctuary on the other side of the wall. She gazed up at the stone box covered with a piece of silk whose embroidery showed a bearded saint in a simple robe, a hermit who wanted to refuse everything the world had to offer, even a bishopric. His desire was so great he prayed for God to excuse him and died of a fever. Would her and Charles's three days of prayers please him? Would the laden purses Charles had left on the altar in the sanctuary after prime Mass?

On the journey, the bumps on her face had swollen, but as she and Charles heard the Rhine's rapids near the Loreley on their approach to the monastery, some of the blisters burst. Her forehead and cheeks were now covered with scabs, but the pain remained. Fastrada touched the silk and felt some strength return. Again, she whispered the prayer. If the saint could not cure her, Fastrada hoped he would at least make her well enough to ride a horse into Worms. She dreaded her return to the litter later that morning.

After Charles helped her to her feet, Fastrada drew her cloak close.

"Have you noticed how strange the abbot is?" she said in a low voice.

Charles snorted. "Probably mortified by his horrid Latin. Even Theodrada speaks it better."

"His Latin is awful, but he's not the first churchman who can't tell *patria* from *pater*. He acts like he's terrified of me, like I'm a witch about to curse his grain stores with a plague of rats."

Charles shrugged. "The man's own shadow frightens him."

At first, Fastrada had dismissed the abbot's actions as timidity or embarrassment, but every time she entered a room he was in, his posture stiffened, his eyes grew wide, and he spoke too fast. What had he heard about her? Still pondering the monk's odd behavior, Fastrada took Charles's

167

proffered arm, more for affection than the need for his support. Even though they wore leather boots, their footsteps echoed as they left the chamber and stepped outside. The morning air was cool but held the promise of spring, even as Lent began and the villagers dined on more salted and pickled salmon.

Looking over her shoulder, Fastrada cast an appraising eye at the church. Charles's earlier donations had helped finish the large structure with square clerestory windows and make it a fitting home for a saint. Other monastery buildings, most of them wood, surrounded the edifice. She and Charles passed the novices' dormitory and kitchen to their right and rounded a corner. The hostel and kitchen for noble guests were more than a hundred paces ahead, beyond the abbot's residence and the school.

Near the abbot's house, a thought struck her. "Remember the story my brother told me about what I supposedly did to Lucas at Oppenheim?"

"So foolish." Charles shook his head. "Where do people get such idiocy?"

"I thought that, too, but maybe the abbot heard that lie. Perhaps I shouldn't have laughed it off."

Charles touched her arm with his free hand. "My dear, if you worried about every absurd tale our people hear, we would accomplish nothing. Pay it no heed."

Fastrada furrowed her brow and winced at the pain. Charles was right. She had heard so many rumors since becoming queen, and this one was silly beyond belief. To concern herself with it would only drain her vigor and distract her from much more important matters, like advising Charles about King Offa and preparing the palace for a visit from Avarian diplomats this spring. The lessons from the children's tutors, the nurses' care of the little girls, settling squabbles among the servants, and the needs of the guards all required her attention.

A few years ago, the abbot's fear would have amused her—she might have even fed it—but now it vexed her. He was a good host and a good man.

When she and Charles returned to their lodging, Fastrada told Nantlind to fetch beer, bread, and dried apples and bring them to the bedchamber upstairs. With her appetite returning, Fastrada realized she would be tired and weak if she waited until afternoon to eat, but she would not let the servants see her break her fast so early.

Her maid sighed with relief. "Saint Goar is healing you already."

After Fastrada finished her meal, she ordered the servants to pack, and Charles sent for the abbot, who arrived moments later. Out of breath, the round-faced man stopped shifting from foot to foot long enough to bow.

The abbot's words came in a rapid fire. "Is all well, my lord king, my lady queen?"

"Yes," Charles replied. "We thank you for your hospitality and will take our leave of you this morning. We ask for your continued prayers for God's grace for us, our queen, our children, and our people."

"As a token of our gratitude," Fastrada added, "we will send two pieces of silk, one of them an altar cloth embroidered by my own hand."

The abbot seemed about to faint.

Fastrada again puzzled over what terrified this man. She wondered if she should ask him about Brother Lucas but dismissed the idea. Charles was right. Such ridiculous tales did not merit her attention. Besides, he might have never heard of Lucas, and if the story enthralled him, he might spread it. The world did not need yet another lie.

March 790, Worms

Charles and Fastrada were both on horseback when they returned to Worms. Each day, Saint Goar had restored a little of her strength, and her rash was receding. She still felt some pain and could not abstain from meat without becoming ill. But the court would see she was not helpless, and she was grateful to Saint Goar for that. Nothing she could give to his church could ever repay him. Yet she resolved to start on the altar cloth as soon as she could and pay a silversmith to fashion a chalice and paten for altar bread.

The children gathered around Fastrada and Charles as soon as they dismounted. Her heart surged. Oh, how she had missed them. Most of them. She didn't dare tell Charles she had not missed Pepin's glowering, which greeted her now. Charles would dismiss her reaction to his eldest son as her humors. Why couldn't her husband see otherwise?

"Any tidings from King Offa?" Charles asked Meginfrid.

The chamberlain shook his head. Fastrada raised her eyebrows. Surely Offa would want to unite his house with her husband's. Offa's lands had rich farms and ports, but Mercia, like Northumbria and Kent, was one of several small kingdoms in Britain. Charles's realm stretched from the sea in the west to Thuringia and Bavaria in east, from Frisia in the north to the Pyrenees and almost to Rome in the south. Karl would inherit all but Aquitaine and Italy. *Could inherit all of it, if Charles's seed doesn't take hold,* Fastrada thought, laying a hand on her belly.

Word from Offa arrived weeks later, after the Feast of the Resurrection, with the return of Charles's envoy, the abbot of Saint Wandrille. Charles decided to hear the message in the royal apartment's reception room. He offered his arm to Fastrada and told Alcuin, Karl, and Hruodtrude to accompany them. Nantlind rushed toward the kitchen. Uninvited, Pepin followed the group.

Fastrada wondered about the envoy's unease. Perhaps Offa's bride price was high or his daughter's dowry low. But that could be negotiated. After all, ridiculous requests were all part of bargaining. No, this was more serious.

Once the door closed behind them, Charles ordered, "Tell me what Offa said."

"They, I mean, he ..."

"They?" Fastrada asked, taking her seat by the hearth.

"His queen is very strong willed." He cleared his throat. "King Offa would like the two families to be joined but not as Your Excellence proposed. He needs his two marriageable daughters free to wed neighboring kings. Nothing I said could sway him."

Fastrada crossed her arms. "How could a king on part of an island be half as good a husband as our Karl?"

Karl grinned. Pepin scowled. Alcuin, a native of Northumbria, straightened his spine.

"What does he want?" Charles asked. His tenor voice was even, but Fastrada felt an undercurrent of annoyance.

The envoy tugged at his dust-covered collar. "He wants Princess Bertha to marry his son, and ..."

Hruodtrude gasped. "Father, you can't! Offa is a brute! He's killing off all his kin except his heir!"

"Peace, Hruodtrude. So help me God and His Merciful Mother, no daughter of mine will live in Mercia." Charles's voice remained calm, his face impassive. Only the squaring of his shoulders betrayed his anger.

"Why was his daughter good enough for me?" Karl demanded.

"Karl!" Fastrada barked. "You don't speak to your father that way!"

Pepin smirked. Hruodtrude gazed at Karl with wide eyes.

Charles waved his hand dismissively at Karl. The prince's frown deepened.

"My son," Charles said, "the Mercian would have lived here, and you would be her lord. She could have studied in the Palace School and refined her ways."

Fastrada noticed Pepin looking at her with hooded eyes. *Trying to goad me, Pepin? I refuse to acknowledge your insolence.* Instead, she asked, "Why does Offa want Bertha as his daughter-by-marriage?"

"My lady queen," Alcuin said, "Offa is extending his realm to Kent. If his son were to marry a Frankish princess named Bertha, it would remind the Kentish people of one of the most powerful kings in Britain, also wed to a Frankish princess named Bertha."

The envoy cleared his throat. "Offa is asking for more. He wants Your Excellence to stop sheltering that upstart. He says he will close his ports if you refuse."

Fastrada frowned. The young man Offa called an upstart was a prince of Kent and the West Saxons in Britain. He had fled to Charles's court about a year ago, claiming distant family ties.

"The king of the Franks does not betray his guests, nor do we yield to threats from petty tyrants." Charles's voice remained steady. "If Offa closes his ports to our merchants, we will close ours to his."

"As I mentioned earlier, Your Excellence," Alcuin said, "Offa and your guest's enmity runs too deep for anyone to negotiate a peace. A dispute with Offa is the Devil's work. Closing the ports will cause scarcity at the Mercian monasteries."

"Whether the ports remain open is his decision," Charles said. "Closing them will hurt him more than us."

"But ..." Alcuin said.

Fastrada pounded the arm of her chair with the flat of her hand. "Enough about Offa! He is no threat to us. The Avars are, and their delegation will arrive in two weeks."

Alcuin scowled.

"Peace, my dear," Charles said. "Alcuin wants only to protect his friends and the churches, and we will help where we can. But you are right. There is nothing more to say about this matter."

"If I'm not going to marry the Mercian," Karl said with a note of eagerness, "can you negotiate with Severinus for the hand of his daughter? I hear she is a beauty."

Pepin's cheeks flushed, and his eyes bored into his brother's back.

Strange. Like Karl is stealing Pepin's betrothed. Pepin, you have seen twenty-one winters. Time to stop being jealous.

Chapter Twenty-six

May 790, Worms

When a guard informed Fastrada and Meginfrid of the Avars' arrival, she hastily inspected her gown and jewelry. The diamond ring and girdle glittered in the morning sunlight pouring through the great hall's windows. Her cross hung from a gold necklace and lay near the enameled bronze brooch with Saint Wigbert's image. Without being asked, Nantlind adjusted Fastrada's headdress and repinned it to her silk veil.

"You are resplendent, my lady queen," Meginfrid said.

Fastrada scanned the great hall, crowded with the guests for the spring assembly. Near the mural of Siegfried slaying the dragon, Charles was chatting with Severinus, accompanied by Richilde, his shapely daughter. Ever since the girl's arrival two days before, Pepin and Karl had sought her attention at every opportunity.

Clever move to bring her to court, Severinus. Now Karl won't stop pressing Charles to betroth her to him.

Fastrada shoved that thought aside for her more immediate concern: how the Avars would see the room, bright on sunny days like this. The shelves gleamed, the result of the servants' days of toil, and the hall smelled of the lemon balm and thyme strewn on the floor. She allowed herself a satisfied smile. Yes, her husband's wealth and power would impress and intimidate these foreign visitors and prove he was just as mighty as an Agilolfing in Bavaria. Once the palaces at Aachen and Ingelheim were finished, any visitor would tremble with awe.

Whispering about the Avars, she and Meginfrid strode toward the courtyard. At the entryway, Meginfrid marched ahead to announce her to their foreign guests, who bowed when she stepped outside. Surrounded by their Frankish and Bavarian escort, the ten Avars had dismounted from their armored steeds. The sturdy horses were the same height as most Frankish animals, about four palm-breadths shorter than Charles's Roman military horses. Even though the withers of the Avarian beasts only reached Fastrada's breastbone, they were majestic. Their bridles had gold discs where the nosebands met the cheekpieces, and feathers from golden browbands floated just above their broad, convex foreheads. And there were those iron objects hanging from the saddles, what Charles had called stirrups.

She turned her attention to the delegation. Meginfrid had described their plumed, conical helmets, the gorgets protecting their necks, and their armor of iron plates sewn onto cloth, overlapping in nine rows, but he had not prepared her for their peculiar appearance. With yellowish brown skin, they had dark, slightly slanted eyes and flat features. Black beards covered their cheeks and chins, and their long hair was plaited.

With the erect posture of men wary of an enemy, they looked like they were trying to hide their apprehension. Fastrada grinned. The Avars apparently feared the Franks enough to agree to a diplomatic visit rather than raid Bavarian lands and steal what they wanted. She needed to be a good hostess to aid her husband's efforts to avoid war.

"Welcome to the court of Charles, king of the Franks and the Lombards and patrician of Rome. We have excellent stables and grooms for your horses, and we invite you to our baths and our table." She could not resist adding, "You will be well protected here. As you noticed, the walls to this city are as thick as the length of a cart. The guards can see for leagues from the towers and are skilled with the bow and the sword. And once the ships being built on the riverbank are finished—you might have seen the hulls as you rode here—we will have superior defenses on the water."

The interpreter Charles employed, a Bavarian with a fair complexion and light brown hair, stifled a laugh before speaking to the Avars in a guttural tongue. Frowning, they said a few words in the same language.

"They thank you and accept your kind invitation, Queen Fastrada," said the interpreter.

As the Avars led their horses to the stables, Fastrada strolled toward the palace guards, who held their weapons for safekeeping. She took special note: sabers, lances, and of course, their flexible, strong bows of yew. *What they've used to pillage Christians.*

***

The apparel the Avars wore to dinner was nothing like Fastrada had seen. They had replaced their armor with calf-length coats that showed off laced leather boots. The noble Avars' belts had gold buckles shaped like a boar's head and were riveted with gold boar's heads to straps tipped with gold, complementing their gold rings, amulets, and S-shaped earrings.

"Gisela," Fastrada muttered, "don't stare."

"But Pepin is," she said too loudly.

Pepin looked away. Fastrada smiled. If only a nine-winter-old girl's observation could affect the gawking Franks and Bavarians so easily.

The midday feast passed with stories of hunting adventures from the Franks and the Avars, the only thing Fastrada could find common to the two peoples. Neither would dare speak of politics yet, and Avars had no books, let alone philosophers and scholars.

When the meal ended, the interpreter said the Avars wanted to present gifts. After servants cleared the tables and set the boards against the walls, Fastrada and Charles ascended to the dais, and the children and courtiers crowded around despite the warmth of the afternoon sun and many bodies. The Avarian envoys bowed and had their servants display an elaborate man's belt, yellow pottery formed like pouches with spout-shaped mouths, a woman's spiral finger-ring of bronze wire, a necklace with beads of melon and pumpkin seeds, and band-like bracelets. All of it showed fine craftsmanship, but Fastrada wanted to shake her head. She would rather have received a weanling of one of their horses. Neither she nor Charles would wear foreign garb or jewelry.

"We thank you for your gifts and will bestow a few of our own," Charles said.

Fastrada gestured for the palace servants to bring a platter made by Rhineland potters along with matching bowls and cups and a gold saltcellar and tiny spoons. The interpreter conveyed the envoys' appreciation.

"Tell us the reason for your errand," Charles said, his tone polite but stern. His question was a reminder for the court, as she and Charles had agreed the previous night.

An Avar with a scar across his nose and a regal bearing spoke in the guttural tongue. "We come to negotiate the border between our peoples," the interpreter translated.

"We welcome these discussions," Charles said, taking Fastrada's hand. "The River Ybbs makes a fine boundary."

Hearing the translation, the Avarian gave a curt shake of the head and said a few words to the interpreter. "The River Inn is better suited."

Fastrada exchanged a glance with her husband. All part of the game. "My lord king," she cried, "there are Christians east of the Inn. They have always been ruled by a Christian and deserve no less!"

Charles patted her hand, but the Avars frowned upon hearing the translation. Did they truly believe Charles would move the border that far west and give up Mondsee and Salzburg with its wealth of salt? Then again, this public part of the bargaining was for Frankish and Bavarian ears.

"They are Bavarian holdings," Charles said, "and will remain so. But surely we can find a river we can agree to."

Negotiations continued until vespers, when the Christians went to prayers. The evening meal was sedate. Perhaps the discussions had tired the

Avars as much as Fastrada, but she noticed they sat a little straighter when the meal ended and the musicians plucked on their zithers, blew a few notes through their flutes, and tapped on their drums. As soon as servants cleared the tables and stacked the boards, the musicians played a melody with driving rhythms, and the guests rose to dance.

Fastrada wished she were not too fatigued to join them. Instead, she remained on the bench. The Avars stood near the wall. In the torch light, they watched the pairs form a line and take three steps forward, three steps back, then three steps forward, with the men twirling the women. The hall soon filled with the pounding of feet against the floor. The Avars tapped their toes then offered their hands to maidservants, who looked to Fastrada. She nodded her permission.

Across the room, she spied Pepin and Karl moving toward Severinus's daughter from different directions. This time, Pepin reached her first and held out his arm. Richilde smiled and placed her pale, long-fingered hand on his elbow. Karl scowled as the two joined the dancers.

Fastrada sighed. *Why, Pepin? Just so you can vex your brother?*

Yet she was surprised by what she saw on his face. Instead of a smirk, he wore a look of joy, like a three-winter-old who had received his first wooden sword. Suddenly, Fastrada felt queasy. *Pepin is truly infatuated with her.*

✳✳✳

As the hounds' barks penetrated the great hall's stone walls the next morning, Fastrada wished Charles and his guests would leave the courtyard and go to the hunting grounds beyond the city bulwarks. Consoling three girls too little for the chase was difficult enough without the reminder of what they were missing—what she was missing. She longed to feel the wind on her face and thunder of hooves beneath her. She shook her head. No use in dwelling on what her body no longer allowed her to do.

"Not fair!" Hruodhaid bawled. "Why do my sisters get to go? I can ride a horse, too!"

"They're older and will stay back when they're told," Fastrada chided.

"I want hunt! I want hunt!" Chiltrude sobbed.

"My lady," Irma said, "stop crying, and Nurse will fetch you a tart."

Fastrada decided not to correct Irma this time. Now weaned, Chiltrude was under the care of the nurse who watched over Hruodhaid and Theodrada, and Irma was one of the queen's maids.

"I want tart! I want tart!" The child's tears were quickly drying.

"Chiltrude, daughter of Charles," Fastrada admonished, "Irma will not get you a tart unless you ask properly."

Her three-winter-old daughter gazed pleadingly. Fastrada crossed her arms and kept her expression stern.

"Nurse, may I have tart?" Chiltrude said in a soft voice.

Fastrada smiled. "Bring tarts for all of us."

Irma headed toward the kitchen.

"Why are you not on the hunt, Mother?" Theodrada asked.

"I lack the vigor." Fastrada hoped she kept the disappointment from her voice.

"But Saint Goar healed you," Hruodhaid persisted.

"He cured my fever, but it's God's will that I still have a malady." She regarded her daughters. Would she live to see them become women?

"Why is it God's will?" Theodrada asked.

A question I have asked many times. "It just is, Daughter."

"Is that why Pepin has a headache?" Hruodhaid asked. "Because God doesn't want him to hunt?"

"I don't know why he's ill. He seemed well last night."

"Why you not know, Mother?" Chiltrude asked.

"God does not always reveal His reasons."

"Why?" Chiltrude stomped her foot.

"Peace, child. It just is."

"Maybe Gomeric and Severinus will make him feel better," Hruodhaid said.

"Let us hope," Fastrada replied.

Pepin must have felt wretched to stay in his bedchamber while the dogs chorused outside. Just a month ago, he had tried to join a hunt when he could not stop coughing. Only his father's order had kept him inside. Gomeric and Severinus were kind to sit with Pepin now, although the prince's manservant did not need assistance. The sound of an opening door drew Fastrada from her thoughts. Pepin's servant emerged from the royal apartment, probably on an errand.

Finally, the barks from the courtyard faded. The hunting party must be traversing the streets of Worms and heading for the forest. Charles had reassured her the Avars had sworn by their swords that they would use their weapons only on a stag, and if the oaths were not strong enough to persuade them, the fact that Franks and Bavarians greatly outnumbered them would. Pepin's man still had not returned to his master. Odd for him to be away so long when the prince was ill. When the girls settled and started playing with their dolls, Fastrada looked for her sewing but couldn't find it.

"I must have left my needles and thread and the shirts Charles needs mended in the bedchamber," she said, rising.

Unbidden, Nantlind followed. They crossed the hall and entered the royal apartment's reception area, dim except for the glowing coals in the hearth. Not wishing to disturb Pepin, Fastrada stepped lightly through the corridor separating the master bedchamber from the children's. Outside the princes' room, she heard voices, all three impassioned. The thick wooden door muffled the words, but what little she could hear sounded like Latin.

Nantlind whispered, "Pepin doesn't seem sick at all."

"Strange." Then she heard Severinus say, "... *filia mea* ..." The rest of his words faded.

He's talking about his daughter. Did Pepin try to seduce the girl? He had seen twenty-two winters, enough to know what an angry count could do on the battlefield. How could Pepin be so selfish and put his father and brothers in such danger? Charles needed all the allies he could get, especially counts who formerly sided with Tassilo. Fastrada clenched her hands into fists to stop them from shaking.

"My lady, what troubles you?" Nantlind asked.

"Something to do with Richilde."

"Pepin seems to like her."

Surely, that wasn't a note of relief in Nantlind's voice, not when the stakes were so high. "I need to talk to Charles. Pepin might like her too much."

It took all of Fastrada's will not to march into that chamber and demand an explanation from Pepin. No, Charles needed to address this, outside of Severinus's presence. She stalked through the corridor and reception room and found Pepin's guards just outside the apartment door.

"You are not to let Lord Pepin be alone with any respectable woman, even if you must drag them apart," she said evenly. "Do not fear the prince's wrath. Fear mine if you fail."

***

Fastrada did her best to conceal her fury from the girls, but she almost pricked her thumb while making her stitches. She tried to tell herself what she had heard was unimportant, but would there be any other reason Severinus would speak of his daughter to Pepin?

At midday, Fastrada choked down her food. She would need her strength when she spoke to Charles. Afterward, she retreated to the archive to read past letters about the Avars. Anxious about Pepin's behavior, she could not concentrate. What if Gomeric could not talk sense into his nephew or placate Severinus? Would Pepin accuse Richilde of tempting him and make matters worse by citing Tertullian's calling women the doorway of the Devil, as he had during Palace School? Severinus wouldn't care, and Fastrada admitted she found no fault in the girl's manners. Richilde had been cordial and proper with both Pepin and Karl. Why could Pepin not be satisfied with the whores his uncle paid for? Judging by the guards' descriptions of fine wool and embroidered girdles, Fastrada surmised Gomeric did not scrimp.

In the late afternoon, Fastrada heard the hoofbeats of the returning party. She stashed the letters in a chest and strode through the manor, ordering maidservants to gather drying cloths and fill basins so the hunters could wash. She went to the royal bedchamber and waited. Soon she heard heavy footsteps, and Charles entered the room with Meginfrid. They were sweaty, and bits of soil and last fall's leaves clung to their skin and clothes. But they were beaming. Apparently, they had killed the stag, and any injuries were minor. She would need to ask the dog handlers about their charges.

Charles's smile faded. "What troubles you, my dear?"

"I must speak to you in private. Meginfrid, I can attend to my husband."

"Wait in the corridor," Charles said to the chamberlain.

As soon as Meginfrid left, Fastrada explained what she had heard when she passed by the princes' room and related her worries.

"That boy thinks with his rod," Charles muttered. "Do we need to concern ourselves with Karl, too?"

Karl was a different story. Courtiers had complained he was too close to a British Saxon man in his retinue, one of Alcuin's pupils, and she had felt relieved when his guards told her they had seen him with a harlot from time to time. "He hasn't threatened a noblewoman's chastity," she said. "How was he with Richilde during the hunt?"

"Boasting of his hunting prowess and showing her how to better hold her javelin, like any young man who wants a beautiful lady, but nothing unseemly. She might make a nice wife for Karl. I won't let Pepin set a torch to our relations with Severinus."

***

Pepin lay naked under the sheets, listening for his brother. When he, Gomeric, and Severinus had heard the party return from the hunt, Pepin had doffed his shirt, climbed into bed, and closed the curtains. Karl soon slammed the door open. *Good.*

"Uncle? What is that noise?" Pepin croaked.

Gomeric pulled back the curtain. "Prince Karl returning from the hunt. A good one judging by the look on his face. How do you fare, Nephew?"

As Gomeric had instructed, Pepin blinked as if the light through the window was too bright. "Better now. I would like to wash and get dressed. Is my man here?"

"Yes."

Pepin emerged from the bed. He spied Karl shedding sweat-soaked garments and handing them to his own manservant.

"Where is Lord Severinus?" Pepin asked.

"Gone to speak with his daughter."

Pepin walked haltingly toward his basin. Gomeric gave him an almost imperceptible nod. While he splashed water on his face and hair, Pepin mentally tried on tunics, leggings, and medallions, trying to decide which would be most appealing to Richilde. He could not compete with his taller, more muscular brother on comeliness, but he needed to show the lady he thought her worthy of his finest garments.

Suddenly, he heard his uncle say a little too loudly, "Lord Meginfrid, to what do we owe the pleasure?"

Pepin hadn't heard the scratch at the door. Karl's man must have admitted him. With his hands in the water, Pepin turned. The chamberlain still wore dirt-speckled hunting garb.

"His Excellence requests Pepin's presence in his chamber," said Meginfrid.

"What does my father wish to discuss?" Pepin asked. *And why is it so urgent you could not take time to wash and change clothes?*

Meginfrid's glance flicked to Gomeric and Karl, who were watching intently. "His Excellence will tell you when he sees you."

Pepin felt the blood drain from his face. *My father knows. It's over.*

"Lord Meginfrid," Gomeric said as if nothing were amiss, "as you can see, my nephew has just arisen after being ill all day and needs a moment to dress."

Pepin and Gomeric locked eyes, but neither could say anything, not even in Latin. Instead, Gomeric asked Karl about the hunt. Barely hearing his brother's boast, Pepin quickly dried himself and fumbled through his clothes. A splinter of pain formed above his right eye. Was he going to lose his throne, his servants, and his chance to lie with Richilde? Was there any way he and Gomeric could escape?

Once dressed, Pepin staggered toward Meginfrid. He could not move quickly or gracefully if he wanted to.

Gomeric strode to Pepin's side. "My nephew might need assistance. Of course, he refuses to ask. You know how stubborn young men are."

With a shrug, Meginfrid led them out of the room and toward Charles and Fastrada's bedchamber. *Say it was only a philosophical discussion.*

His father stood near the hearth, glowering into the embers. He had washed and wore fresh clothes. Beside him, Fastrada clasped her hands as if to stop herself from wringing them.

"Meginfrid," she said, "your man awaits you in your room."

Meginfrid bowed and left.

Pepin's knees buckled. He swayed on his feet.

"Gomeric, you may stay." Charles's voice became a growl, menacing as a boar hound's. "Son, I will say this once and only once. You are not to swive Richilde. Severinus is too important an ally."

Laughter rumbled in Pepin's belly. He clenched his fists and tried to hold it back, but the urge only grew and shook through his body. His relief gushed through his mouth, and he bent forward with the force.

"I fail to see the humor in endangering a lady's honor," Fastrada scolded.

"I-I'm laughing be-because ... it is so ... so ri-ridiculous."

"Show the queen respect," his father ordered.

Pepin could not stop laughing. Fastrada gaped at her husband.

Gomeric's shoulders relaxed, and he cleared his throat. "My lady queen, Pepin intends no insult. He is surprised you would think he threatened a maiden's virtue. He knows I would stop paying for his whores if he did."

Pepin wiped his face with his sleeve and managed what he hoped was a grave expression. "Richilde's chastity is safe with me."

"I heard Severinus say, '*Filia mea*,'" Fastrada said icily. "He sounded angry."

Pepin's mirth deserted him. *Insolent she-wolf! When I'm on the throne, you will be sealed in a barrel and drowned like a witch.*

"What did you do?" his father accused.

"Nothing," Pepin blurted. "Tell them, Uncle."

"Severinus was … wondering about the bride-price. He fears it will be too low."

That is true.

"What did you tell him?" Charles asked.

"Our family always makes fair offers," Pepin answered even though Gomeric had said those words.

A smile flickered on Gomeric's lips.

"So Severinus is not offended?" Fastrada asked.

"My lady queen, he is only bargaining for the best dowry and bride price," Gomeric soothed. "He knows where his best interest lies."

That too is true. Pepin added, "I swear by all that is holy I will do nothing to embitter Severinus."

Chapter Twenty-seven

egotiations with the Avars took four tedious weeks and drew Fastrada's attention away from Pepin. When her health allowed, she was with Charles, the Avars, and the interpreter in the archive, which was across the courtyard from the great hall. Because the room was stifling even to her, she had ordered the servants to open the windows during the day. Maps of Bavaria and Avaria lay on a large table, where Charles and the Avars discussed the border. Occasionally, Fastrada protested that the Avars wanted Christian lands, and Charles reassured her in a voice loud enough for the guards and any passerby to hear that he would never give up Mondsee and Salzburg. One ridiculous demand from the Avars prompted Charles to offer his arm to Fastrada and leave the room. Fastrada suspected the Avars, especially their scarred leader, were unimpressed, but the show was not for them. The Franks and Bavarians milling about the palace needed to witness their king walking away from a bad bargain. Even when the Avars were visibly annoyed, they stayed in the archive. None of their countrymen would see their performance if they stalked out, and Charles would remain unmoved.

Finally, Charles pounded his fist on the table and said the River Ens was the westernmost border he would agree to. "Your khagan can assent to or refuse my terms," he added. "We will not be moved."

Three days later, Charles's legates started their journey with the Avars to speak with the khagan. Fastrada had little hope the leader would accede to the boundary.

As soon as a guard reported the Avars had left the palace grounds, Charles held out his arm for Fastrada and summoned his magnates, Meginfrid, Karl, and Hruodtrude to the archive. Pepin followed like a shadow.

Fastrada had not forgotten his flirtation with Richilde. So far, Pepin's guards reported the prince and Richilde had chatted, often about philosophers and music, and the only time he touched her was to dance. *Pepin wants a girl for something other than swiving? Has a spirit taken over his body?*

Severinus seemed calm whenever he saw Pepin and Richilde together, but Pepin's attention to the girl infuriated Karl. Fastrada knew she and Charles would need to settle the matter between the brothers, but it had to wait. The Avars were a greater threat.

Again, men pored over the maps. Tracing their fingers over roads and rivers, Charles and his magnates discussed soldiers, routes, and supplies.

Charles pointed to the Danube, flowing through Bavaria and Avaria. "We must build more ships."

***

To offset the expense of constructing ships—the wages, travel, and lodging of the master builders and their craftsmen, the men to fell trees, and other workers to extract pitch—Fastrada discreetly sold some of the Avars' gifts: the man's belt Charles would never wear and the jewelry that would never grace her finger or neck. Saints be praised for high-born men and women fascinated with foreign goods.

Each day, Fastrada visited the tower, where she could watch the ships taking shape on the bank of the Rhine. Near partially-constructed boats lay a new skeleton of pine, about half as long as the great hall, and on its back, it looked like a flattened crescent. The shipbuilders were hewing the oaks into thin planks to bend into a narrow hull that curved out from the middle and curled up at each end. Soon, men would hammer iron nails to the overlapping boards.

At the height of the summer, Charles went ahead with his plan to sail the two warships already finished, the result of months of toil, and show their countrymen proof they could conquer the Avars. The dragon-shaped prows and fifteen shields of the oarsmen on each side of the galleys would impress anyone who beheld them, Frank or Avar.

The crowd gathered on the dock as Charles, Karl, and Pepin bade farewell to Fastrada and the princesses. Charles had allowed Pepin to accompany him, with a warning: if the princes quarreled, both would be sent back to Worms on mules normally used by clerics demonstrating their humility. The princes' penance for disobedience would forbid wine, meat, and baths.

"Pepin and Karl are men now," Charles had explained to her earlier, "and the people should see our entire family will defend them, by prayer and sword."

"If Karl and Pepin don't cover each other with bruises," Fastrada muttered.

"The threat of a public penance should be enough to deter them."

With only a few clouds, the day promised pleasant travel. Ducks and geese flew overhead, and about thirty paces upstream, grebes were diving for their dinner. Fastrada touched her enameled bronze brooch with Saint Wigbert's image, hoping for protection for Charles and his sons as they traveled downstream, surrounded by the forest and its innumerable greens on both sides of the river.

Chiltrude's sing-song voice drew her from her thoughts. "Why boats stink?"

"That's pitch," Bertha said.

Any other time, the smell would have annoyed Fastrada. That morning, it reassured her that the ooze and the rags to caulk the gaps would keep the vessels afloat. Hearing the girls chatter about the new, large ships, Fastrada envied them. She wished she could think only of their father's adventure on this vast water with its jewels of sunlight. She pressed her lips together, determined to hide her nervousness. The folk needed to see their queen was confident. But if the ships failed, Charles, Karl, Pepin, and the crews would likely die in the Rhine's swift current. Most of the men couldn't swim, and even Charles's and his sons' abilities would not save them.

"Nothing to worry about, my dear," Charles murmured in her ear. "We hired the best shipbuilders. Had you asked any more questions of them, they might have thought you their confessor."

"You and the boys will be in the abode of nixies," she said under her breath.

"That's why we have a fleece of a black lamb on each mast."

Across the river, Fastrada made out a stork gliding through the air and landing in a nest atop a broken poplar. Perhaps it was the omen she needed.

After kissing her husband, Fastrada watched him stride up the gangplank of one ship while Karl and Pepin boarded the other. The brothers eyed each other hostilely but did not say a word. All took their places under canopies in the back, protecting them from the sun. She held her breath while the men pulled up the anchor. The crews on both ships unfurled the square sails, mainly so the nearby crowd could admire them; the breeze was too slight to move the vessels. Soon, the oars moved to the beat of an unseen drum and the ships skimmed the water faster than a horse's trot. Fastrada slowly exhaled.

With God's help, once the Avars learned the ships were afloat, they would stop dithering and accept Charles's offer.

***

When the estate of Oppenheim came into view at midday, Pepin marveled at the boats' speed. On a journey by land, they would still be in the forest. He had heard about how fast good warships could travel but had not believed it, especially when he thought about the lumbering barges. The oarsmen had slowed to half their pace once the dock at Worms was out of sight, and the captain let the sail and downstream current carry the vessel whenever the wind was strong enough. Now the drumbeat for the oarsmen quickened. In the distance, two figures on the dock rushed toward the fields and buildings.

Saints be praised, Pepin would not need to sit beside Karl much longer. He and his younger brother spoke little to each other. *Richilde likes me better.*

He was glad to have followed Gomeric's advice to talk to her about philosophers and encourage her in her studies. She laughed at Pepin's jokes and seemed to enjoy speaking with him. She politely listened to Karl, but how many hunting and battle stories could the girl bear? Pepin and Richilde's wedding night could not come soon enough. How he longed to hold that body close to his. Unfortunately, the succubus knew it, too, and assumed Richilde's shape in his dreams.

Two blasts of the captain's hunting horn drew Pepin from his thoughts. Oppenheim's inhabitants were gathering near a small dock. Pepin could see a moment of wide eyes and dropped jaws. Then, the servants and tenants were speaking all at once.

After the boats were anchored alongside the docks, the captain again blew his horn and bellowed, "Make way for Lord King Charles and his sons, Lords Pepin and Karl."

Pepin's father descended the gangplank to an ovation. The greeting was polite for Pepin, but to his chagrin, it became louder when Karl followed. Behind them, an oarsman bore a bundle. Pepin guessed it was the silver cup Fastrada had chosen as a gift for their host at Oppenheim. When they reached the bank, the steward bowed and invited the visitors to his table.

"We thank you for your hospitality," Charles said, his tenor carrying through the crowd. He gestured to the warships. "Are they not magnificent? Would a Byzantine or Roman not be awestruck?"

The crowd clapped and shouted.

"Take pride in them, my fellow Franks. They were built by our finest craftsmen, who are constructing more at this moment. These vessels are strong and swift. At sunrise, we were in Worms. At sunset, we will be in Mainz."

Pepin heard many exclamations of amazement, and he tried to contain his own wonder that a journey of two full days by land could be done so quickly.

"If our negotiations with the Avars fail," his father continued, "they will see and feel our might. We will fight to protect our realm, and we will win."

He paused, allowing the waves of applause to roll over him.

"The Avars have an enormous empire and fearsome men," Charles said, "but God has graced us with the best warriors and the best weapons. With the Good Lord's help, they are no match for us."

A frenzy of cheers erupted from the crowd. Pepin kept a smile pasted on his face, but a weight sank in his chest. To these people, his father might as well be Siegfried. How could he ever hope to overthrow him?

Worms, November 790

Even before the Frankish envoys spoke, Pepin could tell they bore grim news from Avaria. Their words only confirmed it: the khagan insisted that the border be the River Inn rather than the Ens farther to the east. Fastrada sat up straight and clenched the arms of her chair, her knuckles white.

His father's nostrils flared. "Unacceptable."

War! Pepin's throat went dry. If he tried to topple his father now, he would be more loathsome than the fiend who slew Siegfried.

After vespers prayers in the chapel that evening, Pepin placed five coins in a cross pattern on the altar, a signal for Gomeric to speak with him later. A few days before, his uncle had returned from settling affairs on his lands in Maastricht and securing money from Pepin's mother in Nivelles.

When Pepin returned to the chapel for compline, he saw Gomeric. Pepin's pulse drummed in his ears. He was about to disappoint his uncle and mother. Still, he wished the priest would hurry through his chants so Pepin could be done with it. As the Mass ended, Pepin knelt near a statue of the Virgin. Gomeric was soon beside him. Pepin listened to the cleric's footsteps shuffle toward the door. Only when the chapel became silent did he risk a glance at their surroundings. The chapel, lit only by the candles on the altar, was empty, save for his guards waiting near the entrance.

In the cadence of a prayer, Pepin whispered in Latin, "Jupiter is between Taurus and Aries. It's a bad omen."

"What foolishness is this?" Gomeric answered in a low voice as if he too were reciting a prayer. "Is Venus not bright enough?"

"When Venus shines in the morning sky, her beauty rivals the sun."

"Then Jupiter wants her."

Pepin nodded. "But he could never lead an army against the Trojans."

"Jupiter doesn't need to. Mars will be his mayor of the palace."

Pepin sucked in air through his teeth. His great-grandfather Charles the Hammer, the hero who defeated the Saracens, had been mayor of the palace. He had been the true commander of the armies, more powerful than his king, and Grandfather Pepin and his brother had succeeded him as mayors before they seized the throne. There had been no mayors since.

"Jupiter will still rule the skies," Gomeric said. "Remember, a people's strength does not depend upon one man. Saturn would be nothing without his magnates."

"Our people don't see it that way. All along the Rhine, the Main, and the Saale, they welcomed him as their champion."

"Then his death must look like an accident."

Chapter Twenty-eight

December 790, Worms

Fastrada woke to Charles shaking her shoulder, calling her name. She smelled burning pitch, stronger than a torch. Smoke scratched her throat. She opened her eyes a crack, and her heart raced. Instead of the faint glow of a night candle, a bright orange light penetrated the crack in the bed curtains.

On the second day of her courses, Fastrada's arms and legs felt as if they were made of lead. Charles grasped the curtains and forced them apart. She winced at the heat. Flames engulfed the door and ate at the wall around it. The maids were stirring.

"Fire! Fire!" Charles shouted. "Awake! Awake! To the window!"

"The children!" Fastrada gasped.

The maids coughed and gagged. Charles leapt from the bed. Unable to move, Fastrada stared at the door as if she could will the flames to stop. A moment later, a metal bar clanged against the floor, followed by slams of wooden shutters flung open. Frigid air rushed in to her right. Heavy footsteps shook the floor. Charles's arms encircled Fastrada in a blanket and bear pelt and swept her off the bed.

"Nantlind! Irma! To the window! Now!" Charles yelled.

The maids dashed to the opening and bounded to the ground an arm's length below. In a few strides, Charles carried Fastrada across the room and passed her to the maids' arms. The wind struck Fastrada's face and forced its ice into her lungs. Nantlind and Irma dragged her several steps into the interior courtyard. Too ill to stand, Fastrada sank to her knees in the snow. Charles jumped out the window, threw on a shirt he had seized, and sprinted in the direction of the girls' room faster than Fastrada had ever seen him move.

Nantlind dug into a pouch at her belt and pressed three objects into Fastrada's hand. The maid met Irma's eyes. "Don't let her follow me."

In the light of a full moon, Nantlind lifted her skirts and sped across the courtyard, through an archway, and around the corner toward the princesses' bedchamber. Fastrada struggled against her own body and Irma's hold.

"My babies!" she cried. "Oh, Mother of God, save my babies!"

Irma did not loosen her grip on Fastrada.

She tried to rise. Her limbs lacked the strength. "Why did God make me so weak and useless?" she moaned.

Maidservants hurled themselves outside.

With quick strokes, Fastrada wiped her tears. How dare she indulge in self-pity! She pointed to the maids as she spoke, "You two, go to the barracks and get the guards to help my husband. You two, go to the great hall, and you two, to the guest chambers.

"The rest of us will pray here." She aimed for an imperious pitch, but her voice sounded frail even to her ears. "We are not leaving this spot until we know our children are safe."

The women rushed to do Fastrada's bidding. The longest distance was the barracks, several cart-lengths away. Soon she heard pounding on doors to the great hall and shouts of alarm.

The maids who stayed with her exchanged worried looks. Realizing she still held the objects Nantlind had given, Fastrada looked down. In her hand were the brooch of Saint Wigbert, a cross, and the diamond ring from Charles. Nantlind must have grabbed them from the small table near the bed.

From the corner of her eye, she saw Irma kick off her wooden-soled shoes. "Take them, I beg you," Irma said in a low voice. "I am better dressed than you right now."

Like the other maids, Irma had slept fully clothed while Fastrada and Charles had lain naked under blankets and furs. Fastrada did not resist as Irma slipped the shoes onto her feet. "I personally will reward you," she whispered. She put on the ring and the cross and pinned the brooch to the blanket.

Behind her, Fastrada heard rapid footsteps, many of them, on the snow-covered ground. Menservants gathered around them.

"Go to the royal children's bedchambers!" Fastrada ordered.

Staring in the direction the men took, Fastrada used what little vigor she had to stave off a collapse. She whispered, "*Ave Maria, gratia plena*," between shaky breaths, over and over. With more fervor than she had ever felt, she promised to leave generous alms.

She did not know how much time had passed when figures appeared in the archway. Soon she made out Bertha, wrapped in a blanket, holding Theodrada's hand.

"Come to Mother!" Fastrada's tears fell unchecked. For once, she didn't care.

She saw Gisela and Chiltrude, then Hruodtrude and Hruodhaid, each wearing not much more than a blanket or cloak. Nurses and maids followed.

"Over here!"

Fastrada touched each of the girls, all unharmed. Sobs wracked her body. *Thank you, Mother Mary.*

"Mother," Hruodtrude said, "are you well?"

"You're well. That's all that matters. Where are your father and brothers? Have you seen Nantlind?"

"Father said he was going to get Karl and Pepin. He commanded us to find you and take you to the bishop's residence."

"What about Nantlind?"

"She woke us up," Bertha said. "I heard her shouting at the nurses when I went out the window."

"I think she was with the king," the little girls' nurse said.

Again, Fastrada heard rapid footsteps and turned toward the sound. Guards, several of them with buckets, long-handled hooks, mats to smother flames, and axes, ran toward them.

Before Fastrada could speak, Hruodtrude barked out orders, her finger sweeping over groups of men. "You help us to the bishop's residence. You assist the king in the princes' chamber and put out the fire. The rest of you salvage what you can from the treasury and archive."

As the men rushed to do Hruodtrude's bidding, Fastrada heard Pepin's voice, winded. "I was in the privies. Where are Father and Karl? Where's Nantlind?"

"Your chamber." Fastrada hated the weariness in her voice.

"I'm going there."

"Father ordered all of us out!" Hruodtrude cried.

"Because you are girls and would get in the way. A man rescues people. My lady queen, please take my sisters to the bishop's residence. They need to get out of the cold."

Fastrada nodded to acknowledge she heard him. Pepin told a manservant to run ahead and advise the bishop, then hurried away. *God keep you safe.*

She did not want to leave. But her daughters were shivering, and her own fingers and toes ached with the cold.

"The girls need their mother," Irma said in an undertone. "Nantlind would want you inside."

Pepin and Irma were right. Fastrada needed to do something useful. Irma and another maid helped her rise and held her upright. Her knees buckled. She staggered forward. The snow barely covered her feet, but it might as well have been to her waist. When she was well, the bishop's residence took a few minutes by foot. At that moment, it seemed leagues away.

"Guard, carry the queen to the bishop's residence." Hruodtrude gave Fastrada a pleading look.

"I will humor you, Daughter."

The burly guard bore Fastrada easily. No one said a word as they crossed the courtyard. Even the little girls did not whine or whimper. *Too scared to cry.*

***

Fastrada awoke to Hruodtrude's urgent whisper. "Father is downstairs."

She opened her eyes, but she could not comprehend her surroundings. She was on a stool leaning against a bed in a strange room, its darkness broken by the light of a hearth and a night candle. Hruodtrude's stricken look and undyed brown dress shook Fastrada from her fog. The fire. It hadn't been a dream. She was in the bishop's solar. She remembered the bishop offering his bedchamber, Hruodtrude pleading with her to retire with the four youngest children but allow the two eldest girls to watch for their father. Fastrada had ascended to the solar to watch over her frightened little girls until they fell asleep. Son of a whore's sow, she had nodded off. Her body had failed her again.

"How is your father?" Fastrada asked. "How are Karl and Pepin?"

"Father and Pepin are well. Karl—" Hruodtrude burst into tears.

A stone sank in Fastrada's belly. She forced the words through her mouth. "Is Karl injured?"

"He's near death!" Hruodtrude bawled.

Fastrada's throat constricted, trapping her voice. After a few breaths, she managed, "Tell your father I will join him soon."

The young woman nodded and wiped her face before descending the stairs twenty paces away.

"Clothes," Fastrada ordered.

"You saw what Hruodtrude is wearing." Exhaustion reduced Irma to a mumble. "The bishop's housekeeper said it was the best she could find."

"It will do. Anything about Nantlind?"

Irma shook her head.

Fastrada's heart raced. "After you help me down the stairs, get a physician and seek out Nantlind. She would have come here by now. She must be hurt."

The maid helped Fastrada into a man's shirt and pulled an undyed woman's gown over it, then tried to slip wood-soled shoes over Fastrada's feet.

Fastrada stepped back. "You need them."

Irma stood, hands on her hips. "The queen of the Franks cannot be barefoot."

"I will not have anyone say the king of the Franks cannot afford shoes for his servants."

"My lady queen, your husband will beat me if he sees you unshod. I will borrow a pair from one of the bishop's maids. I promise."

"Very well."

Fastrada wanted to run down the stairs, across the great hall, and into Charles's arms, but she could only proceed step by clunking step, with Irma at her side to support her. The smell of burning pitch from the torches set the hairs on the back of her neck on end.

After her descent, Fastrada beheld Charles, Pepin, Hruodtrude, and Bertha silhouetted against the light from the hearth, kneeling over a figure in a cot.

Karl. If not for Irma, Fastrada would have collapsed. Turning away from the maid, she wept soundlessly. She could not disturb Charles or let anyone else hear the wails she wanted to let loose. Closing her fists so tight her nails dug into her flesh, she stared at the ceiling, teeth clenched to stop the scream thrusting from the bottom of her belly, the shriek to God, *How could You let this happen?*

Gathering what vitality she had, she wiped her tears, mouthed her thanks to Irma, and staggered toward Charles. He looked up and leapt to his feet. A moment later, she was in his embrace. "My dearling," he murmured.

Even with borrowed clothes stretched across his shoulders, he reeked of smoke and yarrow and wine to wash burns, but Fastrada held him fiercely. How she needed him, his solid frame, his strong arms.

"Charles ..." she began, resisting the urge to sob.

"I am well, just a few burns on my arms and legs."

With a nod, she dismissed Irma to her errand, then approached the cot. Karl slept under a blanket as if given a sleeping draught. He, too, smelled of the wine and yarrow, and bandages covered his hands, arms, and chest. His left arm was in a splint, and so were two of his fingers.

"His leg is broken, too." Charles's eyes misted. "If only I'd gotten to him sooner. The smoke was so thick, I couldn't see anything, couldn't hear anything but the wind and the roar of the flames and the crashes from the roof planks falling to the floor. I was crawling, searching the floor with my hands, calling for Karl and Pepin. Then, I heard a thump. I made my way toward the sound as fast as I could and found Karl. I had to drag him away. He couldn't move himself at all."

"What does the physician say?"

"To pray. It's in God's hands."

Standing across from her, Pepin looked away. "I ... I tried to get Nantlind, my lady queen."

"You should not have sent Pepin back into the apartment," Charles scolded. "If Gomeric hadn't restrained him ..."

"I told you," Pepin snapped, "she didn't order me! I ... it was a favor to the queen."

Charles locked eyes with Fastrada. "You did nothing to stop him."

"Why would I? You and Karl were in there. You needed help." Fastrada's tone was colder than snow.

"From him?"

"I'm not a cripple," Pepin said sharply.

"You were endangering yourself for a servant," Charles retorted, "and calling Gomeric every profane word in Frankish and Latin. It was embarrassing."

Fastrada could not stop the pounding in her ears and could barely see, but she chose her words carefully. "Pepin, thank you for your bravery. Nantlind is more than a servant to me."

***

Fastrada ran through a dark maze of heat and smoke, calling for Nantlind. A woman was sobbing. With a gasp, Fastrada opened her eyes. Her heart raced. She was in a curtained bed. Now she remembered. Downstairs, she had tried to pray over Karl, but her body was too weak to resist sleep. Without a word, Charles had helped her to her feet and to the solar, then carried her to the bed.

Now awake, she labored to push back the blankets and furs and opened the bed curtains. In the gray morning light, Irma held the edge of a small table for support. "Nantlind," Irma whimpered.

A wail escaped Fastrada's lips. She doubled over, trying to suppress the pain that had wrapped its fingers around her heart. How could God take away the kindest, most loyal woman she'd ever known?

Time seemed to freeze in an icy blackness. Finally, Fastrada choked out, "Has a priest said prayers over her?"

"Yes." Irma shuddered as if she was again seeing the body. After a moment, she continued, "The physician said, 'Fetch a priest. There is nothing I can do for her body.' I went to Father Mathis."

The tightness in Fastrada's throat relaxed a little. No matter what he beheld, Father Mathis would presume Nantlind was alive and able to confess her sins silently to God and receive final unction until he felt her throat. At least, Nantlind's soul had a chance in those moments.

"Where is she?" Fastrada asked.

"In the bathhouse. I will wash her myself before we take her to the cathedral."

Fastrada wanted to bury herself under the bedclothes and curl into a ball. But right now, Nantlind needed her as mistress and queen. "Fetch me the finest piece of linen for Nantlind's shroud so I can embroider it. Tell the carpenters they are to build Nantlind her own coffin, and send word to the bishop that I will pay for a Mass to be said for her."

If she could not keep Nantlind in this life, Fastrada would keep her out of Purgatory in the next. And if the courtiers complained she was extravagant with a servant, let them.

Chapter Twenty-nine

Near midday, Pepin was kneeling beside Karl's cot, wondering how much longer he should pretend to pray. His brother had not stirred for most of the night, probably the effect of the hemlock Pepin had tricked him into drinking. When Karl had started to moan, the physician had given his patient a potion with poppy to put him into a stupor. Might Karl's injuries complete what the poison had started? If Karl recovered, what would he remember? Pepin had been careful to make it look like they were sharing a strong spiced wine.

A heavy tread in the bishop's great hall caught Pepin's attention. His father approached, shoulders slumped. About an hour ago, Irma had whispered to him, and he had run upstairs. Now his father's face was drawn. *Is the she-wolf dead?*

Across from Pepin, Hruodtrude rested her hand on the bishop's golden purse-shaped portable reliquary containing dust from the tombs of Saints Boniface and Lioba, among other tiny relics. "What's wrong, Father?"

"Nantlind's body was found. Your mother is heartbroken."

"Fie," Pepin muttered, feeling the heat of a flush spread through his face. Again, he was outside, pinned to the snowy ground where his uncle had tackled him. He had bruises from where Gomeric's fingers had pressed against his arms.

"I will pray for her," Pepin said, rising.

His leather-shod feet crunched against the dried thyme and mint on the floor as he crossed the hall and strode out the door, followed by his guards. He touched the pouch at his belt and felt the edges of the coins his father had given him that morning. Menservants had salvaged most of the treasury and the archives.

Although the day was cloudy, Pepin squinted against the glare from the snow and tried to hurry for shelter from the wind. Once he passed the walls surrounding the cathedral, he was forced to slow his pace. Many worshipers from sunrise Mass had trampled the snow into a surface as hard and slick as ice. Carefully, he ascended the sandstone steps and entered through the double doors.

He had expected the sanctuary to smell of incense and be nearly empty, save for a few priests. Instead, it was crowded, even more than at sunrise, and a little warmer than usual, and the worshippers blocked his view of frescoes of saints in the low-ceilinged windowless aisles to the left and right. Because the sext Mass had already started, Pepin stood in the back, shifting from foot to foot through the Latin chants. In the light from the large, square upper windows, he watched the priest celebrate the Mass.

In front of him, two women wearing sheepskin cloaks spoke in low voices. Pepin had heard bored peasants gossip through the Mass before.

"I tell you it was a plot," said the shorter of the two.

Pepin stopped his fidgeting and leaned forward. The back of his neck prickled.

"Fires happen all the time," said the taller one. "A coal must've fallen onto the strewing herbs."

"Then why could my brother not find the guards to the royal apartment?" Her companion gasped.

God curse gossiping servants.

"He was sleeping in the great hall and heard women shouting and pounding on the door," the servant's sister continued. "He said the smell of smoke was stronger than normal, but he first thought it was a dream. When the noise didn't stop, he arose. He saw the royal apartment was afire. There were no guards. None."

Because they were drugged. Gomeric and his men had dragged their bodies into the shadows.

"Maybe the cowards fled," the second woman said.

The first woman shook her head. "Not these men. They have proven themselves in battle. There's an assassin."

"Who would hire someone to kill the king?"

"One of Tassilo's allies, I bet you. You don't unseat an Agilolfing without paying a price."

I'm going to hell, the gallows, or both!

After the benediction, Pepin rushed to the altar at the curved end of the center aisle and placed a handful of silver coins on the imported marble slab. "May your soul repose in peace, Nantlind," he whispered, his eyes misting. "You were the first maiden to look at me like I was a human being."

He strode toward the gold reliquary for Saint Sencia in the aisle to his left. Kneeling before her, he prayed the Paternoster over and over and over, even as the wooden floor shot pain through his knees, even as the words lost their meaning. In the crowded church, he overheard the talk about the people who had died: an eleven-year-old serving girl, a seventeen-year-old guard, a weak-minded but sweet-tempered manservant. Men were still looking for the dead and wounded.

Pepin wanted to blurt out how one of Gomeric's men had given a sleeping draught to the three guards outside the royal apartment. Hearing a triple tap on the door, Pepin had admitted Gomeric and his henchmen and their dry kindling and pitch. He ached to confess and pledge that when he was king, he would give land to the Church as penance.

Where was that priest his mother had promised? *He said he had a dream of Saint Boniface commanding him to travel to Worms posthaste. I gave him the abbey's best mule and an escort of guards. You must show this holy man your finest hospitality.*

When Pepin had read those words a week ago, he had taken courage to go through with Gomeric's plan, timed for when Fastrada took to her bed. Now, he wondered if the slow strangulation of hanging was worse than this burden on his soul. He needed to talk to Gomeric, but there were so many priests and mourners.

Between nones and vespers, menservants brought two coffins and placed them on metal stands before the altar. One of the coffins smelled of new oak. Pepin turned away and pressed his fist to his mouth to stifle his lament.

For three days, Pepin placed coins on the altar in a cross and spent all day at the cathedral, leaving only to sip water or answer the call of nature. When he wandered into the bishop's residence in the evening, clothes wrinkled, face unshaven, the aromas of fish and bread from the table churned his belly. When he overheard more bodies were found in the rubble, he sweated, despite the cold. Even though Pepin wanted to go to compline prayers, his father ordered him to rest. But all he could see was Nantlind's coffin.

The church was finally empty after vespers on the fourth day, and Pepin saw Gomeric kneel beside him.

"Nephew," Gomeric said too loudly, "you must eat. God surely has seen how you've given alms and fasted and prayed for your brother."

"Do you feel nothing?" Pepin spat. "Fifteen innocents died in that fire."

Gomeric switched to Latin and pitched his voice like a prayer. "Innocents die in war. When Troy fell, women and children were slaughtered with the warriors."

"What about my soul?"

"Many have sins to confess. Minerva's servant will come."

Pepin withstood the urge to glare at his uncle. "The peasants won't stop talking about conspiracy."

"Commoners make up stories out of ignorance," Gomeric said calmly. "It was a tragic accident."

Our original story.

"God's Merciful Mother heard your prayers for the queen," Gomeric said in Frankish. "She attended Mass this morning. You can end your fast."

Pale and gaunt, Fastrada had staggered into the church, looking as if she would fall any moment.

"Saturn is still in the sky," Pepin muttered in Latin.

"Plans don't always come to pass, but we still have cause to rejoice. Saturn's son and Ops are wounded."

"At too high a price. I could have saved that maid!"

"Is that what this is about? A maid?"

"Mars will never again hold Jupiter back when he can be a hero! The people would have loved him. God might have healed ..." Realizing his words were not intoned like a prayer, Pepin snuck a glance over his bent shoulder. His guards stood by the door.

"It is good fortune Mars and Jupiter were both near Pisces," his uncle said.

So he was watching me.

Gomeric continued, "Ulysses's men would not let their master swim to the sirens. Would a man do any less for his sister's son?"

Pepin fumed. After a few moments of silence, Gomeric rose, grabbed Pepin's bruised arm, and tried to hoist him to his feet. Pepin flinched and resisted.

"Stop this nonsense," Gomeric growled in Latin. "Jupiter has suffered enough for the siren. If he wants Venus ... get up."

Pepin stood and yanked his arm from Gomeric's grasp. He strode to the altar and left a few more coins. Staring right at his uncle, he said in Latin, "Alms for Nantlind's soul."

Chapter Thirty

February 791, Worms

Fastrada eyed the abbot of Kremsmünster standing in the church's scriptorium, a small, square room adjacent to the entrance. At more than forty winters, the Bavarian had a graying tonsure that looked like it was caused more by age than a razor. His only adornment was a silver cross, yet he wore a sable-fur lined cloak over his robes. *Tassilo must have been generous indeed.*

The duke had given the property near the River Krems to the Church fourteen years ago and appointed this nobleman as its abbot. No one but an ally would receive such prime land, strategic to the Mur valley.

Was the abbot of Kremsmünster trying to restore his former patron? Was the fire part of an Avarian plot to kill Charles and force the Franks to withdraw from Bavaria?

Charles had agreed with Gomeric and Pepin that a conspiracy was nothing but peasants' babble. Fastrada could not think of anyone in the palace capable of such a thing, but she did interrogate the prefect of Worms about his household. He had responded with a baffled look and stammered that his servants did not know where Avaria was, let alone spy for its ruler.

The fire could have been an accident, Fastrada reasoned, but talk of the absent guards troubled her. They were loyal men who would have braved flames to rescue the royal family. Had treachery lured them from their post? If only they had survived.

The abbot probably had nothing to do with the conflagration, but she and Charles did not trust him. Charles had let him know that when he helped Fastrada to a chair and invited Pepin, Karl, and Hruodtrude to sit on stools. The clerk holding wax tablets and the abbot remained on their feet. The

Bavarian's eyes flitted around the room and its books and letters, like a prisoner looking for an escape. *Good. Let Tassilo's lackey be ill at ease.*

She watched Karl set aside his crutch and slowly sink onto his seat. His lips drew a taut line, but he did not show his usual grimace. God had answered her prayers and Charles's. Karl's burns had healed and left only a few scars under his clothes, but Karl had struggled through the last two months. Even when his limbs were swollen, he wanted to be free of his splints. His bones had mended but his muscles were weak with disuse, and he kept trying to walk without his crutch or a manservant's assistance. Many times, she had seen him baring clenched teeth as if to fight back a scream.

Shivering, Fastrada drew her cloak closer and hoped Irma would arrive soon with mulled wine. She missed the royal apartment's reception room and its hearth. The bronze brazier and its glowing coals were a poor substitute.

"Abbot, tell us the cause of your errand," Charles said with his usual calm.

With beads of sweat on his forehead, the Bavarian reached into his cloak, produced a rolled parchment, and handed it to Charles. "I've come to confirm the donation of land for my abbey."

Charles unrolled the document and scanned it. "A gift from a traitor is useless."

"Our monastery has been steadfast to our king," the abbot blurted. "How could we not support a monarch who brings the light of the True Faith to people who live in darkness?"

"If an army of many Christian peoples—Franks, Bavarians, Saxons, Frisians—sought hospitality at Kremsmünster, what should they expect?" Charles's voice remained steady.

"I swear by the nails in Christ's cross, we would cheerfully give them food and shelter, as Our Lord commands, and pray for God's favor in their righteous quest." The abbot held out his hand, beseeching. "But that is only possible with *your* patronage and *your* protection."

Charles smiled. "The abbey shall have it as long as it remains faithful to us and the Good Lord."

The abbot bowed deeply. "I—and my brothers—thank you. We will serve God's anointed king."

Just like the bishop of Freising, Fastrada thought, *loyal to whoever is stronger.*

"Clerk," Charles said, "write a new charter stating that the king of the Franks donated the land for this fine monastery. Abbot, it is our will you remain at Kremsmünster. Take a seat on one of the stools. We need to discuss how you and your brothers will assist us against the Avars."

"So you are still planning war?" the abbot asked.

"A little fire won't stop us."

Little fire. That was what Charles had called Widukind's attack on Paderborn thirteen years ago. He sounded just as unfazed now as he did when he spoke about the palace in Saxony.

Oh, Nantlind! Even now, Fastrada's throat tightened. Nantlind, who knew what she wanted before she did, who would tell her what she needed to hear, even when she did not want to hear it. Her one true friend. Gone. She squeezed her eyes shut and willed back the threatening tears. But she could still see the charred rooms where the royal apartment used to be, could still smell the stale smoke.

Could she ever think of Nantlind again without icy fingers squeezing her heart?

March 791, Worms

Fastrada knew the messenger bore ill tidings as soon as she saw his flushed face. The young man could barely speak between breaths. "Count Gerold sent me," he said with a Bavarian accent.

Did the Avars learn of the fire and think it opportune to attack?

In the bishop's archive, a cramped room above the scriptorium, she tried to project an air of nonchalance to Charles's magnates, but the pulse in her ears quickened. Charles, Karl, and Pepin looked up from a recently copied map of Avaria. Charles nodded for the messenger to continue.

"Avars ... raid ... River Enns." He reached into his pouch and produced a rolled parchment with Gerold's seal.

"Thank you," Fastrada said. "My maid will show you to the kitchen, where you and your guards can refresh yourselves."

The messenger bowed and left with Irma. Charles broke the seal with his eating knife and held the unrolled letter so they both could read it.

"Of course, those heathens would choose a church," Fastrada said.

"If it's war they want, it's war they'll get," Charles said evenly. "But they won't face defenseless priests. It will be an army like none they have ever seen, and we will show them how our family fights together. Karl, will you be healed enough to blood your sword again?"

Karl's eyes gleamed. "Of course."

Karl now walked without a crutch, but his gait was slow and stiff. Mounting a Roman military horse, once an effortless hop for his tall frame, was difficult. He should use a wooden block, as he did when he was a child, but he refused. Fastrada worried he would try too hard.

"Father," Pepin said, "does that mean I will come, too?"

Charles shrugged. "Very well. You can learn from Fardulf, Angilram, and the other clerics."

A frown briefly crossed Pepin's lips.

"Will Louis and Little Pippin join us at the assembly?" Fastrada asked.

"They are both of an age where their men need to see them in battle," Charles answered.

Already? She knew Karl was close to their age when he went to Saxony, but neither one of them seemed old enough to shave, let alone wield a sword.

Pepin was glowering. Again. Sometimes, she still felt sorry that God had bent the young man's spine, denying him the sword, but his reluctance to accept God's will tested her patience.

June 791, Regensburg

If not for Little Pippin's diadem marking him as king of Italy, Pepin would not have recognized the fourteen-year-old arriving at the assembly. He was taller and broader than the boy Pepin had last seen three years ago. His brother's hair was cut short and curled bowl-like over the top of this head. Like an Italian, he wore a long, loose-fitting tunic extending midway to his calves rather than the close-fitting garb favored by the Franks. At his hip, he carried a sword in a jeweled scabbard.

Pepin snorted in derision. Both of these boys, kings. How could his father think them capable of leading men, yet let his firstborn languish?

The royal family and part of the Frankish army, including Severinus and his men and soldiers from Gomeric's countship, had arrived at Regensburg two weeks ago, and newcomers from Francia, Bavaria, Saxony, and Frisia came each day. The journey from Worms had taken seven weeks. The warships' rowers fought the Rhine's current as they conveyed the crafts to Strasbourg. After a three-day rest, wooden ships, inflated leather boats, and flat wooden ferries took two days to transport thousands of men, horses, and carts across the Rhine, landing them on the road east into Bavaria.

With grunts and groans, the men spent three full days disassembling the ships and placing the pieces in wagons, which portaged the boats for three weeks. When they reached the Danube, the shipwrights reassembled the crafts, and from there, it took but three days to reach Regensburg's dark gray granite walls.

The long, warm days seemed longer and warmer as the counts argued for weeks over whose forces would go where. The she-wolf was never far from his father's side, except for the days she took to her bed. He missed Nantlind's presence. If only Gomeric had not held him back ...

Peasants were cutting hay in the fields when Charles and the noblemen came to an agreement. Little Pippin and his magnates prepared to depart for Italy and secure the border. Pepin, his other two brothers, and his father would ride into Avaria. He suppressed a groan when he learned Angilram would ride with them, probably to further his father's plan for Pepin to succeed the old man as archbishop of Metz and relinquish any claim to the throne. Pepin prayed for the archchaplain's good health, at least until he could claim the crown.

✳✳✳

On the day of departure, Pepin watched his father and the queen linger in each other's embrace. The late summer morning was temperate, yet at sunrise Mass she had crossed her arms over her bosom as if warding off a chill.

"Send me messages," Charles murmured. "Let me know about your health."

"We will all pray for you," Fastrada said.

Charles kissed his wife and hugged each of the girls before mounting his horse. Astride his own shorter steed, Pepin wondered if his life would be like his father's. Would Severinus's daughter truly pray for his safety as Fastrada no doubt did for her husband? Would Richilde be true when he was away?

Did she share his affection? Her letters, written by a clerk, were like his, about happenings that were already public knowledge. He wanted to write poems about her beauty and his longing to see her again, but he could not trust that her eyes would be the only ones to see his messages. The closest he could risk coming to sentiment was to praise her intelligence, encourage her in her studies, and end with "Again, I send you warm greetings in the name of Our Lord."

Pepin still thought of Richilde as he rode with his father, brothers, and the archchaplain at the head of the procession traveling the oak and ash lined road along the Danube. He glanced over his shoulder. The mounted warriors alone seemed endless. They wore swords at their hips and shields on their backs, but in friendly lands, baggage horses carried their armor. Still, their sheer number was enough to deter brigands foolish enough to even consider robbing them. Behind the horsemen were more foot soldiers followed by the baggage train and the wheeled battering rams in their peaked, planked shelters, the catapults and their ropes and buckets, and the tortoise-like structures to shield men undermining fortress walls.

The noise from the army drowned out any sound from the forest. In the river, frightened turtles left ripples near the logs where they had been sunning, and the beavers dared not venture outside their dens on the banks. Between the shiny-leafed black poplars to his left, Pepin caught sight of the Frankish warships, their square white sails full of wind, on the blue river reflecting sky and tree-covered mountains. This would all someday be his! Could someday be his.

Charles's voice cut into Pepin's musing. "Angilram, my sons would like to hear about Saint Arnulf."

Pepin rolled his eyes. *Not again.*

He glanced behind him. Louis sat up straighter. Karl smirked.

"After your ancestor Saint Arnulf took holy orders," the archchaplain began, "he wanted to give the family property to the poor. His elder son was selfish and refused, but his younger son, Anschisus, obeyed. He trusted Christ would reward him, and God did bestow Anschisus with greater riches and has continued to bless his progeny to this day."

"So God preferred the younger son," Karl said.

That means He'd prefer Louis to you.

"God loved each son," the archchaplain said. "The elder found his inheritance could not compare to the joys of serving God. He relinquished worldly fortune and succeeded his father as bishop."

Pepin pressed his lips together to suppress his scowl. *I will not renounce my inheritance or my right to progeny so easily, Father.*

***

After a two-week march, the army stopped at Lorch, the last civilized place before Avaria, with the Danube to the north and Enns River to the east. The travelers rode past wooden houses and huts, where men sharpened spears and arrows. Thick walls and double trenches protected the west side of the city and the towers at the corners and four gates gave the guards a broad view.

Within the fortifications, Pepin stretched his neck to gaze up the slope and spied the church, a rectangular, stone building with small arched windows—the place where the Franks would ask God for victory.

The next morning, Pepin sweated inside the church walls, even with the doors flung open. The place would have been pleasant as summer slid into fall. But the crowd of soldiers and priests, and the smoke from the incense, made the sanctuary stifling. He could barely see the murals and painted wooden statues of saints. In the apse, the church boasted of its wealth with a glass window of cobalt, green, and yellow pieces forming into hexagons and triangles. Along the sides, the windows were composed of green and blue green triangles.

As the bishop and priests approached the altar, Pepin noticed they were barefoot. The three days of litanies the archchaplain had spoken about. How glad he was that Gomeric was rescuing him from a life in the clergy. Angilram paused as if catching his breath, and his shoulders were slumped like he hadn't slept. *Father in Heaven, let him be well.*

During his homily, the priest told the laity what they must do. "If you are not prevented by age or infirmity, abstain from meat and wine or give alms as you can afford."

"We will give alms," Charles muttered.

Karl nodded, but Louis frowned.

Pepin bit his lip. Typical of his father, who loathed the abstinences and fasts of Lent and Advent. They would still give up meat, but the alms would allow them to drink wine. *I will need to do this as well when I am king.*

Pepin and his family attended Mass every three hours, rather than only sunrise and vespers. Midday brought a dinner of bread, beans, and vegetables. Pepin missed the aromas of stews and roasted meat. He hoped God was pleased the royal family ate like peasants.

On the second day, a messenger arrived in the midafternoon at the bishop's residence, where the royal family were guests. From his loose garb,

Pepin surmised he was Italian. His accent confirmed it. "I bear a message from Pippin, king of Italy by the grace of God and his father Charles, king of the Franks and the Lombards and patrician of Rome."

Pepin looked away to hide his scowl. *Brat doesn't deserve a kingdom, doesn't deserve our grandfather's name.*

His father nodded for the messenger to continue.

"King Pippin is well and the border between the lands of the Avars and Italians is secure. As you ordered, his men invaded Avaria on the twenty-third of August."

"Two weeks ago," Charles said.

"They joined the Avars in battle, slaughtered many, and took their fortress and the spoils. They have one-hundred-fifty captives and are awaiting your orders."

Charles smiled. "Praise God and His saints. He is already showing us His favor, and we will reward the men responsible for this victory."

Pepin swallowed. Would God show His favor when he was on the throne?

***

In the bishop's archive, Pepin wrote a letter to his mother to ask for prayers from the monks and nuns at Nivelles. A few paces away, his father dictated a message to Fastrada, telling her about Little Pippin and the litanies that had ended the previous day. Deacon Fardulf scribbled on a wax tablet.

"Tell her I am entrusting her to make sure the litanies are said at home, but she should abstain only if she is well enough to do so," his father said.

Pepin snuck a glance from his parchment.

His father's brow creased. "And tell her I am surprised not to hear from her by now. She should send messages more often and inform me about her health. You will impress upon her that I expect a reply, and you are not to leave Regensburg until you get one."

"I impress upon the queen as much as anyone can, Your Excellence," Fardulf answered, his Lombard accent thick.

"Perhaps you can sway her," Charles said. "She likes and trusts you."

"I merely help her with Latin and annals. I cannot change strong wills, but I try to get answer."

Pepin frowned. He did not know what to pray for. Although he wanted Fastrada out of his life and out of his dreams, Gomeric had insisted they needed her. Yet he worried Fastrada's illness could distract his father from the Avars.

Chapter Thirty-one

In the morning light pouring into the bishop's great hall the next day, Pepin gritted his teeth and watched servants help his father and brothers into leather tunics sewn with tiny metal plates. In a few hours, the Christian army would cross into Avaria—soldiers had already taken bellows to the bank of the Danube, where they were inflating small leather boats for Meginfrid's Saxons, Frisians, and a few Franks to cross to the river's north bank. Pepin would accompany the force his father would lead on the south bank, crossing the Enns near its confluence with the Danube. Refusing to mark himself a cleric and rely only on prayers, Pepin insisted on carrying a wooden shield on his back and having a hunting spear on a nearby baggage horse. If he could not have armor and sword like his father and brothers, he would use the protection he had.

Even though Pepin's father had seen forty-two years, he bore the armor as if it weighed no more than a mantle. Karl stood straighter than before, his eyes gleaming.

"This is so heavy," Louis whined. "It's like bearing a large hunting dog on my shoulders, and this helmet will crush my skull. I will look like Pepin."

"Say it louder," Pepin snarled. "Then everyone will know you're as weak as a little girl."

His youngest brother lunged and stumbled. Pepin pressed his lips to stifle the laugh.

Their father grabbed the boy's arm. "Stop! Both of you!"

Pepin allowed himself a satisfied smile, even though Gomeric frowned. Later, his uncle would chide him about the need to get along with his brothers and keep them blind to their plan.

At midday, the army on the Danube's south bank traversed the blue-green, swift-flowing Enns on a recently restored Roman bridge and trekked through a wood of willows and silver and black poplars. Between the trees to his left, Pepin beheld the wooden warships on the Danube's blue expanse and the marching warriors dwarfed by forested mountains to the north. Somewhere on the road ahead, the Avars awaited.

Six days later, the land became flatter and the Danube shrank. The grasses were brown rather than green. And the army roused a thick dust. *There's been a drought.*

With the sun at its zenith, Pepin's breath caught when he spotted the two-story wooden walls of an Avarian fortress across the river, on a rise near a tributary. Surrounded by a ditch, the stronghold stood amid pastures with a few sheep flocked in a mass and a handful of goats in a thin line except for a few unmoving kids. There were no fields of sprouting winter wheat.

His father raised his hand to stop the procession on the south bank. Behind him, Pepin heard shouts, followed by footsteps, hooves, and wheels coming to a halt and the murmur of men's conversations.

Pepin squinted into the distance. "That's odd. The great gate is open, but the bridge over the ditch looks burned. And why is their livestock outside the walls where our men can get them?"

In front of Pepin, Karl laughed. "They fled. Cowards!"

"Why do you think they fled?" their father asked. "How do you know it's not a trap?"

"Are you jesting?" Karl replied. "We vastly outnumber them, and they would have seen that from the ramparts."

Pepin imagined the sight: armies in clouds of dust on both sides of the Danube and many ships on the river itself. Only a madman would feel no terror.

"Karl, Louis, you need to learn from this," their father said. "What does our enemy's flight tell you?"

Pepin scowled.

Louis spoke up to Pepin's right. "God heeded our prayers and struck fear into their hearts. We should always fast and pray when we ask for His favor."

"Very good, Louis," his father said. "What else? What did we learn from the Saxons and Widukind?"

For a moment, the only sounds were voices in the distance.

Pepin pursed his lips. During the Saxon wars, Widukind had always escaped capture and then ... "Fie! They fled and took their horses so they can gather their forces in greater numbers and fight another day. They will sacrifice their fortress and some livestock to better their chances of defeating us. We think of them as weaklings at our peril."

Karl snorted in derision.

"Don't scoff, Karl," their father said. "Remember the Avars during the hunt when they were at Worms? Men who will charge a stag like that are not cowards. Pepin is absolutely right, and you should heed his counsel."

I don't want to counsel. I want to rule. Pepin glanced at Gomeric. His uncle nodded and smiled. The knot between Pepin's shoulders loosened.

"Whatever is in the fortress will make a nice prize for our men," his father said. "We can let them rejoice and let your mother's annalists boast, but we must stay on guard."

Across the river, some of Meginfrid's men went back to the forest, probably to fell trees and build a new footbridge over the ditch. Pepin wondered what the Avars had abandoned in their haste.

"The Avars will fight another day," his father said, "but they won't have that stronghold."

Charles and the chamberlain had agreed that each army would plunder and destroy whatever fortress it encountered and follow its counterpart the next day. Half of the ships dropped anchor while the other half accompanied the men on the south bank. As the sky changed from blue to violet, they encountered an Avarian town that used to be a Roman fort, judging by the lone tower and crumbling walls of brown and beige mortared stone. Pepin remembered the name Asturius from one of the maps in his father's archive. No straight rows of sprouting grain here either, and the pasture of broad leaf weeds and thistles held only a few huddled sheep and some goats.

"Guards," his father said, "stay close to my sons until we know who's in the settlement."

Pepin and his brothers glowered. As Charles appointed a group of mounted warriors to ride ahead, Pepin pulled his shield from his back and called for his hunting spear. Karl and Louis stiffened their spines and laid their hands on the hilts of their swords.

The scouting party galloped toward the settlement. Pepin leaned forward, his eyes seeking an Avarian arrow in the dim light.

Nothing. Not even a thrown rock. Karl's and Louis's shoulders sagged. Pepin was disappointed as well. He wanted to slay an Avar, show everyone his valor, his worthiness to rule.

Their father summoned messengers. "Tell each count that his men can take whatever they want from the town, but we need the dwellings intact tonight."

Pepin, his father, and brothers led the way past the walls and into the settlement, a collection of wattle-and-daub huts that seemed like they would blow away in a harsh wind. A large wooden structure apparently housed a noble family or served as a place of assembly. After the archchaplain wearily led vespers prayers, the royal family and their servants entered the large building. No murals or tapestries adorned its walls. No parchment covered the windows—only wooden shutters kept out wind and rain. *This is where their nobles live? It's barely better than a tent.*

What the Avars had left behind astonished him: bronze buckets, pottery, looms, and other items essential to a household. "The Avars left in haste. Our men should be happy with all this."

"If they're not fighting each other for it," Karl said.

Pepin flushed. Yet one more reminder of how his younger brother had seen more wars than he.

After sunrise prayers, Pepin and his brothers watched the warriors carry their prizes and lead goats to the baggage train, while tall, broad-headed, pointed-eared dogs bullied the sheep. Dwarfed by the canines, the Avarian sheep seemed smaller and thinner than Frankish animals. Among the men, Pepin saw some black eyes, bent noses, and bandaged arms and legs. Next to a ruined church, priests prayed over a few bodies wearing Frankish and Saxon clothing.

Louis gasped. "How did they die?"

Karl shrugged. "Probably fighting over a bauble."

Pepin frowned.

A shout broke through the rumble of voices and bleats of sheep and goats. "You stabbed a man—your fellow soldier—for this?"

Pepin turned. Severinus, his teeth bared, stood before a groveling young commoner and held up a bronze brooch shaped like a bear's head.

"He ... he tried to steal it from me," the young man sniveled.

Severinus drew back his fist and punched the peasant in the eye, then kicked him in the belly. The man crossed his arms over his middle. The count grabbed him by the back of the collar and repeatedly smashed the peasant's face to the ground. Pepin heard a crack. Severinus's men flinched.

Louis's hand flew to his mouth.

"He has to do this, Little Brother," Pepin muttered, remembering earlier conversations with his uncle.

"Pepin's right," Karl added. "He can't control his men if he doesn't punish wrongdoing. Look at the crowd and you'll see some of the men nodding."

"The brooch will go to the dead man's family as a wergeld," Severinus said.

"But he ..." came the muffled voice.

Severinus yanked the soldier up. Blood streaked the grime on the commoner's face.

"I dispense justice," Severinus growled. "I will not have my men do the Avars' work for them. You are lucky I'm letting you live. Now go confess to Father Justus." He shoved the soldier away.

The peasant landed on his hands and knees with a grunt that sounded like a sob.

Severinus had chosen the priest who pronounced the harshest penance. No meat or wine would touch that soldier's lips for months.

Was Severinus ever that strict with Richilde? Pepin doubted Severinus would risk her beauty and marriageability, but the thought of anyone inflicting pain on Richilde, even to discipline her, caused him to wince.

He glanced at Karl. *Why hasn't he mentioned Richilde to Father? Before the fire, he was all but begging for a betrothal.*

***

The army set off after putting torches to the huts, which took to the flame as easily as dry kindling. *Hardly worth burning*, Pepin thought.

The men marched through a riverside forest of black poplars with leaves starting to turn bright yellow. Briars crept toward the road, and dried leaves crunched under their feet. Late in the afternoon, the army again encountered a settlement. Beyond the few frightened sheep and goats in the pasture, Pepin noticed a stone structure and a few huts.

"Comagena," his father said.

It was larger than Asturius but hardly the city as described in a book of a saint's life. Sunken wattle-and-daub huts sat about the ruins of a Roman fort near the river. The fort's two curved towers with narrow arched windows flanked a crumbling wall of mortared brown and beige stones. The space where the great gate used to be revealed more huts and scavenged Roman structures.

When the scouting party rode toward what remained of the walls, no Avarian arrows came their way. Again.

Pepin let out an obscenity under his breath. The men had no one to fight but each other, and they raced into the town as if they feared nothing would be left for them to plunder. The royal family and Charles's magnates stayed outside the settlement.

"What is that?" Louis pointed to a mountain to the southeast.

With no nearby trees to obstruct his view, Pepin made out a fortress at the summit.

"Cumeoberg," his father answered.

"Will we finally fight the Avars?" Louis stuck out his lower lip.

"Maybe they fled too," Pepin said. "They would have seen us and our dust from leagues away."

"Very good, Pepin," Charles said. "I was just about to ask your brothers. Karl, Louis, what do you think?"

"Two possibilities," Karl said. "They fled, or they're inside the fortress, waiting for us. This one might be large enough to withstand a siege."

"Worth sending scouts?" their father asked.

"Yes," Pepin replied. "We should know what's ahead."

"No," Karl said. "They already know we're here. If it's not deserted, we'll only lose our men."

"Pepin is right," Charles said. "Even if the Avars' hold is empty, they could have left traps."

Pepin smirked, savoring his brother's annoyance, but his pleasure was fleeting. His father would always see him as part of the clergy, fit to counsel but not lead. If only his father had not angered God with his sin; then he would have his rightful place.

***

It took half the day for the army to reach the foot of the mountain where Cumeoberg stood. Again, Pepin saw fallow fields of weeds but no green shoots. *How do the Avars feed themselves?*

The ascent took hours, leaving men and horses winded. Ramparts of timber reinforced with earth and stone greeted them, but the western great gate was open. The bridge across the ditch bore char marks but remained whole, as if the Avars had left before making sure the torch had set the structure afire.

The scouts Charles had sent reported this fortress was deserted. Karl and Louis groaned. *The Avars are cowards. Never faced a real army. Does that mean Karl* ... Pepin shook his head. *Better to presume the enemy strong as Father did.*

"Did they leave anything behind?" Charles asked the scouts.

"War engines!" A scout pointed to a wooden contraption peeking above the wall. "Look at how tall their siege towers are. And their catapults—once we replace the ropes they burned, we could probably throw boulders."

"Those things are bloodstained," another scout said.

"Why?" Louis asked.

"Probably from the fresh hides to protect their men from flaming arrows," Karl explained.

"A trove for us, indeed," Charles said.

"They're scared enough to soil themselves." Karl laughed. "If they plan to fight again, why leave war engines behind? Even those savages can comprehend we will use those weapons against them."

"They didn't have time to destroy them fully or get them down the mountain," Pepin replied.

"Right again, Pepin," his father said.

Inside the walls, they crossed a courtyard with a few wattle-and-daub huts then headed for an opening at the far left of a palisade. On the other side was a large L-shaped wooden structure, about the size of Paderborn's great hall. Just outside the assembly hall stood smaller buildings, one of which resembled a blacksmith's shop, with bellows for a fire pit within and broken tongs.

At least our men will have plenty of booty.

The royal family and Charles's magnates spent the night inside the assembly hall. Its walls were rough-hewn but still better than a tent or the two previous places they had stayed.

Pepin could not sleep that night. His father would not stop pacing, and sometimes he muttered, "Why hasn't she sent a message?"

Chapter Thirty-two

When sunrise Mass ended, Pepin looked down and mouthed a prayer for the archchaplain. The old man had lumbered through his chants in front of the portable altar, a silver gilt box of enamel and porphyry. Covered with an embroidered altar cloth, it was perfect for the chalice, paten for the host, and purse-like gold-gilt reliquary resting atop it.

After warriors and clergy left the hall, the breeze from the open windows dispelled the stuffiness. Pepin was glad for the morning beer and its moistness on his lips and throat. Outside the window, soldiers were running with bundles and chests through the fortress. *Looting what they can before we burn it.*

Charles handed his empty vessel to the cupbearer and dictated a message to Meginfrid, to be delivered by one of the ships between the two armies. "Tell Meginfrid we will continue our march through Avaria," he concluded.

Soon, Pepin's father and brothers were again in their armor. Pepin glanced down at his own fine wool tunic and frowned. He marched outside to a warm day, with a blue sky and a few clouds—good weather for riding. Louis and Karl soon followed and started sparring with wooden swords. Pepin sighed. Louis charged at Karl, who easily stepped aside. The boy pitched forward, using his outstretched hands to break the fall. He cried out.

"Louis!" Charles raced past Pepin.

The boy rose first to his knees then his feet. He rubbed the wrist of his sword hand and winced. Approaching his brother, Pepin resisted the urge to smirk.

"Fetch the physician!" Charles barked.

Pepin heard a servant's hurried footsteps behind him.

"I'm fine," Louis grumbled. His wrist was swelling.

"You need a physician." His father's tone was more order than statement.

Pepin blinked in surprise. His father loathed physicians and almost never heeded their advice.

"No physician!" Louis yelled.

"Louis," their father warned.

The boy pouted.

Pepin modulated his voice so that it fell between concern and a taunt. "Your wrist is puffy, Little Brother. Might be broken."

Louis made an obscene gesture with his uninjured hand.

"Stop that." Their father scowled.

Led by the servant Charles had sent, a monk with wrinkled hands rushed to join the group. He bowed at the waist to Charles and ducked his head to Pepin and Louis. "My lord, let me see."

Grimacing, Louis held out his hand.

The physician's bushy eyebrows drew toward each other as he prodded the boy's wrist. Louis let out a yelp.

"Not broken," the physician said.

Charles let out a breath. *Fie!* Pepin thought.

"But it must be splinted or it won't heal, and he will need to eat cloves," the physician continued. "Your Excellence, your son must not fight in this war."

"No!" Louis wailed. "I've not drawn any blood."

"Your Excellence," the physician said, "I have seen warriors forever weaken their hands when they try to return to battle too soon."

"Address me," Louis snapped. "I'm right here. And I can too go to war."

"Louis," Charles said, "you will fight some other day, but only if your hand heals."

"What good is a sword if I can't use it?" the boy cried.

"Louis, no more complaints," his father said. "You and Pepin will return to Regensburg."

"Why me?" Pepin growled. "I'm not the oaf who injured himself."

"Pepin, let us have a word in private while the physician splints your brother's wrist." Charles's voice had returned to its usual calm.

Surprised, Pepin strode a few steps with his father until they were out of earshot if they kept their voices low.

"Your mother hasn't sent any letter, even with Fardulf as the messenger," his father said. "I need you in Regensburg to write to me about how she fares."

Pepin glared and crossed his arms. He would never have a chance to put his spear through an Avar.

"You're the only one who can tell me what's going on," his father continued. "She intimidates the clerks."

Pepin straightened his back the little his spine would allow. His father was sending him back to fulfill a mission, not because he was a burden like Louis.

He felt a twinge of guilt then shoved it aside. Instead he said, "I will tell you everything about her."

Regensburg, November 791

Seated near the hearth in the great hall, Fastrada tried to read the annalist's writing, but she could not concentrate. Every few minutes, she stared at the entryway and strained her ears for cacophony of hoofbeats, footsteps, cart wheels, and voices from outside. Nothing but the servants bustling about. Her eyes scanned the vast room. The chairs and planks for the table were clean, and the hall smelled of the thyme and mint freshly strewn on the floor.

The children awaited Charles in the courtyard. She wished she could join them, if only she weren't so tired and weak. And cold. Even a fire in full blaze and a fur-lined cloak were not enough.

"I look terrible," she murmured. A pale face with sunken eyes had stared back at her from the polished bronze mirror that morning. Her finest clothes and jewels could not conceal the ailment.

"Your lord needs his strong-willed queen," Irma said.

Fastrada smiled at her maid, glad she had chosen her to take Nantlind's duties. Still, she missed Nantlind, who would have reassured her, told her how happy Charles would be to see her.

"Have some wine," Irma said. "The wise woman says it will help."

Fastrada wrapped her fingers around the warm clay cup and took a draught, allowing it to heat her throat, hoping it would bring some color to her. After getting Charles's letter in September, she had made sure the priests said the litanies. She and the princesses abstained from meat and paid alms to drink wine. She envied the girls. She knew they longed for pork and beef, but they could still chase balls, weave cloth, or discuss scholars. After one day, Fastrada could barely stand through Mass before staggering back to the royal apartment and eating meat in private. Her body was still weak and cold for days, but if that pleased God and protected her husband, so be it.

She regretted delaying her reply to Charles. She did not want him to fret about her health but could not truthfully tell him she was well. When Pepin and Louis had returned, she had no choice but to send a message with Fardulf to reassure her husband that she was managing the household and the princesses were well. She dared not break the seal on Pepin's letter to Charles but guessed that he exaggerated how long she slept and how little she could do. Fardulf had been uneasy, only saying that he would tell Charles the truth.

What were the children telling her husband now? Pepin no doubt would relate to Charles how pale and fatigued she was. Louis would show his father how his wrist had healed and argue yet again how Charles should not have sent him away. Over the past two months, Louis's fuss had been worse than Karl's after the fire, and oh, how the boy had sulked when she had told him his wrist was still too weak for a hunt.

Noise from the courtyard—the voices of many people—floated to her. But something was amiss. Why were there so few hoofbeats? After half an hour, Fastrada heard Charles's footsteps amid the children's chatter. Her heartbeat quickened. She placed the parchment on a small table then set her arms on the chair and steeled her face. Irma held out her hands to help her, but Fastrada shook her head.

A moment later, she rose and watched for her husband. He entered the hall, surrounded by the children and carrying little Chiltrude. Fastrada smiled and wished she had enough vigor to dash across the room. Instead, she kept her back straight and strode toward him, her steps measured.

Charles was whole and as healthy as ever. So was Karl, now as tall as his father. Remembering Charles's letter about meeting Little Pippin in Szombathley, Fastrada noticed the dark-haired youth had grown a little taller in the past few months. Pepin and Louis followed. Bejeweled, Hruodtrude was now as tall as most men, and Bertha likely would be too. Next to their father and Karl, though, they were dwarfed. Gisela, Hruodhaid, and Theodrada all clamored for Charles's attention.

Fastrada had expected triumphant joy, but everyone was somber. Pepin was pale. When Fastrada called to her husband, his eyes misted. He set Chiltrude on her feet and rushed to her, swept her into his arms, and kissed her.

"Why did you not tell me everything about your health?" His voice was level but betrayed disappointment.

"You were fighting a fearsome enemy. I could not burden you."

"Let me worry about the burden, my dear. And write to me more often when I'm away." He held her more fiercely.

"I missed you."

Charles released his hold. After Fastrada embraced Karl and Little Pippin, she turned back to her husband. "What troubles everyone? Did we lose the battles after the Raab River?"

Charles took Fastrada's hand. "My dear, we dealt the Avars a severe blow and got many spoils and captives, but ..."

Fastrada searched his face. "Did Gerold fall in battle?"

"He is well." He hesitated before letting the words spill from his mouth. "A pestilence wiped out the horses in the army I was leading."

The room was spinning. She tightened her grip on Charles's fingers. *We're crippled.*

"It was awful." Karl's mournful voice seemed to come through a fog. "They were coughing and had sores in their nostrils and mouths, on their faces, their legs ... They collapsed in days."

"Barely a tenth lived," Charles added.

Fastrada's throat tightened. "Did Neptunus survive? Did Grane? Alcippe?"

Charles and Karl looked down and shook their heads.

A vision of horses' bodies covering the banks of the Danube swam before Fastrada's eyes. The finest warhorses gone. Even the riding horses snatched away. This was worse than the disasters at Roncevaux and the Süntels. If the Avars attacked next summer, Charles couldn't avenge it, and those heathens would be emboldened to do their worst. Without horses, there could be no war. She wanted to scream, to let hot tears flow down her cheeks, but she felt the eyes of the courtiers upon her.

"With your permission, my lord king," she said, her voice distant and hollow even in her own ears, "we will use the spoils of this war to seek God's favor and buy more horses."

Even with new horses, rebuilding the herd would take years, and the warhorses, bred large enough and brave enough to charge into battle with armored men, would be the most difficult to replace. She tried to calculate how long. To beget strong foals, the few remaining stallions must wait until the vernal equinox to service the mares, and some of the colts and fillies would become mature enough to breed by then. At the same time, the mares already in foal would give birth after their eleven-month pregnancies. The mothers of the surviving foals would spend the next six months nursing them, well after summer solstice—horses conceived then would be weak. Best to delay breeding for those mares until spring. The newborns would take at least two years before anyone could ride them, not to mention the training to get warhorses to not bolt amid the chaos of flashing swords and screaming men.

The fingers of Fastrada's free hand traced her medal of Saint Wigbert. She and Charles had prayed, given alms, deprived themselves of meat. She had sacrificed her vigor for days. Why was it not pleasing enough to God? Why did He let the horses suffer? And why did He leave her people so vulnerable to the enemy?

***

When Pepin heard the lauds bells, he wanted to stay in the warmth of the furs and blankets. Instead, he threw back the bedclothes and thrust the bed curtains open, letting in the cold air and the light from the glowing embers in the hearth. His bare skin prickled.

"What?" Karl said behind him. His sleepiness couldn't mask his annoyance.

"I had a dream." Pepin tried to make his voice sound urgent. "I must pray at the cathedral now."

Karl turned over and his breathing resumed its slow rhythm. Pepin woke his manservant, sleeping fully clothed on a pallet, and dressed quickly.

He strode through the corridor, past his sisters' chamber to the right and his parents' chamber to the left. Soon, he crossed the reception room and was out the door. One of the guards standing near the apartment entrance roused himself from a stupor and elbowed one of his fellows. The pair followed Pepin through the great hall.

"Where are we going at this hour, Lord?" said the older of the two.

"The cathedral! I must pray there."

"The Niedermünster church is closer. Less danger from night creatures."

"My vision told me to pray at the cathedral." He didn't tell the guards the vision was brought on by the coins his uncle had left in a cross on Niedermünster's altar at vespers. Pepin would have preferred Niedermünster rather than the quarter-hour walk to the cathedral. But the nuns at Niedermünster venerated Saint Erhard's relics at all hours and might understand Latin. He'd rather risk demons and other terrors. He patted his dagger. Its cold iron and his cross would protect him.

One of the guards grabbed a birch-bark torch, and both matched Pepin's stride. They traversed the great hall and the portico and left the palace through a man-size door near the great gate. Clouds blotted the moon and stars, and Pepin could see only a few paces ahead as they made their way on the brick-paved streets between houses. When they reached the cathedral, the yawning monks and the priest were mumbling through the Mass. The candles at the altar cast a puddle of light, leaving most of the sanctuary, the two aisles flanking it, and the clerestory windows in the shadows. Pepin discerned the outlines of the painted wooden statues and knelt beside Gomeric in front of Saint Georg.

Pepin listened to the monks' chants, followed by shuffling footsteps of men who wanted to return to sleep. Muttering the Paternoster, Pepin occasionally opened his eyes to check if the priest had left. Finally, he and Gomeric were alone in the church, except for the guards.

"Did you lose your horse?" Pepin asked in Latin.

"Yes, but it's a blessing."

Pepin's eyes popped open, then he quickly closed them. "How?"

"Can you not see? It's a sign from God that He wants Jupiter to be king. Else He would not have rebuked Saturn with the pestilence. When Mars sends out word about this curse, the cause will get much more support."

It took all of Pepin's effort not to grin and rouse his guards' suspicion.

"We will act in a few months," Gomeric said, "and this time we can't fail. There will not be another chance."

"Not with Angilram dead." He had noticed the archchaplain was missing in the courtyard but dread froze his tongue. When Hruodtrude had asked about the old man, his father confirmed his fears. Pepin had felt the blood drain from his face. He could barely eat at the feast Fastrada had planned. "Did Angilram really clutch at his heart and keel over?"

"Yes."

"Why did God not heed my prayers? Maybe He doesn't want ... Jupiter to rule."

"How does the death of one sick old man compare to the decimation of horses?"

"Saturn will not relent. He will insist Jupiter take the vow and give up everything."

"Not without Jupiter's consent. Saturn needs that if he wants support from Mars, Minerva, and their allies. He will understand such a momentous decision requires prayer, months and months of prayer."

Still, Pepin knew, his father's patience would not last forever.

Chapter Thirty-three

February 792, Regensburg

Fastrada was surprised to see Karl in the kitchen, where she was planning dinner. This small stone building twenty paces from the manor was her domain, warm with cook fires and noisy with the clunking of knives against wooden tables and the chatter of servants. Smoke mingled with the aromas of bread baking in the oven built into the back stone wall and wild boar roasting on hooks in the hearth. Neither Charles nor any of his sons had ever set foot in any palace kitchen. With the bewildered look of a man lost in the forest, Karl approached her.

"I must speak to you in private," he muttered.

Puzzled, Fastrada gave her last orders to the cooks and left with Karl, trailed by her maid and their guards. Outside, the roofed passage provided little protection from the cold wind stinging her face or the brightness of the snow assailing her eyes. She drew her fur-lined cloak close as she and Karl walked toward the manor. She snuck a glance up at Charles's heir. His brow was creased. Something distressed him, and it must concern the family. Apprehension gnawed at her. Had he sired a bastard? She and Charles had given him some coins to satisfy his lust with fallen women, and if one of them were with child, why not claim a prince as the father? But all Karl had to do was acknowledge the child. Had one of his sisters lain with a courtier? Or worse, a servant? But how could such a thing escape their guards' notice?

Inside the great hall, she was glad for the shelter from the wind but missed the heat from the kitchen. Her feet were icy, and her eyes needed to adjust to the hall's dimness. Her teeth chattering, she kept a tight grip on her cloak.

"Irma," Fastrada said, "go ahead of us and stoke the fire in the reception room."

As the maid ran toward the royal apartment, Fastrada shook her head. Nantlind would have already been at the apartment door without being told. She swallowed back the tightness in her throat. It had been over a year, yet she still missed her Nantlind. Would this sadness ever leave?

When she and Karl entered the apartment, the guards stayed in the great hall. The fire was strong, adding to the gray light seeping through the parchment-covered windows flanking the room. Irma grabbed a clay cup and said she would fetch mulled wine.

Fastrada tamped down a twinge of guilt. *I'm being unfair to her. Of course she's not Nantlind.* She sat in a chair near the hearth and bade Karl to take a stool.

"I prefer to stand." He started to pace about the large room.

"What so troubles you?"

Karl spun toward her, blushing to the roots of his dark, glossy hair. "You must tell Father not to seek a bride for me. Any bride."

Fastrada gaped at Karl, remembering his odd reaction after prime Mass that morning. While she and Charles had discussed a wife for him, Karl had said nothing, no mention of Richilde, not even an insistence that any woman he married be fair. "Karl, your father and I thought you liked Richilde. Letting her marry into our family would ..."

"It's not her. She's beautiful," Karl blurted. Were his eyes misting? "It's ... me. I ... cannot ... cannot ..."

She waited for Karl to finish the sentence but the words seemed stuck on his tongue. What was he trying to say? A cold horror washed over her. She grasped the arms of her chair to keep herself upright. The floor seemed to give under her feet. "No," she whispered.

"I'm sorry," he mumbled.

She shook her head as if she could will it away. "We'll find a physician to cure you, a wise woman if we must."

"I tried all that. Bleeding, potions, salves, prayers, spells. Nothing works."

"How long?" Fastrada forced through her dry throat.

"Two months after the fire, I wanted a woman. And ..."

She tried not to let her face reveal anything. She did not want to hear details.

Karl cleared his throat. "I thought it was the whore's fault. She apologized so much, I felt sorry for her. Paid her more than I should have." He looked into the distance. "But then it was girl after girl after girl and ..."

She still could not believe what Karl was saying. To look at him, his shoulders and legs thick with muscle, a giant of a man like his father, no one would have guessed he lay near death a little over a year ago. This past summer, he was wearing armor, riding his horse hard, and slaying Avars. Just yesterday, he was shouting in triumph for killing a boar during a hunt. How could he not be whole?

"How did you keep this quiet for so long?" she asked.

Karl shrugged. "Not that difficult. What wise woman wants someone to say she failed? What priest wants to admit God won't listen to him? What harlot wants a reputation that she can't rouse a man, especially if he tells her every other girl could? I tell them I will keep their secret safe and pay them well as a token of my sincerity."

"Does Pepin know?" She shuddered. Pepin could use Karl's ... problem to deny him his kingdom. Rulers needed to be perfect. And that included virility.

"Doubt it." Karl laughed mirthlessly. "Pepin is going into the clergy, and he sards a whore every few days. I am inheriting the kingdom and can't beget a son. Maybe I should ..."

"No!" Fastrada lowered her voice. "Your brother can prove his potency with every whore in the city, but that doesn't make him fit for rule."

"Because he's a hunchback?"

"That's what I thought when I first met him, but his deformity is only a warning that God in His mercy has given us."

Karl raised his eyebrows.

Fastrada leaned forward. "Pepin doesn't see my people as worthy of the king's full protection. He never has. But you do."

"I couldn't have won those battles in Saxony without them."

"That wisdom, among other virtues, is what will make you a good king and why I'm not giving up on you. Maybe God will heal you later."

Karl's voice was near a whisper. "I can't have a wife complaining I deny her rights."

"There will be no bride for now."

"You will tell Father?" he pleaded. "I cannot bear to do it."

"Yes," Fastrada murmured. She slumped, pressing her fingertips to her forehead. *How?*

***

After dinner, Fastrada asked Charles to take a nap with her. She could have insisted on speaking to him earlier, but Karl's visit to the kitchen had raised enough curiosity. She was not about to give the courtiers and servants more fodder for gossip. Better for them to believe Karl's errand important only to him. When they left the royal apartment, she had said loud enough for most to hear, "Let me think about the chestnut colt."

As she and her husband headed toward the royal apartment, Charles cast a worried look at her. "Are you ill, my dear? You hardly touched any food."

"I had a few bites of meat."

"Only a few. You must eat more."

Irma ran ahead. Fastrada and Charles entered the reception room, then traversed the corridor to the royal bedchamber, where a fire burned brightly in the hearth. Fastrada dismissed Irma and Meginfrid before they could help her and her husband undress.

218

"My dear, what is it?" Charles asked. "Is your brother ill?"

Invisible fingers squeezed her heart. If only there were a way to soften this blow. If only someone else could tell him. Fastrada wrapped her arms around him. This must have been how he felt right before he told her that her father had died. "My love, we must never seek a bride for Karl. His wounds in the fire, they left him ..." She forced out the word, not believing what she was about to say. "... unable."

The blood drained from Charles's face. His eyes searched hers. "How do you know of this? Are you certain?"

"Yes. You know I would not tell you otherwise." She explained what Karl had told her.

Charles clung to her as sobs racked his body. Tears ran unchecked down her cheeks. She did not know how much time passed as she held her husband, wishing her love could salve his grief and restore Karl, wishing she could silence the whisper, *Why did God allow this to happen?*

July 792, Regensburg

In the forest's dappled light, Fastrada listened to the cuckoo's call, glad Charles suggested they go riding that afternoon. Two months before, the assembly had planned another war in Avaria, while churchmen in the cathedral had persuaded the bishop of Urgel in the Pyrenees to recant his heresy. *Christ as God's adopted son? Who could believe such foolishness?*

The day was warm enough for Fastrada to leave her cloak in the bedchamber. She and Charles rode at a leisurely gait, perfect for her mare and his middle-aged gelding and easy on the guards who trailed them. The firs and pines freshened the air, and with the beeches, provided a cooling shade.

"Still think Seraphina is in foal?" Charles asked.

"The grooms say she's still gobbling grass and is more temperamental than usual."

Behind them, they heard galloping hooves against the dusty path. Fastrada and Charles turned. It was Meginfrid. What was so urgent? When the chamberlain halted, Charles nodded for him to speak.

"Trouble in Rüstringen," he said between heaving breaths. "A priest from Blexen awaits you in the great hall."

Fastrada's pulse quickened. Charles's kinsman Theodoric, who had fought in the Süntels and helped Meginfrid lead Saxons and Frisians in Avaria, should still be in that district between Frisia and Saxony, seeking horses and warriors to fight the next year. Rüstringen was home to many Christian converts won by the late bishop of Bremen.

"What kind of trouble? Any word from Theodoric?" Charles asked.

"The priest said he would tell you only," the chamberlain replied. "It was difficult to get that little information out of him."

"Meginfrid," Charles said, "ride ahead of us at a canter—let's not show fear—and have our guest wait in the royal apartment's reception room. Then, get a couple of stable boys to meet me and Fastrada at the manor. We will be there shortly, but we will not ride a mare in foal hard."

As Meginfrid obeyed Charles's command, Fastrada smiled her gratitude at her husband. Seraphina was not the only one lacking stamina. If only *she* had more vigor ...

"Has Widukind ..." Fastrada began.

"My dear, we will talk about it in private. We must not give our people cause for alarm."

Or gossip. "Guards," she ordered, "you will say nothing about what you've heard, or we will have your tongues cut out."

Two nodded, and the other two cringed. Fastrada hoped the threat would be enough to silence them. Questions circled her mind as she and her husband rode at a walk along the forest path, past the fields of maturing grain and peasants cutting the last of the hay, and through the gates to the city. There was some sort of fight, but what? A raid, a skirmish, or a massacre? Did Widukind renege on his part of the agreement, a bargain that had cost her father his life? She swallowed back the tears.

She and Charles made their way on paved streets to the royal residence. Outside the portico, the stable boys immediately took the horses' reins. Charles dismounted and helped Fastrada down. She took his arm and let him lead her through the roofed entryway and the great hall. She tried to hurry her pace, but he simply patted her hand and kept his stride steady as if he wanted merely to ask the priest about a Psalm. Only a twitch in his jaw betrayed anxiety.

A guard opened the door to admit them to the royal apartment. A freckled priest in a dusty habit got to his feet so hastily he overturned his stool. He bowed deeply. When he stood upright Fastrada saw a look she knew all too well—the same expression her mother had worn when they had beheld the scorched fields at Büraburg almost twenty years ago. Fastrada fought back a wave of nausea.

"What happened?" Charles asked.

The priest's lips trembled. "Saxons. Frisians. All lost!"

"Worms!" Fastrada spat. "Just like them to hit us with a cudgel when we're lying on the ground, bleeding."

"Count Theodoric?" Charles prompted.

The priest opened his mouth as if to speak but only strangled sounds came out. Finally, he whispered, "Dead."

Charles's lips curled as if he wanted to call curses from the heavens down upon the murderers. He glanced at the door between the apartment and the great hall and clenched his teeth, like a man biting on a leather belt to throttle a scream as a physician set his bone.

Fastrada tried to restrain the rage trembling through her. "Did Widukind break his oath?"

The priest shook his head vigorously, causing the dark blond hair around his tonsure to flare. "I tried to remind them of Widukind's vow. They wouldn't listen. Said he'd betrayed them." The priest drew in a tremulous breath. "They were my flock. I baptized them with my own hands. They promised to renounce the Devil and his ways. I heard them. Then the Saxon soldiers came …"

Fastrada fought for calm. "Tell my husband what happened to Theodoric and his men."

"Ambushed in Blexen," the priest replied. "Then the Saxons burned our church and the cathedral in Bremen. It was only through God's grace that I escaped."

Charles wiped his eyes and leveled his gaze on the priest. "By Jesu, His Merciful Mother, and everything that is holy, we swear to you we will avenge this outrage. But we need your cooperation."

"Anything."

"Do not discuss this with anyone."

"Some people already know. They gave me shelter and food and a mule."

"And I will compensate them," Charles said. "Still, we must say nothing for now and slow the spread of this news."

The priest stiffened. "Why do you want to keep it quiet?"

"You've heard about the horses?"

"Everyone did."

"Then you know why."

"You mean you can't …"

"Do you want to send our people into a crippling panic?" Fastrada snapped. "That's what you will do if you talk about what happened in Blexen."

The priest winced as if he'd been slapped.

"We hear the ashes of the churches crying out for the blood of the infidels," Fastrada said. "But we need God's favor and the horses He will send."

Charles put his arm around Fastrada's shoulders. "Trust us, and we will reward your fidelity. We will have justice."

Chapter Thirty-four

September 792, Regensburg

astrada lifted her jewelry box and slid out a piece of parchment from beneath it. "My most important purchase this morning."

She and Charles were alone in their bedchamber, ready for their afternoon nap. With the shutters closed against drafts, the room was dim. The fire in the hearth provided some heat and light, but she longed for the blankets on the curtained bed. Still, she would delay her rest to speak to Charles in private at one of the few times they would not draw attention.

"You broke Pepin's seal." Charles raised his eyebrows.

"It's for Richilde," Fastrada said with an edge to her voice. "The merchant was chattering about how Richilde would enjoy the letter Pepin asked him to deliver. The merchant thought it was innocent, but I was suspicious. If Pepin learned of Karl's problem, he would be all too happy to let Richilde know."

Charles frowned. "You bribed the merchant."

"It took some haggling."

"And?"

She handed the parchment to her husband. "Nothing about Karl, saints be praised, but read the last two sentences."

"*I long to hear from you. Until then, I leave you with warm greetings in the name of Our Lord.*" Charles shrugged.

"Those are not the words of a man planning to enter the clergy. He won't accept the archdiocese."

"Pepin knows I'm never going to arrange a marriage for him," Charles said. "The girl is his friend, and even archbishops need friends, especially if Pepin is to advise Karl."

"All Pepin and Karl do is bicker. What makes you think they will fare any better than you and your brother?"

Charles squared his shoulders. Fastrada looked down. Her barb had escaped before she could stop it.

"It's for the good of the kingdom," her husband said. "Pepin will accept Mainz. He cannot do any better."

Fastrada doubted Charles's twenty-three-winter-old son cared about keeping the realm intact, with Karl ruling the bulk of it while Little Pippin got Italy and Louis received Aquitaine. *Father would be disappointed.* She shoved the thought aside and focused on the matter at hand. "Any other noble family would give twenty warhorses in their prime and a saint's relic for their son to rule Mainz," Fastrada grumbled. "Pepin has already had four months. How much longer?"

"Patience, my dear. If he needs to show the world he is pondering the matter, let him. I will not tonsure my son against his will, like a traitor with no friends."

"Of course not," she muttered. Charles dared not risk losing support from Gomeric and Severinus or the prayers from the nuns and monks at Himiltrude's double monastery, or from Pepin for that matter. With the Saxons and the Avars, she and Charles needed all the allies and all the prayers they could get.

"If a novice can take a year to deliberate whether to join an order," Charles said, "my son can have a few months."

Gomeric's words. Again. Aloud, Fastrada said, "What is Pepin doing all those hours in the cathedral?"

"Praying."

"In the middle of the night? With Gomeric and Severinus?"

"You said the guards told you it sounds like prayer." His voice took on a note of irritation. "Now that you've satisfied your curiosity, my dear, allow my son to write to his friends in peace. Severinus has no problem with Pepin writing to Richilde. Neither should you."

"Why hasn't Severinus said one word about a betrothal between Richilde and Karl?"

"My dear, let us be happy we don't need to invent an excuse that won't expose Karl or insult the girl and her family."

Two months ago, Fastrada had been so relieved she had not questioned Severinus's lack of interest. But something was missing, like a word scraped off a parchment page. Were Pepin and his companions truly asking for divine guidance all those hours in the cathedral? Time to find someone who knew Latin, even at the risk of Charles's wrath.

***

In the royal apartment's reception room the next afternoon, Fastrada barely saw the letters on the wax tablet. Letting it fall in her lap, she touched her brooch. *Saint Wigbert, let me be wrong.* She shivered, even though the room was warm. She had told her husband she needed to speak to Fardulf about

223

how to include the condemnation of the bishop of Urgel's heresy in the annals and required the room's privacy for such a delicate matter. How she hated telling him only part of the truth, but if he knew what she was going to ask of the deacon, Charles would stop her. *If only Nantlind were here. I could tell her.* Fastrada squeezed her lips together, realizing that she would not breathe a word even to her most trusted maid. This burden was hers alone.

A scratch at the door interrupted her thoughts. As Irma hurried to answer, Fastrada reached into a purse at her girdle. Soon, Fardulf approached her and bowed. She waved the deacon to a stool with her free hand.

"This should say ..." Fastrada switched to Latin. "... The king needs you now, but he knows it not."

Fardulf's brow furrowed.

Fastrada leaned forward and pressed coins into his hand. "I need you to listen to Pepin and Gomeric whenever they speak Latin."

"An unusual request, my lady queen," he replied in the same language. "Your Latin has become quite good. Surely, you would understand them."

"I need to know what they say when they think no one listens, and I cannot do that myself. Everyone knows who I am and where I am. No one would think anything of a deacon in a church at matins and lauds."

"My lady queen ..."

"I don't know whom else I can trust." Fastrada hoped her statement did not sound like a plea.

"Of course I will assist you." Fardulf's shoulders straightened.

"Perhaps, my feeling is nothing but my humors. Pray God that it is. But say nothing of this conversation to anyone."

***

Kneeling before the cathedral's altar after matins prayers, Pepin listened to the priest's wooden soles clunk against the floor. He forced himself to keep his eyes closed and his lips moving. Behind him, Pepin heard a guard say, "Good night, Father." A door opened and closed.

A moment later, he felt Gomeric's nudge at his right, and he opened his eyes a crack. Severinus had not moved from his place at Pepin's left. The candlelight from the altar flickered against stone walls and pillars upholding the arches between the sanctuary and the aisles alongside it, but shadows swallowed most of the wooden statues of saints, the murals, and the clerestory windows. Pepin was alone with Gomeric and Severinus, except for his guards. *Jailers loyal to the she-wolf.*

Gomeric's voice took on the cadence of a prayer. "Jupiter rises tonight, and Saturn will wane."

Pepin's eyes widened. Finally, he would wear the crown, the crowds would cheer for him, not Karl. He closed his eyes again.

"Is your man asleep?" Gomeric asked.

"Always is at this hour."

"Thunder will roll before lauds," Gomeric said.

"Not forget what to do?" Severinus asked in stilted Latin.

Pepin opened his eyes a little and looked about the sanctuary again. "Lift the bar and fold back the shutters. Jupiter is not dim." To avoid guards just outside the royal apartment, Gomeric, Severinus, and their warriors would sneak into the bedchamber Pepin shared with Karl and their menservants.

"And stay out of way," Severinus said. "Hercules and Saturn fall to Mars and Vulcan."

Pepin bit back his retort. *Father and Karl will be asleep. How difficult can that be?*

After Pepin's followers dispatched Karl and the servants, they would move across the corridor and deal with his father. Later, he would send men to Italy to do away with Little Pippin and Louis, the latter ordered to go there by their father to quell the fighting in Benevento.

"What happens to Ops?" Severinus asked.

"Anything you want as long as the she-wolf is gone," Pepin cut in.

"We need her alive," Gomeric said. "Use her until her bones break, if you want, but she must be put on trial to answer for what she has done."

"Then we can seal her in a barrel and drown her like a witch?" Pepin asked.

"Or have four horses tear her apart like the traitor she is," Gomeric answered.

Pepin chanted a Paternoster for his guards to hear.

"Are you ill, Deacon Fardulf?" one of his guards asked.

Pepin's eyes popped open. What had the old Lombard heard?

Gomeric leapt to his feet. Fardulf glanced over his shoulder and sped past the guards. Through the open door, the calls of bush crickets became louder.

"How ill did the deacon look?" Gomeric asked the guards.

"He was pale and shaking."

"Poor fellow. Not well. Not well at all," Gomeric said a bit too quickly. "Severinus, the deacon might need aid."

Severinus gave a curt nod and ran.

"Come, nephew," Gomeric said. "We are finished with our prayers, and you look tired. No need to worry about the deacon. Severinus will help him."

Shaking off the image of stallions tied to his wrists, Pepin tried to mimic Gomeric's lack of anxiety. He forced air through his tight throat as he got to his feet.

Outside the church, the stars and half-moon at its zenith allowed Pepin to make out Severinus's shape moving among the straighter lines of the huts. In the past few months, Pepin had come this way so often, he no longer needed a torch. But his guards refused to be without one.

"Saint Augustine makes an interesting point when he says ..." Gomeric shifted to Latin and told Pepin his plan.

Ahead, Severinus's silhouette shrank and faded into the shadows. Pepin started to quicken his pace.

"We must walk like we're simply returning from prayers," Gomeric said in Latin. "Don't make your guards think otherwise."

Pepin and Gomeric passed more peasant huts and farms before reaching the city's great gates. After a city guard ushered them in through the man-sized door, they headed toward the palace. Pepin clenched his fists to still their trembling. Could Severinus stop Fardulf? What if Gomeric's plan failed? At the palace, Pepin searched the guards' face. Did any of them suspect? He couldn't see any signs. The palace guards admitted them, and they walked toward the royal residence. Pepin's heart threatened to burst from his chest.

After twenty paces, Gomeric said, "Nephew, I must show you something. It's a surprise."

They made a sharp left away from the manor. Pepin kept his stride long. He had rarely gone this way after dusk, where the buildings cut dark blocks against the night sky. Wood smoke told him he and Gomeric had passed the kitchen. He knew the barracks by their large rectangular silhouette, then the smell of horses wafted to him.

Still, they kept walking toward the west wall and a ruined shed Pepin had seen only from a distance. Gomeric had said it might have once been used for weaving. Several times, Pepin thought he had seen a large rat scurry into what was left of the structure. Repulsive—and perfect. What better place to stash armor and weapons smuggled out of the palace's locked storeroom, with the help of drugged wine and easily distracted guards? As they drew near, Pepin made out warped and rotten wooden planks falling in on themselves and wanted to pinch his nose against the dank smell from years of rain pouring through the holes in its thatched roof. He glanced at his uncle. His guards must surely suspect something.

"Now!" Gomeric growled in Latin.

As they had planned, Pepin charged at and tackled one of his guards. The man shouted.

"Silence!" Pepin hissed, trying to pin the struggling man's limbs.

To his left, Pepin heard the rasp of a drawn knife then a liquid, strangled sound. Hands pulled Pepin off the guard, then shadows passed him. The guard's cry was muffled and suddenly silent.

"Dead?" asked Gomeric, smelling of blood.

"Dead," a man replied.

Inside the hut, candlelight within a lantern flickered on Pepin's followers, about twenty-five men. Clad in iron helmets, mail shirts, and leg guards, they were coating their blades with pitch, and using waxed leather gloves, dusting the weapons with a bitter-smelling powder. *The wolf's bane Gomeric told me about.*

Pepin watched his step. Floorboards had been pried off the ground, revealing chests where the armor and weapons used to be hidden. The men looked up.

"Gird our new king with his sword," barked Gomeric.

Pepin beamed. Finally. A sword.

"Change of plans," Gomeric said, his face grim. "We must presume our enemy is awake and knows about our cause. We will enter the royal apartment through the hall. Our prize is now the tyrant's wife and daughters. Their capture is our only chance to force his surrender."

"You are to leave my sisters unharmed," Pepin said imperiously. "Anyone who dishonors them dishonors their king. I—we—will have offenders castrated and sentenced to the traitor's death."

Gomeric glowered. Pepin didn't care. He would protect his sisters.

"The girls are innocent," Pepin continued, "and we will consider your loyalty and obedience when we seek husbands for them."

Gomeric's lips turned up slightly.

"But the queen will answer for her cruelty," Pepin said. "So will her husband for permitting it. That, we swear by Saint Georg."

***

Soon, Charles would be all hers. Fastrada longed to press herself against her husband's broad, sculpted chest, to feel those muscular arms encircle her. For a few hours, they could forget they were king and queen of Francia. They could forget the Saxons, the Avars, the Byzantines, the court.

The light from the candles and the embers in the hearth flickered on the curtained bed and the small table where she had placed her eating knife and the enameled bronze brooch with the likeness of Saint Wigbert. A pace away from her, Charles wore only his linen shirt. He had dismissed his chamberlain, but Irma had just removed her headdress and veil and was still helping her disrobe. Sitting on a stool, Fastrada raised her left leg to allow the maid to untie her garter.

She glanced up at Charles. His bright eyes were a little more round; anticipation lay on his lips. She smiled. Almost nine years and she could still get that look from him.

"How are you feeling, my dear?" he asked.

"Well enough." She let Irma pull off her other stocking.

Voices from the great hall forced their way into the bedchamber. Fastrada and Charles exchanged a look of annoyance.

"Stop him! He is plotting to kill the king!" That was from Count Severinus.

Charles lurched and placed his hand over his heart as if he'd been stabbed. Through a tight throat, Fastrada's breath came in small gasps. She waved her maid away.

"No! He's the murderer!" Fardulf screamed.

Fastrada's pulse raced. It was worse than she had realized.

Without thinking, she was on her feet. Charles drew himself to his full height, and his face fell into stern lines.

"When you come to the hall, stay close to me," he ordered.

He snatched one of the candles from a table and marched out of the bedchamber. Listening to the men's shouts, Fastrada bade Irma to accompany her with a candle, then followed her husband. As Charles's bare feet pounded against the stone floor, she longed to keep up with him, but she dared not run and let her ailment drain her vigor; she would need every last grain of it in a few moments. She passed through the royal apartment's corridor. To her right, she heard the younger girls' nurses whisper for them to stay in the room. She let out a breath. They would be safe there.

She entered the apartment's reception room, dark except for the glow of the embers in the hearth, and beheld Karl, like his father wearing only a shirt. Near the door to the great hall, he barked at his two eldest sisters to stay back. He met Fastrada's gaze.

"Mother, tell them this is no place for a woman," he said.

"It's a place for a queen," she said. "Hruodtrude, Bertha, go to your room and look after your sisters. Karl, come with me."

"But someone is trying to ..." Hruodtrude's eyes welled.

"We'll stop them," Fastrada replied with more confidence than she felt.

Hruodtrude and Bertha scowled but retreated down the corridor. With Karl beside her, she quickened her steps.

"Why would you believe Fardulf? He is a Lombard—a favorite of their former king!" Severinus's voice boomed from the other side of the door.

"God's wounds," Fastrada muttered. She needed to intervene now.

Fastrada entered the great hall and took her place next to her husband. Karl was still protectively close. The sight that greeted her stiffened her limbs. In the light of the birch bark torches, Fardulf knelt, cowering before Charles. The deacon's face was sweaty and ashen; the gray and brown hair around his tonsure stood on end. Two bodyguards stood between Fardulf and Severinus, close enough to grab either of them. Menservants and castle guards formed a half-circle around them. Fastrada's mouth went dry. Behind her, a maid slipped a veil over her hair, then quickly pinned it in place.

"My lady queen, you must help me," Fardulf cried. "Tell them you believe me."

"Fardulf is under my husband's protection," she said in a clipped tone she hoped would conceal the tremor in her voice.

From the corner of her eye, she saw Charles frowning at her. No time to explain.

Fardulf fell at Charles's and Fastrada's feet. His words came in a torrent, and Fastrada could comprehend only pieces. Murder. Pepin as king. His uncle Gomeric holding the real power.

"Ridiculous," Severinus snarled, his eyes crazed. "That Lombard is the would-be murderer."

Fastrada spun toward Charles. He was staring at the deacon. She seized both of Charles's hands. "Husband, Fardulf is faithful to us. He spied on them on my order."

Behind her, she heard the rasp of a blade being drawn. Looking up, Charles freed his hands and shoved her aside. Fastrada stumbled backward. She turned just as Severinus plunged his knife into the eye of one of the guards. A burst of blood. Screams. A shriek ripped through Fastrada's throat. Severinus sprinted into the shadows.

Guards gave chase. Charles lunged and seized the two hindmost men. "Protect my wife and daughters. Karl, once we get sword and armor, you're with me. Fardulf, how many are there? What are their plans?"

"Don't know the number. They were planning to enter through the princes' bedchamber."

Fardulf scrambled across the floor to the prone guard and blurted for him to confess his sins to God.

Fastrada could not stop shivering. If Pepin and his band of traitors succeeded, Francia would tear itself to shreds. No one would accept a hunchback on the throne, and nobles would fight each other for the kingdom. Again, the smoke of Büraburg's scorched fields filled her nostrils, and the village of living skeletons swam into her vision.

Chapter Thirty-five

In the firelit bedchamber, Fastrada kept her panic and rage coiled in her belly. Her daughters and her women needed her to be brave, although she wanted to curl up in a corner of the room. She heard menservants shoving chests and furniture, carrying out Charles's orders to block the windows to the royal apartment. She touched her brooch with Saint Wigbert's image. *Protect us as you protected Büraburg.*

She focused on the matter at hand: helping her husband into his armor. They could not wait for Meginfrid. Wearing only his shirt and leather boots, Charles threw on woolen padding. Fastrada and Irma stepped back from each other, spreading the armor between them. Her arms strained. Charles dove into the garment.

"I'll fetch the leg guards," Irma said.

"No time," Charles said.

"But ..." Fastrada said.

"My dear, this will do."

Stone-faced, he held out his hand. Irma fetched his shield from a peg on the wall and his helmet from an open chest while Fastrada grabbed his belt and sheathed sword. Charles donned the accoutrements. Menservants lifted the chest with the hunting weapons and lugged it to the princesses' bedchamber.

Fastrada kissed her husband. They hurried across the corridor and entered the princesses' bedchamber, crowded with maids, the girls, and their nurses. Karl, armored and girded with a sword, and his man were carrying chests toward the door. Three other chests were stacked in front of the tapestry of the Holy Mother and her child and the shuttered window behind it. The girls gathered around their father.

"My dearlings." Charles's voice cracked. "Stay here until I come for you."

Without waiting for a reply, Charles and Karl dashed out of the room. As soon as the door closed, nurses and maids shoved and stacked three trunks against the entrance. *Karl must have told them to do so.* Fastrada wished the entrance to this room was like the ones to the palace, with locks and metal to reinforce the nailed wooden planks. *Built when the enemy was outside.*

Charles had commanded guards to stay in the reception room and just outside the apartment. Fastrada assessed their other defenses. Open chests with hunting spears and javelins were close. Near the opposite wall were stools, baskets with yarns and threads, and embroidery hoops. At the far wall to her left, two large beds flanked the hearth, and small tables sat on each side of the beds for the girls' night candles, caskets of jewelry, basins and pitchers for washing, combs, and Hruodtrude's and Bertha's jars of perfumes and cosmetics. Chamber pots were stowed underneath. Pallets lay between the beds, the blankets still rumpled upon them.

"Place the tables against the chests by the door and put the pallets on top of the chests," Fastrada ordered. "Move the trunks with our hunting weapons to the back of the room and gather whatever we can throw."

While the nurses moved the tables and maids shoved the trunks, Fastrada and the princesses piled pillows, basins, pitchers, stools, and anything else they could grab near the hunting weapons. Through the walls, Fastrada heard the scrapes of heavy furniture being pushed on the reception room's wooden floor. A barricade for the apartment, she guessed.

Theodrada sniffled.

"It will be all right," Fastrada soothed as much to herself as the girls. "Father and Karl will find the bad men."

"What if Father and Karl don't catch them?" the seven-winter-old asked.

"They will, child," Fastrada said. She tried not to think of what would happen to her babies if Charles failed.

"But what if they don't?" Hruodhaid whimpered.

"Father and Karl are warriors," Fastrada said with more certainty than she felt. "They've slain Saxons, Lombards, and Avars. A few bad men are nothing to them."

Yet the eight-winter-old Hruodhaid's question lingered in her mind. Severinus could still lurk in the hall. Hruodhaid and Theodrada were sobbing, just as Fastrada had sobbed at seven winters old in Büraburg. *We didn't worry about the enemy within then.*

"How could Pepin do this?" Bertha asked, her face pale.

"I knew he was unhappy," Hruodtrude said, her brow creased. "But to betray Father ..."

Fastrada looked away, unable to answer. Her gaze fell on the tapestry mostly hidden by the stacked chests. "We can do something to help Father and Karl. We will pray to the Blessed Mother."

As she and the six princesses knelt near the tapestry, Fastrada glanced up and spied the Virgin's halo. If her pleas would bring Charles and Karl back, she would pray all night, even though exhaustion was already creeping over her limbs. Fastrada bowed her head. She, the princesses, and the women chanted, "*Ave Maria, gratia plena*," over and over and over. She tried to drown out the voice in her mind that railed, *Had you but heeded me about Pepin, Charles ...*

***

Pepin's heartbeat filled his ears. He tried to ignore the unfamiliar heaviness of the sword at his hip and the ill-fitting armor on his shoulders, the awkwardness of holding a shield while trying to rush. The cross swinging from his neck would deter demons, he reminded himself. Sweat drenched his face. Even though he strained to breathe, he tried to keep up with the group sneaking along the south wall, prove to them his worthiness to rule.

Near the royal residence, Gomeric held up his hand to halt. Pepin heard feet pounding against stones and shouts: "I think the murderers are over there."

He muttered a profanity. Severinus had failed. He turned his head this way and that to ascertain the sound's origin.

In the starlight, Gomeric's posture stiffened. He pointed to two warriors, then Pepin. The men nodded as if they had discussed something before. Pepin frowned. What had Gomeric not told him?

Gomeric gestured for the remaining men to follow, then sprinted through the arch. Metal slammed into wooden shields ahead of him. *No turning back.* Pepin squared his shoulders as much as his twisted spine would allow and strode toward the manor, the two fighting men flanking him.

At the edge of the courtyard, he beheld shadows of his fellows and the guards hacking at each other. A few already lay dead. Pepin could not tell whether they had been his men or his father's.

The warriors next to Pepin grabbed his arms. "Go no farther, Your Excellence," said the fighter with a deep voice.

"Unhand me. I must fight for my crown."

"Mayor Gomeric's orders. It's too dark and too risky. Especially with poisoned blades. Even a scratch could kill you."

Pepin scowled. The knot of pain tightened between his shoulder blades. "The men should see my bravery."

"They can barely see anything."

Pepin tugged against the men's grip, but they held him fast.

"Keep thrashing," said the other, who had a nasal voice, "and we will beat you senseless. Mayor Gomeric's order."

"Don't talk to me like that. I am your king."

"Mayor Gomeric said we are to protect you by any means, my lord," said the second fighter.

Pepin stopped struggling. He would rebuke Gomeric for denying him his glory. Maybe he would let Gomeric think he would not be mayor of the palace. As Pepin watched the warriors hack their swords into shields and parry blows, he still could not tell which soldiers were his. Whose soldier just cried out? Another shadow joined the fray.

A few men, perhaps castle guards, dropped their swords. Another bent over and spewed. The poison was working! A fighter chopped through the sick guard's neck. Other men soon were heaving and couldn't hold their weapons, and Pepin's warriors slew them.

A smile spread on Pepin's face. Gomeric, blessed Gomeric, would win him the throne. But then Pepin heard the marching of many men. He spat out an obscenity.

"Inside!" Gomeric bellowed.

The two men holding back Pepin now shoved and dragged him. Pepin ran through the courtyard. His belly lurched at the stink of carnage and vomit. His fighters, covered with blood, regrouped in the great hall and dusted their weapons with powder from pouches in their belts. In the torchlight, Pepin saw fewer of his own warriors, but Severinus had joined them. His clothes and face splattered with gore, he held a bloody sword, perhaps taken from one of his father's dead guards.

"The king and Lord Karl left the hall to search for you," he said hurriedly, keeping his voice low. "The fight at the door drew most of the guards, but a few remain near the royal apartment."

"To the royal apartment," Gomeric said.

The men's footsteps rumbled across the dark hall. After a few strides, Pepin fell behind; the two warriors exchanged an anxious glance, then seized his shoulders and hauled him. In vain, Pepin tried to gulp air. Ahead, metal struck metal and wood. At the royal apartment, blades and armor flashed in the torchlight. Warriors grunted and sobbed for breath.

Wielding an ax, one of his soldiers chopped the door where it met the hinges. Soon, the scene from the courtyard repeated itself. The castle guards' swords clunked to the floor. As they reached after their weapons, they vomited, and Pepin's men easily dispatched them. The door fell to the floor, and Pepin heard the enemy at the other end of the hall.

"Tell His Excellence the traitors are in the manor!"

✳✳✳

The crash from the reception room sent Fastrada's heart racing. Vigor surged through her, banishing every trace of weariness. She rushed through the Ave Maria, crossed herself, and leapt to her feet.

"Gisela," she said in a low tone, "get the little girls to the far corner of the room, near the beds, and stay with them. Hurry!"

Gisela grabbed Theodrada's and Chiltrude's hands and ordered Hruodhaid to follow.

233

A thump like the toppling of a heavy chair came from the reception room. Shouts, then clashes and scrapes of metal against metal penetrated the plastered stone walls. Men cried out. Objects fell to the floor, followed by retching.

"Why are so many so ill?" Hruodtrude asked. "They were well earlier."

"They're experienced fighters, not boys who have never seen battle. Unless ..."

"Unless what?"

"Poison!" Fastrada whispered.

Hruodtrude and Bertha blanched, and Fastrada felt the blood drain from her face. *Charles' legs are exposed!*

"Don't say anything," Fastrada muttered. "For your sisters' sake."

The two eldest girls nodded.

Fastrada dashed to the back of the room and grabbed her javelin. Hruodtrude and Bertha took their weapons. The other women clutched something to throw from the pile of improvised missiles.

In the low light from the hearth and candles, Fastrada watched the chests at the door, half hidden in the shadows. Her body was as tense as a bowstring. Feet pounded against the reception room's floor. Metal smashed against metal. A heavy object slammed into the bedchamber door again and again and again. Wood cracked.

With her free hand, she touched her brooch. *Saint Wigbert, we need God's help.* She tightened her grip on the javelin.

No one spoke, and the clashes and shouts dominated the room. Wood splintered. Someone dragged the door away. Fastrada squinted at their makeshift barricade. The top chest inched its way forward.

Her breathing quickened and became loud in her ears. Bertha raised her arm, ready to throw.

"Not yet," Fastrada said in an undertone. "Wait until you see their heads."

The clanging and yells continued in the next room. The women stared at the chest. The pallets atop it slid off, then the trunk fell, hit the small tables, and crashed, landing on its side. The intruders were silhouetted against the torchlight.

"Now!" Fastrada yelled.

She loosed the javelin with all her strength and struck an invader in his right shoulder. He cried out and staggered back. Soon, two more javelins, a basin, chamber pot, basket, and pillow followed. Two more fighters fell while other warriors cursed as the pottery shattered against helmets. They disappeared, and after a moment, the middle chest started to move slowly forward.

Bodies thudded to the floor in the other room.

"Nurses! Protect my children!" Fastrada shouted.

The nurses retreated. Fastrada clutched a pitcher in her right hand and Charles's hunting spear in her left. Hruodtrude and Bertha flanked her, and the maids stood nearby. Fastrada knew any order to hide would be futile. She glanced at the women. All held something harder than a pillow.

The chest hit the tables and stopped. Their foes raised their heads above the barrier.

"Again!" Fastrada shouted.

The women hurled their missiles. Still grasping the spear, Fastrada blindly flung anything within reach. The room filled with the scent of lavender from a broken jar.

"Keep pushing," Gomeric bellowed from the other side of the door.

The tables resisted then scraped against the floor. So did the upended chest. In the narrow space between the trunk and the door, a figure with a drawn sword and raised shield clambered over the bottom trunk.

The women launched whatever they could, but his shield caused most of the objects to break or bounce harmlessly away. A second figure with a curved back—Pepin—entered the room with his weapon held aloft. Other men remained in the doorway.

Soon the women had nothing left to throw. Fastrada gripped the spear in both hands and pointed it at the first man's neck. From the corner of her eye, she saw Hruodtrude and Bertha do the same and heard the rasp of eating knives being unsheathed.

The intruder lowered his shield. Fastrada fought the urge to recoil at the sight of blood splattered on Gomeric's face and clothes.

"Surrender," he said between breaths. "Your husband is dead. Pepin is king."

Fastrada heard muffled sobs and shushing from the far corner of the room. Hruodtrude and Bertha both sucked in air through their teeth. Although her mouth and throat were dry, Fastrada stiffened her spine and raised her chin. *Be brave. Be brave for the girls.* She spoke to Gomeric as if he were a stubborn servant. "You lie."

"Surrender to me, and your daughters will be safe."

"Why not kill the she-wolf?" Pepin asked.

"Hold your tongue!" Gomeric snarled.

Was that a tremor she saw in Gomeric's hand or a trick of the firelight? Strange that the traitor had not moved to harm her or anyone else in the room. Three women with spears were no match for an armored, experienced warrior with a shield and poisoned blade. He needed them alive, and she suspected it had something to do with the sounds of renewed fighting outside this room. Her fingers ached from clenching the spear, but she dared not let go.

Stall for time. "The only way I will surrender is if you and Pepin swear an oath. You must swear to Jesu, His Merciful Mother, Saint Martin, Saint Wigbert, Saint Ursula, Saint Peter, Saint Paul, Saint ..." Her mind went blank.

"Saint Dionysis," Hruodtrude continued for her, the words tumbling from her mouth, "Saint Rusticus, Saint Eleutherius, Saint Germanus ..."

"That's enough!" Pepin barked.

"You are in no position to make demands," Gomeric growled.

The shouts and clangs grew louder. Pepin's eyes widened. Gomeric had the look of a cornered boar determined to gore its way out.

Fastrada focused on keeping the stammer from her voice. "How is asking you to take an oath to be true to your word a demand? You betrayed my husband. I presume you are a good enough Christian not to turn on God and His saints."

"I swear to God and the Blessed Mother no harm will come to your daughters," Gomeric spat.

"Not good enough," Hruodtrude said. "You must also swear not to harm my mother."

"And Karl," Bertha said.

Gomeric bared blackened teeth. Drops of sweat ran down his face.

Fastrada smiled at Gomeric, the way she did at Charles's enemies at court. "Pepin, too, must swear an oath to all those saints. Three times."

In the shadows near the door, swords clashed. Fastrada planted her feet and locked eyes with Gomeric. Her foe stood still. Over his shoulder, she saw the silhouette of a warrior slump and be shoved aside. Then, a hulking figure leapt on the chest.

"Charles!" Fastrada cried. The girls' gasps were distant in her ears. Fastrada blinked back the tears blurring her vision. God be praised! Charles was alive and whole!

Chapter Thirty-six

Charles sprang at Gomeric. The traitor turned, using his shield to fend off Charles's blow. With all her strength, Fastrada thrust the spear into Gomeric's exposed side. The barb crunched against his armor and penetrated only a little, just enough to draw blood. As Gomeric flinched, she heard clangs nearby, then a thump.

"Wife, out of the way!" Charles ordered.

Fastrada stepped back, keeping her spear in front of her to block Gomeric's path. She glanced to her right. Pepin stood against the wall, weaponless, with Karl pointing his blade at his brother.

Charles raised his sword and aimed to split Gomeric's skull. His foe jumped away. Gomeric swung his weapon toward Charles's face. Charles countered with his shield—saints be praised, it held. He thrust his blade toward Gomeric's heart. His foe parried, then aimed for Charles's legs. Charles knocked the blow down with his own weapon, then drove his sword into Gomeric's throat. A burst of blood. The traitor fell.

Pepin howled, an unearthly sound.

Fastrada dropped her spear and raced to her husband.

Karl raised his sword. Fastrada gasped. *He is going to slay his brother!*

"Stop!" Charles barked.

"He betrayed us!" Karl snapped. "He and his ilk deserve death!"

"Kill me now!" Pepin screamed, tears streaming down his face. "I've nothing to live for."

"Neither of you gets to decide." Charles's voice was eerily calm.

"Traitors are scum," Fastrada added, "but we need intelligence. We need to know how far this conspiracy goes. They can't talk if they're dead."

Scowling, Karl lowered his weapon. "Show no mercy."

"If they must hang from the ceiling until their arms tear out of their sockets, so be it," Charles said icily.

The girls were pale and trembling but otherwise unharmed. *If only their hearts could be as untouched as their bodies.*

***

Fastrada heard the rustle of the bed curtains, and the air was slightly cooler on her face. Still, she did not move. Her limbs felt as if lead weighed them down. Even her eyelids were heavy.

"Has your lady gotten out of bed at all today?" Charles asked.

"I begged her to awaken, if only to eat," Irma moaned. "To no avail."

Fastrada could no longer distinguish nightmares from the waking world. Had Pepin tried to assassinate Charles two days ago? Or had it been another dream like the one of the Saxons shattering Büraburg's walls? The sadness in her husband's voice was all too real.

When the excitement of battle had been fresh in her, Fastrada had done what she could. She ordered maids to scrub away every trace of blood and vomit and prepare another chamber in the royal apartment to be fit for the princesses. She dictated a message to the abbess of Niedermünster, promising the sisters a generous gift if they washed the bodies of Charles's slain warriors and prepared them for burial. She told menservants to cart the dead renegades to a crossroads and leave them to the rats and crows. The world would know what happened to traitors, body and soul. All too soon, her vitality had drained away, and she had collapsed on the bed still clothed.

Charles touched Fastrada's shoulder. "Awake, my dear. It is well past sext."

She considered not moving. She was still vexed with her husband for ignoring her suspicions about Pepin. Had he listened to her, she would be in the princesses' room, telling them to stop bickering about who had the nicest gown, not stuck in this bed making weak attempts to comfort them when they spent a few moments with her. Had Charles listened to her, Chiltrude would not scream in the middle of the night.

Fastrada opened her eyes a crack. Mother of God, Charles's face was drawn, despite his efforts to show the world the rebellion had not hurt him. If only God would restore her vigor so she could do the same. With the little strength she had, she turned toward her husband, for his sake.

Charles helped her sit upright against the pillows and adjusted the sheets. He stroked her cheek.

"Irma, fetch your lady food and wine," he said.

Behind him, the maid bowed and ran.

"You will eat, my dear."

"I will do my best. Sometimes it takes all my effort just to eat."

"You must restore your strength. I need you. Your children need you."

At the mention of the children, Fastrada again saw her babies quaking in the corner. Her face crumpled. Sobs racked her body, and she was too exhausted to stop them. She didn't know if she wept for the girls' fear, for Charles's heartbreak, or her rage against Pepin.

Charles hugged her to his chest. "There, there, my dear. We will obliterate this conspiracy, every last bit of it. No one will hurt you or our family ever again."

Fastrada vaguely remembered her husband telling her that Pepin and his fellow traitors were in a cell under the palace's northwest tower, and Meginfrid was working with the guards to extract information. Charles had ordered the chamberlain not to torture Pepin, but from what she heard, Fastrada surmised the prison was unpleasant enough.

When she finally could stifle her tears, she asked, "What has Meginfrid found out?"

Charles frowned.

Her heart started to beat faster. "Tell me."

He let out a sigh. "Dreck at first. They said they couldn't tolerate your cruelty and repeated that rooster-and-jackass story about the monk at Oppenheim. Then they protested the treatment of the Thuringian rebels, as if they cared one whit about them before.

"Meginfrid tired of the horse dung and told Severinus if he wanted to protect his wife and daughter, he needed to tell the truth. That worked better than the beatings. We finally had some useful information."

Charles confirmed her worst fears—the conspiracy spread beyond the walls of Regensburg and included many of Tassilo's allies in Francia, Bavaria, and Lombardy. Yet she was shocked by a few of the names, like Charles's cousin Wala, Count Theudald, and the bishop of Verdun.

"Severinus says Himiltrude provided money for arms and spies, but Pepin denies it." Charles snorted in derision. "Good to see he's loyal to someone."

A shiver crawled up Fastrada's spine. If Pepin had succeeded, Himiltrude would have become the most powerful woman in Francia. Fastrada had thought of how her own life might have changed if she had borne a son and God had taken Charles in battle. As queen mother, Fastrada would have ruled part of the realm as regent. But at what cost? Would the hunger for power supplant the love among Charles's children? Her mouth filled with a bitter taste. "Praise God and His saints for giving me only daughters. I understand now why you prayed for them."

Charles squeezed her hand.

"There is something else, isn't there?" she said.

He looked down. "The fire in Worms. It wasn't an accident."

"You mean, the traitors ..."

He nodded.

A wave of dizziness coursed through her. "Nantlind was murdered! And Karl ..."

Tears slipped down Charles's cheeks.

"Charles?"

"I thought my sons would grow out of their squabbles and become allies," he muttered. "Instead, one of them wants me dead. Maybe I should have sold Pepin into slavery as soon as I saw his shoulders start to stoop."

Fastrada looked at her husband, speechless. The Franks would have been better off if Charles had done such a thing, but she would never even think of condemning her own child to that fate. This was not the Charles she knew, which made her loathing for Pepin sink its fangs deeper into her heart.

***

Getting through sunrise Mass at Niedermünster two days later taxed Fastrada's strength, just as vespers Mass had the previous evening. After the benediction, Fastrada told her husband that she would meet him at the manor and bade Karl, the girls, and the servants to go ahead without her. Some bodyguards remained. While Charles approached the altar with a purse full of coins, she trudged toward a painted, wooden statue and sank to her knees. The Virgin, her face serene, held her doll-like Child. Against the flowing folds of her veil and robe, the infant Jesu gazed up at His mother. *If only our family could be like that.*

She shook her head. How naïve. Caressing her brooch, she murmured a Paternoster, an Ave Maria, and a prayer of thanksgiving for her family's safety. As she rose and made the sign of the cross, she glanced at another statue, the Pietà. The lines on the Virgin's face bespoke her sorrow as she cradled her limp Son. It was the same anguish Fastrada had seen in Charles.

Her throat tightened. She wanted Pepin to hurt as much as Charles did. She wanted him as terrified as Hruodhaid and Theodrada when they begged her not to leave at bedtime. She had spent an hour whispering to them that the bad men would never return, that she and their father would protect them. She would keep that promise—and she would get some answers in the few hours of vitality she had that day.

Trailed by two bodyguards, she left the church and headed for the palace. Once she entered the grounds, she turned right and strode past the barracks to the northwest tower. With a straight back and lifted chin, she entered and ordered the guards within to bring Pepin from the room under the floor. They opened the trapdoor, releasing an odor of mold and mildew. Moments later, Pepin was dragged before her in chains. His shoulders slumped more than usual under a torn and filthy tunic.

She winced at the sight of Pepin's bruised and swollen nose. A scab had formed where his lip had split, and both eyes were blackened.

Turning to the guard, Fastrada demanded, "Who beat him? My husband's will is to leave him untouched."

"No one defied the king, my lady queen," the guard stammered.

"My father did this," Pepin said tonelessly.

Her eyes widened. Her Charles? The realization sunk in her belly. Yes, her Charles. He had forbidden everyone else from harming Pepin, but they needed information to save their people, even if that meant thrashing it out of his own son.

"Tell me, bastard," Fastrada snarled, "why should I not prove you right about me? Why should I not persuade your father to have you tied to four stallions and send for a mare? You know I want to. You killed my maid!" Her voice ragged, Fastrada swallowed back the tears that threatened. She would not weep, not in front of the guards, not in front of her enemy.

"I tried to save her," Pepin mumbled. "Uncle Gomeric held me back."

Rage shook her. "You caused that fire! Your little sisters could've died in their beds. And for what? A crown that would have been yours in name only."

"Not true," Pepin muttered.

"Your uncle would have ruled, not you. Do you truly think the nobles would have tolerated a king bearing God's curse?"

"God would have cured me." His voice cracked. "We were doing His will."

"Father in Heaven! You believe that!" She lowered her voice. "If murdering your father and your family is God's will, why are you still a pathetic, twisted little man?"

She turned and left. She wanted to hear Pepin beg for mercy, shriek as the horses tore him apart. But she could not get Charles's pained face from her mind.

***

Fastrada stared at the glowing embers in the hearth. Alone with Charles in their bedchamber, she took a sip of mulled wine to warm and to steady herself. She had not yet related her conversation with Pepin the previous day. It had drained her so much she had to sleep right after dinner. She had dreamt that she was searching for Nantlind in Worms's royal apartment but could not find her.

Today was not any easier. As they dressed that morning, her husband had spoken of how he had sent the Lombard king and Duke Tassilo to the cloister. *But we never thought them loyal. Pepin's treachery is worse.*

Life in a monastery would make Pepin more miserable than the archbishopric he had tried to avoid. He could no longer threaten the realm, and Charles would deny the rebels a martyr. Yet a fist squeezed her heart as she thought of Nantlind and Karl and the girls. How could she not demand justice?

All morning and all through dinner, she had agonized over what she would counsel Charles to do. Now, during the time for their midafternoon nap, she could no longer delay. They had dismissed Meginfrid and Irma and were still fully clothed. In the dim light of the shuttered room, she set the wine aside and turned toward her husband. Mother of God, he had become haggard. She knew what she needed to do.

"It's about Pepin," she said, reaching for his hand.

"I would have rather lost my sword arm than see what I've seen of Pepin these last few days." He squared his shoulders. "You're going to advise me to execute him with the rest of the traitors."

"No." Fastrada's voice was barely audible, even to her own ears.

The tense line in Charles's brow relaxed. "You approve sending Pepin to the cloister?"

"We must. It's best for our people." *Nantlind, forgive me.*

Her husband squeezed her hand. "Everyone will see it as mercy, but Pepin will be wretched—and still hate me."

His words were a hot poker in her entrails. Fastrada had long stopped caring if Pepin despised her. But for that ingrate to loathe Charles, his own father, who had done so much for him, was still doing what he could ... "What does Pepin expect? To go free and inherit a kingdom?"

"My dear, he is as obstinate as a pagan clinging to false gods."

She shivered. "He left you no choice. The tonsure is the only way to redeem his soul."

"You care about his soul?"

Tears swam into her vision. "I care about *you*. He is your son, and you love him. Still. I cannot—will not—let his betrayal destroy you, even if we must sacrifice vengeance."

He held her face between his large hands and kissed her, then embraced her fiercely. At that moment, she knew their people would heal—Charles's heart would heal. They would root out the traitors and defeat the Saxons and the Avars. They would construct palaces and churches, and build an empire to rival Byzantium. And someday the world would call her husband Charles the Great.

I learned about Fastrada while researching my debut novel, *The Cross and the Dragon*. Charlemagne's biographer Einhard attributes the plots against his lord to "the cruelty of Queen Fastrada." *What did this woman do?* I thought. Einhard never elaborated, and since Hildegard was Charles's queen at the time of my first two books, I set the question aside, figuring that whatever it was, Fastrada must have been a bad person.

That is, until I encountered Fastrada again in the Royal Frankish Annals, when she and Charles were overjoyed to see each other upon his return to Worms from Rome.

Maybe there was more to this story. I got to wondering: was Fastrada truly cruel or was she the victim of a backlash against strong-willed, influential women, a backlash we've seen in the twentieth and twenty-first centuries with Nancy Reagan and Hillary Clinton?

What's known about Fastrada: she was King Charles's fourth wife, whom he married in October 783, a few months after the deaths of Queen Hildegard and Queen Mother Bertrada. She was from East Francia, an area where Charles needed an alliance during his ongoing wars with the Saxon peoples, but we don't know where exactly in East Francia. The fortress of Büraburg existed at the time, but there is no evidence Fastrada was from there. Documentary evidence indicates she and Charles loved each other and that she was influential—only people with power or influence attract enemies. Her age and appearance are my invention.

Allegations of her cruelty come years after the deaths of Fastrada and Charles. In addition to Einhard, the anonymous writer of the Revised Royal Frankish Annals cited her bad behavior as the reason for Pepin's rebellion. Neither specified the alleged atrocities, and the author of the revised annals implies skepticism about the rebels' motives. Cruelty, by medieval standards, was persecuting one's own people—massacring the enemy was something to brag about.

And there is no evidence to support that she mistreated her stepdaughters. Nor is there any proof that Fastrada became jealous that Hruodtrude would be empress and thwarted the girl's marriage to Byzantine Emperor Constantine. Charles and Constantine's mother, Irene, both take credit for the breakup. Both Frankish and Byzantine sources say Constantine was upset to lose Hruodtrude, but history is silent on Hruodtrude's sentiments.

Little is known about Charles's first wife, Himiltrude, a Frankish noblewoman and, if we are to believe Pope Stephen, the bride picked for Charles by his father, King Pepin. Later called a concubine, Himiltrude was set aside so that Charles could marry a Lombard princess. Scholars disagree on whether Himiltrude was a concubine or a spouse. The reason I believe she was a wife is that Charles's younger brother, Carloman, had wed Gerberga on his father's order, and no one disputed the validity of that marriage. Had Carloman's son been born out of wedlock, there would have been no war in Lombardy. It makes no sense for Pepin to arrange a marriage for the younger heir but not the elder.

Himiltrude's skeleton was found at Nivelles, and she lived to be thirty-five to forty years old. Because one source compares Pepin to the Old Testament character Abimelech, who killed his brothers and usurped his father, one scholar has speculated that Himiltrude was involved. It is possible. Deposed medieval queens did not always go quietly. Gerberga is one example. After Carloman died, she crossed the Alps with two little boys in tow in an attempt to restore their father's kingdom to them.

An unknown number of Thuringians (sometimes called East Franks) rebelled in 786, and several leaders were blinded. Fastrada's role in administering that form of justice, also practiced by the Romans and the Byzantines, is not recorded. Nor does anyone know when or how her father died or if she had siblings.

The annals record the fire at the Worms palace as accidental. Why Charles did not rebuild the Worms palace is a mystery. After all, he rebuilt the Paderborn palace twice.

Another mystery is why Karl (called Charles the Younger by scholars) never married. A couple of scholars have speculated about Karl's relationship with Osulf, a member of his retinue and pupil of Alcuin. Were Karl and Osulf close friends, drawing the jealousy of courtiers, or was there something more? Even if it was the latter, Karl still could have wed a high-ranking woman. What mattered is that he could do his duty as a husband and engender children. What he did outside the marriage was between him and his confessor. In many medieval minds, homosexuality was just another sin, like adultery or premarital sex. Karl was named duke of Le Mans in 790 and led several forces in Frankish wars before his death in 811.

To keep the story focused, I simplified the politics in Italy, including Benevento. I omitted the seneschal bringing the Breton leader to the 786 assembly in chains, Grahamannus and Otgar fighting the Avars in a 788 war in Bavaria, and Charles having a sister, the abbess of Chelles. I also left out court intellectuals such as Paul the Deacon, Theodulf, and many others, and downplayed Bishop Felix's heresy, even though it was important to the theologians.

The Franks' speculation about Tassilo's involvement with Adalgis's attack is my invention, but Charles thought he had just cause to depose his cousin. The Avars with the fearsome reputation were weakened by drought and infighting, but Charles likely would not have known the extent.

The historic Fardulf revealed the conspiracy to Charles, and he was rewarded with the abbey of Saint-Denis. That he was working with Fastrada is another authorial liberty.

Fastrada's role in the composition of the Royal Frankish Annals is possible but unproven. The RFA's authors (perhaps three or more of them from 787 to 829) are unknown to us. The first part might have been composed between 787 and 793, while Fastrada was queen. The annalist includes the year she married Charles and that they were overjoyed to see each other when he returned to Worms from Rome in 787, an unusual entry.

Fastrada died in 794, possibly before her thirtieth birthday. The cause of her death is not disclosed. There is a clue of a chronic illness in a 791 letter, in which Charles asked her to write to him more often, specifically about her health. As an author, I chose chronic anemia from Fastrada's second pregnancy. This condition can prevent conception, and it forces the heart to work harder and, if untreated, causes an early death.

Charles married a fifth and final time in 794 or 796 to Luitgard, who did not bear him any children. After Luitgard's death in 800, Charles had a string of mistresses and more children. He died in 814.

Everything Charles did in his personal life was political. When Fastrada died, Charles likely did not want any more heirs, sons born in wedlock. He already had three adult heirs and would divide the kingdom among them, as was the Frankish custom. He may have wed Luitgard because she could not have children and did not marry again after her death to ensure there were no more claimants to the throne. None of Charles's daughters married, but they likely played an important role in the court and may have assumed the responsibilities of the queen.

Charles apparently did not mind if a daughter took a *Friedelmann*, which I will loosely define as almost-husband. Hruodtrude had a son with Count Rorico, and Bertha had two sons with the courtier Angilbert. Three other daughters might have had relationships as well.

The name of Hruodhaid's mother is lost to history, and Hruodhaid's birth year of 784 is an estimate. The concubine was given a name in this story for the ease of both the author and reader.

Little information is known about Charles's eldest son, Pepin. (To lessen confusion with his younger brother of the same name, I used a variant spelling, Pippin, and called him Little Pippin. His original name, Carloman, was changed in 781.) Was eldest son Pepin, often called Pepin the Hunchback, truly deformed? Einhard and Notker (Mr. Unreliable) say so, but no other source does. However, it would make sense. A deformed son would give Charles a reason to divorce his wife and free himself for a marriage that would build an alliance with Lombard King Desiderius. It would also give Charles a reason to have at least two sons by Hildegard anointed, where Carloman was renamed Pepin. Kings could not have any deformities, which were believed to be a curse by God, retribution for a parent's sin such as conceiving the child on a Sunday. After churching, a woman avoided looking at someone with a deformity, fearing her child would also be afflicted.

Assuming Pepin had a curved spine, he was treated well by Frankish standards. Infants with deformities were thought to be changelings, and you only need to read a few of Grimm's folk tales to find out the horrors done to them: sticking them with a hot poker, letting them die of exposure. If the mother instead blamed the deformity on her sin, she might kill the child or sell them into slavery.

Compared to that, Pepin's fate was much better. He lived in Charles's household and was educated, perhaps to prepare for life in the Church. Abbots and bishops lived as aristocrats and were influential. They ate well, dressed well, had servants, and could go hunting. Those who followed a more austere lifestyle did so by choice.

Pepin did take part in a rebellion against his father, but many details are lost to us. Gomeric and Severinus are inventions, as is the battle at the end of this story. Charles might have wanted Pepin to become bishop of Metz even after the conspirators were caught. The king left the see unfilled. Might Charles have been waiting in vain for Pepin to formally renounce his claim to the throne? The answer remains unknown. The historic Pepin spent the rest of his life as a monk at Prüm and died in 811.

Pepin's compatriots were executed and their lands confiscated. And, I suspect, some innocents were caught up in the affair. Charles's cousin Wala was banished from court for a while, although he later became a close aide to the king. The bishop of Verdun and Count Theudald went through trials by ordeal in 794 and 797, respectively, to restore their good names and royal favor. Trials by ordeal were not for sissies. One method would have a defendant (or their champion) grab a stone in a pot of boiling water. If their hand got infected and did not heal, that was seen as God's condemnation.

Sometimes a historical novelist finds that the only information about people is their mention in the annals such as Radolf, Fastrada's father; Amalwin as the palace official who delivered hostages to Widukind; and Hardrad as the ringleader of the Thuringian rebellion. But oh, what an opportunity for fiction.

For more about the history behind this fascinating era, visit kimrendfeld.com or kimrendfeld.wordpress.com.

—Kim Rendfeld, Muncie, Indiana

Acknowledgments

My name is on the cover of this book, but I could not have created and refined it alone.

As with my other fiction, I am indebted to scholars who've studied this era. Dame Janet L. Nelson (also called Jinty Nelson) has written academic papers that are gems for this novelist. My library also includes Einhard's *The Life of Charlemagne*, translated by Evelyn Scherabon Firchow and Edwin H. Zeydel; *Carolingian Chronicles*, which includes the Royal Frankish Annals and Nithard's Histories, translated by Bernard Walter Scholz with Barbara Rogers; P.D. King's *Charlemagne: Translated Sources*, and Pierre Riché's *Daily Life in the World of Charlemagne*, translated by Jo Ann McNamara. Any mistakes, goofs, and misunderstandings are mine alone as are the outright fabrications.

For assistance with the storytelling, I thank my critique partners, authors S.K. Keogh and Tinney Sue Heath, and author and freelance editor Jessica Knauss (who also writes as J.K. Knauss). In addition to being helpful partners, they are wonderful writers, and I encourage you to check out their work.

As always, I am grateful to my family for their faithful support. Special thanks go to my husband, Randy.

And dear reader, I am grateful to you for spending time with *Queen of the Darkest Hour*.

About the Author

Kim Rendfeld has made a career in journalism, marketing and public relations, and fiction. She grew up in New Jersey and attended Indiana University, where she earned a bachelor's degree in journalism and English with a minor in French. She was a journalist for about seventeen years at Indiana newspapers, then spent about eighteen years in public relations in higher education, including a leadership role in Southern Illinois University Carbondale's communications team. In retirement, she plans to spend more time with her family, her community, her fiction, and her garden.

Kim, a member of the Historical Novel Society and the Alliance of Independent Authors (ALLi), lives in Illinois with her husband and their spoiled cats. The couple has a daughter and four grandchildren.

For more about Kim, visit kimrendfeld.com.